Yesterday nobody said anything at all. It was how they looked that made me sick.

I lay back down on the cot.

Footsteps echoed down the hallway. The door slid open.

"Hey, kid!"

I didn't answer.

"Kid, um . . ." He shuffled some papers. "Kyle Caroll? You sleeping?"

I opened my mouth, but no words came out.

"Caroll, you got visitors here. You gotta get dressed and come out. They're not gonna wait all day."

I looked at the cop. I thought about the next scene of the movie. Everything got blurry then and went black. But that was the moment that everybody wanted to hear about. Over and over again. What could I say? I didn't know what had happened.

I thought about it again. The air smelled like iron and fire. I saw gray powder and heard a thundering boom. But I couldn't see.

One time Jase and I rented a movie called *Groundhog Day*, where the guy woke up every day on the same day. He had to get the day perfect, because if he didn't, he'd wake up on the same day again.

I kept wishing that would happen to me.

FREEZE FRAME

HEIDI AYARBE

LAURA GERINGER BOOKS
HARPER TEEN
An Imprint of HarperCollins Publishers

HarperTeen is an imprint of HarperCollins Publishers.

Freeze Frame
Copyright © 2008 by Heidi Ayarbe
www.harperteen.com

Library of Congress Cataloging-in-Publication Data
Ayarbe, Heidi.
Freeze frame / by Heidi Ayarbe. — 1st ed.
p.   cm.
Summary: Fifteen-year-old Kyle believes he does not deserve to live after
accidentally shooting and killing his best friend.
ISBN 978-0-06-135175-4
[1. Firearms—Fiction. 2. Violence—Fiction. 3. Death—Fiction. 4. Best
friends—Fiction. 5. Friendship—Fiction.] I. Title.
PZ7.A9618Fr 2008   2007049645
[Fic]—dc22   CIP
                                                                           AC

Typography by Carla Weise
10 11 12 13 14   LP/CW   10 9 8 7 6 5 4 3 2 1
❖
First paperback edition, 2010

For my big sister, Carrie, and husband, César.
Thank you for believing.

Gray slats of light slipped between the bars, only to be swallowed by blackness. I shivered and pulled the colorless blanket around me, squeezing my eyes shut, holding my breath until the pain swelled and exploded in my chest. I exhaled and counted. Each breath took me farther away from where I wanted to be. But I had to go back. I had to change it.

Almost all of yesterday played like a movie in my head. I could start it, rewind, stop, fast-forward, and replay scenes—except for one. That scene never came clear. It was as if the film from the reel had been exposed to sunlight and gotten blotchy.

In some scenes, I even thought about making changes, doing a director's cut.

Melanie, go back and flip your hair to the other side.

When I thought about it like that, I felt like I had control, like it was a Quentin Tarantino movie, all out of order. I could change anything. But then I would remember. No matter how much changed inside my head, it was the same everywhere else.

October 8, 8:52 A.M., Scene One, Take One

We got up from the table because Jason had used all the syrup. The guy really poured it on. Dad ran down to the store to stock up, as if he knew I needed breakfast to be perfect.

Mom ordered us to get ready for the homecoming game and scooted us out of the kitchen. "You can eat in a couple of minutes."

"Sorry about the syrup, Mrs. Caroll," Jason said.

I shook my head. "My pancakes are gonna get cold. You could've saved a drop."

"Big deal, Kyle." Melanie flipped her hair. "God, Mom, he can be such a dumbass."

"Mel, watch your language." Mom glared.

Jason swallowed a laugh. In his house, he'd be nailed for saying *dumbass*. "Sorry, man. I like a lot of syrup."

"I guess so." I rolled my eyes. "Pig."

"You shouldn't insult your *guest*," Melanie huffed. "Grow up, Kyle."

2

Jason wasn't a "guest." You can't consider your best friend since kindergarten a guest, even if he hasn't been around for a while.

I glared at Mel. "It sure wouldn't have hurt you to save some either." I puffed out my cheeks and gut. "If I were you and had to wear that cheerleading skirt, I definitely wouldn't be eating pancakes—and especially not with syrup."

"Mom!" Melanie yelled. "Did you hear what he just said?"

Mom shot me her you're-a-step-from-deep-shit look.

"What?" I asked. "I didn't do anything. I swear!" But by that time Mom was after me with a spatula, and Jason and I ran out the kitchen door before she began screaming too.

"Oh, man," I grumbled, standing barefoot out on the frostbitten grass. I danced from one foot to the other. The cold burned my toes.

"Things don't change around here, huh?" Jason's teeth chattered. "It's cold, man. I'm, like, still in my pajamas." He looked around. "Remember when we decided to go snow camping out here after watching *Vertical Limit*?"

We'd thought it'd be pretty easy, pretend like we were mountaineers or something. Eat beef jerky for breakfast. We didn't even last an hour. We might've lasted longer if Jase hadn't insisted that he had frostbite. And I didn't want to have to explain to his mom why his toes fell off.

I laughed. "Maybe the coast is clear. Let's go back inside."

Jason and I peeked in the kitchen window. We saw Melanie blabbering away at Mom. Mom pushed a plate of half-eaten pancakes in front of her.

"It doesn't look good. Mel's pretty pissed." Jason turned toward me. "You might not get to go to the game."

"Nah." I shook my head. "You think?" I was standing on my toes, trying to keep my feet from freezing off.

"Yeah, man. That's the kind of shit that gets me sent to Pastor Pretzer."

Jason's family was really churchy, and he always had to talk to his minister when he got in trouble. Whenever we did something wrong at his house, Mrs. Bishop quoted something from the Bible. Her favorite was "Do unto others as you would have them do unto you."

When we were in ninth grade, I asked Mrs. Bishop if that meant we could do unto Kayla Griffin as we would have her do unto us, and she sent me home. I didn't think Mrs. Bishop would get so worked up. It's not like we were twelve or anything, and it *was* pretty funny.

Mom told me I was being disrespectful. I had to write a letter of apology to Mrs. Bishop and was put on Jason's "probation friend" list. After nine years of being best friends, I became a probation friend. Only Mrs. Bishop could think of crap like that.

4

"Well, I wouldn't have called her fat if she really was," I told Jason. "I'm not *that* big of an asshole." I looked back in the window. "Plus, when did our sisters become such freak shows? I mean, Mel used to be pretty cool before all the cheerleading and diets and shit."

Jason shrugged. "I dunno. So, what's next?"

"Let's hang in the shed until things cool down, unless you want to go around through the front door."

"Our feet would freeze off before we got there."

We crossed the backyard to Dad's work shed. The dew soaked my pajama pants. The door was locked, but I knew where Dad kept the key and grabbed it from the ledge. The shed had metal doors, kind of rusty; they screeched when we opened them.

"*Shhhh,*" Jason said. "Keep it down."

The shed smelled like a mixture of oil, fertilizer, and wood shavings.

If I were a director, I could change everything. Jason and I could've gone into the garage and waited. We could've sucked up the cold and snuck in the front door. We could've gone down the street to his house. Maybe I wouldn't have told Mel she was fat. As a director, I had so many choices.

That's why this movie in my head sucked. It didn't change. Nothing was under my control.

I shoved the palms of my hands into my eyes, pushing so hard, I could feel the thumping in the back of my brain. I heard the *tick, tick, tick* of the seconds marking the time in my head.

I smelled burning.

October 8, 9:03 A.M., Scene Two, Take One

Jason and I sat on the workbench. Light filtered through the grimy windows; everything looked distorted and gray.

"It's not much warmer in here than outside, Jase." I shivered.

"Yeah, but it's all right. We should come in here more often. We could call Alex and the guys over. There's a lot of cool stuff." Jason got up and started to look around.

The hair bristled on the back of my neck. "Last time we got busted."

"Well, we wouldn't have if you hadn't set the wood shavings on fire. Your dad and mom just about shit when they saw the flames."

"I didn't really think I could do it with a string and stick like they do in the movies. It was kinda cool, though."

Jason rolled his eyes. "Yeah."

Mom and Dad had acted as if we'd set the whole state on fire. They came running out with the fire extinguisher, screaming and hollering. The side of the shed turned black.

And Jason and I had to go to a fire safety course at the community center.

"What's your dad do in here, anyway?" Jason opened some drawers.

I shrugged. "Stuff, I guess." I looked around. Shelves sagged with the weight of paint cans, tools, tattered boxes, and unfinished projects. "I think he likes it because he doesn't have to clean it up. Mom doesn't even come in here."

"Check *this* out." Jason handed me a huge pair of curved, rusty scissors. They looked like a medieval torture tool.

"Let's see what else there is." I jumped off the bench and started going through drawers and boxes. "Hey, look!" I pulled down Grandpa's old 8 mm film projector. "I'd forgotten about this." A box of home movies was tucked behind it. I pulled out some reels and blew off the dust. The film still looked pretty clean. "Maybe we can set it up later, huh?"

Jase didn't answer. He was distracted.

"Whatcha got, Jase?"

Jason jimmied the lock on a metal box. He whistled. "Check this baby out."

I put the movies down. Jason's find was much better.

I opened my eyes. The tiny cell was bright. The sun had risen, but I wished it hadn't. I didn't know how long I was going to have to stay here or what I was supposed to do. It wasn't like Mom and Dad had sent me there as a punishment.

I could just hear how stupid that would've sounded. *Kyle, you really messed up this time. We're locking you up.*

Yesterday nobody said anything at all. It was how they looked that made me sick.

I lay back down on the cot.

Footsteps echoed down the hallway. The door slid open.

"Hey, kid!"

I didn't answer.

"Kid, um . . ." He shuffled some papers. "Kyle Caroll? You sleeping?"

I opened my mouth, but no words came out.

"Caroll, you got visitors here. You gotta get dressed and come out. They're not gonna wait all day."

I looked at the cop. I thought about the next scene of the movie. Everything got blurry then and went black. But that was the moment that everybody wanted to hear about. Over and over again. What could I say? I didn't know what had happened.

I thought about it again. The air smelled like iron and fire. I saw gray powder and heard a thundering boom. But I couldn't see.

One time Jase and I rented a movie called *Groundhog Day*, where the guy woke up every day on the same day. He had to get the day perfect, because if he didn't, he'd wake up on the same day again.

I kept wishing that would happen to me.

I looked at the cop standing at the door. I wondered how fast he could run. Sometimes these guys seemed a little too thick around the middle to catch anyone.

"There's a lot of people with a lot of questions, kid. You need to get ready."

He didn't look too tough. He looked kind of bored, actually. I wondered if he had been up all night. His face looked scruffy. My face never looked scruffy, but I shaved anyway, just 'cause the other guys did. My razors usually lasted about five or six weeks unless I forgot to take them out of the shower and they got all rusty. They lasted way longer than Mel's. It kinda sucked to have a sister hairier than me. Once I asked Jase if Brooke was hairier than he was. "I won't dignify that with a response," he said.

Dumb question. Jason was one of the hairiest guys in tenth grade.

"I don't have any answers." I turned my back to the cop.

October 8, 9:16 A.M., Scene Four, Take One

There was a terrible noise. And a smell like burned matches. Hundreds of them. I choked. Then everything got quiet except for a sharp ringing in my ears—like one of those emergency broadcast tests.

"Oh, shit, Jason. Shit, shit, shit, shit, shit. Mom and Dad are gonna shit." I looked around the shed. "Did anything break?"

But Jason didn't move.

"Jesus, Jason, help me out, man. We're in deep."

Jason was slumped against Dad's workbench.

He didn't say anything. I couldn't hear much anyway, but I would've at least seen his mouth move if he had said something, like in one of those silent films. It was all wrong. He just looked at me funny.

"Jason, don't be an asshole. Help me out. Jason?"

At that moment, I felt like somebody had drained all my blood. Why the hell was he doubled over that way?

The shed door screeched open. Mom blocked out all the light.

"What's going on, Kyle? What was that noise?" Mom

looked at me, at Jason. "Oh my God, Kyle, what happened?"

I stood there.

Mom pushed me out of the way and ran over to Jason. "Mel! Mel, call nine-one-one!"

Mel stood in the doorway, gaping.

We were all stuck, like somebody had hit the pause button, only Mom didn't pause. Mel stood. Jason slumped. I froze. And Mom moved, flittered, vibrated.

"Jesus, Mel. Get out of the way, then." Mom ran out of the shed and into the house. I could hear the hinge of the kitchen door. It squeaked and stayed ajar. Dad needed to fix the door. Mom came back with a blanket and sat on the shed floor. She held Jason's head in her lap.

Mom whispered something to Jason. It was a deep chant—humming, murmuring, rocking back and forth.

The cop came closer. "Kyle Caroll? Kid, you hafta get up now."

I had to stay still. I had to stop time. Freeze frame. Pause.

"You've got some lawyer, your PO, and your folks here."

The film wasn't pausing.

"PO?"

"Yeah, kid, Mark Grimes, your parole officer. He was

12

here last night with you."

"Oh, yeah, that's right."

"Get up."

I couldn't see my parents. I shook my head.

He leaned over me. "Get up and get dressed. C'mon, kid."

I looked around the cell. They'd told me it was a holding cell—someplace I'd be for only a night or two until they figured out what to do with me.

I turned to the cop. His nametag said BYERS. "What's the date?"

"October ninth." He scowled. "Let's go, kid. They're waiting."

I looked at him. How was it possible to keep moving forward when everything had stopped yesterday?

The same two officers from yesterday were in a cramped room with a smudgy plastic clock hanging crooked on the wall. I looked down at my wrist. They had taken my watch the night before.

The cops were drinking their coffee black. The fatso cop drank in slurps, steam fogging up his glasses. He had to take them off and wipe them. The glasses, thick and heavy, left red indentations on the bridge of his Silly Putty nose.

Mom hugged me—too tight. "We're going to figure this out, Kyle."

I shuddered. It didn't seem like there was a lot of figuring out to do. They pulled out a chair for me.

"Michael, we need to ask your son some questions,"

said the fatso cop. They knew Dad. I don't know how or why, but they did.

Dad nodded.

I sat between Dad and our lawyer—Mr. Allison, who Dad golfed with every Thursday afternoon. I guess Dad had called in a favor.

Mark held out his hand and introduced himself. "I'm Mark Grimes, the parole officer assigned to Kyle's case. We have a detention hearing tomorrow during which I will recommend that Kyle be left in custody until all his psych evaluations are complete and I can better assess the situation."

Mark crossed his arms. He wore a blindingly white shirt that showed his muscles. His head glistened—the perfect kind of bald and tan that you only see on Harley guys. There was a tattoo on his wrist of some Chinese writing or something.

Mark had come to the detention center when they processed me the day before. "Everything is just procedure," he said. "Follow the directions of the detention staff when they're booking you."

They photographed, fingerprinted, and strip-searched me.

When they finished, Mark was waiting. He looked me up and down. "Basically, kid, you belong to the state of Nevada. I work for the state, so now you belong to me."

"Yes, sir."

"We're going to be spending lots of time together until things get worked out around here, so you might as well call me Mark."

I nodded. "Okay."

They took a mug shot. If Jason had ever had to get a mug shot, Pastor Pretzer would have sent him to hell or something. Maybe I could get him a copy. I was about to ask Mark for my one phone call when I remembered. My stomach lurched and I almost threw up. I leaned my head against a cool brick wall.

"Kid, you okay?"

I nodded.

"It's late. You'd better get some sleep. We have a big day tomorrow. Any questions?"

"Um, is my mom okay?" The lump returned to my throat when I thought about how Mom had looked in the hospital parking lot.

"Your family is fine. You'll see them tomorrow. Get some rest." Mark clapped me on the back, closing the door to the tiny room.

I hadn't realized how tired I was until then. I couldn't sleep, though. My mind replayed the day over and over again, always getting stuck at that one scene. A black screen faded to forms of gray, as if the shed had been dipped in murky fog. Jason's body was blurred, lying in a black pool. Then the screen became red.

"Kyle, are you ready?" Mr. Allison asked. "We need you to focus now."

"Oh, yeah. Sure." I nodded, looking around the small room.

The skinny cop stared at me with buggy eyes. He reminded me of Gollum from *The Lord of the Rings*. Fatty, on the other hand, looked more like Igor. It was like *Clash of the Movie Tools*.

> *"Igor, bring me the brain."*
>
> *"Yes, master." Igor rubs his hands together and hobbles down the dark corridor to the deep freeze.*
>
> *"My precious. My precious," Gollum says, limping after him.*
>
> *"Rubbish, Smeagol. Bloody fool," Dr. Frankenstein mutters. "You'd think he could find something appropriate to wear over those putrid rags." He pinches his nose and sneers down the hall after the receding shadows. He flips through a thick medical book, then looks over his spectacles at the body, prone on the metal slab.*
>
> *The sky flashes with streaks of lightning. For a split second light illuminates the corpse's pasty face.*

I jerked my head sideways and gasped. Everybody in the room stared at me. Dad's hand was on my shoulder.

"Do you need me to repeat the question?" Gollum leaned back in his chair. "Can you take me through what happened yesterday, step by step?"

Both of the officers pulled out their little notebooks at the same time. It looked like one of those choreographed moves in Bollywood. I wondered if one of them would get up on the table and sing. They looked at me in the way adults look at kids on those after-school specials before the kid admits to having tried beer at a party. Do directors tell them to make those faces?

I looked at Dad.

Dad nodded.

I told them everything I knew, up until the blurry scene. Their pencils whirred. They flipped the pages and scratched more.

"We need to know what happened next. Do you remember pointing the gun? Squeezing the trigger? Anything like that?" Gollum leaned in.

"I don't know." I shook my head. Scene Three was gone—a snippet of the film cut and thrown out. I'd seen a movie called *The Final Cut* where people had these implants in their brains that recorded their entire lives. After people died, cutters would edit their lives and present the recordings to the dead people's friends and family in

the form of a movie. It was like my scenes had already been edited.

Igor looked up over his glasses. "Hmm . . . ," he grunted.

"Okay, let's skip to what happened next. We'll go back to that part later. What do you remember after that?"

October 8, 9:18 A.M., Scene Four, Take One, Continued

Mel and I watched Mom and Jason.

I heard Dad's car drive up. "Dad's back with the syrup, Mom." Now we could have our pancakes and go back to our regular day. I remembered I hadn't eaten yet. I wondered if we'd have time to eat before the game. I felt hungry—starved.

"Mel, get yourself together and go get Dad." Mom held Jason's head in her arms. She still rocked back and forth. "Now, Mel. *Go!*"

Mel moved in slow motion. She rested her hand on the doorframe and stepped back out of the shed.

"Hurry!" Mom shouted.

Mom changed at that moment—she became a still image. Everything in the shed lost the illusion of motion, as if the film had slipped off the reel.

Freeze frame.

Fast-forward . . . Pause . . . But there was no rewind.

Play.

"Hurry!" Mom hollered again, the film spinning back on the reel.

Mel jerked into action. Her ponytail bobbed up and down with each step. The kitchen door slammed shut. I heard distant shouts and hollers.

Jason and I were the only ones left on pause. Stuck. I started to worry we'd never catch up.

Come on, Jason. Get up, get up, get up, get up, get up.

Dad got to the shed in three strides. Mel ran behind him. Dad wrenched the shed doors open all the way. The rusty metal and hinges moaned. Light streamed in. The gray disappeared and I felt relieved, squinting in the bright October light. Maybe the dream was over.

"Oh, Jesus, Kyle." Dad gripped my shoulders and slipped the gun out of my hand. The gun was hot, burning through my palm. When it was gone, I felt like I could step away. Rewind everything and start again. But the rewind button was jammed, and we just moved forward—without direction, without a script.

This wasn't supposed to happen.

"God, Maggie, what's going on?" Dad held his fingers to Jason's neck. "Jesus Christ, oh Jesus," he whispered.

"I've called the ambulance. There's a lot of blood. I, I—" Mom's chin wrinkled and her voice wavered. "Michael, you need to go get Gail and Jim."

Why did Dad have to go get Mr. and Mrs. Bishop?

I glared at Mom. I knew they'd be pissed. But they never said *pissed* at the Bishop household. So they'd probably be "totally disappointed."

Jason was just messing around. He was gonna get up soon. I waited for him to say something.

"Kyle, come on." Dad pulled me out of the shed. Mel stood outside, shivering. "Melanie, get a coat. You need to wait out front for the ambulance. I'm going to get the Bishops."

Mel nodded dumbly, and Dad left me standing outside the shed in the wet grass. By then, I couldn't feel my toes. I couldn't feel anything.

5

Gollum scratched his pointy chin. He looked at Dad, at Igor. "Michael, are you the legal owner of the gun?"

Dad nodded.

"Can you tell us why you had the gun?"

"Yeah. Ray, my brother; he had a pawnshop in Reno." Dad cleared his throat. "He had some problems, so I bought him the gun."

The officers exchanged a look. There's something about the word *pawnshop* that makes people get weird, like they're embarrassed about it.

"When he closed the shop, he returned it to me." Dad's voice got real quiet. "I didn't even remember. It was so long ago."

"We need to get your registration and permit. Can

you get that for us?"

"Of course. Certainly. I brought it with me. Yesterday . . ." Dad's voice trailed off. "I couldn't seem to find anything."

The cops wrote furiously. Dad's hands trembled, handing over the registration and permit. I felt like my sense of time was off again.

I wanted it all to be over. I wanted the policemen to leave everybody alone. I wanted the sick feeling to leave my stomach. I wanted to stop smelling the burn. I wanted the movie to stop.

"Kyle." Gollum leaned in. "I really need you to take us back to yesterday."

The rewind didn't work. Didn't he know that?

"Can you do that?" His eyes widened, the lids peeling back.

I rubbed my eyes. My throat tightened. It was hard to swallow. "But," I stammered, "but the movie. It's missing a scene."

October 8, 9:24 A.M., Scene Five, Take One

Mrs. Bishop brushed by me. "Maggie, what happened?" she asked. She dropped to the floor. "No, my baby! Hold on, hold on, hold on." Her words barely made it through her tears.

Mr. Bishop came right behind the men with the stretcher. They pushed Mom and Mrs. Bishop out of the way. They talked fast into walkie-talkies, hoisting Jason onto the stretcher.

"Gunshot wound to the chest."

"Fifteen-year-old boy."

"Nine millimeter."

"Massive blood loss."

"How long ago did this happen?" They looked at me. "Kid, can you remember?"

I shook my head. "I don't know." How long ago did what happen?

Mom stepped forward. "We heard a loud noise around nine fifteen. I ran out, saw what had happened, and called nine-one-one."

The blanket dripped black with blood. A crimson pool formed on the floor.

Jason blinked every once in a while. I could hear him gasping. He made a terrible, wheezing, choking sound, worse than anything I'd ever heard.

Stop it. Stop making those noises. Say something.

His eyelids fluttered.

I reached out to touch his arm, but the EMTs pushed me away.

The Bishops ran behind the stretcher. Mrs. Bishop heaved herself into the back of the ambulance and sat next

to Jason. The paramedics turned on the lights and siren and peeled out of the driveway. Mr. Bishop and Dad followed the ambulance.

"Mom, you need to change," Mel said. I looked at Mom's shirt, then down at my pajamas, stained with the same red-black color. I felt splatters on my face and started to scratch at the dried blood spots.

"And the pancakes are burning," Mel said.

Was that the terrible burning smell?

Mom pushed me to Mel. "I've got the pancakes. You help Kyle."

Mel nodded. She steered me through the kitchen door and upstairs. "Christ, Kyle, *snap out of it!*" Mel looked nervous. She threw some clothes at me. "Get dressed. Wash your face. We have to get to the hospital."

My toes were blue—the same blue as Mel's cheerleading uniform, as Mom's eyes, as Jason's lips. Why were his lips so blue? I pulled my socks on and shoved my feet into my orange sneakers.

"Come on, Kyle. We need to get going." Mel yanked my sweatshirt over my head. She took a cold washcloth and scrubbed at my face. She jerked back when she touched my hair and gagged. "Put on a baseball cap." Her voice quaked.

"I didn't—" I couldn't finish the sentence. "He isn't—?"

Mel wiped her cheeks. "Come on. We've gotta go."

We rushed downstairs. In the kitchen, Mom held on to

an old towel and wiped her hands, over and over again. The pancakes were burned and the kitchen looked as disastrous as the morning I bet Jase he couldn't eat seventeen pancakes. I never thought he'd actually go through with it. I ended up losing out on an entire semester of Twinkies from my lunch for that bet.

Jase was the biggest sophomore in all of Carson City. At Carson High School, all the coaches drooled over him. Jase liked sports enough. He just had other shit he wanted to do more. They didn't get that. I did.

Mom led me to the garage. "Kyle, get in the car. Mel, go over to the Bishops' and get Brooke and Chase. We're going to the hospital."

I climbed into the very back of the Suburban. I pulled my knees in tight and tried to squeeze the pain out of my stomach.

Mel came back with Brooke and Chase. Brooke and Mel cried all the way to the hospital. Chase didn't say anything.

He passed his Jack Sack from one hand to the other. *Swish, swish, swish, swish.* I could tell he was scared. Even though he was only eight, he did everything with Jason and me. He was a great kid. Chase unbuckled his seat belt and turned around. His head popped over the seat back, and he held out his hand.

I took it in mine.

"Kyle, is that what you remember?" Gollum smiled.

"Yeah, those Jack Sacks *swish* when you pass them back and forth. You know what I mean? All those little pieces of sand—tiny, tiny pieces of sand, trapped in that leather cover. They *swish*."

"I do. I do." Gollum nodded.

He was lying. He probably didn't even know what a Jack Sack was.

"Can you remember anything else? Besides the sounds of the Jack Sack, of course?" Igor looked nervous. Sweat rings soaked through his gray shirt. He paced back and forth and wiped his forehead with a coffee-stained hand-kerchief. Maybe he was hungry. I hoped they had more bagels for him in the other room.

"You know Chase can say every word, line for line, from the X-Men movies?" I shook my head. "Every damn word."

Thinking about Chase made everything much worse. I chewed on my lip. I wondered how they'd explain all this to him. Who'd tell him?

"Okay, Kyle. We need to get back to what happened yesterday." Gollum and Igor exchanged a look. Igor rolled his shoulders back in circles and moved his head side to side. "Let's talk about what came next."

"I don't know. I guess. The hospital. Yeah, we waited at the hospital."

27

I looked over at Dad. He nodded, like I was doing okay, like I should keep going. He tried to smile, but his eyes looked like the Nevada road map—red lines and dark circles. He hadn't shaved and his shoulders curved in. Dad shrank that day. And it was all my fault.

6

October 8, 9:39 A.M., Scene Six, Take One

Dad waited for us at the emergency room entrance. He held a cotton ball to the crook in his arm. He threw his heavy coat over his shoulder. "Maggie, we're donating blood. He needs blood. Melanie and Brooke can go too."

"Why can't we?" Chase stepped forward, holding my hand.

The emergency room doors opened and shut. People hurried in and out. Doctors and nurses rushed up and down the hallways. Cushioned footsteps echoed on the linoleum floor. I listened to the crinkle of cheap hospital gowns being put on and clothes dropping to the floor with soft thuds.

It smelled like sterile plastic, a kind of sickly new smell.

I'd come here two years earlier when Jason bet me the Fourth of July sparklers his grandma brought him from Mexico that I couldn't jump from the roof onto the porch. I missed the porch and landed in the hedges, breaking my ankle. I had to wear a cast for ten weeks and then do another five of physical therapy. We both got in big trouble for that one. Jase shared his sparklers with me anyway, just because he felt so bad. But I didn't remember the hospital being so loud.

"Mr. Caroll, I want to give my blood, too." Chase looked up at Dad. He pulled on Dad's sleeve.

"You're too young, Chase. You need to be bigger." Dad took us into the waiting room. "You can help by sitting with your parents."

Mr. and Mrs. Bishop sat in the far corner, holding tightly on to each other. Chase tugged on my arm. "C'mon, Kyle."

The Bishops looked up at Dad and me. They had these empty, expressionless eyes. Mrs. Bishop held a Bible.

Dad put his coat on. "Let's give them some space. We'll wait outside."

Chase let go of my arm. He ran over to Mr. and Mrs. Bishop.

"Is he okay?" Chase asked. "What happened?"

Dad led me outside. I felt better in the bitter October cold. The wind chafed my cheeks, and my fingers turned numb again. I didn't move closer to the building.

I didn't want protection.

Mel and Mom joined us. Mel pulled her jacket up high and hugged herself. She was still wearing her cheerleading uniform. The four of us stood in the cold silence. The doors whirred open and shut with each patient coming and going.

We waited.

October 8, 10:02 A.M., Scene Seven, Take One

Dad and Mom didn't speak. Mom chewed her nails. She went to the hospital chapel. She lit candles. She brought back cheap vending-machine cocoa for all of us. I singed my tongue and the skin peeled back, raw and burned. I liked the feel of the burn. It was the first thing I'd felt all morning.

We waited.

I peeked through the windows and my breath fogged the glass. The Bishops sat huddled together. From the outside, they looked like a normal family, just sitting in an ugly room. Grandma and Grandpa Bishop had come. Every now and then, Grandpa Bishop would walk outside and light his pipe. He'd nod at us, puff on his pipe, and return to the warmth of the waiting room.

Inside, the machines beeped and footsteps padded down the hallways. Telephones rang. Children cried. When

the doors zipped open, the sounds amplified by thousands, but then the doors would shut again.

"That's his ER doctor." Dad's words shattered the underwater silence that surrounded us.

I didn't want the waiting to be over.

Please be okay. Please, please, please be okay. Please. I clenched my fists.

"Should we go in?" Mom asked. She stepped toward the door.

"Maggie." Dad shook his head. He pulled her into his arms. The four of us pressed our noses against the cold glass. My heart accelerated. I bit my burned tongue.

October 8, 10:46 A.M., Scene Seven, Take One, Continued

The doctor approached the Bishops. He shook his head. He didn't say anything. He didn't have to.

I looked at my watch: 10:46.

10:46.

I yanked out the winder. The hands froze.

We didn't have to wait anymore.

Dad's shoulders slumped. He struggled to catch his breath. Mom leaned into him, clutching his shirt. Mel threw up right outside the ER doors. My heart stopped.

I hadn't even seen the cops until then. I didn't pay attention to the tapping on my shoulder. I kept staring into

the waiting room, hoping that everything was a mistake—a horrible mistake. We needed to do another take of the scene. Throw out this script. Write another one.

Time of death: 10:46.

Mom looked really confused. She grabbed my shoulders and shook her head. She looked right through me, eyes wild.

Nobody made any sense. Everything moved in slow motion and everybody had warped kidnapper voices.

Dad shouted something and threw his coat over my shoulders. Mel puked again. The officers talked to me. They pushed me toward their car. But the sound track I heard was the quiet gurgling noise Jason had made earlier.

Cold metal handcuffs tightened on my wrists. I felt thankful for the warmth of the police car, but I couldn't stop shaking.

I saw Mom holding on to Dad; Mel's hand was on her stomach; Dad slouched around both of them. They looked like they were drowning out there. My head pounded. I watched through the back window as the car turned a corner and my family faded out, disappearing from the screen.

October 8, 10:46

The End

7

Gollum and Igor cleared their throats.

"Kyle," asked Gollum, "how long had you known about your dad's gun in the shed?"

"I—I don't know."

Dad shifted in his chair. Mom dropped her head.

"We're just trying to clear a few things up, okay?" Igor dabbed sweat off his forehead with a yellowed handkerchief, took off his glasses, and rubbed his eyes.

"Kyle," continued Gollum, "whose idea was it to look for the gun?"

My chest constricted. "I don't know. I don't know."

"Did you point the gun at Jason knowing it was loaded?"

"I don't, I don't remember." I closed my eyes, but all I saw was the gun in my hand, like the camera had

zoomed in for a close-up.

"Who taught you how to shoot a gun?" They looked at Dad, and the camera zoomed out: an aerial view of us sitting around a wobbly table, the steam of the coffee curling up, fogging the lens, blurring the scene.

Igor raised his left eyebrow. "Did you aim the gun at Jason?"

Did I? Did I point and aim and shoot and kill? I squeezed my eyes shut, only to see the red lens and a pool of blood.

"Can you tell us who taught you how to shoot a gun?" Gollum smiled. His lips stretched thin across yellowed teeth.

"I—I—I never—" I stuttered. "I don't know." I didn't even know I *had* shot the gun.

"Please help us out here. We just need to get some answers." Igor paced back and forth. He drummed his fingers on his fat belly.

"Kyle," Gollum said, his eyes boring holes through me, "had you and Jason been getting along all right lately? Did you have any fights or disagreements you'd like to tell me about? Maybe some things happened at school?"

I thought back.

"Hey, Jase! Where're you heading?" I had caught up to him leaving the building after science.

35

"Hey, I looked for you by your locker. Me 'n' the guys are going to Taco Bell."

"Again?" It slipped out. I cleared my throat. "Cool."

"There's room, man. C'mon."

We'd joined up with Alex, Pinky, and Troy as we made our way to the parking lot. Alex rolled his eyes and said, "Yeah, Shadow, there's room. You don't take up much space."

Jason laughed. "C'mon, Kyle." He lowered his voice. "Dude, they just mess around like that. They're pretty cool when you give them a chance. Plus, *yo quiero Taco Bell*." The perfect Taco Bell Chihuahua impersonation. "I'm dying for one of those triple-bean burritos."

"What, so you can drop a bomb in math?" I cracked up, picturing Mr. Rivera running around the room frantically to open all air vents and windows before we met our demise from Jason's toxic gas.

Alex exchanged a look with Pinky and Troy. "Real mature." Pinky and Troy grunted.

I shrugged.

Jason looked back at Alex and rolled his eyes. So now Jase didn't even laugh at fart jokes?

Alex laughed. Then Pinky and Troy did. It was like Alex was the brain for the three. One brain. Three heads.

"C'mon, Kyle."

"Nah. Brown-bagging it today. Got some homework to do before math."

"Okay then. See ya after lunch."

"Yeah, see ya." It felt like somebody had just punched me in the stomach.

I watched them walk to Alex's new four-door truck. Alex was one of the only tenth graders with a driver's license. And for his sixteenth, his parents had given him a sweet cherry red truck.

Jason turned around and shouted, "I'll bring you something back. We're still cool for after school, right?"

I smiled. "Yeah, we're cool."

Igor cleared his throat. I came back to the same small room with the stench of sweat. "You remember anything at all, kid? Anything we should know about?"

I thought about Jase and the guys and felt the sting of tears. I shook my head. Jesus, I was such a tool.

"Did you and Jason struggle in the shed? Did you fight?"

"No." My chest felt like Igor was sitting on top of it. "I know we didn't fight. We never fight."

"Fought," Igor corrected me.

"Yeah," I whispered.

Mr. Allison stood up. "I'd like to know where this line of questioning is going. We're talking about a

fifteen-year-old boy here and his best friend." Mr. Allison clenched his jaw.

"We're talking about a fifteen-year-old corpse, okay?" Igor snapped back.

Mom gasped.

Dad stood up. "We've talked to you enough today. My son, m-my son . . ." He stammered. He kicked his chair out of the way and paced the room. "I just went to the store for more syrup, okay. That's all they wanted that morning—maple syrup."

Fucking maple syrup.

"Let's settle down, everybody—take it step-by-step," Gollum said in a soft voice. He hummed his words like music.

Mr. Allison stood up. "What are you trying to do here?"

Everything started to sound scripted, like in *The Truman Show*. I half expected Igor to hold up his pen, grin, and say, *It's a good thing we have these brand-new Swick permanent marking pens to write down this boy's statement— the only kind of pens the Carson City police department uses.*

Then Gollum would pipe up, *Oh, and these bagels from the Kaufmann Bagel Shop, all natural, all kosher, using only the finest ingredients purchased from local farmers, are de-e-e-e-licious.*

I listened for a catchy jingle. Mr. Allison pulled me

back to the room by squeezing my shoulder.

Gollum stood up. "We're trying to find the truth, Mr. Allison—what really happened in that shed yesterday morning. We think that the Bishops deserve at least that much."

The room spun. The officers cleared their throats and scribbled in their notepads. Mr. Allison looked angry. Mom buried her face in her hands.

"Don't even start to play that power game with me." Mr. Allison's eyes narrowed. His comb-over flopped the wrong way.

We'd gotten to that part in the movie where the innocent guy tells everything or the guilty one lawyers up. But I didn't know which guy I was.

"Like we said, we're just looking for the truth." Igor gnawed on a toothpick. The clock ticked, rattling the walls. Louder. Louder. Deafening.

Then Gollum snapped his notebook closed and put his pen away in his breast pocket. "Mark," he said, looking at my PO. "He's all yours."

Mark finally spoke. Until then he'd looked like he was meditating. Or napping. This all had to be pretty routine to the guy. "Tomorrow morning, at eight A.M., you will stand before the juvenile master. Kyle, that's the kind of judge who handles cases like yours. But as I said, until I have the full psych evaluation, Kyle will not be going home." Mark

uncrossed his arms and snapped his gum.

"Mr. and Mrs. Caroll, we appreciate your time." Gollum held out his fingers and wrapped them around Mom's small hand. "We hope to resolve this quickly."

How can you resolve a dead body? Dead is dead, right?

The two policemen left. Mr. Allison stood up. "Michael, call me if you have any questions. We'll figure this out."

"Thanks, Bob. We really appreciate it." Dad shook his hand. Mom hugged him.

"Kyle." Mr. Allison came over to me. I looked right through him. I wanted him to disappear too. "I'm real sorry about Jason. I know he was your best friend."

I'm sorry, too.

My throat constricted and everything went out of focus. Fade to black.

Mr. Allison left with Mom and Dad. They took me back to my holding cell to wait for Mark. I counted the seconds and a scene flashed through my mind, then stuck there.

I tried to erase it, because it scared me. I had never thought about death like that before. I had never wished for it to come and get me.

8

Mark and I walked down a hallway. We passed by other cells and a social room. Everyone wore the same blue-gray jumpsuits, like the kind auto mechanics use. There were some kids lying down on bunk beds playing cards. A skinny girl lay on a cot facing a concrete wall. Her shoulders jerked up and down like she was crying.

"What's wrong with her?" I asked.

Mark looked at her, then back at me. "Not my case."

"Are there a lot of us?"

"What do you mean?"

"Cases? A lot of cases?"

Mark nodded. "Too many, I'm afraid."

"Oh." My sneakers squeaked on the linoleum. I was glad they had let me keep my orange sneakers. It was this

pair of knockoff Vans I'd won when I went to the International Chili Cookoff with the Bishops last spring. I was the only one who could eat the whole bowl of Tasmanian Devil–Breath Chili from Down Under without asking for a glass of water. After winning, I couldn't feel my mouth, and I guess my lips and tongue looked pretty swollen, because the Bishops rushed me to the emergency room. Jason was pretty pissed.

"I didn't even get a chance to eat my Indian fry bread."

"Thanks for your concern, asshole."

"Man, Kyle, you did this for a pair of butt-ugly shoes."

"They're not ugly. They're tight." I was sucking on ice, so when I spoke, drool dripped down my chin.

"They're orange."

"So. Orange is tight."

"You'll never wear 'em."

"Yeah, I will." I pulled off my high-tops and put on the orange chili shoes.

"You'll never wear 'em in public."

"Wanna bet?" By that time, a tingling numb feeling had crept into my throat. Blisters popped out on my lips. I have to admit I was a little worried. I chomped on the ice and let it trickle down my throat.

"Yeah. I bet you won't wear 'em."

"I'll wear 'em. Every day."

"For how long? A weekend?"

"A year. I'll be the fashion trendsetter this year."

"Yeah, right."

"Bet your 1948 Captain Marvel Adventures number eighty-one."

Jason paused. "And if I win?"

"You get any film collection I have."

"Any?"

"Yep."

"You're not gonna stick me with that Bollywood shit."

"Like I said. Your pick."

"Okay. I want your David Lynch collection, including *Twin Peaks*."

I paused. This was big.

"What? Stakes too high?"

"Deal."

"You're on." Jason grinned.

I looked down. The orange sneakers contrasted with the gray jumpsuit thing. They were pretty dirty. So far I'd worn them for 170 days straight.

"Kyle!"

I turned around and saw Mark standing in the middle of the corridor, fifty feet away.

"Have you been listening to me?"

I shook my head. "Sorry." I looked down at my shoes. "I was just thinking."

Mark nodded. "Come on. Dr. Matthews is going to help you work through some things now. She'll be good to talk to."

It was better to think about my shoes.

"You seem like a pretty good kid, Kyle." Mark clapped me on the back. He liked back clapping. I guessed it was the manliest way he could hug a guy. "You're going to be okay," he said.

Who cares if I'm okay? What about Jason? What about Chase? What about Mom? It was like the world had taken a freaky turn and I'd ended up with all cameras focused on me.

We arrived at a dinky office at the end of a long hallway. It didn't have the doctor's name on it or anything, so I kind of figured she just came every now and again. I peeked in the window.

Dr. Matthews's matted hair was swept up into a knot on the back of her head. It actually looked like a spider-webby doorknob from a 1930s horror flick—like in an old Boris Karloff film. Wisps of gray around a rubber band, smack in the middle of her head. She wore a shapeless dress with bright colors and jungle prints. She jingled when she walked because of the loads of jewelry that covered her body, head to toe. The office smelled like burned cinnamon.

I looked at Mark. "She's the one who's going to

decide if I'm sane?"

Mark pushed me through the door and introduced me to Dr. Matthews. "I'll be waiting for you when you're done."

"You'll have to excuse the makeshift office. I'm getting mine redecorated. It should be done sometime next week." Dr. Matthews smiled, and lines webbed from the corners of her eyes to her temples.

She cocked her head to the side and said, "We have a lot to talk about. Why don't we just jump right in."

Jump.

"Jump!"

That's what Jase and I shouted to Mel and Brooke when we went barreling down Elm Street in Dad's rickety firewood wagon. We were in fourth grade and thought it would be fun to tear down the street. We just never thought about the steering part. Or the stopping part. Jason took the helm, and just as we hit the turn going onto Richmond, Jase shouted "Jump!" He knew we'd never make the turn, and a wall of rosebushes was straight ahead. Jase and I jumped, but Mel and Brooke didn't. They catapulted forward into the rosebushes, and it took about three hours for Mom to dethorn them. That time neither of us was too bugged about getting busted because it was worth a lifetime of laughs to watch them fly into the bushes—a

classic Buster Keaton moment. But I kind of think Brooke still holds a grudge because of some lame-ass scar she has on her forehead.

They should've jumped.

"Jump," I whispered, and shook my head. "Jump."

"Kyle?" Dr. Matthews raised her right eyebrow. "Would you like to take a seat?"

She sat on a colorful couch and leaned against the pillows. I sat on the far end of the same couch. There was nowhere else to go.

"Can you tell me how you're feeling right now?"

I looked down at my sneakers. God, I was glad to have those orange sneakers.

"Okay. Maybe you could walk me through what happened yesterday."

So I told her the same stuff I'd told the police. She just listened and nodded. When I finished, she didn't say anything for a long time. I kinda thought she was asleep until she sighed. It wasn't a regular sigh. It had kind of a hum to it. Maybe it was a hum and not a sigh. I really couldn't tell. She might've just had some kind of respiratory problem.

"Can you remember anything at all between finding the gun and Jason being shot?"

Scene Three. All I saw were split-second images, like in the old days when the movies flashed subliminal messages

of popcorn and Coke on the screen. Nobody saw the popcorn or Coke images—they just got really hungry. That's what I saw when I tried to remember Scene Three. Flashes that I couldn't splice together to make the scene whole. And it made me feel sick.

I shifted on the couch. "I'm trying." I picked at a callus.

She laid her hand on my arm. "That's okay. You'll remember."

But what if I don't want to? What if I really did it? On purpose? What if I'm a killer?

"I'm here to help you fill in the blanks—put the pieces of that day back together."

I looked up at her and clenched my jaw.

"Why don't you tell me how you feel about what happened?"

Everybody wanted explanations. Everybody wanted to "get" it. Get me. I never had to explain myself to Jase. He got that on Tuesdays I'd always be late showing up to his house to go to school because I had to watch the first five minutes of the re-reruns of *The X Files* to make sure it wasn't episode 6X07, "Rain King," where Mulder is almost killed by a cow that's dropped into his hotel room—the only one I haven't seen in all nine seasons. A fucking cow, of all things.

Most people would just think I should rent it and get it over with. But Jason understood. He knew that renting it would be like giving up. He just got stuff. Or he used to.

Dr. Matthews cleared her throat. "Can you tell me how you feel about yesterday?"

It's like I hit the fucking delete button. *Zap!* He's gone. How was I supposed to feel about that? I looked at Dr. Matthews and shook my head.

"Okay, let's try this. What's the first thing that comes to your mind as we speak?"

Sorry.

"It doesn't have to be anything you think I want to hear. Feel free to let your mind wander and grab onto the very first thought you have."

Sorry.

I started to feel pretty hot in that closed-in office. It was about the size of Grandma Nancy's linen closet—with a lumpy couch and schoolroom desk squashed into it. There were no windows, just the one that was on the aluminum door. Sweat stung my eyes, and I wiped it off my forehead.

Dr. Matthews cocked her head to the side. "Are you okay?"

No. I mopped the sweat off my forehead and stared at my shoes.

Then we sat quietly until Dr. Matthews said, "We'll have a chance to get to know each other better. If you need to see me, even when it's not your appointment time, you can always ask for me. Do you have any questions?"

How long will it take the state to build up the case so they can put me away forever? What will it be like to live in prison? Did I do it? Did I kill Jason on purpose?

She had a kitchen timer on the desk. She picked it up and slipped it into her pocket. "Our time's up for now, Kyle."

Mark knocked on the door. Dr. Matthews invited him in. Some kid stood in the hallway with a brown-uniformed cop. The kid had piercing holes all over his face: eyebrows, lips, nose, chin. He stuck out his tongue—split down the middle like a snake's to match the tattoo that coiled up his neck to his ear. He glared at me.

"I'll be right with you, Simon." Dr. Matthews smiled a tired smile.

Simon? Talk about the wrong name. A kid like that should be named something meaner, tougher, like Damian. But then again, Arnold Schwarzenegger doesn't look much like an Arnold.

Dr. Matthews closed the door behind Mark.

"It's my turn, you mad cow! It's my hour! The judge said." Simon had a high, piercing voice, like it had never gotten around to cracking. The door didn't do much to muffle his shouts.

Dr. Matthews winced and sighed. She turned to Mark. "Please take a seat."

Mark looked really uncomfortable sitting behind the small desk.

"We need more time," she said. "I want to see him every day."

Mark looked at me. I shrugged. I kinda figured that Simon could use more Dr. Matthews time than me; he was a human colander, for God's sake.

"Kyle's not quite ready to talk." She smiled at me. "The mind is a wonderful thing. It has a way of protecting us from the truth sometimes."

Why can't I remember?

I dunno.

Dude, do you remember?

I'm the dead one.

So dead people don't have memories?

I haven't really thought about it.

Some help you are.

You could cut me some slack here. I am *the dead one.*

Yeah. You mentioned that.

Dr. Matthews stood up. She looked like a prism; her body shattered into thousands of colors. If she were one of Jase's superheroes, she'd be Mega Matthews, the huge psychiatrist who wraps her enemies in straitjackets, then poisons them with cinnamon incense, erasing their memories.

"Kyle, are you listening?" Dr. Matthews asked.

I looked up and shook my head. I had forgotten where I was for a moment and squinted. Dr. Matthews was pretty "mega."

God, I'm such an asshole.

"I'm going to give you some medication for a few days to keep you on an even keel. It's nothing to worry about. Just standard procedure, okay?" Dr. Matthews swayed in the middle of the room, and I focused, pulling all the color back together to make her whole again.

"Okay. Sure. Standard procedure."

She squeezed my arm. "We'll talk tomorrow."

Great. Mega Matthews, take two. How many takes would I need to get it right? I guessed as long as the state wanted to pay for it.

Mark led me back to my cell. "I'll see you tomorrow morning. We have the detention hearing first thing. I'll come for you at seven forty-five."

Tick, tick, tick.

Everything kept moving forward.

Stop. Just push the stop button.

But Mark's lips moved. People walked by us in the hallway. The afternoon light grew dim. And I was stuck on play.

That night they gave me Dr. Matthews's pills with my food. My world lost its colors. The brightness turned to shades of gray and forms lost their edge. But my dreams were filled with red, black, and deep purple. Veins, tendons, arteries, muscles, and blood, pumping, flowing, and then clotting and stopping. I woke up when the room was so

51

black, I couldn't even see my own hand. I stayed awake and listened to some girl cry down the hall. Another kid tapped a pencil or something against the wall.

I counted backward, wondering if I could turn everything around if I concentrated hard enough, but I couldn't. The sun rose, and I was two days away—farther from Jason than I ever thought I'd be.

9

The courtroom smelled like lemon furniture polish and old men's cologne. It was too small for a jury. And the judge was a surprise. You always think judges are gonna be some balding fat guys with mustaches or something, but not this one. Jason and I used to talk about what jobs would be good for meeting hot women. Judge would've been one of them.

"You know what would be cool?" Jason said one day when we were in seventh grade, out of nowhere. We were just hanging out in Jase's room. "Teaching."

I looked at Jason. "Teaching what?"

"Art . . . or something."

"C'mon! That's so lame. What teacher have we ever had that's hot?"

Jason shrugged. "I dunno. I think Miss Simpson isn't too bad. And Mrs. Carmichael is a pretty good-lookin' old bird."

"Mrs. Carmichael? She's gotta be at least thirty-five! And way far away from being Hooters-hot. You need a job where you meet Hooters-hot chicks. Like a cop or fireman. Think *Backdraft*, not *Stand and Deliver*. Plus, when I get picked for Carson City's hottest firemen calendar, the chicks will be all over me."

"Hottest firemen calendar?" Jason shook his head and cracked up. "Whatever, Mr. December."

"Dude, why not?" I did my Mr. Universe pose.

"You're hopeless."

I punched him, and he put me in a headlock. "C'mon, Jase." I tried to break free, but he had me tight. "It's way better than playing school with Miss Simpson in her plaid vests."

He let me go. "Okay, seriously. Have you ever thought about what you wanted to do? I mean for real?"

"Not Mr. December?"

"Kyle, I'm serious."

I thought for a while. "Not really. It just seems so far away. Plus, all I like are movies. And I don't think having a managerial position at Blockbuster is a babe-magnet kind of job." I shrugged. "What about you?"

"An artist."

"An artist? Like painting and art galleries and shit?"

"More like graphic design and comics. Grandma Peters

54

is teaching me to draw with charcoal. She said I had to get the basics first. It's pretty cool."

"Dude, so that's what you've been doing. I mean, when you say you're busy and don't want to watch old movies."

Jason nodded.

"Will you show me your stuff?"

"It's not any good."

"C'mon, just show me."

"Don't laugh." Jason pulled out a notebook of chalky black drawings. At first they weren't so great, but then by mid notebook, the apples really looked like apples. He had even drawn a picture of an old tennis shoe with the toe worn through. "Check these out." He had a separate notebook filled with Marvel comic characters.

"*You* drew these?"

He nodded. I flipped through the pages and started noticing familiar faces. "Dude, that's me."

Jason cracked up. "Yeah, I drew you as a movie director."

I whistled. "And check out the actresses. Nice, Jase."

He grinned. "I thought you'd like that."

"You know, you could draw those caricatures of people—like they do at Disneyland."

Jason shrugged. "Maybe."

"Definitely. These are good."

"You think?"

"Shit, Jase. You're going to be the hottest new name on the comic-book market." I already pictured his stuff in a series. Or maybe he'd even have drawings hanging up in some kind of cool New York art show with people milling around eating cheese and crackers off silver platters.

"Grandma Peters signed me up for art classes after school this year, three nights a week. Dad's pretty bummed I won't be playing basketball or anything. His oldest son, an art pansy."

"Drawing superheroes is definitely not pansy. It's cool, Jase. Really. When are your classes?"

"Mondays, Wednesdays, and Fridays."

I felt a twinge of sadness. What would happen to our Friday Night Flicks club? "Then you *really* must like this."

"Yeah, I guess so."

Before Jason closed up the book, he tore out the sketch of the movie director. "Here." He handed it to me. "Only if you want it." He scuffed his shoes against the wall, leaving a black smudge.

"Yeah, I want it. This will be worth a mint someday." I still have it hanging up on my bulletin board. He never signed it, though.

The judge cleared her throat. "What do we have on the agenda today?"

A lady tapped things on a black machine, and a man

sat in a little box next to the judge. He handed her a file. She flipped it open.

Mark stood up. "Juvenile Master Brown, at this time I don't think we need to remand Kyle to West Hills Hospital because I don't believe he is a suicide risk. I do, however, request that he be placed in the juvenile detention center until I can better assess the situation."

"Where's the jury?" I asked.

Mr. Allison leaned in. "There is no jury. You're in juvenile court. You will have a disposition before Juvenile Master Brown in the next two weeks. She'll review your case and then determine your . . ." His voice faded. "Your sentence. Do you understand?"

I nodded. Twenty to life without the possibility of parole. I tried to remember how the defendants acted in all those movies when they're sent away. Most of them don't even cry. They're just stone-faced.

How will I react?

I looked at all the people crowded into the small courtroom.

"Do you have any problem with that, Mr. Wiley?" the judge asked the other lawyer across the room.

"No, Juvenile Master Brown, I don't. When should we meet again?" Mr. Wiley shuffled his papers and nodded at me. He wore a much nicer suit than Mr. Allison.

"Can we meet Wednesday afternoon or Thursday

morning?" Mark said, looking at his calendar.

"So soon?" Judge Brown raised her eyebrows.

"The Carolls, from what I've seen so far, are good people. My main concern is the psychological welfare of Kyle, and I don't think that the juvenile detention center can offer him more support than his family. I do, however, want to take the time I need to visit the home and make sure there is no longer a risk factor."

"Mr. Wiley?" Judge Brown looked over her glasses at the other lawyer.

"That's fine. Thursday morning?"

The man who sat next to the judge said, "We will meet here Thursday at ten-thirty A.M."

"Good. Next." The judge didn't even have a gavel to pound on her desk.

Mr. Allison patted me on the back. "See, it's going to be okay," he whispered.

I glared at him. How was it possible that things would ever be okay after what I had done? I needed to edit that day. It didn't matter about Jase and the guys. We didn't have to hang out anymore. I just needed to go back and edit that one day—one scene. Scene Three.

But how could I edit what I couldn't remember?

Mom and Dad rushed over to me. "We'll get you home Thursday."

Mark was waiting for me outside the holding room. "Let's go," he said. "Back to Dr. Matthews."

10

I walked to Dr. Matthews's office. She had a stack of pictures on top of the small desk. A guitar leaned against some boxes in the corner. "Hi, Kyle."

"Hi."

She smiled and motioned me to sit at the other end of the couch.

Then we had one of those weird silences that Jason told me happen a lot on first dates. Dr. Matthews wasn't a date, of course, but just sitting with her like that on the couch made me as nervous as hell.

"I like your couch."

She smiled. "I've had it since my college days."

"A long time, then, huh?"

She raised her eyebrows.

"Sorry, Dr. Matthews. I, um, didn't mean it like that."

She laughed. "Pretty long, actually."

I nodded. I wondered if she'd ever changed the upholstery or anything, because it looked pretty ratty. I picked at a loose string and unraveled part of a faded purple flower.

"Can you tell me what happened last Saturday?"

"Again?"

"This time, I want you to close your eyes and talk about everything you remember—the color of your clothes, the smell of the grass—everything."

I closed my eyes. The images came back to me in flashes—like I was looking at film negatives—and ended with the red-black pool of blood and the blue of Jason's lips. All I could smell was the burn. All I could hear was the ringing in my ears. I opened my eyes and shook my head. I gave her the abbreviated version—like a movie preview.

"Jason and I were cold. We went to the shed. Now Jason's dead. End of story."

She laced her fingers together and sighed. I traced a bumpy leaf with my finger. I wished she'd say something; instead we sat there in that cramped office, listening to the ticks of the kitchen timer.

"Kyle, this is a place where you can say anything that's on your mind."

I'm sorry. I'm sorry. I'm sorry. My lip quivered and I took a deep breath.

"Or nothing, too. That's okay."

Nothing. That was better.

Dr. Matthews looked at the time. She stood up and stretched a little. "I still want you to take your medication. It will help you feel better."

"Okay."

"I'll see you tomorrow, Kyle."

"Sure, um, see you tomorrow."

Mark wasn't waiting for me in the hall that time. Some guy in a brown uniform took me back to my room. "Where's Mark?"

"He'll be here tomorrow. Some of the kids are going to play checkers and Parcheesi in the common room. You game?"

"No, thanks, sir." I couldn't imagine playing Parcheesi with Colander.

I counted the bricks that lined the cell door until it got too dark to see. The next couple of days were gray. Everything seemed blurred, like in those old 8 mm home movies Mom and Dad had from when they were kids, the ones I had found in the shed. No sound. Just the snap of the film spinning around the reel.

When I was little, Dad once showed me his record collection. We sat and listened to music in the den. The sound was crackly, and one record got stuck. Just when I thought the song would continue, it moved back to the same spot.

"It's scratched here, you see?" Dad shook his head and pulled the needle off the black disc. He showed me the record, and I ran my fingers across smooth vinyl and felt a hairlike scratch. It didn't feel like anything big at all, but it was because of that tiny little mark that the song just wouldn't go on.

"Can't we fix it?"

"I don't think so." Dad gently held the record in his hands. "Maybe I'll bring some records to the café. What do you think?"

It was the first time Dad had ever asked me what I thought about his café, The Hub. I imagined how cool it would be to have The Hub packed with people, listening to the crackly music. "I think it would be great, Dad."

Dad smiled.

October 8 was the place where my needle got stuck. There was no way to go on. And it couldn't be fixed.

That Thursday, I stood before the judge again. Mark requested that I be put on house arrest and released to my parents until the disposition. I had to continue psychological counseling and was given a prescription for the gray pills. Dr. Matthews explained they didn't want me to have severe spikes and drops in my moods. The pills would level me.

But I hadn't felt anything but emptiness since October 8. And the pills didn't fill the hole in my stomach. They just

made the days gray, my nights black-red.

I had to check out of the Kit Carson Juvenile Detention Center like it was the Ritz. They made sure I didn't swipe any of the stained sheets or anything. At the counter, they handed me a list of my stuff: one PEDRO FOR PRESIDENT T-shirt, one pair of jeans, one pair of socks, one gray Wolfpack baseball cap, one navy blue Carson High sweatshirt, one watch. Beside the word *watch*, somebody had written "broken."

I pulled all the items out of the yellow plastic bag, one at a time. Everything smelled burned. The cap still had splotches of brown blood on the inside. The watch was at the bottom of the bag.

October 8, 10:46.

"Everything there, Kyle?"

I held the watch in my hands. The brown smudges flaked off.

10:46.

I wished I had set it at 10:45—at 10:45 Jason was still alive. I rubbed the face of the watch, smearing the brown spots with my sweaty thumb.

"Is there a problem?" Mark looked at the inventory and the clothes that I had pulled out of the bag. "Kyle?"

"No." I shoved the stuff back into the bag and put the watch into my pocket. Mom had brought me fresh clothes to wear.

Mark shook my hand. "We have a week before your

disposition, where I'll be making a sentencing recommendation. As long as you're doing what you need to be doing, you and I won't have problems."

I nodded. But I didn't know what I was supposed to be doing. Maybe not killing any more friends. Everything else, though, was pretty vague.

When we got home, Mel ran up to her room, closed the door, and turned on the radio full blast. I went upstairs, too. Everything looked the same. My *Attack of the Killer Tomatoes!* poster hung on the door, taped together from the time I had torn it up after my cine club had failed in eighth grade.

"Kyle, that's a cool poster, and you just ruined it." Jason shook his head.

"Nobody else seems to think it was cool. Nobody even came."

"I was there."

"That makes two of us, then."

"Dude, most kids want to see *The Lord of the Rings* or something. It was pretty out there to debut with *Attack of the Killer Tomatoes!*"

I threw the scraps of the poster in the trash. "Whatever. I just wanted to try something different."

"Nobody knows how good that movie was. You're just a visionary, man."

"A visionary, huh?" I bit my lip, not wanting to cry in front of Jason. Not all guys would be so cool about their best friend being a total loser. "Want a tomato?" I had bought twenty pounds of cherry tomatoes to sell during the movie instead of popcorn.

Jason laughed. "Dude, let's tape this up." He picked up the pieces of the poster out of the trash.

The poster got all hazy and I pushed the memory away. How come I could remember that but not the shed?

I shoved the yellow plastic bag of clothes from the detention center into my dresser, put the watch on, and went downstairs. Five days of unread *Nevada Appeal*s were piled on the coffee table.

I flipped through them until I saw Jason's picture on the front page of Tuesday's paper. "C-11" was printed under his picture. The headline read "Tragedy Puts Carson City on the Map: Is Any Community Immune from Gun Violence?"

My hands trembled as I opened to page C-11.

Obituaries.

The words blurred on the page.

You're dead. You're really dead.

Yeah. Big surprise?

It's here. In writing.

Well, you can't believe everything you read.

I tore out his obituary, crumpling it up and shoving it into my wallet.

"Kyle?" Mom hollered from the kitchen.

Stay cool. It's just the fucking newspaper. Keep your voice steady. I walked into the kitchen, wiping my sweaty hands on my jeans. "How come Mel's not at school?"

"We thought we could all take a break this week."

I slumped into a chair. Maybe they all hoped that things would change if we stopped our lives, too. But the same Carson High was there with the same teachers, same students, same secretaries—same, same, same. All except for Jason. None of us could escape that.

Dad went out to the shed. I sat in the kitchen while Mom worked.

"Do you want to help me out?" She passed me a bowl.

I squished the ricotta cheese and eggs between my fingers. Mom had made two lasagnas and was starting her second pie and a batch of cookies by midafternoon.

Melanie slumped into the kitchen. "Is there anything to eat? I skipped lunch."

"I don't have anything prepared. You'll have to get something on your own." Sweat trickled down Mom's temple. She concentrated on her egg whites.

Melanie looked at the table, heavy with food. "Where's Dad?"

"He's in the shed." I stirred the chocolate chips into the

dough. Dad had spent the whole day there since we got back from the courthouse. He'd taken a bucket and bleach. The police had taken all the photos they needed and said Dad could clean it up.

Mel sat next to me. I handed her the bag of chips.

"Thanks," she whispered. "I'm kinda hungry."

"Me, too." It felt strange to want to eat something. Wrong.

We heard the shed doors screech closed. Dad put a padlock on the outside and snapped it shut; then he stood and stared. He held a bucket of water in his hands. Bloody rags hung over the side. Dad looked like a frame still. He didn't even move.

"Mel." Mom's sharp voice interrupted my trance. "Come with me. We're going to take this food over to the Bishops'."

Mel looked at Mom. "What am I supposed to say to Brooke?"

Mom paused. "I don't know, Mel." She shook her head. "We need to take things one day at a time."

I remembered how when I was little, Mom and Dad had the answers to everything. Or maybe I just thought they did.

It was easier being little.

Mel and Mom left with two baskets filled with food. I tried imagining the conversation on the Bishops' porch. I

watched out the front window as Mom and Mel walked down the street, slowly, deliberately. They returned fast. Mel ran up to her room, crying. Mom put the still filled baskets down on the table and dished out lasagna.

She knocked on Mel's door, screaming over the latest boy band's music, "Mel, turn that down! Come out and eat some lasagna!"

"I'm never leaving my room again." Mel had said this millions of times before, but this time I believed her.

Mom came back downstairs. She went to the door and hollered at Dad. "Michael, come inside! It's late. It's cold. You and Kyle need to eat."

I looked at the wavy noodles, doused in tomato sauce and melted cheese. "I don't know, Mom."

Mom sat across from me, dark circles ringing her eyes. "I love you. We love you. You need to know that."

Dad came inside from the backyard and stood behind Mom.

I shrugged and took my lasagna into the front room. I looked down the block at Jason's house. It seemed so weird that just yesterday . . . no, not yesterday, but—I counted on my fingers—five days ago . . .

Dong, dong, dong, dong. Four o'clock. Too much time had passed. I ran upstairs to the grandfather clock and held the pendulum in my fingers, watching the hands come to a halt.

STOP. I needed to stop time.

11

I returned to my plate of cold lasagna and watched the cars line up in front of Jason's house. People streamed in and out.

They looked down the street. Some pointed. A couple of high school kids tried to get into our backyard. Dad hollered at them and threatened to call the police. The phone rang nonstop. Dad finally unplugged it.

Streetlights blinked on. I went out and sat on the porch. It was really cold for October. Colder than the morning Jase died. I hid in the shadows and listened to the slow crunch and scuffle of sad footsteps on chewed-up asphalt. People walk differently after somebody dies. They speak in whispers.

It's not like you're gonna wake the guy up, I thought. *Man, you couldn't even wake Jason up when he was alive.*

I bit my lip and clenched my fists. I hadn't realized how hard it was to be alive. Since it had happened, I'd been in a cell, going through the motions. But here I was, looking at Jason's house, breathing, living. And it hurt. It was wrong. Jason's life had stopped. So should mine.

It wouldn't be long before they sent me away again, though. "I don't remember" is about as lame a defense as anybody can present. And Mr. Allison was no Atticus Finch. At least from a prison cell I wouldn't have to look at the Bishops' house. In prison, I was just as good as dead.

In eighth grade, when Jason's grandma died, I spent the day with him. He was pretty down. Grandma Peters wasn't a blue-haired kind of grandma. She took country-western dance classes, wore leather pants, and sometimes smoked cigars. And she taught Jason how to draw. She always said stuff like "I wonder how the hell I got a Bible-thumping daughter" when we were about to say grace at the table. Grandma Peters seemed too young to have a stroke like that.

Jason and I watched everybody come in with those same plates of cream-colored food—something Grandma Peters would *never* have served in her life. We called it "dead food" and wondered why, when somebody died, people didn't bring pizza. Or at least that person's favorite food. Maybe it had too much color. Pizza was way better

than some chicken hot dish made with cream of mushroom soup baked dry in somebody's oven. Even Mom's soupy lasagna was better than that.

That day, I couldn't get a smile out of Jason until I bet him my new Swatch that I could drink seven Cokes and hold out on going to the bathroom longer than he could. I got to the point that my sinuses burned from holding it. I ran to Jason's bathroom, but his old aunt pattered up behind, tapped me on the shoulder, and stepped ahead of me.

I couldn't wait, ran out back, and peed right on Mrs. Bishop's rosebushes—two seconds before Jason joined me. *Two seconds.*

"Dude, I thought you'd never go. I was dying."

I sighed. "Two seconds. Two seconds, man. That sucks."

Jason laughed. "Yeah, but how much would two *Matrix* seconds cost? You're getting off easy."

"Yeah, but I was thinking more along the lines of two *Brick* seconds."

"You and your movies. Is there a movie you haven't seen? " Jason held out his hand.

"Plenty," I muttered, unclasping my Swatch. Jason unhooked his cheapo Dimex and we traded.

"It looks good on me." Jason whistled. He stuck out his wrist and did his victory dance—the same dance he'd been

doing since we were five.

Later that evening, I helped the Bishops clean up. We sat down to watch *The Amazing Race* when Mom called. I heard Mrs. Bishop laugh and say, "I've got three, what's one more? No. No. You know, Maggie. They're like brothers. Yep. He's on his way." Then she hung up.

"Time to go." Mrs. Bishop got my coat. "Thanks for your help."

"No problem, Mrs. B."

Jase walked me to the front door. "Hey, Kyle, um, it was a shitty day. Thanks for hanging out. I mean, I feel better."

I raised my eyebrows. "Dude, Jase. Are we having a greeting-card moment?"

"Forget it, man." Jason shook his head and laughed.

I started to leave but then turned back around. "You're welcome," I said.

He grinned. "Okay, Hallmark. See you tomorrow."

"See you."

I looked at the Dimex on my wrist: 10:46. I was glad to have it—something of his.

Jason would be bummed to think everybody, even my mom, was bringing dead food to the house because of him—because of me. Maybe next week I'd have pizza sent over there—Jason's favorite. Pan-crust five-meat supreme with extra cheese. Maybe Dad would spot me some cash.

My breath came out in cloudy puffs. I didn't realize I was shivering until Dad sat down next to me on the porch and threw his jacket over my shoulders. He fidgeted. Then he lit a cigarette and puffed. I kind of wished I could smoke. I wondered if it made him feel better.

"You haven't smoked for a long time."

He exhaled gray smoke. "Some things might change, you know. A lot of things, actually." The cigarette glowed.

I nodded.

"I don't blame you. But sometimes, when things happen, people want to blame someone." He looked at me and inhaled, deep and long. The ashes burned crimson and crept toward Dad's fingers.

"The Bishops have the opportunity to talk at your disposition. They might say some things you don't want to hear." Dad snubbed out the cigarette. His breath smelled burned. Everything smelled black. "It's cold, Kyle. It's late. Let's go inside. We can talk tomorrow." We went back indoors.

I wanted to tell him not to worry. I wanted to show Dad I could be a man and handle being sent away to prison. The words caught in my throat.

"Tomorrow is school," I said. I thought about walking in through those same front doors as if nothing had changed. I wasn't supposed to be here. Not like this. My stomach churned.

"We're all going to take a few days off." Dad squeezed my shoulder.

He gave me one of Dr. Matthews's pills, but I spit it out after he left. My mind raced. I closed my eyes and tried to remember everything, but all I saw were pools of blood and Jason's blue lips. I got up to go to the bathroom. That's when I heard them.

"You forgot about it? You *forgot* about it? Jesus Christ, Michael. It's a gun, not a goddamned dental appointment." Mom was sobbing.

"I don't understand why we have to go over this every night. You don't think I've asked myself this? You don't think that's the first thing I thought about?" Dad sounded like he was crying, too. "Blame me. Blame me for everything, because I already blame myself."

"That's not fair."

"Our son shot his best friend with *my loaded gun*. He will be sentenced in a week, and we don't know what will happen to him. *That's* not fair."

I heard someone rummaging around the room. "Where are you going?"

"Out. I need some space right now. I need to clear my head."

"Michael, don't."

"I need space."

I slipped back into my bedroom and closed the door,

putting on my headphones and pumping my stereo up as loud as I could stand. I ripped my clock from the wall; its red numbers blinked and faded to gray. I crushed it under my foot.

Jason's watch glared at me from my bedside table.

10:46.

I'd stop, too, once they locked me away. Freeze frame. Just like Jase.

"There isn't one clock working in this house, Michael." Mom rushed down the stairs, tugging on some pantyhose, holding Dad's jacket and two ties in her hands. She came back up. "How come the stove is the only . . . Never mind."

Dad came out of the bathroom with a mouth full of toothpaste. "What time is it?"

"It's eight thirty-two. We can't be late," Mom said.

"We won't. Okay?" he replied.

Mom handed me the jacket of Dad's suit she was making me wear and held out a retro, tie-dyed, seventies tie in one hand. "Kyle, you need to wear a tie. Pick one." The tie in her other hand looked like something Mr. Hammons would wear on parent-teacher night—blue with diagonal rusty-brown stripes. Jason and I cracked up when we saw

Mr. Hammons in a button-up shirt and tie, because he always wore jeans and SAVE TAHOE T-shirts. Funny how he thought wearing a tacky tie and an old suit might impress parents more than his SAVE TAHOE stuff.

"Kyle? Kyle! Listen to me. We don't have time for your dawdling. Which tie do you want?" Mom held them up against my shirt.

"This one's fine." I grabbed the retro tie.

"I don't know if I can do this. I haven't even talked to Brooke yet. What are we supposed to do?" Mel came out with curlers in her hair. She was stuffed into a tight black miniskirt and a tube top. Charcoal black paint lined her eyes.

Mom took a deep breath. "You're not going to wear that. You're going to wash off the clown face and put on your dark green dress."

"Maggie," Dad whispered.

"And Kyle," Mom added, "you're *not* going to wear those filthy orange shoes with your dad's suit."

"Why do you even give a damn about what anyone's wearing on a day like today?" yelled Mel. "Are you worried we'll attract too much attention? I might be wearing an outfit you don't like, but, Jesus, Mom, Kyle *killed* Jason."

She did have a point. I had killed Jason.

Dad winced. Mom turned crimson. I really thought she was going to smack Mel. But she didn't. After all, Mel

77

had only said what we all wanted to pretend wasn't true.

"Melanie Ann, calm down. Everybody is upset today. We just need to get it together as a family and be there for the Bishops, okay? This isn't about you. It's about Jason and the Bishop family." Dad turned Mel around and walked with her to her room. I held Dad's tie in my hands.

"Dad will knot that for you in the car. I need to get ready. Why don't you wait downstairs?"

I hoped Mom's face would lose the bright red color before we got to the church. At least Mel's scene was a good distraction from my sneakers. They peeked out from under my pinned-up pant legs. I hoped Mom wouldn't notice them at the funeral.

176 days down, 189 to go. A bet's a bet.

We had to walk four blocks to get to the church. Mel tripped all the way in her new high heels. When we finally got there, we could only find room in the far back corner. *Everybody* from Carson City was there. I think I even saw Jack, the guy who mows the Bishops' lawn.

I used to be invisible. Jason's friend, the skinny kid, the shadow, the tagalong. But now they all looked at me. They stared. They hummed and clicked their tongues.

My eyes burned when I saw the shiny wooden coffin draped with white flowers and green grassy stuff. Purple light slanted through stained-glass windows, giving everything an eerie glow.

I didn't see the Bishops anywhere. I didn't see Chase. There were two rows of empty pews right next to Jason.

"Kyle, stand over here." Mom motioned me back into the corner.

People crowded in, pushing, trying to get a spot, craning their necks to see above everyone's head. The air reeked of perfume, incense, and funeral flowers. I pushed my way to the very back corner of the church to get more air. My chest felt tight.

Don't lose it.

Mom's tiny hand closed around my wrist. She pulled me over and put her arm around my shoulder. I could still see the coffin. I couldn't believe Jason was in there. I wondered what Mrs. Bishop had made him wear.

Does it matter what he wears now?

I bet Mrs. Bishop hadn't put on the Swatch. She said gambling was a sin and wouldn't let Jase wear it after she found out where he got it. But he'd earned it. By two seconds. He'd earned it, even if they wouldn't let him wear it. I should've called her and said to put it on. He really liked that watch. But I didn't call. I didn't do anything.

One by one, people went up, looked inside, and left something by the coffin. Even Sarah McGraw brought something. She never even talked to Jase at school.

I tried to loosen Dad's tie but couldn't figure out how to slip the knot down.

"Kyle," Mom whispered. "Would you like to go up?"

I hadn't seen Jason since Saturday. It was almost like he was on one of his family vacations—just gone for a while.

I swallowed hard and nodded.

"We'll go together." Dad and Mel walked ahead of Mom and me.

People stared and then looked away. It was like a bad TV movie, the kind they air on all major networks the same night at the same time.

ABC: *Killing Jason—The Kyle Caroll Story*

NBC: *The Murder of a High School Student*

CBS: *Kyle the Killer*

I had turned Jase into the movie of the week.

"Come on." Mom pushed me along.

Mel clutched Dad. My legs felt weak, and I had to stop several times to catch my breath—it came in short bursts. I grabbed my chest to make sure my heart still worked. A numb feeling spread through my body.

Why did I, Kyle Caroll, Mr. Nobody, live, when Jason died? It should've been the other way around. The main character never dies in the movies. It's always his sidekick. This movie was definitely fucked up.

It took forever to get to the front of that church. The

coffin hadn't looked so far away a few minutes before.

Melanie sobbed when she saw Jason. She teetered and started blubbering, "I'm so sorry. I'm so sorry." Dad held Mel in his arms, and they walked to the back of the church.

I'm sorry. It sounded so hollow, echoing off the church's bare walls.

Mom and I got to the coffin, and I looked in. It was Jason. But it wasn't. Mom started to pull me away, but I had to stand there for a while. It didn't make any sense.

His eyes were closed. His hands were crossed in front of his stomach.

They had cut his hair. He had been growing it out since December. He wanted to look like a real artist, and *they cut his hair*.

He wore a blue suit I had never seen, with the sleeves so long, they covered his wrists. I touched Jason's hand to check for the watch and recoiled from the waxy skin. This wasn't Jason. It couldn't be.

I couldn't have done this. I couldn't have killed my best friend.

I leaned into the coffin and put my head on his chest, listening, hoping that somehow this was a sick joke. Like when your parents really want you to learn your lesson the hard way, so they help you pack your bag to run away. But they fill it with all sorts of stuff, so you drag it halfway down the block and you realize you can't go any farther

because the suitcase is too damned heavy.

Maybe somebody would say, *See, you shouldn't play with guns.* And all of Carson City was in on it. Like in that movie *The Game*—a total setup. We'd laugh, feel relieved, and eat cake or something while listening to some police guy talk about gun safety.

But Jason didn't move. I grasped his suit, my tears staining his starchy white shirt. "Wake up. Please, Jason. Get up. I can't . . ." The words were icicles in my throat.

There was a powdery, lavender smell in the coffin that itched my nose, like an old-grandma smell. Definitely not a Jason smell. Everything was wrong, out of place. He wasn't wearing the watch.

"You can't be dead," I whispered.

But he was.

Mom pulled at my scarecrow suit. "Kyle, let's go."

I stood back, fighting to catch my breath. My heart stopped. I know it did. It stopped pumping blood throughout my body. I gasped for air and yanked on my tie.

How could I say good-bye?

I was ready to walk away with Mom when I turned back and leaned toward Jason one more time. His face looked weird. "Dude, are you wearing makeup?" I'm not the most brilliant guy in Carson City, but I know dead people can't have pink cheeks. I'd seen Jason. He was gray in the shed. Blue-gray, and he hadn't even died yet.

82

I wiped my hand across Jason's pink cheeks. Powdery blush and brown stuff rubbed off on my fingers. They cut his hair. They blew off the watch. They put makeup on him. I pulled out Dad's old handkerchief and tried to clean it off.

I wiped and wiped, but it was like the makeup was applied with some kind of freakish permanent spray. I had to get it off, though. Nothing else mattered.

Then I felt a heavy hand on my shoulder that ripped me around. Mr. Bishop towered over me. The Bishop family stood behind him. "What do you think you're doing? To my son?"

I held the limp handkerchief in my hand. Nothing made sense—none of it.

"My son is dead. You and your family have no right to be here. *You* have no right." Mr. Bishop shook. "You have no right," he whispered, clenching his jaw.

People got quiet. They moved around in their seats. Papers rustled.

"Kyle." Mom pulled on my arm. "Honey, we need to go sit down." Dad had turned around and started walking back toward us.

"Kyle," Dad said, coming up to me, "let's go sit."

I couldn't move. It was like in the shed. Freeze frame. Pause.

"Get out of here." Mr. Bishop came closer. My hands

were still stuck on the coffin.

"Enough!" Dad stepped between us. He pried my fingers from the glossy wood. "Let go of it, Kyle. Just let go.

"We're going to sit down," he said to Mr. Bishop, his voice cracking. "We loved Jason."

I looked away. I hated to see Dad cry.

Play.

Everything started to spin around me like weird special-effects lighting. Blackness crept through my brain, turning the church blotchy gray with pinpricks of white light. My knees buckled, and I grasped onto the front rail. My body shivered and icy sweat dripped down my back.

Pulling myself up, I stumbled down the aisle, past my parents and the Bishops. I tried to breathe without inhaling the sickening church smells. I yanked at my tie and ripped off the suit jacket. The exit looked so far away. Everybody's faces were blurred and distorted. Dizzying light streamed through the stained-glass windows. Squinting, I kept my eyes on the heavy wooden doors, ignoring the whispers. I rushed outside, tripped down the concrete steps, and collapsed on the lawn behind the dried-up rosebushes. My body heaved and hiccuped until all that came out of me was acidic yellow bile.

I lay on the dead grass and gasped for breath. My head throbbed. The deeper I inhaled, the less air I got.

I'm gonna die. Please let me die.

"Take it easy. Slow your breathing." Mom's cheeks were wet with tears. She held a paper bag to my mouth and nose.

The world stopped spinning, and everything came back into focus. Dad and Mel stood over me. "You okay?" Dad asked.

No.

I nodded.

Dad helped me up. "Let's go home."

We walked slowly to the car. "I didn't say good-bye," I whispered.

I listened as the organ played "Amazing Grace" from behind the heavy church doors. I wondered what other music they would play. What would Jason have liked?

I looked back. Mr. Bishop was right. I had no right. I had no right to be there. I had no right to be.

"**K**yle! Kyle, wake up!" Mel leaned over and shook my shoulders.

I sat up and grabbed her. "I can't," I gasped, struggling to steady my breathing. Nightmare images came back to me: choking, the inside of a coffin, being buried alive.

"You're okay." She sat down next to me.

I held her tighter.

She circled her arms around me. "I was walking to the bathroom when I heard you."

I nodded, still hanging on to her pajamas.

"I still kinda need to go."

"Go where?"

"To the bathroom."

"Oh. Oh yeah. Sorry." I didn't let go.

"Kyle?"

I let the fabric slip from my fingers. "Yeah, thanks. Sorry about that."

"G'night."

She closed the door and I was blanketed in darkness. I grabbed my pillow and waited until the first purple shades of dawn seeped through my window before I closed my eyes.

"You look tired today." Dr. Matthews handed me a glass of water. "Did you sleep well?"

"Sure."

Mom and Dad had called an emergency Matthews session. "We're going to try something called association. When I show you a picture, I just want you to tell me the first thing that comes to mind." She held out an ink-stained picture. "What do you see?"

"A stain."

She raised her eyebrows. "A stain of what?"

"Black ink."

She scowled. "And this one?"

"A bigger stain."

She did one of those hum-sighs. "Think of it like cloud watching. Have you ever done that? Looked up at clouds and found figures?"

Chase, Jason, and I had done it all the time. With stars, though, instead of clouds. We named our own constellations. Chase's favorite constellation was the *Taraxacum officinale*—the dandelion. He said it was a very misunderstood flower. At first I thought he was shitting me, but the kid actually found the same group of stars every night. One year for Chase's birthday, Jason and I bought him a star and named it Dandelion because we couldn't remember the scientific name. We thought he'd like it, but he said, "How can you buy something that belongs to everybody?"

We tried to return it, but we couldn't. I kinda felt like shit after that.

Dr. Matthews cleared her throat. "You know what I mean, Kyle, about the cloud watching?"

"No. I've never watched clouds," I said.

Dr. Matthews put the cards away. "Can you tell me about the funeral yesterday?"

I bit my lip.

"Can you tell me about the makeup?"

Trying to save my best friend from an eternity of lip gloss and blush didn't seem so unreasonable to me. I didn't know what the big deal was. Everybody'd just flipped out.

"Did you read Jason's obituary?" she asked. It was as if she knew I'd torn it out the week before and carried it around, too afraid to read the words. "What did you think

about it? The obituary?"

"I didn't read it."

"Why not?"

I bit my lip harder, until I tasted metal. I looked away, out the tiny door window.

"Would you like to read it?" She handed me a fresh version of the clipping I had crumpled in my wallet.

I blinked, hoping that everything would disappear, that the words would morph like they did in that movie *The Butterfly Effect*. All he had to do was look down at his notebook to change the words, and he'd change the past.

I concentrated on the obituary, but the print stayed the same. The words didn't change.

JASON GABRIEL BISHOP

Jason Gabriel Bishop, 15, of Carson City, Nev., died from a gunshot wound on October 8, 2008. He was born July 17, 1993, to Gail and Jim Bishop in Dayton, Nev.

Jason was an accomplished student at Carson High School, and first in his class. He belonged to several school clubs. He was an active member of his youth group at the Foursquare Church and a mentor to younger church members.

Among his survivors are his parents, Gail

*and Jim; paternal grandparents, Jacob and
Marlene; and two siblings, Brooke and Chase.*

*Services will be held Saturday, October 15,
at 10 A.M. at the Foursquare Church, followed
by a reception. The Meyers Crematorium and
Funeral Home is in charge of arrangements.*

The obituary depressed the hell out of me. What does any of that say about Jason? Nothing. All it talked about was his church and his mentoring. But what about who Jason really was for the other 163 hours of the week? What about the Jason who was the next Marvel comics artist? What about the Jason who was the best big brother to Chase? What about the Jason who would make a bet on just about anything—and win? What about the Jason I knew—not some made-up, Bible-toting, preachy mentor Jason? It seemed so sad that Jason's parents didn't even know him, like they were missing somebody who wasn't even real.

"What do you think?" Dr. Matthews urged.

Having it in print made it feel cheap—nothing more than headline news. All *Nevada Appeal* subscribers would have read this and thought, "Oh, too bad." Maybe over coffee they'd *tsk-tsk* and talk about the dangers of Carson City, sorry about the churchy dead kid. Then they'd go on with their regular day because, to them, it was just words on a page.

I handed the obituary back to Dr. Matthews. "I think they didn't know Jason."

Dr. Matthews nodded. "And you did?"

"Well, yeah. He was my best friend."

"Would you have written something different?"

I would've written about the first time Jason and I got to go camping on our own, up at Marlette Lake. We hiked the five miles up from our families' campground and hung out the whole afternoon, swimming, fishing, and skipping rocks. We started a campfire and ate sizzling, charred hot dogs off sticks that tasted like pine, then bet on who would see the most falling stars. We hadn't even set up camp. We weren't gonna because we wanted to sleep outside, under the stars.

Then it started to pour, one of those Nevada rains that come out of nowhere. We hadn't seen a cloud before the first drop pelted us. We ran like mad to get the tent up when I realized I had forgotten the poles. We ended up scrambling five miles down to our families' camp in sheets of rain, up to our ankles in mud.

Most guys would've been pissed. Jase just said, "Yeah. I could've brought them, too. Whatever."

That's the kind of stuff I would've written about. It says a lot more about a person than being on the honor roll.

91

"What would you have written, Kyle?"

"Something else. Something real."

Then we had another one of those awkward silences when Dr. Matthews waited for me to keep talking but I didn't.

She cleared her throat. "Your hearing is coming up soon. What are you feeling about that?"

Maybe it would be easier for everybody not to see me anymore. I shrugged. "It's not really up to me. After what I did and all, I guess it depends on the laws."

"What do you hope the outcome will be?"

I deserve to be sent away. My life needs to be put on pause. "I guess I don't hope for anything, you know? Just waiting."

"Waiting is hard."

"I guess so," I said.

"It might help to fill in the blanks on that day."

It doesn't matter anymore. Jason is dead, so whatever happened in the shed doesn't matter.

Scene Three.

Erased.

Jason.

Erased.

Now it's my turn to fade out.

When I got home from Dr. Matthews's, Mark and Mr. Allison were waiting for me.

"I'm here. I'm not happy. Remember what I said?" Mark asked.

"Um, not really."

"As long as you stay in line, you and I won't have problems. Your performance at the funeral yesterday isn't what I consider staying in line." Mark snapped his gum. A blue vein bulged across his temple every time he clenched his jaw. *Snap*, bulge, *pop* . . . *snap*, bulge, *pop*.

"Kyle, Mr. Grimes is talking to you. Please look at him." Mom brought out a pot of coffee for everyone. Dad had picked up a dozen donuts. Grease seeped through the box.

"We need to talk about your behavior." Mark sat down.

Eight days had gone by. Eight days of meetings with Mark, Mr. Allison, Gollum, and Igor. Eight days of Dr. Matthews and gray pills. Eight days of nothing but *tick, tick, tick*. And we had finally gotten to Sunday morning.

Mr. Allison paced back and forth. "Kyle, we need to talk about everything. Tuesday we stand before the court and Juvenile Master Brown. This is your future—your life."

Some life.

"You know that the Bishops can speak at your disposition. They have the right to address the juvenile master," Mark continued. "This can be good or bad. I don't know the Bishops very well, but after the stunt you pulled yesterday at the funeral, I don't suppose they're going to talk very favorably."

"Kyle, this is really important," Dad said, sitting next to me.

Snap, bulge, *pop* . . . *snap*, bulge, *pop*. Mark spit his gum out into a napkin and took a bite out of a greasy donut. Glaze stuck to the corners of his mouth. "A homebound teacher will be with Kyle until after the disposition. I don't see how it would do any good for him, at this time, to go to school. My recommendation will be probation—no time served—until he is eighteen years old. This probation, though, can be successful only if he has heavy psychological counseling. I don't see why Kyle should go to a detention center."

How can I not be sent away?

"So he'll be able to come home? For sure?" Mom asked. She had chewed her nails down to nothing.

"It's ultimately up to the juvenile master—the judge— after she reads through all statements. Usually, she'll sway toward the PO and psychiatrist's recommendations. But there are times when things don't necessarily go the way we believe they should. That could happen, for instance, if the DA and the Bishops put forth compelling reasons why Kyle should serve time."

"Oh, God." Dad's voice was just a whisper.

It was like I had broken something inside him.

"Let's not even go there for now." Mark clapped Dad on the back. God, he had to get this back clapping under control. "I have faith in the system," he said. Obviously

Mark hadn't seen *The Shawshank Redemption* or *The Count of Monte Cristo.*

"These things happen," Mark said.

These things happen.

"But what about college? Getting a job? Voting? Will Kyle be a felon?" Dad rubbed his temples.

Voting? Dad's worried about me voting?

"Juvenile records are sealed. No future employer will have access to Kyle's past. What happened here stays here."

Buried with Jason.

Dad sighed. *Relieved, I suppose. Good thing murder won't get in the way of a college education.*

"Okay, then," Mark said. "I'd like to have a little time with Kyle."

Everybody went to the kitchen. Mark and I sat in the living room, the box of donuts between us. "This is your one chance. I'm doing my best to help you, but you've gotta help yourself. And what you did yesterday doesn't help. All of this can count against you. Everything you do from here on out will be put under a microscope, analyzed, and dissected. You've got to shape up."

I nodded.

Mark scratched the back of his head. "I'll be coming by to help you prep for the disposition. A lot of us here are working hard for you, but your future is in your hands."

So was Jason's future. In my hands.

Mark said good-bye to Mom and Dad. He put on his black leather coat. "We'll talk soon."

And then they all disappeared, one by one—Mark, Mr. Allison, even Mom, Dad, and Mel—leaving me alone, staring outside at the Bishops' house.

Neighborhood kids ran up and down the street, playing football like it was a regular Sunday. Like nothing had happened.

Only eight days had passed. Jason was already forgotten.

I figured I knew, then, what death felt like. Nothing at all.

For the disposition, Mom wore the blue dress she saved for teacher conferences. Dad wore the suit I'd borrowed for the funeral. They had bought me a new shirt and tie and a pair of gray slacks. Not like it mattered.

Mr. and Mrs. Bishop came in. They shuffled into the back row. Mrs. Bishop strained to keep her head up and ended up resting it on Mr. Bishop's shoulder. He had black circles under his eyes and fidgeted with his wristwatch. I never really knew what sadness looked like until then.

The judge had declared it a closed hearing, open only to family. That was good. I didn't want anybody bugging Mom and Dad. They had enough shit to deal with.

The lawyer at the other table shuffled papers. Mr. Allison whispered things to Dad. Mel sniffled and blew her

nose. Mom leaned over and straightened my tie. "Things are going to be okay."

She had been saying that the past ten days, like some kind of mantra.

But they weren't.

I looked down at Jason's watch and rubbed its face. I almost felt relieved. Soon it would all be over. The end. My end. Roll the credits.

Judge Brown came in, and we stood up. She turned to the lawyer standing across from Mr. Allison and me. "Mr. Wiley, I've reviewed the case. Would anybody for the prosecution like to make a statement?"

We all turned to the Bishops. Mrs. Bishop held a crinkled handkerchief and dabbed at her eyes. Mr. Bishop sat with his arms crossed in front of him, a roll of skin bulging over the top of his shirt collar.

The courtroom was silent.

Say something, I thought. *Tell her about what I did; about the "probation friend" list; about Jason's new friends. TELL HER.*

Mr. Wiley shook his head. "No, Your Honor, the Bishops don't wish to make any statement. You have everything before you."

"Would you like to say anything to the court?" Judge Brown looked at me.

I took a sip of water and looked back at the Bishops.

Mr. Allison and Mark had prepped me the past week about what I should say. They said it's really important to show remorse. "Look sorry," they'd said. "You really need to look sorry in court."

What does *sorry* look like? Does it have a color? A shape? Is it dark or light? I knew what it felt like, but what did it look like?

"Mr. Caroll, would you like to address the court?" Judge Brown asked. She leaned on her desk.

Mrs. Bishop stared at her lap, her head too heavy to hold up. Mr. Bishop's eyes darted back and forth from the judge to the stenographer. Mom's knuckles turned white from squeezing Dad's leg so tight. Dad wrapped his arm around Mel, and she leaned into his shoulder. I looked at Mr. Allison.

"Go ahead," he urged.

I'm sorry.

Mr. and Mrs. Bishop looked up at me. Mrs. Bishop didn't even try to wipe her tears.

"I—" I cleared my throat. "I, *um*—"

I remembered Mr. Bishop trembling in the church, saying, "You have no right . . . you have no right." I heard Brooke's sobs and Chase asking if Jason was going to be all right. I saw splatters of blood all over Dad's shed and the burning flesh. I saw Jason's body doubled over, lying in a pool of blood.

Jason would never graduate from Carson High or go to college. He'd never get to backpack around Europe. He'd never have a fancy New York art show.

I had no right.

If I didn't look sorry, they'd have to send me away. Judge Brown would see that I deserved to go to a detention center.

I turned from the Bishops and shook my head. "No."

"Just a moment, Judge Brown," Mr. Allison said. He turned to me. "Don't you want to say something?" He leaned in. "Remember what we talked about."

I squared my shoulders and swallowed. "No. I have nothing to say." I heard a sob from the back of the courtroom.

Judge Brown paused, then nodded. "Then I'll proceed." She flipped through a file on her desk. "From the evidence presented by the Carson City Police Department, letters received, and the recommendations of Mr. Grimes and Dr. Matthews, I remand Kyle to three years' probation under strict supervision of his parole officer, Mark Grimes, and continued psychological evaluations by Dr. Matthews or any other state-appointed psychiatrist. I also recommend counseling for both families, the Bishops and the Carolls. This was an unfortunate incident." Judge Brown looked at me. "Do you have any questions?"

"But," I said, shaking my head, "but they have to tell

you about me—about what I did."

Judge Brown nodded. "I know what you did, and your sentence is appropriate."

I killed Jason. How could that sentence be appropriate? I turned to the Bishops. "You *saw* what I did. Tell her! *Tell her!*"

Mr. Allison yanked on my shirtsleeve. "Enough!"

"I don't get it. I kill Jase and get a get-out-of-jail-free card? Like nothing? What the fuck is wrong with everyone here? I *did* it. He's dead because of me."

Dad grabbed me by the shoulders. "We're going home, Kyle. We'll deal with this there."

I looked around the courtroom. It didn't make sense. It was an open-and-shut case. I killed him. I confessed. And they send me home because it was an "unfortunate incident"? I felt numb. It was like everything had turned upside down again. Everything was wrong. I squeezed the watch, my heart pounding in my ears.

"Look at me, Kyle. Look me in the eyes." Dad held my jaw in his hand. "We're going home now."

I shook my head. "No. No. No."

Mark came forward and said, "Juvenile Master Brown, clearly Kyle is not himself, and he is reacting to the intense pressure he's under."

The judge looked at him, then at me. She said almost in a whisper, "You are one step away from being in

contempt of this court. You have a second chance because this court believes you deserve it."

Second chance? Tell that to Jason—the dead one.

"This court does not hand out second chances lightly," Judge Brown continued. "You have an opportunity to make something of yourself—to redeem yourself. I never want to see you in my courtroom again. Understood?"

I felt cheated. My life was supposed to have been put on pause, just like Jason's. It wasn't supposed to turn out this way. I wasn't supposed to be allowed to go on. *Freeze frame.*

Every morning since October 8, I'd wished I could wake up to the smell of pancakes and the sounds of Mel's blow-dryer and Jason's snoring. I'd wished that I had a chance to make that day right. It would be so easy if life could be edited. But the movie never changed. And there was no way to erase what I had done or to go back.

"Court adjourned." Judge Brown stood abruptly and left.

The courtroom settled into an uncomfortable silence, something you wouldn't find in a real courtroom drama. I looked back to see Mr. and Mrs. Bishop slip out the door.

Mom muttered, "Thank God. Thank God," all the way to the car.

Mark caught up to us. "Kid, I don't know what the hell that was all about."

Mom stepped forward. "He's upset. His best friend is dead."

"I'm aware that he's upset, but that's the kind of thing that gets a judge doubting a kid. Dr. Matthews is going to have to reevaluate whether or not we should send him to West Hills."

"The mental hospital? Aren't we jumping to some conclusions here, Mark?" Dad opened Mom's door. He was in charge now. "Aren't we expecting a lot of a fifteen-year-old? Under the circumstances, I'd say Kyle is handling things pretty well."

Mark nodded. "It's not an easy time for anyone. But you need to know what I expect of Kyle."

Dad waited, arms crossed. He stood head and shoulders above Mark.

"Kyle's job is to get good grades and stay in line." Mark turned to me. "You still belong to the state. Understand?"

I nodded.

Mark turned to Mom and Dad and softened his tone. "After a while, these kinds of cases tend to take care of themselves. I'll be in contact with Dr. Matthews. I want to see Kyle's progress reports. I'll be talking to you about his behavior and grades, but I hope I don't have to come around too often."

Mom and Dad nodded. Mark shook my hand. "See you later this week, okay?"

"Okay."

We got into the car. Dad's hand shook too hard to put the key into the ignition. "Christ," he whispered.

Mom steadied his hand and guided the key in. Dad rested his head on the steering wheel.

"You okay, Dad?" Mel asked. She leaned forward.

His shoulders shook with silent sobs.

15

The house was quiet. I trudged up to my room and stared at my poster of *Sin City*. Jase had been a Frank Miller fanatic, and it was the only movie poster he ever really wanted. But I didn't give it to him. I never bet him for it, either. Some part of me liked having something Jase wanted.

Did that mean I had pointed the gun at him? On purpose?

I took the poster off the wall, leaving a glaring white spot. One by one, I tore down the rest of my posters, piling them up in the corner. I didn't deserve to have anything anymore. I should've given the fucking poster to Jason.

I looked at the blank walls. Nothingness. That's what I deserved. My mind returned to the scene I thought of at

the detention center—my death scene. There was only one way to make things stop now. The ultimate freeze frame. Could I do it?

Shivering, I pulled my knees to my chest and remembered that Jason's duffel bag was pushed into the back corner of my closet from that last night he'd stayed over.

What did he pack? Would I have to return the stuff to his parents?

Jason had used the same duffel for every sleepover since fourth grade. It was blue and white and had a purple stain on the bottom from the time that Jeffrey Mason barfed up his Kool-Aid.

I pushed my shoes out of the way and reached back to drag out Jason's bag. The duffel was heavy. I had forgotten that he had come over right after school. He hadn't even stopped at home. His gym shoes and sweaty clothes were inside. He had brought home his math, science, and history notebooks with every white space filled with drawings and doodles. His doodles were art, not just squiggles.

He had a library book: *The Metamorphosis*. I flipped through the first few pages. Jase read the strangest shit. And the book was way overdue. I bet Scarface Cordoba, the librarian, had already sent out a hit on Jase for not returning it.

Too late, Scarface.

I wiped my nose and wondered if the library had one

of those drop-off slots like they have at Blockbuster so I could drop it off and run. Or maybe if I got to school at five A.M., I could leave it propped against the door.

Leave it to Jase to stick me with facing Scarface with an overdue book. Shit.

Dude, Jase, nice touch. It was overdue before all this happened.

Suck it up, Kyle. Things could be worse.

Yeah, can't argue with a dead guy.

You never could argue with me alive, either, man.

Whatever.

I pulled out his sketchbook and portfolio. They were his latest comics characters: Infinity Detention, Split Infinitive, Formaldehyde, Sketch, Kite Rider, Line Runner, and Freeze Frame. My hands felt clammy; my sweaty fingers smudged the notebook. I put it down, and an application for UC Berkeley's teen summer comic-book art program slipped out. Jason had already filled it in.

So he was going to apply after all.

Jason had big dreams.

Poof! Now they were gone.

I sat with the empty bag on my lap and my hands shook. It smelled like Jason—a combination of peanut butter, damp socks, and chalk. There wasn't a day that went by that Jason didn't eat a peanut-butter sandwich. The guy was obsessed with them—the chunky kind. And the damp

socks and chalk smells were everywhere else. I don't know why, especially since damp socks are kind of raunchy, but it was more of a damp-socks-after-going-through-the-wash kind of smell. Damp, clean socks. And the chalk came from all those pastels he used for his art.

I buried my head in Jason's bag and breathed deep. I didn't even hear Mom coming up the stairs.

She opened my door and gasped. "Kyle! What are you doing with your head in a duffel bag?"

I pulled my head out and shoved the duffel and Jason's stuff under the bed. "I'm just thinkin', Mom."

"With a duffel bag on your head?"

"Yeah. I read about it somewhere. You know, to help me think."

"Are you okay?" Mom scanned the bare walls. Dad's frame filled the doorway. He hadn't said anything since we'd left the courthouse.

The smell of Mom's perfume drifted through the room, erasing Jason.

"I guess I kinda want to be alone for a while. If that's okay."

Mom came toward me. Dad pulled her back. He nodded. They backed out of the room. Did they smell Jason too?

"Don't forget we have a family session with Dr. Matthews later today," Mom said.

"Sure. Okay."

Dr. Matthews had a new office. A big one with that same lumpy couch and tiny desk. But she also had beanbags and Legos and stuff like that. Every session with her got worse. It was like she wanted to direct the movie in my head. But she didn't get that the most important scene of the movie had been deleted, and there was no way to recover it.

She wanted us to do family therapy once a month—including Mel. Mel glared at Dr. Matthews the whole visit.

"Now, then. I want to talk about Kyle." Dr. Matthews focused on me and smiled.

She was obsessed with my issues and ticked them off for my family.

I wanted to interrupt and say, *Actually, I killed my best friend. No matter what I do, that's what happened. And I can't go back. And when I close my eyes, all I see is blood and Jason stuffed in a coffin. And his mother made him wear makeup for eternity. That's my real "issue."*

But I didn't say that.

Dr. Matthews leaned back. I wondered if her knotty hair might get caught up in the buttons on the couch cushions. She started talking to my parents, and I played their conversation in fast-forward, listening as the shrill words blended together. Then I stopped and played it backward, so everything sounded like a different language.

".gnilaeh ot pets tsrif eht si gnirebmemeR"

"?rebmemer ot deen elyK seod oS?"

".ti deen ew nehw su stcetorp taht enihcam lufrednow a si dnim ehT .oN"

"?aisenma ekil ti sI"

".emit emos etiuq rof deneppah tahw yltcaxe rebmemer ton thgim elyK"

".sseug I ,gnimlehwrevo neeb lla s'tI"

I looked at the wall. Framed diplomas hung all around the room. I couldn't believe she had actually gone to college for this stuff.

Dad put his arm around my shoulders. Mel rolled her eyes and kept looking at her watch. I let their conversation play in real time.

"We're going to get through this, Kyle." Dad nodded firmly, with confidence.

Dr. Matthews's bright dress blended in with the colorful sofa, and she looked like a blob with frizzy hair. If I squinted, I couldn't tell where the sofa ended and she began.

"Kyle needs to get back to school and start normal activities again. He's been on homebound since the incident and has not progressed. One of the terms of his probation is that he do his homework and get passing grades." She flipped through a folder. "Kyle needs to get moving. Inertia is *deadly*." She leaned over when she said that last part, ruining the sofa-dress-blob effect.

"Okay," Mom agreed. "Kyle will start on Monday."

110

16

Inertia is deadly.

Life is deadly too. Just ask Jason.

After Mom, Dad, and Mel had gone, Dr. Matthews said, "The disposition was pretty tough."

"It was okay."

"Do you really think you deserve to be sent away for what happened?"

For killing another person? Yes. "The judge didn't."

"But do you?"

"I dunno."

"Can you tell me why, then, you reacted the way you did at the disposition?"

I unclasped the watch, then clasped it again. "I guess I was surprised."

"What surprised you?"

"It's not like I expected to go home, you know."

She pushed a loose strand of hair behind her ear. "Were you disappointed that the judge didn't send you to a juvenile detention center?"

"Yeah," I said, then caught myself. "No. I mean, I dunno."

"Can you explain?"

"I killed Jason." I picked at a hangnail. It started to bleed. I sucked on it, letting the copper taste coat my tongue.

"Did you mean to?"

Since tenth grade started, I had eaten lunch alone in the cafeteria most days; the only time Jason called was to see if I could hang out with him and Chase. So really, it was probably just Chase who wanted to see me. Jason had only hung out with me alone one weekend, and he ended up dead.

Did I mean to?

Is not sharing lunch a motive for murder?

It would make the perfect film noir, like *The Maltese Falcon*. An old black-and-white detective movie with high-contrast photography and over-the-top acting.

Mark, the tough and gritty PO, moonlighting as a private eye, sits behind a desk. Smoke curls up from his unfiltered cigarette while he pours himself another stiff drink from the half-empty bottle of whisky. Sirens wail and a neon sign blinks in the background.

He hears the sound of high heels clacking on the stairway. The door flies open and in walks Dr. Matthews, clad in fishnet stockings and a dress that probably cuts off her oxygen supply. She bats her eyelashes. "Did he mean to? Will you help me, sir?"

Mark looks up at her and tips the brim of his hat.

Dr. Matthews throws herself into a chair, sobbing uncontrollably.

Mark coolly hands her a handkerchief and a piece of paper. "Here are my rates. I'll find out. I'll find out if he meant to. But know this: I won't play the sap for you!"

"Kyle?" Dr. Matthews tapped my shoulder. "Are you listening?"

"Yeah. Sure." The only problem with that movie is that Sam Spade never had a tan. Maybe I could convince Mark to stay away from the tanning beds on Fifth Street before shooting.

"Was there something you wished you could've said to the Bishops?" Dr. Matthews asked.

I'm sorry.

But I didn't say it, and now it's too late—just another scene I screwed up and can't edit. What a fucking mess.

"Okay. Let's try it another way. Are there things you

113

would've liked to say to Jason but didn't?"

Why did you ditch me for Alex and the guys?

Why didn't you want to hang out with me anymore?

Do you know what happened?

That's what I especially wanted to ask him: *Do you know what happened?*

"Maybe you can write those things down. Write them when you think about them. You don't have to show me," Dr. Matthews said.

I leaned back and stared at the water stain on the ceiling. "Okay."

"Your first day back at school will be tough." She handed me a card. "You can call me if you need to talk."

I hesitated.

"Take the card. You don't have to call. I just want you to know that you can."

The minutes slipped away. I lay in bed and listened to the house, its walls moaning in the wind, the familiar creak of the third step. Every evening the sun dropped behind the mountains, only to come back the following morning, streaming light into my bedroom. Every goddamned morning.

That Sunday, I sat by the front window and watched Chase run up and down the street with one of his kites. There was no wind, but the kid didn't give up. He was out

all day long from morning until evening. Nobody helped him at the Bishops' house. Jason would've. Jason was always there for Chase.

My stomach ached, watching Chase drag the tattered kite across the asphalt. His cheeks and nose turned red, flushed from the cold. Once in a while I saw him look toward my driveway.

Help him out, dude. Don't be an asshole and just watch him like that.

Easy for you to say. Your parents don't hate you.

Get over it. His kite's gonna get torn to shreds, and you know Mom and Dad won't get him a new one.

I got out to the porch but then I saw Mrs. Bishop, wrapped in a thick sweater. She called Chase inside. His kite hung limp. He dropped his head and went in just as the sun slipped away.

Don't forget about Chase, man.

I sometimes wished I could shut off the Jason in my head. Especially since he talked to me more often dead than when he was alive this past year.

Mark came by that evening. "Just wanting to check in."

No. He definitely couldn't pull off Sam Spade.

"You're a smart kid. It's time to get back on the bike, Kyle."

I nodded. He loved to talk about bikes. I wondered if he'd ever seen *The Great Escape*, but then figured a PO isn't

likely to watch a movie about escaping prisoners, regardless of the cool motorcycle stunts.

"Every action has a reaction," he continued. "Everything we do or say has an effect."

No shit, Sherlock. I bit my tongue.

Mark glared at me, like he knew what I was thinking.

"I'll see you Friday. Time to move on, Kyle." Mark left the house, his motorcycle rumbling all the way down the street. I had to be the only kid with a PO who looked like he belonged on the set of *Easy Rider*.

That night I listened as Mom and Dad argued. The wind rattled the windows, and birch tree branches scratched up against the house.

Time to move on, Kyle. Yeah, right. I thought about stopping time. And I only knew one way to do it. Everybody would be better off. Dying couldn't be so terrible—so hard to do. Besides, maybe then I could be with Jason.

Dawn came when I wanted it least, when I had finally found a quiet moment to escape my thoughts. Mel's alarm clock beeped. Dad had finished showering; his electric razor buzzed across his face. The smell of coffee drifted upstairs and turned my stomach.

I picked Jason's watch up off the nightstand and put it on. It would keep me where I needed to be until I could work up the guts to get there myself.

17

"**K**yle, come down for breakfast." I looked up to see Mom peeking in the door.

Mel thundered down the steps. "I can't do this, Mom. Brooke doesn't even talk to me. Everybody whispers when I walk down the hall. They all stare at me because of—" Mel turned and saw me at the top of the staircase. She looked away.

Mom gave Mel one of those another-word-and-you're-toast looks.

"Well, I'm *not* showing up with him at school today. It's just too weird. It's too—I dunno," she whispered. Like I wouldn't be able to hear her. Cheerleaders definitely don't have volume control. And Mel had freakishly developed vocal cords; she was the only one on the squad

who never used a megaphone.

"That's fine—I'm riding my bike." They stared at me.

"Kyle, it's late October. You can't ride your bike." Parents always come up with arbitrary shit like that. What does October have to do with riding bikes?

I didn't hear what else Mom had to say, because I walked into the garage, got on, and rode, taking Elm Street down to Crain to get to Fifth. I didn't want to pass Jason's house.

I checked in at the front office. Mrs. Brawn jumped up and grabbed my shoulders. "Oh, Kyle! How *great* to have you back!" It was weird to have her happy to see me. Mrs. Brawn was about ninety years old, and she had been the school secretary since Charlie Chaplin's silent-movie days.

Supposedly, Mrs. Brawn had once stapled a kid's tardy record to his forehead and made him walk around all day with it. I figured it was a rumor and told Jason it was impossible. "Plus," I said, "it's illegal for adults to staple things to body parts. That's abuse." Though it would make for a wicked scene in some kind of horror flick.

Jason had shrugged and said, "In the old days, teachers and secretaries could beat up kids. Believe what you want, but I'm not gonna piss off Mrs. Brawn."

I always felt a piercing pain in my forehead when I saw her. Jason had told me it was psychological. I supposed I could check with Dr. Matthews about that one.

That morning, walking in through the school doors, I wondered if the knot in my gut was psychological, too.

Mrs. Brawn patted my hand. "You don't want to be late, now. Not on your first day back."

I inhaled the soupy school smells: rusty metal, musty carpets, greasy food, sour sweat. I swallowed and rushed to first period, stalling in the doorway. Almost everybody had settled in. The desk between Catalina and Tim was glaringly empty. I wondered if Mrs. Beacham had erased Jason from her seating chart.

Catalina Sandina   XXXX   Tim Tierney

Was it that easy to do? Just a line through a name and he's gone? I backed up, figuring Mom and Dad could home-school me. Then I wouldn't have to see that empty desk every day. Or maybe I could get out of first period. It was the only class we'd had together.

"Hello, Kyle!" Mrs. Beacham squealed, walking up and squeezing my shoulder. "I'm delighted to see you back in class." Her nicotine-yellowed nails dug into my back as she nudged me into the room.

Everybody stared, then went back to their little gossip circles.

"Uh," I muttered to Mrs. Beacham and shrugged her claws off my shoulder. "Thanks."

I walked past Jason's desk, running my fingers across it, feeling the bumpy etchings other students had carved. Jase liked graffiti. He said it was an art form, rebellion against the establishment. I found my seat between Judd and Marcy. Marcy stared at me, and when I looked up at her, she pretended she was reading.

Judd grunted, "Hey, Kyle." He slumped over his English book and picked his nose.

Jessie Martinez came up to me after third period. "Kyle?" She looked around. "Do you think they're gonna make a movie about this? I, uh, wouldn't want to look bad on the day they film."

"Yeah, Michael Moore's coming this afternoon," I muttered.

"What? Did you say . . ." She flipped her hair and globbed on some sparkly lip stuff that smelled like grapes.

"What's the deal with chicks and fruity-smelling lip stuff?" I'd asked Jason one day.

"It's for hookin' up. Don't be a moron."

"Yeah, like you'd know."

"You've gotta be joking. You've never hooked up? Not even once?"

I hadn't really thought about it much, except for in the bathroom. "Well, yeah, but she didn't have a whole bunch of strawberry shit all over her lips."

Jase grinned. He knew I was lying but didn't call me on it. "It's better with the lip gloss. Try it sometime," he said.

God, I hope Jason had sex. I mean, I hope he didn't die a virgin. I hadn't thought about that before.

I thought about Dr. Matthews's "things to ask Jason" list. *Can people who are dead talk to other people who are dead? That's another one.*

In gym, we played handball. It felt good to throw the ball as hard as I could. Coach Copeland came up after class. "Kenny—no, Karl—no, excuse me, Kyle! You ought to think about indoor-track tryouts."

What a tool. He couldn't even get my name right.

"I don't know, Coach Copeland. I'm kinda busy lately." I went into the locker room to shower and change.

A group of guys, Jason's new friends, hung out by my locker. Jase used to be like me, kind of a loner. But since high school had started, he had friends from all over the school.

"Hey, Shadow." Alex Keller shoved Pinky and Troy out of the way. He came right at me.

The locker room cleared out. I was left alone, trying to get dressed with six assholes staring at me.

Then I thought about Chase. Who made sure nobody messed with him? Who watched out for Chase now that Jason was gone? How could I not have remembered about

121

those kids? The ones who bullied him?

I told you. Don't forget about Chase.

I didn't. I just—

Alex pushed me against the locker. "Kenny—no, Karl—no, excuse me, Kyle, I'm talking to you." Alex and his friends snickered.

"Yeah, what?" I pushed him off.

Alex stood in front of my locker and pushed me back. "You're a freak, dude. We saw you at the funeral. You're a freak. And nice fuckin' shoes."

That was it? That's the best he could do? I'm a freak with bad taste in footwear?

Alex blew a bubble and it popped, *smack*, in my face. He chomped his gum. "You weren't even friends anymore. Why was he over at your place?"

That stung. I felt blood rush to my face, and my lip quivered. I replayed the last two sentences.

"You weren't even friends anymore. Why was he over at your place?"

"You weren't even friends anymore. Why was he over at your place?"

Just because I wasn't a tool and didn't want to ride along in Alex's dumb-ass truck to make Taco Bell runs, that didn't mean Jase and I weren't friends. So they'd shared a couple of taco pizzas. Big fuckin' deal.

I came back to the scene. Alex and Pinky were laughing

about something. I looked down to see a glob of slobbery chewing gum slide down my leg.

"And you just walk around like nothing happened." Alex leaned in closer. "Well, I won't forget what you did to my friend." He shoved me. "Ever."

Yeah, neither will I, I thought. Then I realized that it was a lie, since I couldn't remember to begin with.

I went back to that moment: My pajama pants were wet. I kneeled down to squeeze out the dew. Then Jase was dead. The end.

A crushing pain ripped through my head when Pinky flicked my temple. "See you in math," he said.

Alex sneered. "Like I said, fucking mental." Then they walked out of the locker room like some B-movie bounty hunters.

If I concentrated hard enough, would I disappear? I squeezed my eyes shut.

"Kyle?" Ricky Myers tapped me on the shoulder.

I jumped. Not invisible. "Yeah?"

He looked around. "What's it feel like, you know?"

"What's what feel like?"

"What's it feel like"—he looked around again—"to kill somebody?" Ricky swallowed hard, and his Adam's apple bobbed up and down, bulging out of his neck.

"I don't know," I muttered, and left.

18

The hallways hummed with that prelunch electricity. I walked into the cafeteria. Everybody sat in the places they had staked claim to at the beginning of the year. Plastic trays banged on tabletops. Students ripped into their utensil packs, dropping the plastic bags on the floor beside them. The smell of greasy synthetic cheese permeated the air.

I scanned the tables, looking for a place that looked safe. Kids stopped eating. They whispered. They stared at me until I looked over, then they pretended that I wasn't there. Backpacks filled empty chairs, and guys spread their stuff out, marking territory like dogs pissing on trees.

Alex slammed into me. "Sorry, Shadow. Didn't see you there." Pinky and Troy laughed. "Doesn't look like there's

any place for you here." He said it loud.

Everybody looked up and focused on me, the one-man freak show. It was a classic scene, starting with a shot of me holding my lunch bag and a library book. The camera swish-panned the cafeteria, and all I could see was a blur of faces. Then the camera swiveled back to me for a closeup.

Sweat trickled down my temple and back. My face felt flushed.

Fade out. Fade out. Fade out.

That's what I wished I could do. Fade out and go away. Forever. I couldn't handle this anymore.

But the cafeteria stayed the same, with all those faces looking at me. Everyone knew that I wasn't the one who should be standing there. The wrong guy had died.

Rewind, then. Back up. Get out. I reversed into the hallway.

"Hey, kid. Where are you going? Lunch is that way." The hall monitor pointed to the cafeteria doors.

"I, um, I forgot I have to return a library book. And I don't have time after school." I pulled *The Metamorphosis* out of my backpack. "I can't return it late. Mr. Cordoba will have my head."

The monitor laughed like he understood. Nobody returned books late to Mr. Cordoba. "Okay. Go ahead."

I exhaled, not realizing I had been holding my breath, and hurried away. I stood outside the library in the empty

hallway, opening the door a crack. Scarface sat hunched over the newspaper. Rumor had it he was in the Witness Protection Program; the Feds wouldn't let the school get rid of the guy.

Some seniors had told Jase that when Scarface was young, he worked with one of the largest cartels down in South America smuggling drugs and shit. That's where he got the nasty scar that ran from his left eye down to his jaw. He was offered a shitload of cash and lifetime protection to testify against the *patrones*.

"Yeah, but why'd he become a librarian? Man, Jase, they'd never give a guy like that a job with teenagers. That's, like, well . . . Couldn't happen."

"I don't know, but that's what I heard," Jason said. "Some seniors said they saw five passports hidden in his office."

No seniors ever talked to me, so I didn't know that kind of stuff.

"Yeah, like the school board would hire him with that past. Don't you figure they at least ask for references— noncriminal ones?"

"Don't be a shithead. The Feds always create these new identities. It's not like his real name is even Cordoba."

Jason had a point. We kept an eye on him freshman year, but in the end, Scarface Cordoba didn't have any of

the telltale mob-assassin signs. He didn't even wear nice suits.

"I think he's just a regular old librarian, Jase."

"Maybe."

"Are you in or out, Mr. Caroll?" Mr. Cordoba asked. His left eye sagged a little, pulled taut by the scar. I followed the bumpy, purple skin from the corner of his eye down to his jaw. It zigzagged by his nose, then stopped right below his chin. "Mr. Caroll, are you going to stand there gawking at me all day? In or out?"

"In?" I answered. I couldn't believe he knew my name.

He nodded. A group of students played chess in the far corner of the library. Almost every table had somebody at it. "What can I do for you today, Mr. Caroll?"

I pulled *The Metamorphosis* out of my backpack. "Mr. Cordoba, this is late. Um, a friend of mine had it, and I, uh, just found it."

Scarface took the book from my hands.

"I'm sorry." I figured the late fee would be, like, $245. I'd have to empty my savings to cover Jason's stupid book.

Scarface scanned the book into the system and nodded. "You're set."

"How much do I owe you?"

"For what?"

"The late fee. It's about four weeks late, I think."

"Nothing." Scarface set the book on top of a pile of books. "Find a seat if you'd like. But don't eat and read at the same time. When you're done eating, wash your hands; then you can read. Don't make a mess of my books."

I looked around. Nobody stared at me. Most kids were already reading and doing homework. The only empty table was the one right smack in front of Scarface's desk. I sat down and pulled out my lunch, staring out the window while I ate. The last leaves clung to the spindly branches of the birch trees in front of the school. The grass had already turned yellow from the cold.

When we were in seventh grade, Jason and I went around and raked people's lawns for cash. I was saving up to buy a video camera, and Jase wanted some vintage comic book. But we ended up wasting more time than working, because once we'd raked up the leaves, we couldn't resist jumping in the piles. We came up with some sweet moves: the half pike, the forward flip, the back bend, and the cannonball. I once did a cannonball on a leaf pile in Mr. Bachman's yard and bit through my lip. It bled like hell, and he called my mom, flipped out because he thought we'd sue him. I think he spread the word, because after that, nobody would hire us. My lip swelling to the size of a basketball didn't help with our corporate image. Neither did the fact that I walked all messed up because my ass hurt.

"What's worse, Jase: not being able to eat or not being able to sit?"

Jason laughed. "Well, you've got them both. You tell me."

I would've laughed, too, if my lip hadn't hurt so freaking much.

"Mr. Caroll, are you going to sit there daydreaming all day or actually get something done?"

I jumped. Scarface peered over the top of his newspaper.

"I'm, um, sure. I'll read something." I grabbed the first book I could reach from the shelves.

The Baby-Sitters Club. Shit. I looked over at Scarface. He buried his head in the paper. I sighed, relieved he hadn't noticed.

Scarface cleared his throat. "Mr. Caroll, I didn't know you were a babysitter."

"I, um. I just grabbed something."

"Okay." He went back to his paper.

"Mr. Cordoba?"

"Yes?"

"I don't really know what to read."

"What do you usually read?"

"I don't." I shrugged. "I watch movies."

Scarface raised his eyebrows and peered over the top of the paper. "Well, then, try this." Scarface handed me back

The Metamorphosis. "I assume you haven't read it."

I sat down and started the book. I was still on the first page, where some guy wakes up as a bug, when the bell rang. The library cleared out. I took a deep breath and got ready to go, tucking *The Metamorphosis* into my backpack.

"See you around, Mr. Cordoba."

"I look forward to it, Mr. Caroll."

As I headed out the door, Mr. Cordoba swept through the library, cleaning crumbs off the tables, straightening books, tucking in chairs.

The last two periods dragged. Pinky Deiterstein, the genetic mutant, sat behind me in math. He had enormous thumbs, almost as long as his pointer finger, twice as wide, and really hairy. During the eighth-grade Thumb War Finals, Pinky broke Tim Preston's thumb. We heard the crack when the bone was crushed.

If Pinky hadn't flicked me in the head and whispered, "Murderer . . . murderer," I might've been able to pay attention.

Murderer . . . murderer . . . murderer . . . murderer . . . I replayed the words over in my head. It was the voice-over to my movie—one line, one word: *Murderer . . . murderer . . . murderer . . . murderer.* It echoed against the walls of my mind.

Don't forget about Chase.

Murderer . . .

Don't forget about Chase.

Murderer . . .

I rubbed my temples; my head ached.

While everyone around me was working on some complicated problem with tangents and cosines, I leaned as far forward as I could, out of Pinky's reach, and pulled out one of the notebooks Jase had left at my house.

I thought about *Run, Lola, Run*, the perfect movie. Lola gets this call from her boyfriend, and everything is messed up. So she gets to do the scene over and over again until it turns out the way it's supposed to, always starting with the phone call. I closed my eyes. I remembered my pajama pant legs sticking to my ankles. That's where the scene would have to begin.

Since I couldn't remember that scene in the shed, maybe another director could, like Tarantino, Lynch, or even Hitchcock. Yeah, Hitchcock. That would be sweet, to have him direct a scene in my life. He'd probably get it right.

Don't forget about Chase.

I won't.

You already did.

I was just . . . I didn't . . . I just . . .

I closed the notebook, hoping I could turn off Jason's voice. Announcements crackled over the loudspeaker before the final bell. I gathered my stuff and decided to

head over to Chase's school just to make sure he was okay.

It was Monday. I'd see Dr. Matthews the next day and Mark on Friday. All these people had become a huge part of my life because of just one scene. The final bell rang. Pinky brushed by me and pushed my books off the desk. Jason's notebook flipped open to a page where he had drawn Sketch, his latest superhero version of himself. A sinking feeling settled over me.

There was no editing real life.

19

I picked up all my papers and stuffed them into my backpack. I left without stopping at my locker for homework.

Orange doors opened and slammed. The halls filled with students, but I pushed my way through. Buses lined up and I darted between them, ignoring the teachers' shouts, "Hey, you, get back over here! Hey! Stop!"

I got onto my bike and rode as hard as I could. My lungs burned from the cold air. I looked at my watch: 10:46. *Shit!*

I knew I only had about ten minutes, so I pumped hard until I got to Chase's school. The buses were already lined up, idling, belching out puffs of black smoke. I hid my bike behind a bush and walked between the buses until I found bus 12. It was the first in line. There were some Dumpsters

right at the corner—perfect for hiding.

The bell rang and kids spilled out of the school, running around with macaroni art projects in their hands and winter hats with pom-poms on their heads.

Then I saw a familiar green hat with multicolored stripes. Chase was walking and reading a book at the same time, probably science fiction or something about kites.

Every year he picked a new thing. Last year it was dinosaurs. Two years ago it was space travel. He was a walking encyclopedia. The kid would be great for *Jeopardy!* someday.

The same bullies who had been giving Chase shit since kindergarten walked behind him, stepping on the heels of his shoes, shoving him along. Jesus, those kids were only eight, but they were already total jerks. Didn't their parents know? Do parents know when their kids are shitheads?

Julian, the leader of the pack, was a short, freckly punk with greasy red hair. He had buckteeth and warty hands. It was kinda sad, really. I didn't remember the others' names. One looked like he had flunked a few grades. He was shaped like a bowling pin. And the other kid looked pretty normal except for this really irritating eye twitch. I listened for the trill of the whistle from that old Clint Eastwood western. This one would be called *The Warty, the Fatty, and the Twitchy.*

Bowling Pin pulled off Chase's hat. "Thanks for the hat, Chase-Basket-Case. I needed a new one. Tomorrow I'll need a scarf."

Chase didn't do anything. He didn't turn around. He didn't stop them from taking his stuff. He just dropped his head and walked on.

Keep your head up, Chase. Keep it up.

Tears stung my eyes. I hated those kids for making Chase feel so small. I scanned the area. None of the bus-duty teachers were looking my way, so I stepped from behind the Dumpster, cutting the three off.

"Hey, cool! It's a high-school guy! What are you doing here?" Julian wiped his hand across his face. A glistening trail of snot stuck to his jacket arm.

Why are the snottiest kids the bullies?

I didn't say anything. I looked over at Chase getting on the bus and looked back at the three kids. "Leave Chase alone. Got it?"

Bowling Pin stepped forward, then looked like he changed his mind mid stride and stared at the ground. "Okay." His voice cracked at the end.

Poor kid.

Twitchy stood behind. I noticed his lip quivering.

Jesus, they were just kids. I felt like such a tool messing with eight-year-olds. But they were mean little shits. And Chase didn't have anyone else.

"Leave him alone."

They nodded, turned, and ran to their buses. Julian dropped the hat.

The buses chugged out of the lot. I picked up Chase's hat and waited for all the teachers to go back to the building.

I looked across the empty field, remembering how big I used to think the playground was. I walked over to the swings and sat down for a second, the chains pinching my fingers. They were the same swings we'd played on; the same ones Jase had fallen off and gotten a concussion.

I had about two hours until Mom and Dad would be home. I hated counting hours and minutes. I needed someone to talk to. I wanted to see a friend. So I got on my bike and rode until I got to the cemetery.

20

Nobody was around. I guess not many people take time to visit the dead. It's hard enough to get people to visit their great-aunts and grandmas when they're alive. Plus graveyards are creepy.

I opened the gate and wheeled my bike in. The gate *chink*ed closed behind me. I jumped.

"A little nervous, boy?"

Some old guy holding a rake stepped out of a small office.

"Uh." I looked around. If he hadn't talked, I would've probably thought he was a zombie. This guy was straight out of *Night of the Living Dead*. He had to be a thousand years old.

"Looking for something?"

"Yeah." I nodded. "A friend."

"Here's the map." He pointed out a map that had the names of people and their grave numbers. There were hundreds.

"Thanks."

I skimmed over the names. I'd never known a dead person before, except for Jason's grandma Peters. But she was old dead. That's different. I found him. Jason G. Bishop—R—317.

"Find it?"

The *Living Dead* guy was still there. It was like he didn't breathe or anything, he was so quiet. Maybe he didn't want to wake them all up. Couldn't really blame him. It didn't look like it'd be too long before he'd be joining the ranks.

"Yeah, thanks."

I walked along the winding paths. Tufts of dying grass grew around cracked tombstones. The farther I walked, the fewer tombstones there were. Most graves had stone plaques marking the ground, covered by dirt and dried leaves.

An old oak tree stood in the middle of a bunch of graves, and I pictured its roots webbing around coffins like gargoyle claws. I shivered.

Then I saw it. Jason. The earth was fresh, a rusty color, loosely piled. Flowers surrounded the grave. They were

pretty wilty, but they still looked okay. There was a wooden box with water-stained, muddy pictures inside, CDs, a bag of marbles, a Jack Sack—all sorts of things. Tattered satin ribbons were tied around the box with popped balloons on their ends.

I hadn't brought anything.

I dug around my pockets and pulled out a quarter and a wad of chewed gum that had stuck to my pocket lining. I had nothing for him, not even a comic book.

"Fuck," I muttered. My voice sounded like an invader in the heavy graveyard silence. Plus I didn't think *fuck* was the most appropriate thing to say. "Excuse me," I whispered, looking around.

Jesus, who was I talking to?

I stared at Jason's grave.

Jason's grave. My stomach lurched. I could feel the acid work its way up. I swallowed hard and breathed. My legs felt heavy, but I forced myself forward.

Jason G. Bishop
SON, BROTHER, FRIEND
He walks with God

I ran my fingers across the black granite set flush with the earth. I think I would've put ARTIST on the stone, too. Some people think that you have to actually be famous and

stuff to call yourself something. But Jason really was an artist, even if he hadn't sold anything yet. Yeah: Jason G. Bishop, ARTIST, SON, BROTHER, FRIEND. He would've liked that. I wasn't so sure about the *He walks with God* stuff though.

The slate gray sky darkened with heavy clouds. My fingers burned from the cold. I crouched down.

"Hey."

Leaves rustled.

"So this is it." I rubbed my arms and sat by the stone, pulling my knees to my chest. "Thought you might like a little company."

It was actually a peaceful place. Maybe that's what bugged people so much about graveyards. They were silent. Nobody hollered or shouted in a graveyard. The traffic was miles away. And dead people were a quiet bunch.

Silence is pretty shitty when you don't want to hear your own thoughts.

BROTHER: I traced the word with my finger. "I haven't forgotten about Chase. I'm gonna take care of him. Somehow I'm gonna make things okay for Chase. I promise."

The wind whined in the trees. I opened my backpack and pulled out a crumpled paper. "I, uh, I have a few things I've been wondering about. And things I guess I've wanted

140

to say to you. I don't know if it's anything you can help with, but, well, I've just been writing this shit down as it comes to me."

I waited. The wind picked up a little, and one of the ribbons came loose and skipped across Jason's grave. I was never big into signs, but I figured that anything was better than nothing. Maybe Jason was around.

"Okay. Well, first of all, it's been a hundred and eighty-five days. You know. The orange shoes and all. I betcha you didn't think I'd go through with it, huh?"

I cleared my throat and straightened out the paper. "I'm also just kinda wondering if you're lonely. Is it the same kind of lonely we have down here?"

I paused. I had been lonely way before Jason died, but it wasn't like this.

"This is the thing. If I wait for a sign every time, this might take all year. So I'm just gonna read through the list, okay? Just thoughts and stuff. No big deal. All right. Here goes: Are there angels? Like with wings? Are there ghosts? Are you a ghost? Can you pick to be a ghost or angel or is it kind of assigned?" I paused. "Can you, um, talk to Grandma Peters? Can you hang out with other dead people? Like if I died, could we hang out?"

I looked around. It had to be the loneliest damned place on Earth. I shivered and zipped up my jacket. I held Chase's hat in my hand and shoved the questions into my pocket.

141

"Do Alex and the guys come?" I wiped my nose. "Were they really good friends? That good?" Well, they didn't fucking kill him. That's gotta top the shitty-things-to-do-to-your-friend list. I breathed in deep.

"Dude, I messed up. Big-time. I just don't know what to do. These questions and stuff, they're just dumb. Dumb shit I think about so I don't have to think about this. About you. Here, you know? I just don't know how—how that could've happened. Anyway, I fucked up. I know I did." I closed my eyes and slumped against the pile of dirt. I thought maybe I could just never get up. Simple. Just sit and sit until I became one of the dead.

When I opened my eyes, the sky had turned purple-black. The first stars had popped out. My teeth were chattering.

I stood up and my feet tingled from the cold. I blew on my stiff fingers. "I've got Chase covered. I guess that's the most important thing, right? That's the one thing I can do right."

I looked at the headstone again. *Jason G. Bishop.* At least they hadn't spelled out Gabriel. He hated his middle name.

I turned back. "Hey, Jase? What's worse: killing your best friend or being killed by your best friend?"

No answer.

I kinda think the first one is worse. But that's because I don't know what the second one is like. Jase probably had his own ideas about that.

21

Riding home, I felt a little bit of relief. I had one thing under control: I could keep Chase safe. Maybe if I did that, kept my promise to Jase, I'd have a reason to stick around. I coasted into the driveway and saw Mark's motorcycle.

"Shit."

I threw open the front door.

"He's home now. He's here." Dad was talking to someone on the phone. Mom and Mark rushed toward me.

"Where have you been? We've been worried sick!" Mom shook my shoulders. Dad came over and pried her fingers off. "Do you have any idea what time it is?"

I looked at my watch: 10:46.

"Kyle, are you listening? Do you have *any* idea what time it is?"

God, I hated questions like that. If I knew the time, I was screwed. If I didn't know the time, I was screwed. Parents always get pissed because we don't have the right answers. They never figure that they have the wrong questions.

What if I didn't give a shit about the time?

I shrugged. This was definitely a scene I wanted to skip. Fast-forward.

They paced up and down the hall in jittery movements, their words coming out in high-pitched screeches. It was like watching one of those old quarter-machine westerns in Virginia City where you get to crank the action, and it goes as fast as you want.

I returned to the scene when Mark was getting ready to go.

He glowered. "Kyle, you messed up."

"I was just riding around."

"You don't get it, do you? You can't be anywhere without telling us where you are. *Anywhere.* If you pull another stunt like this . . ." Mark didn't finish the sentence. It was one of those if–then statements, without the *then*. Those were the worst, because you knew the *then* had to be pretty awful. "I'll call tomorrow." He looked from Mom to Dad. "And get him a damned cell phone." He left; his Harley rumbled down the street.

"Where were you?" Dad asked, steering me into the kitchen. "We were worried."

"I was just riding my bike around. That's all." I suppose they figured I had nowhere to go but school and home now that I'd killed my only friend.

"In the dark? Riding your bike?" Dad rubbed his eyes and leaned on the counter. "Things are—" he started to say. "Kyle, we don't—" He couldn't finish a thought. "We're really worried about you. We're just . . . is Dr. Matthews helping? Do you need to talk to someone else?"

The only person I needed to talk to was Jason. I couldn't shake the cold and stomped my feet on the kitchen floor, shivering.

"You're freezing. Go upstairs and get a sweatshirt. We can talk about this after homework and you eat your dinner. It's in the microwave."

Dad went to his office and closed the door. I walked upstairs. Mom was slumped against Melanie's door. I could hear Melanie's sobs. "They all hate me, Mom. They do," she bawled. "Brooke decided to quit cheerleading. She can't stand to be around me. And then you and Dad . . ." Her words were muffled by a new wave of sobs.

"Honey, I'm so sorry. You have to expect that things will be different for a while." Mom's voice sounded raw.

Different? Painting a room is *different*. Killing Jason could hardly be called *different*.

Mom turned and tried to smile at me. It was one of those forced it's-not-your-fault-you-ruined-our-lives smiles.

Through her door I heard Melanie say, "I hate Kyle. He ruined everything."

I went into my room and closed the door. At least she said what everybody else thought.

Somebody knocked.

"Come in." I flopped on my bed.

Mel walked in with puffy, red eyes. "I didn't mean that."

Yes you did.

"I just never want to go back to school again. I'd rather die." Melanie buried her face in her hands.

I knew how she felt.

"Things are that bad?" I asked.

She wiped her sleeve across her eyes. "I guess they aren't much better for you."

I shrugged. "I'm not a cheerleader. I'm pretty low profile, you know."

She sighed and sat next to me on the bed. "I didn't mean that. Really."

"It's okay." It felt good to sit next to Mel. Almost like things were before she got boobs.

"Maybe we can change our identities and move away," she said.

"Don't think I haven't thought about it."

"And I can't believe you're getting a cell phone." She punched me in the arm. "God, life is so unfair."

Mel had wanted one for about a year. I elbowed her. "Yeah, unlimited minutes with my PO."

She shook her head. "God, everything sucks. Life sucks."

I wanted to ask Mel if she thought it was always going to be this awful, but before I could, she got up and left.

I thought about Clock Westergard. Everybody at school laughed at him. He had stringy black hair and was too skinny. One arm was longer than the other, so when he raised his hand in class, it looked like either six o'clock or twelve thirty. He smelled like photo chemicals because he spent most of his time in the school's lab. He always walked around with this beat-up camera.

The "cool" kids messed with him. They hit his books out of his hands, shoved him into lockers, and gave him cans of soda shaken up. In ninth grade Troy Beckett slipped snow through the vents in Clock's locker. Kids laughed, like getting schoolbooks wet was the most hilarious thing ever. We knew that Clock's grandma didn't have money for new books and shit. All Clock did, though, was take out his books and dab them dry with a dirty gym shirt. Then he stood up and looked Troy in the eyes. We thought they'd fight, but all he did was hold his books and stare Troy down. Troy backed up and left. Then Clock looked each one of us in the eyes. It was like he was saying, *Fuck you*. I avoided him after that.

147

I wondered if I should talk to him, ask him how he got up to go to school each day. Christ, I didn't even know his real name. I think even the teachers called him Clock.

I stared at the words in my history book: *The Egyptians were among the greatest architects in the history of the world.*

I read that sentence seven times before I closed the book and looked out the window. A porch light flickered on at Jason's house. It was funny how from the outside everything could look the same.

Tuesday morning was more brutal than Monday, like the day was being played in slow motion.

At lunchtime, I headed straight to the library, but the door didn't open. I jiggled on the knob, thinking maybe it was jammed or something. Locked. Kids streamed by.

I zoomed in on the sign on the door: LIBRARY CLOSED FOR LUNCH ON TUESDAYS.

Fuck.

I held my lunch and *The Metamorphosis* in my hands and looked down the hall toward the cafeteria. I definitely didn't want to repeat the scene from the day before. The hall monitor had gone, so I snuck back by the science classrooms. Nobody ever hung out in the science hallway, because it smelled like chemicals and dead animals.

I leaned against some lockers and started to read.

"Mr. Caroll?" Scarface towered over me, holding a pile of science books.

I jumped. "Oh, um. I, um, was just on my way to the cafeteria." *The Metamorphosis* slipped from my hands and thunked on the floor.

Scarface nodded. "That's unfortunate. I could use some help in the library today." He turned to go down the hallway.

"Oh. I've got time." I cleared my throat.

He nodded.

I carried Scarface's books and followed him into the warmth of the library.

"Eat lunch—then you can help me with the books. You should have time for a little reading before the bell rings."

I sat at the table in front of Scarface's desk. He pulled out a Tupperware container of salad and some pita bread.

I chewed on my ham sandwich. I like it when the bread gets smooshed with the ham, cheese, and mayo and sticks to the roof of my mouth. Then I try to peel it off with my tongue without breaking apart the bread-ham-cheese mass. Jason used to do the same with peanut butter and jelly.

"What do you think about the book?"

I was in mid peel when Scarface spoke. I choked down the bite. "What?"

"The book. *The Metamorphosis.*"

"Oh. It's pretty weird, you know." Who would direct *that* movie? Maybe David Cronenberg. He was real into disease and weird transformations. Maybe he'd film it in a seedy downtown motel off Fourth Street in Reno. It would make a wicked flick.

Mr. Cordoba watched me. He didn't say anything but waited. Shit, he probably wanted a report or something. "I don't really remember where they are, um, which city." I opened the book, looking frantically for something about the setting, themes, main conflicts, and all the other crap Mrs. Beacham harped on.

"Mr. Caroll, I'm not asking for a presentation. Just tell me what you think about the book—about what you've read so far."

"Um, well, I'm not far or anything, but I kind of think it's . . . not too believable."

"How so?"

"Like who's gonna wake up a bug?"

"Don't you think somebody's life can change drastically from one day to the next?" Scarface asked. "One moment to the next?"

I paused. "I never thought about it like that."

"Sometimes you have to look beyond the words." He took a sip of water and said, "If you woke up one morning with your reality horribly altered, what would you do?"

I thought for a long time. "If I turned into a bug, I'd do anything to feel normal, I guess."

Scarface nodded and turned back to his work.

"Mr. Cordoba?"

He looked up.

"Do you think they ever made a movie out of this book?"

"Most likely. But I don't really know." He pulled some books out of a box. "We need to code these for shelving."

I helped him organize books, then read until the bell rang. "Mr. Cordoba?"

"Yes?" He looked up from his computer.

"Is the library open at lunch tomorrow? You know. It's kind of hard to read in the cafeteria. Lots of noise and all."

"Yes."

"Okay." I picked up *The Metamorphosis* and put it in my backpack. "It's a pretty cool book after all, huh?"

"That it is. See you tomorrow, Mr. Caroll."

"See you." I walked down the hall, thinking about all the ways *The Metamorphosis* could be filmed.

23

"**H**ey, Shadow!" Pinky came up to me and threw me into the wall. He kneed me in the stomach, over and over. I gasped and could feel my air shutting off like a valve.

Alex and Troy stood behind him, laughing.

"Dude, Pinky. We don't wanna kill the guy. Jesus Christ." I wondered if it could end like this; then it would all be okay. It would be over.

But what about my promise? What about Chase?

I fought to hold on as his knee kept jabbing me. Major fade-out. Just as everything started to go black, he stopped. I slumped to the floor, choking.

"Yeah, real tough, punk," Troy said. They walked off laughing, and the hallway cleared out.

Crash! Bang! Pow! Back to reality, comic book–style.

Nice friends you've got there, Jase.

They're not bad, once you get to know them.

Not bad? Pinky just tried to de-entrail me.

They're just . . . They're probably bummed too.

Oh yeah. I forget you were Mr. Popular. You know, you didn't need them.

Dude, I wanted to do other stuff.

What's that supposed to mean?

I just didn't want to watch old cult movies with you every Friday night for the rest of my life. What's the big deal?

Sorry to have cramped your style.

Whatever.

"Murderer . . . murderer . . ." The sound track kept playing, like one of Dad's scratched records.

The days passed. It didn't take long for teachers to start giving me notes to take home. "Dear Mr. and Mrs. Caroll: I'm concerned that Kyle has not turned in homework since his return to school."

I shoved the notes into my backpack. I didn't figure my teachers would cut me any slack if I told them I was too busy rewriting that scene. Dr. Matthews was still on a big memory kick, wanting me to remember everything about Jason, but black thoughts crept through my brain, staining everything.

"Why don't you try thinking of it as a movie," Dr.

Matthews had said. "Write the whole movie and see what happens when you get to that scene."

But I didn't want to write the whole movie. I wanted *Run, Lola, Run,* a chance to redo that scene until I got it right.

SCENE THREE: Take One—Tarantino style
"Comanche," by the Revels, is blasting in the shed and fades out completely before fading in again when the action begins.

FADE IN: Kyle's pajama pants are wet, sticking to his ankles. He crouches down to squeeze out the dew. He breathes in deep. Jason holds the gun out for Kyle to get a closer look.

CLOSE-UP of Jason twirling the gun in his hand.

> JASON
>> Check it out, Kyle. It's pretty
>> tight, huh?

> KYLE
> Sweet, Jase. That's sweet.

CUT TO: Kyle's mom framed in the doorway, silhouetted by the October light.

FADE IN: Jason lying in a pool of blood, then the camera cuts to the gun in Kyle's, alias Shadow's, hand. The camera pans the shelves of the shed and focuses on an old suitcase and a samurai sword.

WIDE-ANGLE SHOT: The Mexican standoff between Kyle, Jason, and Kyle's mom. Kyle holds the gun. Mom holds a pancake spatula.

CUT TO: CLOSE-UP of the gun in Kyle's hand.

WIDE-ANGLE SHOT: The entire shed is coated in blood. Blood sprays from Jason's bullet wounds like in a Manga comic strip.

FADE OUT: Jason lying in a pool of blood.

I reread the scene.
Wrong.
It was like failing a test about the memories of my own life. How pathetic could I get? Maybe I had early-onset Alzheimer's.

Dude, you're really calling it Scene Three?

Yeah. So?

So that last scene of my life is called Scene Three?

I can't think of anything else right now.

You've gotta do better than that.

Give me time and I'll come up with a name for the whole thing.

Jesus, Kyle. Scene Three.

My teachers' notes padded the bottom of my backpack. I looked at the blanks of missing homework. Egyptian pyramids just didn't seem all that important. When I woke up, the only thing that got me through the day was Chase. Lady Macbeth and her damned spot seemed pointless. All she needed was a little bleach. It had worked in the shed.

I had to be totally mental. Maybe I *did* need Dr. Matthews after all. Even if she didn't seem to help.

I saw Clock one day on my way back from the nurse's office. I was in a hurry to get to Chase's school.

"Dude, you okay?" Clock asked. He pulled his hair back into a ponytail and leaned against the wall, his arm outstretched.

Six fifteen, three thirty, six fifteen, three thirty.

Clock stared at the bag of ice I was holding to the back of my head. "What happened?"

My head throbbed. The nurse had said ice would stop the swelling, but the ice was melting, dripping all over me.

Clock shrugged and left. I didn't get how anybody could be like Clock. Carson High was a school of sheep, but Clock didn't give a shit.

"Clock!" I shouted, and ran after him. "Man, I'm sorry."

"About what?"

"Dude, I don't know. Just stuff, just life."

He turned to go.

"Clock, uh, what's your name, anyway?"

He grinned. "Clock."

I had to get to Chase's school, but I needed to know who Clock was. "Your real name, I mean. What's your real name?"

"What's it to you?"

"I dunno. It's just . . ." My voice trailed off. What *did* it matter? "I guess I'd just like to know."

He leaned against some lockers and didn't say anything for a long time. He just stared at me, like the time he had stared at Troy, with his black eyes. Icy eyes.

But I didn't look away.

Then he smiled. "It's Kohana."

"That's different."

"It means 'fast' in Lakota." Clock zipped up his coat and walked away. "I'm gonna be late."

I looked at my watch: 10:46.

"Shit, what time is it, uh, Kohana?" I called after him.

He looked back at me. "Time to get a new watch."

"Yeah, yeah. What time is it?"

Clock pulled out one of those old-fashioned pocket watches on a rusty chain. He flipped open the lid.

"That thing works?"

"Better than yours. It's two fifty-five."

"Shit! I've gotta go."

I rode as fast as I could and got to Chase's school just as the lines of kids were piling into the buses. Chase got on and found his favorite seat, three rows from the back on the right-hand side next to the window. He sat with his head leaned up against the pane, his breath fogging the glass.

He was okay.

24

I *shade my eyes, trying to block the glare of the fluorescent light.*

All I can hear is the spinning of a gun cartridge and a click when it's shoved back into place. "One bullet; one chance." Jase holds the gun out to me, twirling it in his fingers. "Take it, you fucking pansy. Do it."

Canned laughter from an audience. My eyes adjust and I see Alex, Pinky, Troy, and Jase sitting in a circle. Each holds a gun to his neighbor's head. The entire school is watching us.

"Sit the fuck down, Shadow," Alex sneers.

Sweat beads on my forehead and I take the last empty chair. Jase shoves the gun into my hand. "What're you gonna do?"

The lights dim and it's just Jase and me, facing each other

in the shed. "*Whaddya wanna do?*" *he asks.*

"*Whaddya wanna do?*"

"*Whaddya wanna do?*"

I jerked awake and stumbled to the bathroom. The porcelain felt cool on my face. Everything was blurry. I tried to stand, but my knees buckled. Clutching the toilet, I retched, squeezing my eyes shut, trying to erase that day. What did we do in the shed? How did it happen?

My nightmares were getting worse. It was easier not to sleep.

I listened to the darkness and watched Jason's house through the window. Mrs. Bishop had put a candle lamp in the window. She never turned off the light. I read that's what people used to do for sailors or soldiers, waiting for them to come home.

Didn't she know he was never coming back?

I walked out to the shed, locked with a padlock now. I touched its cold metal doors and leaned my face into it. Did it smell burned inside, like ashes and fire?

I imagined Jason and me switching places, him having shot me. Things made more sense when I thought about it that way. People loved Jason and would understand. People would forgive. Dying wouldn't be so hard.

Then I thought about Jason gasping for breath, his eyes glazed over, the blood seeping through his T-shirt and

pooling on the shed floor.

It took him ninety minutes to die. Less time than a movie. Ninety minutes from the bang to time of death.

How long did they work to revive him? Did he hurt the whole time?

I sat in the shadows, writing in the dim light of the streetlamp, trying to remember, returning to the same place, the same moment, the same scene. I needed to remember.

SCENE THREE: Take Two—Lynch style
The theme song of Scene Three by Angelo
Badalamenti plays softly in the background,
leading Jason and Kyle to the shed. The light
sputters on and buzzes, never giving the
viewer a full view of the scene. The shed is
bathed in green by the flickering fluorescent
light that hangs from the shed's rafters. The
hum is barely audible above the haunting
score.

CUT TO: Man in a cowboy hat behind the shed,
peering in through the window.

POINT OF VIEW: Viewers see the shed through
Kyle's point of view. The camera pans the

shelves of the shed. They are blurry because Kyle is trembling. The music fades out and changes to "Dance of the Dream Man."

FADE IN: Kyle's pajama pants are wet, sticking to his ankles. He crouches down to squeeze out the dew. He breathes in deep. Jason holds the gun out for Kyle to get a closer look.

> JASON
> (Holding the gun out to Kyle)
> Check this baby out. It's pretty tight, huh?

> KYLE
> Sweet, Jase. That's sweet.

> JASON
> What do you wanna do?

> KYLE
> I dunno. What are we s'posed to do with it?

> JASON
> (Pulling his collar up to look like a minister)

Well, Kyle, let's see what our
options are. We could put the gun
away and continue to freeze—

FADE OUT: The shed doors wail, and Kyle's mom
comes in, blue box in her hand. Behind her,
Jason's mom is holding a ring. Their dresses
are identical.

MAN IN THE COWBOY HAT
Just say, "He's the one."

KYLE'S MOM
He's the one.

CUT TO: CLOSE-UP of the gun in Kyle's hand.

FADE OUT: Jason lying in a grotesque position.
He is deformed, so a sheet covers his face.
There is no blood.

I read the scene. At least I got a little more dialogue this
time. "What are we s'posed to do with it?"
Did Jase want to put the gun away?
Or did I just take the gun and squeeze the trigger?
Any way I wrote it, Jason ended up dying.

At school, everybody was pumped after a crazy Halloween weekend. Somehow dressing up like a ghost didn't seem that fun anymore. I biked over to the cemetery.

"I'm on a pretty tight schedule now, with Dr. Matthews and Mark. It's hard to get away."

I rubbed my eyes and crouched down to pick up the red M&M's that were scattered everywhere. Chase had been there. He only ate the red M&M's. I put them back in the small jar and gathered a few rocks to keep it steady.

"Anyway, I read *The Metamorphosis*." I waited. "I liked it."

A family walked by and gathered at a fresh grave. They piled flowers on the black soil. "And Chase is doing good. I mean, I haven't talked to him or anything. But I can tell he's doing good. Those kids stopped messing with him. He leaves you these M&M's." I jiggled the jar. "Have you ever wondered what he does with the other colors?"

I wiped the mud off Jason's marker.

"I'm still wearing the orange shoes. It's been a hundred and ninety-five days, counting today."

I scuffed my shoe on the patchy grass. "I still feel bad all the time, Jase. And I have these dreams. *Nightmare on Elm Street*. It's awful." I wiped the tear that dripped down my nose. "Is it better there? Where you are?"

The wind cut through my jacket. The family huddled over the other grave, humming, praying. I kneeled down

and leaned my forehead on Jason's marker, waiting for an answer.

Then I heard soft footsteps padding down the walk. I turned to see the Bishop family—all of them. Mrs. Bishop held a bouquet of bright flowers in her arms.

I jumped up and knocked the M&M's all over the grave. "Shit!" I looked for a place to hide. Leave it to the Bishops to bury Jason on the only treeless hill. The only way out was across the graves.

I ran, hopping from grave to grave. "Sorry, sorry, sorry, excuse me, sorry, sorry." The last thing I needed was to piss off half of Carson City's dead. "Excuse me, sorry. Sorry." I didn't stop running until I got to my bike. It took me a while to steady my hands to unlock the chain. As I pulled my bike out, I noticed that somebody had put a small jar of red M&M's in the drink holder. I looked back. The Bishops had disappeared behind a short hill. I put the jar in my pocket and rode home.

25

Lunchtime in the library was like a frame still. I could always count on the chess club taking over the back table; the skinny girl with glasses sitting at the table kitty-corner from me; Brady, the junior class president, coming in to read the newspaper; and Joaquín Sánchez, the center for the varsity basketball team, coming in twice a week to tutor his little brother in math. It would've made a great publicity shot.

At the end of the period on a Friday, I handed Cordoba *The Metamorphosis*.

"Mr. Caroll, do you need another book?"

"Yeah. Maybe."

He pulled down books from the shelves. "What would you like to read?"

I picked up *The Time Machine*. "Maybe this one." I looked at the names of those who had checked it out but didn't see Jason's. I wished I had asked him about more of the books he'd read. Maybe Mr. Cordoba knew.

"That's a classic, Mr. Caroll." Mr. Cordoba stamped the book. "See you Monday."

"Sure. Thanks." I sighed, glad to have something to read over the weekend.

Mel met me out on the porch that day with her you're-in-deep-shit look. "Kyle, you messed up. They got your progress report today, and Mom freaked out. Big-time. She won't even talk."

"What shade of red is she?"

"God, Kyle. This is huge. It's about as bad as it can get."

"Man, I didn't think progress reports came until mid-November. That's weird."

"Kyle, it *is* mid-November."

I imagined a scene where the camera cuts to pages of a calendar flipping through the days, stopping on November 11. Somebody tears out the date; the camera zooms in on the piece of paper drifting into the wastebasket. I go back and change the scene. It would be better to stop and tear out October 8.

"Thanksgiving is in two weeks." Mel snapped her gum and grabbed my arm. "Jesus, I sometimes wonder what planet you live on. What have you been doing all these weeks in your room after school?"

Nothing, I thought. Absolutely nothing. Could Mel understand how much energy *nothing* took?

I heard Dr. Matthews's voice saying, "Inertia is deadly." It echoed down the streets.

At least it was a better voice-over than *murderer . . . murderer . . . murderer.*

"C'mon, Kyle." Mel pushed me through the door. Mom held on to Dad's hand so tight, you could see the white in her knuckles, just like at the disposition. Freeze frame: Mom and Dad on the couch.

I wondered if they were trying the whole stay-still-so-the-Earth-swallows-me-up thing. I could've told them that it doesn't work. Mark had his arms crossed in front of his chest. I concentrated on the bulging Chinese tattoo. Jesus, the guy even had muscular wrists. I hadn't even noticed his Harley at first. It was as if all my life scenes were blurry.

"Kyle, we need to talk."

Nothing good ever follows *We need to talk.*

"We received your progress report today." Mom rubbed her temples.

"We didn't realize things were this bad." Dad leaned on the coffee table.

Mel shoved me into the easy chair and sat down on the arm next to me.

"You haven't turned in one homework assignment for over a month, since October." Mark's temple vein pulsated. His tattoo twitched. What if the tattoo guy had written *Dog*

shit in Chinese instead of *Control, Determination, Peace,* or whatever the hell it said? How would anybody know? Anybody not Chinese, I mean. I pictured Mark visiting Carson City's Golden Chopsticks Chinese Palace and having all the waiters laughing at his *Dog shit* wrist. "You're failing every class." Mark looked back at the progress report. "Every class but PE."

Mom clenched her jaw and glared at Mark.

I looked from Mom to Dad. How could I explain to them how pointless homework seemed?

Dad said, "Remember what Dr. Matthews said? Remember how important it is to get back into life?"

Back into life? As if I ever got out of it. That was Jason. Out of breath. Out of time. Out of life.

It was like somebody had shouted, "Cut! That's a wrap!" as soon as that ER doctor walked into the waiting room at 10:46.

That's a wrap, Jase.

Yeah. Scene Three.

I don't have time for this shit right now, okay?

Whatever. Scene Three.

"What work did you bring home this weekend?" Mom asked, and reached for my backpack. She opened it and pulled out *The Time Machine,* my notebook filled with Scene Three, sixteen tardy notes, seven notes from my teachers, and a detention warning. "What the— Jesus, Kyle.

170

Why didn't you give me these notes?"

I shrugged.

"Why didn't your teachers call? What the hell is going on with the school? What happened to open communication?" Mom paced back and forth, reading through the notes.

"It's not a big deal," I muttered.

"Being sent to a juvenile detention center? Not a big deal? Is that what you want?" she cried.

To go away forever and never have to face anyone again? Never have to look at the shed again? Never have to look at the Bishops' house again?

But then again, I had Chase. And a promise to keep.

Plus, I had seen some raunchy movies about prisons. Maybe I'd end up being some fat guy's bitch. That would suck. Alex and "the guys" were better than that.

Mark leaned in and skimmed through some of the notes. "You've been given a second chance here, and look what you're doing." He pulled a faded piece of paper out of his pants pocket. "This is a grade contract. Sign here. If you blow your grades again, we'll have to come up with some alternative plans."

"What's that supposed to mean? Alternative plans?" Mom clutched my backpack.

Alternative plans probably mean a place in the Willow Springs or West Hills psych wards. White walls. White tiles. White jackets. White noise. Stanley Kubrick.

He turned to Mom and Dad. "Kyle needs to learn that he is responsible for his own actions and poor choices."

Did I choose to point and aim and shoot?

Dude, I still can't believe you're calling it Scene Three.

Ah, fuck you, man.

Mark glowered at Mom and Dad. "Probation is about monitoring, listening, keeping track of what's going on. And that's obviously not happening here."

"So we're supposed to know everything about a fifteen-year-old boy who hardly speaks? He walks into his room and sits there all afternoon until the next morning. What am I supposed to do about that?" Mom turned a deeper shade of red.

I could've made a sweet documentary about what happens to parents after their only son fucks up their lives.

Mom's eyes darted between Mark and me. "Kyle, we want to help you. I'm afraid—" She gripped the notes in her fist. When she realized that they had formed a sweaty ball, she let them drop to the table, then tried to straighten them out. "You're just so disconnected," Mom said. She kept her head down. Mom didn't like to cry in front of anybody.

Dad cleared his throat. He sat on the end table next to my chair. "It's not just the grades."

Then the room fell silent. No comic relief for this scene. Finally Mark stood to go. "I'll set up a meeting with Kyle's teachers and Dr. Matthews for next week." He shook

Dad's hand. "We'll get things worked out." Mark thumped my shoulder. "Last chance, kid." He motioned to the grade contract.

Mom finally looked up from the crumpled notes on the table. She nodded. A solution had been placed on the table. A meeting. With adults. Talking about how to fix me—the one who broke everything else.

Mark left and Mom returned to my backpack. She picked up the copy of *The Time Machine* and ran her fingers along its crooked spine. Her voice trembled. "Are you reading this book for a report?"

"No."

"Okay. Then what are you studying in your classes?"

"I don't know."

She sighed. "Okay. Okay. This is my fault."

Why did they always want to take the blame for the things I did wrong?

"We need to get this homework in order," Dad said.

We, we, we, we, we . . . I wondered if Hannibal Lecter's parents said shit like that. "Hanni, honey, we need to try to stop killing people, then doing nasty things like broiling them for supper. . . ."

"Can't you call a classmate to ask for some assignment—any assignment?" Dad asked. He rubbed Mom's shoulders.

I shook my head. "I don't have anyone to call."

173

26

Tuesday morning, Dad took me to school. "Kyle, you need to stay after school for a while today. We arranged for you to go to the library. Mom and I are having a big meeting with your teachers. You need to get back on track."

Back on track.

Back on the bike.

Back from the dead.

The day sucked. I thought about all of them—my teachers, my parents, Mark, and Dr. Matthews—sitting in Principal Velásquez's stuffy office. I hoped *all* my teachers didn't have to be there.

After the last bell, I rushed to Chase's school and came back as fast as I could. It took longer running, since I didn't have my bike that day. I looked at the clock in the hallway

outside the library. I was forty minutes late. Maybe Mr. Cordoba didn't know what time I was supposed to get there.

I stood outside the library in the empty hallway. Lunchtime was one thing, but almost nobody went to the library after school. Nobody who didn't have to, anyway.

"You're late."

I jumped. It was like the guy could see through his newspaper and the door. I cleared my throat. "Sorry."

"Get in, then."

I handed *The Time Machine* to Mr. Cordoba.

"Well?" he said.

"Well?" I echoed.

"Tell me about the book."

I paused. "Really, I guess I was kind of disappointed. I expected to get answers, you know?"

"Disappointed? Answers?"

"It didn't help me much, Mr. Cordoba." I cleared my throat and stared down at my shoes. The orange had faded, so they looked more like a dirty peach. I had to find a way to glue the peeling rubber back on.

"What do you want help with, Mr. Caroll?" he asked.

"Um, I dunno. It's just that I guess I wanted something else. Something about being stuck in time."

Mr. Cordoba put his paper down. "Stuck?"

"Have you ever wanted something so bad, you thought there had to be a way for it to happen?"

That's one of the last things Jason had said to me. We ran into each other Thursday after school. He was hanging out by the flagpole, waiting for Alex to pick him up.

"Where're you guys heading today?"

Jase shoved his books into his backpack. "Nowhere." He looked real down.

I sat next to him. "What's up?"

"Have you ever wanted something so bad, you thought there had to be a way for it to happen?"

I shook my head. "Whaddya mean?"

Jase pulled out a letter from UC Berkeley. He handed it to me. I skimmed it over.

"Oh, shit, Jase. I'm sorry."

"I thought I could get into the winter comic-book art program for teens, you know? I've even been working on this new portfolio." He pulled out a sketchbook of school superheroes and villains. "But I'm just not good enough."

"Dude, there had to be major competition. Plus you submitted your old stuff. It's not as good as this." I pointed to Infinity Detention, who shaped his body into the infinity sign, zapping his enemies to the detention room forever. Split Infinitive was awesome. Her body would divide in two, and she'd crush her enemy's brain if he messed up on grammar.

Jason smiled. "Check out Formaldehyde. He's the master villain. He doesn't even kill his enemies, but preserves

them in these massive jars and leaves them in the science hall on exhibit."

"And you?"

Jason flipped the page. "I'm Sketch. I can draw anything the superheroes need. So if Kite Rider needs a kite that spouts fire and shit like that, I draw it and it comes to life. Or if Freeze Frame needs a stopwatch, I draw it up."

"Freeze Frame?"

He turned the page. "Check him out. Look familiar?"

I grinned. "Freeze Frame rocks."

He nodded. "I was debating between Freeze Frame and Director's Cut. I went for Freeze Frame so you could stop time. You're the only force that can stop the *zap* of Infinity Detention."

I flexed. "Freeze Frame. This is sweet." I skimmed through the notebook and saw Line Runner. Some lame-ass basketball guy who looked like Alex. I cleared my throat. "You should try again for next year."

Jase shrugged. "I was thinking about the summer program, but that one's even harder to get into than the winter one. I'm not even gonna try."

"Don't quit. You'll get in. I'm sure of it. Especially with this new stuff."

Jason bit his lip. "Nah. You just like being a superhero."

"Who wouldn't?" Alex probably did, too. "You'll get in."

"Probably not."

"For sure. What's worse: never trying and never knowing, or trying and getting your ass kicked once in a while?"

Alex drove up. He rolled down the window. "You tagging along, Shadow?"

I didn't get why Jase would even bother being friends with those ass wipes. I shook my head. "Nope. Busy today." I got on my bike.

"Hey, Kyle?"

"Yeah?"

"You still thinking about trying out for basketball?" Jason asked.

"Yeah, maybe." Basketball was my latest lame-ass effort to keep up with Jase and his new friends. My friendship with Jase had become a pathetic game of follow-the-leader with him sitting in the director's chair.

Alex snickered.

Jason lowered his voice, like he didn't want Alex and those guys to hear. "Wanna shoot hoops after the homecoming game, then?"

"Cool." Then it slipped out. "You can stay over tomorrow night if you want. I just got the uncut version of *A Clockwork Orange*." Fuck, why did I invite him? He probably had a few parties to go to with Alex.

"Yeah. Sounds good. See you tomorrow."

"See you."

I hadn't really known what Jase had meant when he said he'd wished for something so bad, but now I did. I wish I'd never seen Jason after school that day or that the dialogue was different. It would've been an easy scene to fix. All I had to do was leave it at playing basketball after the homecoming game. Easy.

Mr. Cordoba tapped a pencil on his desk, waiting.

Maybe he would understand. "Have you ever wanted to go back and edit something in your life?" I asked, staring at the carpet.

"Yes, I have."

I looked up. "Really?"

Mr. Cordoba was nodding. "Really."

I waited for a while, hoping he'd tell me. But he sat quietly behind his desk, watching me.

"So what did you do?"

"To what?"

"To change the past? Or"—I paused—"to delete it."

Mr. Cordoba frowned. "Delete it?"

"I guess. I mean, I dunno. It's confusing."

"The past will never go away, Mr. Caroll. But you can make peace with it."

"How?"

"By facing it."

I sighed and sat down. As if it were that easy. I pulled out the notebook and wrote:

SCENE THREE: Take Three–Hitchcock style
A carnival organ pipes "It's a Most Unusual
Day" in the background. FADE IN: Kyle's
pajama pants stick to his ankles. He crouches
down to squeeze out the dew, then sits next
to Jason on the workbench. The contents of
the shelves blur behind them.

DOLLY ZOOM/HITCHCOCK ZOOM: the shelves. The
shelves overwhelm the foreground. The viewer's
attention is taken away from Kyle and Jason
and directed to the contents of the shelves.
The viewer sees a newspaper clipping, with a
picture of Hitchcock advertising a weight-loss
product, lying on top of an old dollhouse.

CLOSE-UP of the dollhouse staircase.

WIDE ANGLE: Jason is facing the camera. The
viewer sees the back of the murderer. He has
shaggy brown hair. He is short and thin. He
looks like Kyle from behind, but the viewer
does not see his face. He breathes in deep.
Jason holds the gun out.

CLOSE-UP of gun in Jason's hands.

180

CUT TO: Kyle wiping his hands on his pajama pants, trying to keep his hands from trembling.

                    JASON
          (Jason holds the gun out to Kyle.)
          Check this baby out. It's pretty
          tight, huh?

                    KYLE
     Sweet, Jase. That's sweet.

                    JASON
     What do you wanna do?

                    KYLE
     I dunno. What are we s'posed to do
     with it?

                    JASON
          (Pulls up T-shirt collar around
          his neck, making him look like a
          pastor. He scowls.) Well, Kyle,
          let's see what our options are.
          We could A: put the gun away and
          continue to freeze, or B: put the
          gun to good use.

                    181

CUT TO: the gun passing from Jason's hand to
Kyle's.

HITCHCOCK ZOOM: to a mirror behind Jason. The
viewer's attention is directed to the mirror,
where he sees, reflected, the face of the
killer. The killer is holding a glass of
brandy and the gun.

I was just up to the part of the scene where I was going
to drink the brandy when Mr. Cordoba interrupted me.
"Mr. Caroll, you have a lot of catching up to do, from what
I understand." He eyed the notebook.

I put it away. The master of suspense would have to
wait. Nobody argued with Cordoba. Ever. I opened my history book and started on the day's assignment. It wasn't as
boring as I thought it would be. The only noise for the next
hour was the sound of Mr. Cordoba working on the computer and the scratch of my pencil on paper.

"Mr. Caroll, it's time to find your parents."

I looked at the clock: 4:45. It was the fastest hour I'd
had after school since— Well, for a long time. As I was
packing up my stuff, my parents appeared at the library
door. For a second they looked like strangers. Mom looked
skinnier. Dad's shoulders slouched. He opened the door.

"How did it go?" He was looking at Cordoba.

"Give us a few more minutes." Cordoba nodded his head in my direction. Dad closed the door. "So, Mr. Caroll, I think our trial period went well. I'll expect you here every day after school as well as at lunch. On time."

Our trial period? Every day? On time? What about Chase?

"Uh, Mr. Cordoba. I can't."

"You can't what, Mr. Caroll?"

"I, um, I can't be on time."

Mr. Cordoba arched his eyebrows and cracked his knuckles. "Because?"

Because I stand behind a Dumpster to watch out for my dead best friend's brother. Too weird. I didn't want to sound like a stalker. "I just need a half hour."

He waited for me to get my arms through my backpack straps. "So it looks like you'll be getting up a half hour earlier, then, to get here before school."

I groaned. I didn't mean to, but it escaped out of my throat. I didn't care about lunchtime and after school. Getting up to spend even more hours at school—that kind of sucked.

Mr. Cordoba lowered his voice. "You need your half hour after school? I need your half hour before school." He cracked his knuckles again. "Do you need another book?"

I nodded. "Yeah. Thanks."

Mr. Cordoba nodded and handed me *A Separate Peace*.

"Don't we have to read this in eleventh-grade English or something?"

"Probably."

I raised my eyebrows.

"Read it twice."

I didn't argue. I looked at the signatures of kids who had checked it out. Jason hadn't.

"Mr. Caroll, your parents are waiting." He opened the library door. "I'll see you tomorrow morning."

"Okay, Mr. Cordoba." For a moment, just a moment, I felt almost normal.

27

After Mom and Dad's conference with all the Carson City school district's employees, I became every teacher's project. I couldn't go anywhere without being mobbed by somebody who wanted me to be *involved*.

At home, things weren't much better. Uncle Ray came down from Reno at least once a week so he and my dad could have breakfast. They invited me once, but I couldn't stand the breakfast smells: syrup, pancakes, fried sausage. I felt nauseous and had to go sit outside. The only things I could stomach for breakfast anymore were cereal and Pop-Tarts.

I went to Dr. Matthews's office every Tuesday, the only day I had left to visit Jase because I got out of library duty for the shrink.

At Dr. Matthews's I hardly ever spoke. Every week she asked me to tell her about October 8. Over and again. Once I asked, "Tarantino or Hitchcock style?"

It threw her for a loop. That afternoon, neither of us said much.

The days dragged. At school, I couldn't understand how Karen Jacobs and Maria Ramirez were excited about Sadie Hawkins. I couldn't understand why nominating the winter homecoming court was so important. The only things that made sense were watching Chase, going to the graveyard, and the library.

Then I saw the flyers.

MEMORIAL ASSEMBLY FOR JASON BISHOP:
5TH PERIOD

How long had the flyers been up? Why hadn't I seen them before? They were pasted everywhere with a picture of Jason from freshman year, when he didn't have long hair. He hated that picture.

The sophomore class officers handed out flyers and balloons that read: JASON, YOU'RE IN OUR HEARTS FOREVER. They all wore black, and Sarah McGraw, class president, dabbed her eyes with Kleenex. I'd never even seen her talk to Jason. They swept through the hallway like storm-troopers.

Jesus, they were probably going to read some bad poetry, the kind you find on greeting cards and bumper stickers. I bet I was the only one who knew that Jason's favorite poet was e. e. cummings.

All of last year, Jason had refused to capitalize his name in English class. The student teacher, Miss Torrence, marked Jase down for bad capitalization one day. He brought in e. e. cummings's poems and said, "If he doesn't have to, why do I?"

A few months ago, I saw Miss Torrence working at Costco. I think she decided not to be a teacher after all.

The flyer felt like lead in my hand. The first bell rang for fifth period. "Shit," I muttered. I crouched down between some lockers, behind a trash can, waiting for the tardy bell to ring. The halls emptied as kids rushed to the gym. I had to get out of school before the assembly began.

When I stood up, prickles of light ripped through my skull. For just a second everything went grayish black. Steadying myself on the lockers, I walked down a side hallway nobody used except for the smokers. They had rigged the door of the emergency exit so the fire alarm wouldn't go off. The hall smelled like potpourri spray and old cigarettes. I saw Clock walking across the field and thought I could catch up to him. I almost made it through the door when I felt a hand on my shoulder.

"Going somewhere, Mr. Caroll?"

Cordoba.

"Mr. Caroll, are you lost, perhaps?"

There was no escape. My eyes darted around the hallway.

Cordoba leaned over and picked up the flyer. "I need some help reshelving books in the library. I think you just got the job."

He didn't smile. He didn't give me one of those bummer-you-killed-your-friend looks. He didn't give me a Mrs. Beacham–style sympathetic shoulder squeeze. He just pointed toward the library. Relieved, I followed Cordoba down the hall. I took out *A Separate Peace* and handed it to him.

"You finished quickly."

"Yeah."

Cordoba raised his eyebrows. I knew the drill; it was book confession time.

"It was so-so."

"Why so-so?"

I sighed. "I dunno. I didn't get it. How could Finny be so okay with everything after what Gene did to him?"

"So Finny shouldn't have forgiven Gene?"

"I think there are some things . . ." I cleared my throat. "Some things aren't forgivable."

"Even between best friends?"

I thought for a bit. "Especially between best friends."

"How so? What isn't forgivable?"

Living. Being alive. Breathing, eating, sleeping, jacking off.

I heard "The Star-Spangled Banner" blaring out the gym speakers. Mel slumped into the library and sat next to me. "Didn't feel much like an assembly today." Her mascara was smeared underneath her eyes. I was relieved to see her. I didn't want to talk about Cordoba's books anymore.

"Me neither," I whispered.

"They're all assholes, Kyle. You know that."

I didn't know who "they" were, but I figured it had to do with her cheerleader friends. It sucked to see Mel so sad all the time.

Sorry, I wanted to say. But it just seemed like such a copout.

"The Bishops are coming. They're planting a tree with a plaque or something."

The knot in my stomach moved up to my throat. My eyes burned. It was like everybody wanted to relive it over and again. But they weren't there. They didn't know how awful Jason had sounded—gurgling, gasping, dying. It wasn't like it was in the movies. It was final. It was over. What good was a fucking tree? Trees died too. And it was November. You can't plant a tree in November.

They should've made some kind of cockroach memorial. Those prehistoric fuckers never die. They'll live way longer than the whole human race. It could be the cockroach memorial to Jason Bishop. It would've been perfect

because of *The Metamorphosis*. Jase would've liked that.

Mr. Cordoba watched Mel and me whispering. He cleared his throat. "Mr. Caroll, why don't you help me reshelve these books? Miss Caroll, I assume you've got a note."

Mel handed it to him.

"Are you ready to work too?"

Mel nodded.

I liked the smell of the library. I liked the feel of the book pages between my fingers, and the crinkly sound of the plastic covers. We spent the afternoon sorting and shelving books.

"It's time to go now." Mr. Cordoba pointed toward the clock: 5:00.

It was weird how the library was the only place where time meant nothing to me. There were no ticks or pings. I felt like I could sit there forever without wanting to go backward or forward.

"Let's go home, Kyle." Mel grabbed her keys and put on her coat.

"Yeah. Wait a sec. Um, Mr. Cordoba. Do you have a book by that poetry guy, e. e. cummings?"

"Poetry guy," he mumbled, shaking his head. "Interesting choice." He pulled a book down and handed it to me. I should've taken the time to read e. e. cummings while Jason was still alive.

All evening, something didn't feel right. As I listened to

the sounds of nighttime, I saw the jar of red M&M's on the nightstand and realized what it was. Chase. I'd forgotten about Chase. I couldn't even keep the simplest promise.

"I'm so sorry," I whispered. "I'm so sorry."

28

I stood behind the Dumpsters. The bell rang and kids came running out with construction-paper turkeys in their hands. Some class had made stick mobiles with glittery winter scenes dangling from the tips. A little girl tripped and crushed her mobile. Poor kid. She couldn't stop crying.

I saw the circus act. They looked over at me. Julian looked especially pale and ran to his bus, leaving Bowling Pin and Twitchy behind.

No Chase.

Kids piled into the buses. The crusty snow looked dirty and tired after being trampled by little feet. The buses pulled out.

No Chase.

My heart raced.

Maybe he's sick. Yeah, he's probably sick.

An icy tightness gripped my stomach. I had missed yesterday and now there was no Chase. I stood up to leave when I felt somebody tugging on my coat sleeves.

"Chase, what are you doing here?"

"I didn't see your orange shoes yesterday." Chase had a huge bruise on his left cheek. His eye was a little swollen.

"What happened? Who did this to you?"

Chase shrugged. The kid could talk a thousand miles a minute, but only when he wanted to. "What happened to your neck, Kyle?"

I had gotten so bruised and beaten lately, I had lost track. A few days earlier Alex had elbowed me in the neck and left a huge black-and-blue mark that was fading to a yellowish green. I'd been wearing turtlenecks so my parents wouldn't see. They didn't need anything else to worry about. But there was no fooling Chase. Looking up at me, the way he was, he saw the bruise where it poked above my shirt.

"So? What happened to your neck?"

"It doesn't matter. Are you okay? What are you doing here? Why aren't you on the bus?"

"Where were you?"

"I blew it. I didn't come."

"Yeah, they didn't see you and kicked my butt. Plus it was a GCP day. Not good."

"GCP?"

Chase nodded solemnly. "Green corduroy pants day. Whenever Julian wears his green corduroys, somebody gets beaten up. Usually me." Chase pulled out a piece of paper. "This charts the days Julian beats me up. Here, you see what he wears. Sixty-two percent of the time he beats me up, it's a GCP day. You can't refute the facts."

I studied the chart. "Maybe it's a coincidence."

"Kyle, in life there are no coincidences."

"Maybe he doesn't have a lot of pants."

Chase took the chart back and tucked it into his notebook. "So where were you?"

Chase looked so small. I crouched down. "I'm so sorry," I said, trying to control my voice. "It won't happen again. I'll always be here."

"Even if you're sick?"

"Even if I'm sick."

"Even if you have to have an emergency appendectomy?"

"Oh. In that case, maybe not."

"So you won't always be here."

"I'll always . . ." I sighed. "I don't know. Chase, buddy, you can't let them do this to you. You've got to stand up for yourself."

"Do you?"

"Do I what?"

"Do you stand up for yourself?" Chase pointed at my turtleneck.

"That doesn't matter."

"Do as I say, not as I do?"

I tried to smile, but only one side of my mouth curved up. Chase was one of a kind. "Do you know how to throw a punch at least?"

Chase shook his head. Another boy came around from the Dumpster. Chase nodded at him. "This is Mike. He's my best friend. He has a GCP chart, too. His is forty-one percent."

Mike shrugged. "They just kick my butt a lot." He gawked at me. "Geez, you're big."

I stifled a laugh. I was 5'8" and weighed 120 pounds. Real big. "Nice to meet you, Mike."

"How much do you charge?"

"For what?"

"To be Chase's bodyguard?"

Chase looked at Mike as if he'd asked the dumbest damned thing. "He does my work pro bono."

Chase killed me. Where'd he come up with this stuff?

"Okay, this is the thing, guys. These kids—that freckled guy, Julian, and his friends—they'll never leave you alone if you don't stand up for yourselves."

"Maybe they'll grow out of it." Chase shrugged. "Maybe he won't buy any more GCPs after this year."

"No, Chase. They won't grow out of it. Never. You have to stand up for yourself. I'll be here. But what if I'm not here forever?"

"Will you go away like Jason?"

Tears stung my eyes. "No, not like that. But maybe I'll have to get a job or something."

"Oh. This isn't your job?" Mike asked. He was even smaller than Chase. "Is that why you come late sometimes?"

Chase nudged him. Then he pulled a red Spiderman watch out of his pocket and handed it to me. "This is for you. I bought it with my allowance."

I held the watch in my hands. "For what?"

"To tell the time, Kyle."

"I've got a watch."

"Oh." He inspected my wrist. "That's Jason's old watch—the one you traded. It's broken. I knew the watch was the problem—why you come late."

"It's not—," I said.

"Did you really think it was ten forty-six?" Chase asked.

10:46.

"Anyway, I had to decide between Spiderman and the Hulk and decided Spiderman fit your profile better. The Hulk is entirely too conspicuous. This should help you get here on time, every day." Chase took off my old watch and fastened Spiderman around my wrist. "It's already set and has a new battery. Do you want me to throw this one away?"

"No!" I snatched the watch from his hands. "I, uh, maybe I can fix it." I stared at the two watches. One stopped at 10:46. The other ticking away, like nothing had ever happened.

"Okay." Chase looked at Mike, and they both shrugged.

The Bishops' minivan was idling in the school driveway. "There's Mom. She wanted to come pick me up today because of yesterday. I don't think you're supposed to be here."

I bit my lip and ducked back down behind the Dumpsters. "I know. I know." I swallowed hard. "Go on. I'll see you tomorrow."

Chase's eyes got really big.

"I promise, Chase," I said.

A large shadow blocked the sunlight. Mr. Bishop towered above me.

"Dad!" Chase said. "Kyle was just—"

"Chase, Mike, get in the car."

"Dad, but—" Chase said. He reached out for my hand.

Mr. Bishop pointed to the minivan. "I said '*Get in the car!*' Now."

Chase nodded. He and Mike looked back at me.

"What the hell are you doing here? At Chase's school?"

I couldn't even begin to explain. "I, um. I . . ."

Mr. Bishop clenched his fists. "You are to stay away from my family. Understood?"

I tried to stand, but my legs wouldn't hold me. I swallowed. *I'm so sorry*, I wanted to say. *I'm sorry.*

My hands burned with the icy snow. Mr. Bishop kept talking, but I couldn't hear him. I only heard a buzzing in my ears, like when I shot the gun. His mouth moved, but no sound came out. Someone had muted the movie.

I finally got the strength to stand and get to my bike. Mr. Bishop stood behind the Dumpsters staring at me, fists by his sides.

I rode to the library as hard and fast as I could, the cold air piercing my lungs. My hands trembled, and I could barely open the library door. I sat in the first chair I found with my head between my knees, trying to control my breathing.

Mr. Cordoba peered over his newspaper. "Everything okay?"

"Sure. Yeah." My voice wavered.

"Do you need anything?"

"I just want to sit right now, okay? Just sit," I whispered. Vertigo. The floor spun, the colors of the carpet blending. I squeezed my eyes shut, hoping that life could stop, but all I could see was Jason's dead body crumpled up in Dad's shed.

I hugged my knees, listening to my heart thud against my hollow chest.

Mr. Cordoba set his newspaper down on his desk and

half read, half watched me.

The minutes ticked by. Fiery orange light streamed through the windows, and pink clouds streaked from behind the mountains. Everything became blanketed in purple. I got up and started to pull down book after book, searching for Jason's name. Which books did he take out? What did he use to read?

Cordoba watched as the tables piled with books.

"Are you looking for something?"

"I just need to find," I said, choking out the words, "I just need to find a book. That's all. I don't need your help. I don't need anybody's help. I'm just looking for a . . ." The titles blurred before me. My voice cracked.

"Why don't we call your folks?"

"No." I shook my head. "I just need a book."

Mr. Cordoba approached me. "Can I help you pick one out?"

"I don't want *your* books. Don't you get it?"

He put his hand on my shoulder. "Mr. Caroll, it's time to go home."

"No." I pushed him away.

"Why don't you get your things out of your locker and come back here? We'll find whatever book you want."

"We will?" I whispered.

Mr. Cordoba nodded. "We can look all night if we have to."

"Okay," I breathed. "Okay."

The hallways were empty. Most teachers had gone home. Sometimes after the library I could hear a vacuum in the distance. Sometimes, if varsity basketball practice was running late, I could hear the pounding of rubber balls on the court and the squeak of basketball shoes.

Something felt wrong. It was later than usual, too dark. Too quiet.

I was walking down the hallway when I heard glass shatter; then I felt thunderous pain in my head.

"Fucking pansy. Hiding out in the library behind that freak, Cordoba. Didn't even have the balls to show up at the assembly."

I staggered back and felt blood trickle down behind my ear, matting my hair. Dripping. Clumping.

"What's the matter, Kyle? Not so tough without your gun?" Troy asked.

"You're the one who shoulda died," said Alex. "You're the fucking loser who followed Jason around. You're the fucking shadow."

A quiet rage surged through me. Troy, Pinky, and Alex turned crimson, erasing the gray of the hallway and the purple of the evening light. I reached for Alex's neck and shoved him against the locker.

He trembled, his breath rank with fear.

29

"**H**ow could you do this, Kyle? This isn't you." Mom paced back and forth. "This is— Jesus, I need some air."

Who am I, then?

I held an ice pack to my head.

I didn't remember the explosion. I didn't remember anything but Cordoba holding on to me. Holding me back. Bringing back the gray. And Alex. Whimpering, crying, begging, pissing.

That would be some mess for Janitor Parker to clean up.

Principal Velásquez tapped her fingernails on the desk. *Tackity-tackity-tackity . . .* pause *. . . tackity-tackity-tackity.*

Mark stormed in through the door. "What happened?"

My head throbbed. Alex's mom held him in her arms. He sobbed in the corner of the room, far away from the rest of us.

We waited for Troy's and Pinky's parents to come. When they arrived, we all sat around an oval table in the meeting room, Alex included. Mom and Dad stood behind me.

"Kyle, why don't you begin?" *Tackity-tackity-tackity* . . . pause.

"I, um—"

"He was gonna kill me!" Alex shouted. "That's what was gonna happen. He had me in a choke hold. He wouldn't let go. He's a freak. A killer. He probably killed Jason on purpose too." Alex wiped his nose.

The hair bristled on the back of my neck and my breathing became shallower. Maybe he was right.

Mrs. Keller hugged Alex and stroked his hair. "My baby, my baby," she whispered. She was one of those hairspray casino moms. Lots of makeup, glittery jewelry, and high heels.

"Kyle," Dad said, moving forward. "Can you tell us anything at all?"

Indiana Jones was named after George Lucas's dog. Fuck or derivatives of the word are used 272 times in Reservoir Dogs. The Blair Witch Project *was filmed in eight days.*

"Kyle, I'm talking to you." Dad pulled up a chair beside me and put his hand over mine.

I jerked my hand back, then felt embarrassed for Dad. His only son couldn't stand to be touched.

Jesus, I'm a freak. They're right. They're all right.

Dad crossed his arms and sighed. "Kyle, can you tell us anything?"

I thought of the soft library light, the quiet dark hallway, and the thundering pain. "I don't know."

The other parents started to talk at once about my mental instability; my obvious psychopathic tendencies; my explosive temper. "I demand that he be expelled today, right now. I will *not* have my son go to school with such a violent boy." Pinky looked really small next to his parents. Even his thumbs. So much for genetic engineering. They were a family of mutants.

What's worse, Jase: being a freak or a mutant?

What's the diff?

Good point.

"He didn't do anything wrong," Mr. Cordoba said. "As I said before, he was protecting himself. Do I have to point out that Kyle is the only one here bleeding?"

Nobody said anything. The meatheads' parents glared and stayed quiet for a while.

"Who, then, hit you with the bottle today?" *Tackity-tackity-tackity* . . . pause.

"I don't know." That was the truth. It was too dark. "One of them, I guess, since they were there and all. But I don't know who."

"Principal Velásquez, every student has a right to defend him- or herself from harm. Kyle was, in my opinion, doing just that." Mr. Cordoba crossed his arms. He looked even bigger than Mark.

Mr. Cordoba's defense propelled Dad and Mom into action. They were exempt from guilt—from having to live with the possibility that their only son was a serial killer, stalking popular kids throughout high schools everywhere, ruthlessly murdering them. "Kyle, have they attacked you before? Do they bully you?" Mom asked.

I wasn't gonna rat. Rats sucked more than the fucking jock squad. "Um, in PE things get a little rough sometimes. Normal stuff, though. No big deal."

"Bullying?" Pinky's mom pushed her chair out and stood tall. Everybody else followed suit, leaving me alone at the table. It was like a scene from *12 Angry Men*. I could've renamed it *12 Angry Parents, Parole Officers, and School District Employees*. Pinky's mom towered over everyone except for Mr. Cordoba. "There's no proof that my son has ever laid a finger on your son." She glared at me. "And only one boy in this room has a parole officer." She flashed Mark a look.

I kept my mouth shut.

"Well, if there's bullying going on at this school, I think we need to address it, Principal Velásquez. Here and now." Mom was on fire. She didn't even reach Pinky's mom's shoulder. I hoped she'd be able to run fast in case we needed to bolt. I looked at Pinky's mom's thumbs. Huge. And she had the arm span of an ape.

"Bullying? In this school? It has never been brought to my attention." *Tackity-tackity-tackity, tacka-tacka-tackity.*

The only thing separating these guys from gangsters was their letterman jackets.

"Are these boys the perpetrators, Kyle?" Mom asked.

Perpetrators? "It's just PE class. No big deal."

"But he tried to choke me," Alex whined.

I didn't remember that part. I just remembered the red—the anger.

"All of you get in-house suspension. All four of you." *Tackity-tackity-tackity.*

"What about basketball? We haven't lost a game all season." Alex jumped from his chair. Snot bubbles formed and popped.

Principal Velásquez crossed her arms in front of her. "Well, I guess you'll enjoy watching it from the stands. You're all off the team until after your suspension."

"Oh, you'll be hearing from us, Principal Velásquez." Pinky's mom stomped toward the door. Principal Velásquez's diplomas rattled against the walls. "We're not through here."

"Oh, Ms. Deiterstein, I do believe we are finished." Principal Velásquez didn't take shit from anybody—especially parents. "And all of you will complete these anger-management and conflict-resolution packets. Due after winter break in January."

Nobody said anything.

"Tomorrow you gentlemen will begin your in-house suspension. I've got a couple of phone calls to make tonight—including one to Coach Copeland. Thanks for coming, everybody." She grabbed each parent's hand. I wondered if her nails dug into them when she squeezed.

Mark nodded triumphantly and shook Mr. Cordoba's hand. "Thanks." Then he clapped me on the back . . . again. "Never again, Kyle. This can never happen again. Got it?"

"Sure, Mark. It won't."

"You've got to let it go. Let it go when these kids go after you like that."

"Yeah, okay."

"Okay, Kyle. Good. We're good now." Mark put on his jacket.

Pinky, Troy, and Alex followed their parents out the door.

"I can't believe she thinks she can kick me off the basketball team," Alex muttered.

Mr. Cordoba cleared his throat. "I don't think it would be prudent for the four of them to be together. Kyle had

better do his suspension in the library."

Tackity-tackity-tackity . . . pause . . . *tackity-tackity-tackity.* "Sounds reasonable."

Mom, Dad, and I walked to the parking lot. It was like the reels of our lives had been taken and filmed over—just blurry images were left on the film. I wondered if Jason's death would eat us away, bit by bit, until we crumbled into nothing.

Mark rumbled off on his Harley. Mom and Dad got into the car.

Mr. Cordoba walked next to me. I half waved and said, "Thank you."

He stopped and looked me in the eyes. "A book must be an ice axe to break the seas frozen inside our soul."

I sighed. "What?"

"Kafka," he said, and handed me a book.

My head hurt too much to even think about some nutty novel. I looked down. *The Catcher in the Rye.* I flipped it open and saw Jason's crooked signature—no caps. Tears burned my eyes. "Thanks," I whispered.

Mr. Cordoba put his hand on my shoulder and nodded.

30

They wanted to take me to the ER to make sure I wasn't brain damaged or something. But they calmed down once my head stopped bleeding.

We dropped Dad off at the Hub. He had to relieve some worker who'd called in sick. Everybody called in "sick" around the holidays, especially Thanksgiving.

When we got to Richmond Avenue, I looked in the Bishops' front window. Mrs. Bishop still had that candle lamp lit, waiting for Jason to come back. Mom didn't talk until we walked in the door. "Sit. Now." She pulled out a kitchen chair. "We need to talk."

Not that again.

"Look at me." Mom crossed her arms.

I rolled my eyes. "It's not a big deal." I went to the

fridge for some peanut butter and jelly.

"Kyle Michael Caroll, I want to know what's going on with you. You're distant, withdrawn, and now this? I'm worried about you."

"So, what? I can't defend myself?"

"You know that's not what I'm talking about," she said. "It's . . . it's everything." She paused. "That boy was terrified, Kyle."

My jaw muscles tightened. I clenched my fists around the jar of jelly, feeling an electric surge shoot through my body. It was like I was at the edge of a cliff and any minute, any second, I could jump and crash to the ground.

"We just—" She sighed. "We want things to be normal for you again."

"Why? Why do you want things normal for me? So life can be easier for you?" The burning started up in my stomach again.

"Kyle . . ." Mom's voice trailed off.

"Why doesn't anybody have the balls to say that things will *never* be the same again? How come that's so hard to say?" I felt the sting of tears in my eyes. I swallowed and bit my lower lip.

"You keep pushing us away. You won't let us help. You won't move on. We don't know what to think, Kyle."

Move on? Move on? I have no right to move on.

I felt the heat creep up my body and fill everything with

crimson red. The edge of the cliff was a step away. I jumped into the void. "I'm sick of all the bullshit." I clutched the jelly jar. "You have no idea how I have felt every single day since then. You have no idea," I whispered. Sweat beaded on my forehead. "And you want me to move on? Tell that to Jason. Tell that to Chase. Tell that to the Bishops!" I squeezed the jar. It shattered and fell to the floor. I looked down. Drops of blood mixed with globs of raspberry jelly.

Everything went into slow motion. Mom and I looked from the blood to my hand to outside the front window. We watched Mel drive up and run into the house. She came into the kitchen and looked from me to Mom. "Oh, wow, Kyle. Are you okay?"

I nodded.

"Can I help?" She came forward.

I shook my head. "I'm fine."

"Okay." Mel stepped out of the kitchen.

Mom grabbed a towel. "Put your hand over the sink. I need to pull out the glass."

I wanted to close my fist and grind the pieces into my palm. But Mom looked horrified, so I held my throbbing hand over the sink, watching the blood trickle out of the cuts.

"Kyle?" Mom said. "What can we do? What can we do to help you?" Mom held my hands in hers.

I looked down at where my orange sneaker tips poked out from under my pants. I didn't know if I'd make it another 144 days. I didn't know if I could even make it

one more day. "Nothing."

Mom ran her fingers through her hair. "Okay. I, um, maybe we should call Dr. Matthews?"

I sighed. They hadn't realized that my visits with Dr. Matthews were a waste of time.

On the way to my room, I turned around at the top of the staircase. Mom looked so far away, like I was seeing her through a camera lens.

In my room, I flicked off the lights, threw myself onto the bed, and stared up at the ceiling. Somehow, I finally fell asleep.

The rope burns, scraping across my neck. "Nah, you do it."

"*Fuck, why do I always have to do things first?*"

"*You're taller.*" *I loop it around his neck.*

"*See, that's not so hard. Watch this.*" *He jumps, swinging back and forth, back and forth, a happy grin on his face.*

Then his body jerks.

Hiccups.

Spasms.

He smiles.

I watch the smile fade—first the lips disappear, then nose, eyes. A blank face. Nothingness.

I jerked awake and gasped for air. I grabbed a blanket and crept into the hall. Lying outside Mel's door, I waited until the first light of morning.

When light from Mom and Dad's room spilled into the hallway, I tiptoed back to my bed.

"Kyle? It's time for school." Mom called through my door.

I faked a horrible cough and lay under the covers, working up a sweat.

Mom knocked on the door. "Can I come in?"

"Yes," I said in my most gravelly voice.

Mom came in and placed her hand on my forehead. "You have a fever."

I nodded. It wasn't too hard to look sick, since I'd lost about fifteen pounds over the past eight weeks and had hardly slept in days. My face had taken on a kind of skull-and-crossbones look.

Dad came in. "He'd better stay home today."

Mom looked worried. "I can't miss another day of work. Are you covered at the Hub?"

Dad shook his head.

"I'll be fine," I whispered. "I just need sleep."

Mom bit her lower lip and scowled. She looked at her watch.

"It's just a few hours. I'll come home after the lunch rush," Dad said. "And he can call me if he needs anything. You'll call, right, Kyle?"

I closed my eyes and pretended to drift back to sleep.

"I'll tell the school." Mom's heels clacked down the stairs.

The familiar sounds of breakfast drifted to my room. Mom burned Dad's eggs again. I heard Mel laughing at something Dad said. They actually sounded happy. Free. Free from Kyle.

Before leaving for work, Mom slipped into my room and kissed my cheek, her eyes filled with concern. "Will you be okay for a few hours?"

I grunted. "Yeah. Don't worry."

She put my cell phone on the bedside table. "You call Dad if you need anything, and he'll be home before you know it." She bit her lip. "You know how much we love you, right?"

I listened as they left the house, the front lock clicking

and car doors slamming. Then I got up and grabbed my notebook. Maybe if I remembered, it would be okay.

SCENE THREE: Take Eleven—Chinese fantasy
(Zhang Yimou) style
Dissonant violins play in the background.
The sound of bullets ricocheting off objects
overtakes the score. FADE OUT score.

WIDE-ANGLE SHOT of the scene. The shed is at
the left-hand corner of the shot. It's a
high-contrast color shot; the white of the
shed stands out against the green grass and
bamboo in the background.

CUT TO: Kyle crouching down to squeeze out
the dew from his pajama pants. He pauses,
catches his breath, then stands again.

CUT TO: Jason, holding the gun, twirling it,
and shooting at various targets in the shed.

The camera ZOOMS OUT, and we see light streaming
into the shed like crisscrossing strings,
surrounding Jason. Kyle is in the background,
hardly visible in the shadows.

ZOOM OUT: Jason shoots, the bullet piercing
the roof of the shed.

CLOSE-UP of Kyle. He pauses, then does a
martial-arts triple flip and pokes his finger
through the bullet hole in the ceiling,
landing safely on the ground.

> JASON
> (Holds the gun out to Kyle.)
> Check this baby out. It's pretty
> tight, huh?

> KYLE
> Sweet, Jase. That's sweet.

> JASON
> What do you wanna do?

> KYLE
> I dunno. What are we s'posed to do
> with it?

> JASON
> (Pulls up T-shirt collar around his
> neck, like a pastor. He scowls.)

Well, Kyle, let's see what our
options are. We could A: put the gun
away and continue to freeze, B: put
the gun to good use, or C (and my
personal favorite): rob the local
convenience store, frame Mel and
Brooke, move to the Cayman Islands,
and never, ever have to work again.

                    KYLE
(Relaxes his shoulders and laughs.)
We don't work now, you moron.

CLOSE-UP shot of our hero—Jason.
Blindfolded.

                    JASON:
Do it! Just do it!

Silence. The ricocheting bullets have stopped.
We hear a sickening sound as the bullet
pierces Jason.

ZOOM OUT. The shed is in the left-hand corner
of the shot. Fall turns to winter to spring,
then summer, then fall.

ZOOM IN. Jason lying in a puddle of blood.

CUT TO Kyle, staring at Jason.

CUT TO the gun in Kyle's hand.

The dissonant sound of violins begins again, accompanied by the sound of the wind through the trees. FADE OUT.

I reread the entry. More dialogue, but still incomplete. I closed my eyes. *Remember,* I thought. *Just remember.* But nothing came. Just the shrill sound of the bullet as it left the gun's barrel, and Jason buckling over. I put my notebook away and got dressed. I walked out to the shed and held my hands against the door. The cold seeped from the metal surface through my gloves. Snowflakes tumbled from the sky. Gusts of wind whipped them into a whirling frenzy. I clasped my hands in front of me and closed my eyes.

What are you doing out here?

The whine of the wind grew. My teeth chattered.

I blew it, you know. With Chase.

The snow fell faster, like it was in some kind of hurry to get where it needed to go. A film of snow covered my body. My teeth knocked hard against each other. Jason didn't say anything,

Do you believe in signs? Like dreams that tell you what to do?

I waited.

What am I supposed to do?

Silence.

It doesn't matter anymore, anyway, does it? Nothing matters anymore.

Silence.

Asshole.

God, I'm such a freak show. I'm pissed off at a dead guy. I brushed the snow off my coat and pants. "See you soon," I whispered.

Chilled, I walked back inside, changing out of my snowy clothes into dry ones before Dad got home to check up on me. *You'll catch your death,* he would say.

That's the point. But that's the kind of stuff a kid really shouldn't say to his parents.

32

I woke up to Mom and Mel arguing in the hallway.

"But Mom, you guys promised you'd go."

"We can't leave him here alone. One of us has to stay."

"He's just sleeping anyway. And you promised," Mel cried.

My door opened a crack. "Kyle?"

I didn't answer.

"Don't wake him," I heard Dad say. "How long is the program, Mel?"

"It's just a couple of hours. And we've been practicing since September."

I had forgotten it was Mel's regional cheerleading competition. Carson High had made it to the finals.

"We need to go, Maggie," Dad urged Mom.

"But you didn't see him." Mom's voice sounded strained. "You didn't see the look in his eyes yesterday."

"We were all tired. It was a long day, and he was coming down with something. I've been here all afternoon, and he hasn't moved. He just needs sleep."

"Please," Mel begged. "Please, Mom."

Mom came in and touched her cool hand to my forehead. I lay still. She walked back into the hallway.

"Well?" Mel's voice had a whiny pitch to it.

"He was fine alone this morning," Dad said.

"How about if I stay just through your performance, Mel?"

"That's perfect."

I listened as they put on their heavy jackets and winter boots. Downstairs, Mom, Dad, and Mel shuffled out the door and got into the car. I took out my notebook and read through each scene. The words ran together. Tears smudged the writing.

I can't do this anymore.

Then don't.

You always have the answers, huh?

Depends on the questions.

Fuck you.

I threw the notebook across the room. The lamp teetered on the edge of my nightstand and shattered on the floor. I crawled to the corner and squeezed my head

between my knees. The pounding had to stop. The hurt had to stop.

"Go away," I said. I rocked back and forth.

Every time I closed my eyes, the walls closed in.

"Breathe. Just breathe," I whispered.

I looked around the room, desperate, and pulled out the phone book. "Cordoba, Cordoba, Cordoba."

Fuck, what's his first name?

I dialed the first number I saw under Cordoba. Maybe we could talk about books. I just needed to talk—to hear somebody besides Jason.

Three rings. Four rings.

"Hello?" Out of breath, low humming voice.

Deep breaths, slow deep breaths. Count to ten.

"Hello?" she repeated.

"I—" I cleared my throat. Inhale, exhale, inhale, exhale, inhale, exhale . . .

"You kids have nothing better to do than this?" She hollered to somebody, "It's another one of those prank callers. We need to get caller ID."

"Please," I whispered.

Click.

I went to sit at the top of the stairs. Mrs. Schneibel had already strung up her Christmas lights. The glow of the colorful lights reflected off our living room windows.

'Tis the season. Fucking holidays.

Mom had left the radio on in the kitchen. It was a crackly old radio—you had to turn the dial and mess around with a duct-taped antenna to hear anything. And if you moved it, even the tiniest bit, you lost the station and had to start again.

I walked into the kitchen and cranked up the staticky Christmas carols the radio stations had been playing since October. I stared out at the Bishops' house. The candle was lit. A warm light glowed between the slats of the blinds. They were home. Shadows moved behind the Bishops' curtains. Maybe they were watching TV.

"'Tis the season to be thankful. 'Tis the season for forgiveness and love. It's time to reach out." The DJ was really caking on the love and forgiveness stuff. He was taking calls and listening to everybody's sappy reconciliation stories.

I bit my lip and looked at the calendar.

November 23.

Last year at this time, Jason and I were probably eating the crust off Mrs. Bishop's homemade apple pie. Last year Jason and I had a Coen brothers movie marathon. Last year, as soon as Jason got back from church, we spent the rest of Thanksgiving weekend sledding up on C-Hill.

I laid my head on the cold countertop. Tears pooled on the tiles.

The DJ ho-ho-hoed in some hokey Santa voice. "Come on, everybody! What are you waiting for? I challenge each

and every one of you to—" I bumped into the radio and it went fuzzy.

I pulled on my winter hat and coat and walked down the street. I fought to steady my breathing. My stomach burned when I saw that Mrs. Bishop had hung up her old wooden turkey. It was the same one she hung up every year.

My hand trembled when I rang the bell.

I heard shouts inside and Brooke opened the door.

Freeze frame.

I opened my mouth. The words got trapped in my throat. I struggled to breathe, fighting to push the words out.

I'm sorry. I'm sorry. I'm sorry. I'm sorry.

But nothing came out. As soon as I tried to say them, I knew the words wouldn't change anything. They wouldn't bring him back. Sorry was the cheap way out.

Brooke narrowed her eyes. "Who the hell do you think you are, coming here? At Thanksgiving?"

"Who's there, honey?" Mrs. Bishop hollered from the kitchen. The house smelled like pumpkin pie and apple cider.

I tried to say something, but nothing came. Not even tears.

Mrs. Bishop came out from the kitchen with a plate of cookies. "Kyle!" she said. She dropped the plate and it shattered on the hardwood floor. Her mouth quivered

and her eyes closed. She covered her face with her hands and muffled a sob.

The next thing I knew, I was standing in front of the shed again. I had no clue how I'd gotten there.

33

I stared at the shed. It had been there since before I was born. The hinges never worked on the right-hand door, and the white paint had flaked off over the years, giving it a splotchy look, like it had psoriasis or something.

I looked for the key above on the ledge, but it wasn't there.

Maybe that was one of Mark's suggestions. "Hide the fucking key, man. Don't let your kid in there."

Not a bad suggestion, really.

I stepped back and punched the doors. My knuckles cracked on the cold metal. The padlock rattled and clanged. I kicked and punched the doors again and again until my hands were bloody and numb. The metal dented and crumpled under the weight of my fists and boots.

Fucking piece of shit cheap shed.

I went around to the back, where a small window faced the neighbors' yard.

Crash!

The rock ripped through the flimsy glass, leaving jagged edges. I punched the glass and heaved myself inside.

It smelled the same. It smelled like damp wood and fertilizer. It smelled like grease and dry grass.

It smelled like death.

I pulled the cord hanging from the fluorescent light. The light sputtered on, and the whole shed glowed an eerie green.

The floor was filthy except for one really white spot.

I kneeled down and touched where his blood had pooled.

I tried to replay it all. But I still didn't know how it happened. How could something like that happen? It was just one second. Not even a second, really. Then the burn, the powder, the ashes.

Ashes, ashes, we all fall down.

What had I done?

I circled the shed and moved toward a box of rope. Frayed ends and knots, lots of rope. Lots to tie. Lots to hang.

You're the one who shoulda died.

You're a nobody.

You did this.

You have no right.

You're a freak.

I hate Kyle. He ruined everything.

Stay away from my family.

Everything seemed clearer. My breathing evened out. I held the yellow rope in my bloody hands. They'd all be better off.

I just wanted to stop thinking about whether I had done it on purpose. How I had ruined everybody's lives that day. I wanted to get away from that scene—that moment.

I grabbed a pencil and scrap of paper and wrote: *The End.*

My heartbeat steadied. I made a loop. The perfect size.

The rafters were too high to reach from the bench. God, I was so fucking short!

Jumping up, I tried to loop the rope around. Wood splintered and creaked, and the bench collapsed.

I crashed to the floor and felt the rope, raw in my fingers. I clenched the rope between my teeth and curled into a ball. Hot tears spilled down my cheeks and into my ears, my sobs trapped in my throat.

I couldn't even kill myself. I couldn't even do that right.

My body trembled.

What would Jason do?

What would Jason say?

Dude, Kyle, don't be a shithead. Don't do it.

But what else is there? What if I meant to kill you?

Shit happens, Kyle.

Shit happens?

Yeah. So what?

You come to me with the great philosophy of "shit happens"?

Man, you'll figure it out.

Cold seeped through my clothes. My teeth chattered; I shivered. My hands throbbed and bled.

Suppose, I thought. *Suppose I lived.*

The light in the shed wavered, dimmed, then died. Everything was bathed in night, and objects became formless shadows, lumps on drooping shelves. I don't know how long I stayed in the shed, replaying my death scene in my head. After a while, I slipped out the broken window and walked into the house, welcoming its familiar smells of toast, vacuum dust, and Mel's perfume.

My hands ached and shook when I cleaned off the blood, wrapping them in bandages. I stared at myself in the bathroom mirror, pushing my hair behind my ears. He said I'd figure it out. Maybe—just maybe—I would.

I walked up to my room and opened my shades. At night, snow made the world seem like day. The bright white filled the room with reflected moonlight.

I put my notebook back into my drawer and hid it under some CDs. I buried my head in Jason's duffel bag and breathed deep. It was losing its smell.

I didn't even hear the car pull into the drive.

Mom opened my door. "What are you doing?"

I looked up at her. Her cheeks were flushed from the cold. "Are you feeling better?" She came in and put her hand on my forehead. Her breath smelled like peppermint. I shoved the duffel under the bed and hid my hands under the covers.

Dad came in with a steaming cup of peppermint chocolate. Mel bounded up the stairs. "We won, Kyle! Look!" She barreled into the room.

I smiled. "That's great, Mel. It really is."

She plopped next to me. "You look like shit."

"Thanks."

"Are you feeling okay?" Dad asked.

I think so. Maybe. I nodded.

"Why don't we let Kyle rest?" Dad motioned Mel and Mom to leave the room. He put his hand on my shoulder. "Do you need anything?"

I shook my head, still hiding my hands.

"Sleep. Maybe you should get more sleep." Dad looked into my eyes.

I looked away. "Yeah."

He paused. "Can I sit here for a while?"

I concentrated on the streaks of peeling paint on my bedroom wall. "Sure."

He sat on the edge of the bed. I felt him watching me, like he was looking for a sign that I was okay.

I turned and smiled. "I'll drink this when it cools down. Thanks."

"You're welcome." He got up. "I'm right down the hall if you need anything."

"Sure."

He left me alone. I flicked off the lights and stared at the glow-in-the-dark planets that Jason and I had pasted on my bedroom ceiling. We each got a set for Christmas when we were in fifth grade. When we were sticking mine up, Jason slipped on the ladder and pasted Pluto overlapping Saturn. My solar system was totally lame. We tried to scrape it off, but it stuck. So Saturn looked like it had an extra moon and Pluto didn't exist.

I was pissed at the time, but now I actually liked my Pluto all wrong. It was better. It made me remember something other than the shed. I let the memory wash over me and I held on to it as long as I could, hoping it wouldn't disappear into blackness. I was just about to remember what Jase sounded like when he laughed when I fell into a dreamless sleep.

I woke up to the sound of pebbles hitting my window. Chase stood below with his hands cupped over his mouth, hooting like an owl.

"What are you doing here?"

He held up an orange card, then hid it under a rock in the yard. He waved and ran away. I slipped out the front door and opened up the card.

> Dear Bodyguard,
>   Your presence behind the Dumpsters has been missed. Luckily, we haven't had any GCP days, and we're learning tactics to get through the school day unscathed.
>   We look forward to your rapid recovery.
>   Our best, Chase and Mike

I smiled. Getting through the day "unscathed" took a lot of energy. They had included a drawing of me with my orange shoes, a hole in the left one.

My stomach growled, and I went inside to get breakfast. Mom dropped the raw turkey on the kitchen floor when she saw my hands.

We spent the rest of Thanksgiving morning in the emergency room getting X-rays and a cast for my broken left hand.

"Sorry about Thanksgiving, Mom."

"It doesn't matter. We'll order Chinese."

When we left the ER, Dad and Mom walked ahead of me, whispering to each other. They looked like an old 1920s silent movie, their black jackets a stark contrast to the fresh-fallen snow. Dad wrapped his arm around Mom's hunched shoulders. The snow muted the sound of our footsteps.

He opened the car's back door for me and helped me tuck my head in so I wouldn't whack it on the doorframe. I clicked my seat belt and turned to look out the back window. Everything looked the same as that day. The outside of the emergency room had the same concrete walls, painted white and stained with exhaust fumes and who knows what else.

We walked into the house. Melanie was watching the Macy's parade. She flicked off the TV. "What happened?"

I covered the cast with my jacket. "I'm fine."

Dad shook his head. "I just don't know what to say."

"I think we might need to see Dr. Matthews. Maybe today? Should I call her?" Mom tipped my chin up so she was looking into my eyes.

"Dr. Matthews. Sure, Mom. That sounds good." Not like she helped any.

Dad pulled the note out of his pocket. "What does this mean, Kyle? 'The End.' I found it in the shed beside the broken bench."

"I just had a bad night, Dad. No big deal." I turned my face away from Mom and took the note. I crumpled it up and tossed it in the garbage. "It didn't mean anything."

Yesterday I'd wanted to die.

Today I didn't.

How can you explain that to your dad?

"I'm just gonna hang out in my room until we go."

"Okay, honey. Sure." Mom stepped forward like she was going to hug me, but I moved back. I felt like I was directing a part in a movie where the camera goes from close-up to wide angle, pulling away from the actors. I saw Mom, Dad, and Mel at the end of a long tunnel, far, far away. I went up to my room.

Mel knocked on my door. "Can I come in?"

"Yeah."

She hesitated, then came and sat on the bed. "What do you think Dr. Matthews and Mark will say?"

I shrugged.

She puffed out her cheeks. "Kyle, how do you feel about what happened? Would you like to talk about it?" She actually did a pretty good impersonation of Dr. Matthews.

I tried to smile.

Mel grabbed my hand—not the broken one. "Do you want talk about it? For real?"

"Not really."

"Those guys roughed you up pretty bad."

"Nah. I'm okay."

"What happened last night?"

I pulled my hand away. She scooted closer to me.

"Just a bad night, I guess."

Mel looked into my eyes. "Don't do that, Kyle. Ever. Okay?" She laid her head on my shoulder. "Promise me," she whispered, her voice cracking.

I squeezed her hand. "I promise." Somehow I knew this was a promise I'd keep.

She looked up and moved my bangs out of my eyes. "Growing your hair long?"

"Maybe."

She wiped her nose. "Looks cool."

"Thanks."

"Talk to her, Kyle."

"Who?"

"Dr. Matthews. Or Mr. Cordoba. Anyone, really. Just talk, okay?"

Dr. Matthews leaned back and laced her fingers around a steaming cup of tea. I sat across from her in a retro chair shaped like an egg. The orange plastic was pretty hard on my ass, and she kept asking me questions I didn't want to answer. "How would Jason like to see you today?"

"Whaddya mean?"

She pointed to the notebook I always carried around: the one with Scene Three. "What would Jason like to see you doing? Maybe you can write about it."

"Writing doesn't help."

"What do you write about?"

"That day. I need to figure out if I—" I stopped.

"If you what?"

"Nothing."

"Maybe you could write about other things."

I chewed on my lip. The edges of the notebook curled in. I had filled every page but one with that scene.

"Just think about it, Kyle. What would Jason wish for you?"

"Does it really matter?"

"I think it does."

I glared. "Why? Why would that matter?"

"Because you were friends. I think you forget that sometimes."

I shook my head. "I never forget that Jason was my best friend."

"No. But you do forget that you were *his*."

36

It was weird to be alive. Everything was under my control that night in the shed. I was even relieved. It made sense to me. I wanted to die.

Then I didn't.

I had Chase. I had books and Mr. Cordoba. And I didn't want to leave them. But I was stuck. I didn't want to be Freeze Frame anymore. I didn't want to live my life in Scene Three. But I didn't know how to move forward, either. Jase had said, *Shit happens*. Maybe that was his way of telling me I hadn't killed him on purpose. Jase would be the first to hold that against me if I had. He'd have probably found a way to haunt me, like in *The Amityville Horror*, or possess me like in *The Exorcist*, if that were true. And so far I hadn't projectile-vomited green baby food.

Over the weekend, most of the snow melted, leaving patchy spots of dirt and ice all over the graveyard. If I squinted, it almost looked like a winter quilt. I brushed a pile of slush from Jase's marker.

"Chase left me this great drawing." I sat on the least snowy spot near Jason's grave. "He might be an artist like you someday." I pulled out the drawing. "See? He even drew the orange shoes."

I tucked the drawing into my pocket. "I guess I just wanted to tell you I'm still here. That's pretty dumb, I know. If I weren't, you'd probably be the first to know." I tapped my fingers on his grave. "And, um, thanks, you know, for the message. I think I get it."

When I got up to go, I left a piece of apple pie on his grave, without the top crust. "I miss you, Jase," I said.

I returned to the library early Monday morning to start my in-house suspension.

"Mr. Cordoba?" I peeked in the door.

Cordoba sat reading the *The Nevada Appeal*, sipping his morning cup of coffee. "Nice to have you back, Mr. Caroll."

Relief flooded my body.

"Well, get in and close the door." He handed me a pile of worksheets and instructions from my teachers. "It looks like you'll be busy."

"Yes, sir." I picked up my assignments and took them to the table.

"What happened to your hands?"

"Just an accident."

Mr. Cordoba looked at my cast and bandaged hand, then back into my eyes. "Are you okay?"

"Yeah, I think I am." I sat down and stared out the window. The buses pulled into the parking lot, spewing students out into the winter grayness. My notebook lay in front of me. One page left to fill—one director left to use. And then I'd need a title. I'd written fourteen different versions, from Tarantino to Iñárritu. None of them, though, had turned out quite right. I flipped through the pages, scene after scene, until I got to the last page. Blank.

"You returned the book of poems," Cordoba said.

I nodded.

"What did you think?"

I shrugged. "I've never really read poetry before." I looked around the library. This was definitely not something any self-respecting fifteen-year-old guy would want people to know about him.

"Most people don't."

"Don't what?"

"Read poetry."

I nodded. "I can see why."

"Why is that, Mr. Caroll?"

"Well, um. It's kinda weird. Words missing. A little confusing. No connectors. Mrs. Beacham is big into connectors."

"Connectors?"

"*And. But. However. Whereas.* You know."

"Were there any poems you liked?"

I thought for a while. "I liked the one called 'Suppose.' I really liked the title."

"Why?"

I leaned close to the radiator, warming up. "Because *suppose* means, I dunno, I guess it means there're other possibilities." I remembered the shed. *Suppose I lived.*

Mr. Cordoba nodded.

I got up and tossed my notebook into the garbage. *Suppose. Suppose I forgot about it. All of it. Suppose it didn't matter if I remembered.*

That afternoon, I crouched behind the Dumpsters and peeked around the corner, watching the kids trudge to the buses.

"Hey Kyle. *Pssst!*" Chase stood in front of the Dumpster.

"Chase! What're you doing here?"

"What happened to your hands? How come you're wearing a cast?"

"Nothing."

"Did they do that to you?"

"Who?"

"The ones who hurt you before?"

"No, Chase. I don't think I have to worry about them anymore."

"Oh." He let out a slow whistle. "Then what happened to your hands?"

Unless I told him, he'd never quit asking, and we'd be out there all afternoon. Chase could go on for hours, and I had to get back to the library. "I punched the shed the other night. No big deal."

"Oh. That's not a smart thing to do."

"Yeah, I know."

"Is it scratchy?"

"What?"

"Your arm."

I knocked on the cast. "No. Not really."

"That's good, then." Chase looked relieved.

"Anyway, thank you. For the card and the drawing." The buses started to pull out of the lot. "You're going to miss the bus, Chase."

Chase shook his head. "I'm going to Mike's today. He's over there keeping watch." I peered around the corner. Mike was on his hands and knees staring at something in the grass with a magnifying glass. Great lookout.

Chase opened his backpack and pulled out some duct tape. "We noticed you could use this."

"For what?"

Chase pointed to my shoes. "The sole is coming off. And neither of us are cobblers. But we saw on the FX Channel that duct tape is great for everything."

"You're allowed to watch FX?"

"Mike's family has DISH, and his big brother let us watch it the other day. We watched *The Man Show*. It was quite informative."

"Yeah, I bet."

Chase pulled out some scissors, and the two of us taped the sole of my left shoe back together. He stood back and admired the patch job. "That stuff is really great." He eyed the tape I held in my hands.

"Why don't you keep it? If I need more, I'll borrow it."

He grinned. "Good idea. I think I'm more organized than you, anyway." He looked down at my shoes. "I've been thinking you need a bodyguard name," he said. "Like . . . Orange Dragon."

"Orange Dragon, huh?" It sounded like a superhero Jase would've drawn. "I like it."

"Me, too," said Chase. "Very scary."

A car pulled into the parking lot. Mike whistled three times, then hooted like an owl. Chase hooted back. "That's our signal."

"Yeah. I remember."

"Listen closely. Mills Park. Saturday. Noon. Fly kites."

"On the sly?"

He nodded. "It's BYOK."

"BYOK?"

"Bring your own kite."

"Oh. Yeah."

Mike hooted again and Chase left.

37

One morning, Mr. Cordoba was busy in his office. I wandered around the library, browsing the shelves, looking for other books Jason had checked out. I'd already read *The Catcher in the Rye* twice but didn't want to let it go just yet.

The back windows of the library faced the track. The cheerleaders were practicing some pyramid thing. Mel's cheeks were flushed in the chilly December wind, her hair pulled back in a ponytail. I didn't see Brooke anywhere.

Kohana walked by with his camera hanging around his neck, his black hair sticking out of the bottom of a stocking cap, green jacket flapping in the wind. He had his hands shoved into the pockets of his baggy jeans. He'd stop and stare at something for a while, fidget with his camera, then snap a picture. After a while, he made his way to the

flagpole and sat at its base.

The radiator clicked on, its heat fogging the windows. I leaned against the pane, icy glass cool against my forehead. I returned to the tables and started on the day's assignments.

"It looks like you need a new notebook, Mr. Caroll." Cordoba held my notebook in his hands. "I found this in the garbage."

It was like the damned scene was chasing me. "Did you read it?" I grabbed it from him.

"No."

I sighed, relieved.

"I noticed that you write a lot."

"This? It's just, um, director's notes." How lame did that sound?

"Director's notes?"

"Yeah. It's a dumb thing I started to do. Writing out a scene from my life, but trying to figure out how some of my favorite directors would direct the same scene."

"So that entire notebook is just one scene from your life?"

I flipped through the pages. "Yeah."

"That's impressive."

"Not really."

"How many directors did you use?"

"Fourteen."

"Is it finished?"

"No. I still have room for one more director."

"And?"

"Couldn't think of one." I moved to throw the notebook back in the garbage and hesitated. "Besides, no director can edit the past. These directors can't even remember it."

Mr. Cordoba took a sip of coffee. "Why don't you just set it aside?"

I walked to the garbage can. "That's what I tried to do until you took it out of the garbage."

"I see. You're throwing away the past."

"I'm trying."

Mr. Cordoba went back to his desk and opened up a book to read.

"What?"

He looked up from the book. "What, what, Mr. Caroll?"

"Aren't you going to come at me with one of your philosophies? About making peace with the past?"

"What would you like me to say?"

"I don't know."

Mr. Cordoba closed his book. "Will the past make sense if you throw it away?"

I shook my head. "I don't know. Maybe." I chucked the notebook in the garbage.

Mr. Cordoba's fingers slid over the bumpy scar. He went back to his office and returned with a notebook.

He handed it to me.

"I can't write that scene anymore, Mr. Cordoba."

"Then don't. New notebook. New scenes." He returned to his book.

What scenes? I was already a master of forgetting, not even counting the shed. It was like in *Eternal Sunshine of the Spotless Mind*, when a guy gets his memories erased. One by one, and no matter how hard he tries to hold on to them, his memories disappear.

That had started to happen to me. I was forgetting what Jason looked like. His face got blurry in my mind, like in those old family photos. You knew who the people are, but they aren't in focus. Same with his voice. I tried to remember how he sounded when he laughed. I didn't think I'd ever get his voice back.

It made me so sad to see that Jase was fading away. Fade out. Jason.

Mr. Cordoba had put his book on the desk. He watched me and motioned to the notebook in the garbage. "Can I hold it for you? If by the end of the year you don't want it, you can throw it away."

"Whatever." Cordoba could be really weird sometimes, fishing old notebooks out of the garbage. I flipped through the blank pages of the new notebook. "So which director should I use for the new scenes?" I asked aloud, kind of to myself.

247

"Why not you? You could direct your own memories." Cordoba looked at the clock. "It's time to get to work, Mr. Caroll."

I worked through my day's assignments. The new notebook lay on the desk, hundreds of blank pages before me. I had a lot of scenes to write.

My pajama pants stuck to my ankles. I crouched down to squeeze out the dew. I did that only to catch my breath. I'd never seen a gun before.

"New notebook," I whispered, crossing out what I wrote. "New scenes." Now I just had to remember.

38

In-house suspension were some of the best weeks I'd had. I finished my work early, then read. Sometimes I'd practice remembering. Something—anything—about Jase that didn't have to do with the shed. But all the memories got mixed up, out of order—just like that guy in *Memento*. He had to write notes all over his body to remember, and he still got it wrong in the end.

Leaving the library one afternoon, I ran into Kohana sitting at the base of the flagpole. "Miss the bus?"

He nodded, cleaning the lens of his camera.

"How long do you have to wait?"

He pulled out his watch. "Just a few more minutes. Then my grandma will be here."

We sat for a minute in silence. I messed with my bike gears.

"You still stuck at the library with Scarface? I heard what happened with Alex and those guys."

I leaned my head against the flagpole. "I'm not suspended anymore, but I go to the library a lot."

"Does Scarface ever talk to you?" Kohana asked.

"Cordoba? Sometimes. I don't think he likes to talk, though."

Kohana wasn't big on talking, either. He looked at my cast. "What happened to your hand?"

"I, um, punched our shed."

"Shitty day?" He put his camera away.

"Yeah. I guess you could say that."

"So how do you ride your bike?"

I smirked and showed him how I managed to balance and steer with my cast while using my bandaged hand for brakes.

"Impressive." He nodded. "Very Cirque du Soleil."

"So"—I motioned to his camera—"what do you take pictures of?"

He arched his eyebrows. "Everything. Some might say nothing."

"What do you mean?"

"I take pictures of things—things most people don't pay attention to. Objects tell stories, you know." He

shrugged. "You probably don't get it."

"Yeah, I do." I touched the Dimex in my pocket.

"Maybe your shed has stories," he said.

The metal from the flag clinked against the pole. "Too many."

He zipped up his backpack. "You get it."

"So, um, who started calling you Clock?" I asked, just to get away from the shed's stories.

He smirked. "I did."

I must've looked pretty shocked, because he laughed aloud. "Irony, man. Irony. You're the only one at school who calls me by my name."

"Really?"

"You're the only one who knows it."

"Why?"

"No one else ever asked." Kohana shivered and leaned against the flagpole. I sat next to him and picked at the tape on my shoe.

His grandma pulled up in an old two-tone Dodge Dart. She had long black hair clipped behind her ears, and black eyes. She wore tight jeans and a tighter sweater. Kohana's grandma was hot.

"Dude, that's your grandma?"

Kohana nodded. "It kinda sucks to have a grandma better-looking than me. Like, she's way out of my league."

I cracked up. "And I thought a cheerleader for a sister was bad."

"Yeah, Melanie's pretty sweet-lookin'."

I cringed.

"Well, you're the one checking out my gram."

Then we both laughed.

Kohana's grandma leaned her head out of the car. "Kohana, are you ready?" she asked.

He turned to me. "Gotta go. Thanks for the company."

I was biking off when Kohana shouted, "Wait! Just a sec." I pedaled over to him. He pulled out his camera, lay on the asphalt, and snapped a picture.

"What'd you take the picture of?" I asked, looking on the ground.

"Another story," he said, getting in the car. "Maybe someday you'll tell it to me."

I looked under the bike and all around.

"See you tomorrow, Kyle." He waved.

"See you."

I held Jason's Dimex in my hand, just one of the many things he had left behind—one of the many stories. I liked how Kohana thought about objects.

The planet set on the ceiling told a story—like the *Attack of the Killer Tomatoes!* and Frank Miller posters, my orange shoes, a ton of things I hadn't thought about. I scanned my bedroom and saw the pieces of paper sticking out from the pages of the R volume in the encyclopedia set my parents were so excited to get me for my thirteenth birthday—now with one volume missing. All I wanted was the original poster from Mel Brooks's *Silent Movie* that Jase and I saw on eBay. That or a dog. Hell, even a T-shirt would've been okay. But Mom and Dad had gone on a

better-my-mind-and-purge-it-of-popular-culture kick.
Probably because I had gotten four Cs the first semester.
I pulled the pieces of paper from the encyclopedia and
smiled.

Only Jase could turn a disastrous thirteenth birthday
into something cool.

I brought out the notebook and wrote.

UNTITLED: SCENE ONE—PTBP Syndrome (Post-
Traumatic Birthday Present Syndrome)
A blazing cake glows through the window. A
family gathers around the table singing "Happy
Birthday."

CLOSE-UP: Kyle has his eyes closed.

CUT TO: scene in Kyle's head: He's hanging up
Silent Movie next to his *Blazing Saddles* poster
to complete the Mel Brooks movie poster collection.

WIDE ANGLE: Camera pans the faces of everybody
at the table, brimming with expectation. The
gifts are passed down the table and Kyle rips
open a comics-wrapped DVD of *Plan 9 from Outer
Space.*

KYLE

Thanks, Jase!

FADE OUT: "Happy Birthday" music, then, like
Ravel's "Bolero," background starts softly
with John Williams's theme to *Jaws*. The music
gets louder and louder.

CUT TO: Scene where Kyle's parents unveil the
encyclopedia set.

KYLE

[Milk-curdling scream.]

A later scene, not filmed at this time, shows
Kyle's mom throwing all dairy products out of
the refrigerator.

MOM

So you really like it. That much?

DAD

We just *knew* you would.

He lovingly takes Mom in his arms and they stare
at the new encyclopedias in the bookshelf.

Background music fades out. Silence. No music.

CUT TO: Kyle's bedroom. Kyle and Jason sit on the bed, staring at the books. Camera pans the encyclopedias in the new bookshelf and returns to Jason and Kyle.

                    JASON
        That sucks.

Kyle nods his head. Eyes glaze over, looking at the shiny bindings. Jason waves his hand in front of Kyle, but Kyle doesn't flinch.

                    JASON
        Dude, it's your thirteenth. And
        you're going through PTBP Syndrome—
        Post-Traumatic Birthday Present
        Syndrome. Unreal.

Kyle's eyes dilate, then do that swirly, bulls-eye cartoon thing. In the background we hear the *boing!* cartoon sound.

                    JASON
        It's supposed to be a cool birthday.

We gotta do something about this.

Dazed, Kyle walks over and pulls out the R
volume of the set. He flips the book open,
and there's a deafening crack from the new
binding being opened. Jason claps his hands
over his ears. Kyle winces. Then he begins to
read aloud.

> KYLE
> R. "Rickets. Rickets is a softening
> of children's bones potentially
> leading to fractures and deformity.
> Rickets is among the most frequent
> childhood diseases in many developing
> countries. The main cause is a vitamin
> D deficiency, but an inadequate supply
> of calcium in the diet may also lead
> to rickets." (He looks at Jason.) I
> don't figure we have rickets.

> JASON
> C'mon. I've got an idea.

Jason pulls out two sheets of paper from a notebook.
He hands one to Kyle with a pen and takes one.

                              KYLE

      Great. Homework already.

                             JASON

      Rip the paper in half. We're gonna
      write about where we'll be in ten
      years. The same thing on each half.
      Then we'll each keep one of each.
      But we can't read them until your
      twenty-third birthday. Deal?

Kyle raises his eyebrows.

                             JASON

      For real. None of that Mr. December
      shit, either. Where are we gonna be
      in ten years? Ten years from today.

ZOOM OUT: Kyle and Jason are writing on their
slips of paper. They fold them up and
exchange papers.

                             JASON

      Now put your two pieces in here. R.
      Rickets.

KYLE

Where'll you put yours?

JASON

Give me a letter.

KYLE

(Sweeps his hand over the encyclopedias
like Vanna White) Well, Mr. Bishop,
pick a letter. There are twenty-six.

JASON

(Jumps up and down and squeals like
a game-show contestant) GIMME AN X!

KYLE

OOOH! Risky. (He hands him the
volume that includes X words.) I
still don't get how these (he shakes
his papers in the air) makes *this*
(he motions to the encyclopedias)
less uncool.

JASON

Ahhh, young Luke. (Perfect Yoda
impersonation.) This is not merely
an encyclopedia set. It's the crypt

that holds the secrets of our
future.

                    KYLE
Yoda, Yoda, how could I ever have
doubted your wisdom? (He bows down
and hands over the WXYZ volume.) But
first please read us something from
those ever-so-informative pages.

                    JASON
(Clears his throat) X. "Xerophagy.
Xerophagy means 'dry eating.' In
some cases, this means bread and
water, especially if being used as a
form of discipline or hunger
strike." (Jason looks up.) I guess
like that Gandhi guy.

                    KYLE
Forget the commentaries, O wise one,
and just read it.

                    JASON
Look who's loving his new
encyclopedia set. (He laughs, then

returns to the encyclopedia to
read.) "Involuntary xerophagy" (Jason
looks up), aka starvation, "is
imposed as punishment to heretics,
infidels, and evil-doers, adding to
the misery of their imprisonment."

                    KYLE
I thought for sure you'd go for
xylophone.

                    JASON
Dude, xylophone would've been so
obvious.

                    KYLE
(Laughs and places "R" back in the
bookshelf) X. Xerophagy. Good word.
Want more cake?

                    JASON
Now we're talking.

I held the pieces of paper in my hand. I couldn't bring
myself to read Jason's page and slipped our futures back
into R. Someday. Not today. I hoped Mrs. Bishop hadn't

thrown out that XYZ encyclopedia. Maybe I'd ask Chase.

I read over the scene and smiled. It felt good to remember—to have a piece of Jason back. Maybe my mind could get him back, more than just Scene Three.

Everybody was psyched for Christmas break and the Winter Ball. The school looked like it had been transformed into some kind of *Hallmark Hall of Fame* movie set. But those movies always had happy endings. It had never occurred to me before that the holidays could suck for some people.

Later that week Mark came over and said, "Your grades are better. You're up to date on your homework. Your teachers say you've never been a better student. What's up?"

I couldn't win with this guy. "Nothing. Just studying."

"Spending lots of time in the library, they say." Mark flexed his biceps. I wondered if he did it subconsciously. "What about sports? What about extracurricular activities?" Mark rubbed his head.

"I dunno, Mark. I don't think I'll be elected class president anytime soon."

"You know what I mean."

"I like the library."

Mark leaned against the doorframe. "Dr. Matthews says you still don't talk about any of it."

"Isn't there a law against doctors talking about their patients?"

"Not when they belong to the state of Nevada. So what's up? Why don't you talk?"

I'd seen a show called *Taxicab Confessions*. The cabdriver just drove around like normal, but people told him everything. It's not like he even asked them anything. They started blabbing and blabbing about all their problems and stuff. It was funny, but weird.

"Maybe I should take a ride in a taxi." I shrugged.

Mark rubbed the back of his neck. "It's Christmastime. It's a tough time for everyone, I know."

Shit happens. That's what Jase said. But just because it happens doesn't mean it's okay.

I looked down the street at the Bishops' house. "Maybe I'll make some popcorn strings to wrap around the tree."

People on Richmond Avenue strung up their holiday lights as if nothing had happened—all except for the Bishops. Mrs. Bishop hadn't even put out her nativity scene.

I held the poinsettia in my hands. I had bought it the week before but couldn't bring myself to face them, especially after what happened when I went over at Thanksgiving. The leaves had gotten pretty wilty, even though I'd watered it every day.

Sorry about Jason.

No.

I thought you might want a poinsettia. And, well, sorry.

No.

Every time I tried to cross the street to go to their house, I'd feel a dizzying wave of nausea and would have to lie down on the ground until my world stopped spinning. It took me an hour, but I finally worked up the courage to go. I stepped off the porch and faced their house, clutching the poinsettia.

But the movie got all messed up again. I had almost made it to their house when I saw Mr. Bishop walking out, carrying a suitcase in each hand. His shouts echoed down the street. "There's no way to get him back! He's dead!" The last word hung in the air like one of those cartoon bubbles. *Dead!*

I pictured Mrs. Bishop holding on to fifteen years of birthdays, Christmases, family holidays—fifteen years of memories and photos. They'd all fade away, though. And maybe a day would come when we wouldn't think about him. Not once.

Then he'd really be gone—dead.

The camera panned down the street. Chase sat on the corner, rocking back and forth, his hands covering his ears. Brooke hugged him, begging him to go back inside.

It was a slow-motion shot of all of them turning to look at me—Jason's killer—holding a half-dead plant. Pause. Nobody moved. Nobody said anything. Mr. Bishop looked like he was suspended in time.

Play. Brooke ran at me. She screamed, "A poinsettia! You come to us with a fucking poinsettia!" She ripped the poinsettia from my hands and threw it at me. The pot shattered on the street, the plant's roots curling in the dirt.

Mr. Bishop pulled out of the driveway. Mrs. Bishop looked at me, her eyes filled with tears. I couldn't let Jason be gone forever. I had to find a way to bring him back to them—to Chase. And Mrs. Bishop.

I'd be the one to remember.

I tried to find Chase at school, but Mike told me he was home sick. "Do you maybe wanna come around anyway?" Mike scuffed his boots in the snow. His ears turned red. "Just, you know. So you don't lose practice at being a bodyguard."

I smiled. "I'll be here, Mike."

"Really?"

"Sure."

"Wait a sec." He pulled a sweaty dollar bill out of his pocket. "This is all I've got." He looked worried. "Will that cover it?"

"Keep it, okay? I'll be here."

Mike wrapped his arms around my waist and squeezed. "Thank you, Orange Dragon."

"Don't miss your bus."

"I won't!" He skipped to his bus and waved at me from the window. Real discreet.

Every time I saw Kohana taking pictures, I thought of the stories that went with each one. He showed me a picture he had taken of my backpack, my notebook poking out the top. "I want this story," he said, pointing to the notebook.

I laughed it off. Nobody could have those stories.

Jase had a bunch of stories because he had a shit-load of stuff: his art supplies and favorite jeans. And his secrets—the leftovers that Mrs. Bishop would've found.

The secret stash.

You forgot about it, huh?

Yeah. You still got everything?

Yeah. Mom'll probably flip out when she finds the stuff.

Maybe she'll get them to change your headstone. Turn WALKS WITH GOD into ROAD TO PERDITION.

Ha ha. Quite the comedian.

I do what I can. And the book?

Yep. The book.

You're so screwed when Brooke finds out it was you.

A little late now, huh?

I guess.

UNTITLED: SCENE TWO—The List

FADE IN: Kyle and Jason are whistling tuneless songs while rollerblading up and down Elm Street. They skate, pause in front of Jason's driveway, and continue to skate.

CLOSE-UP: Jason's front door. Brooke and Mel leave the house. Off camera we hear laughter and car doors slamming. Camera remains focused on the front door.

CUT TO: Jason motioning to his eyes, military style, and back at the house.

CUT TO: Kyle nodding.

FADE IN: Larry Mullen Jr. and Adam Clayton's score from *Mission: Impossible*. Jason and Kyle slip ski masks over their faces, and their Rollerblades turn into climbing shoes. Jason and Kyle elbow-crawl up to the house. Jason opens the door and the hinge creaks. The *Mission: Impossible* music ends with the sound of a needle scratching across a record.

MRS. BISHOP

(Off camera.) Boys? Is that you,
Jason? Do you need a snack?

KYLE

Real incognito, Jase. Smooth.

JASON

Should we call off the mission?

KYLE

No way. Not now.

JASON

You won't really do it.

KYLE

Watch me.

FADE IN: *Mission: Impossible* sound track. Kyle
sneaks past the den, where Mrs. Bishop is
watching TV, and slips up the Bishop staircase. He stands in front of a door.

ZOOM IN: to sign on the door. "KEEP OUT. That
means you!" Kyle slips his library card into

the doorjamb and clicks it open. Soundless.
(Homage to classic *Mission: Impossible* scene
where Ethan Hunt/Tom Cruise dangles from a
cord while retrieving information from the
computer.) Kyle dangles from a bungee above a
dresser. Sweat drips from his brow as he
plunges his hand into the top drawer.

JASON

(Speaking through the door) What's
taking you so long?

KYLE

You didn't tell me I had to look
through her underwear drawer to
get it.

JASON

Dude, you'd better not be checking
out my sister's underwear.

KYLE

(Has a pair on his head and rips
them off). No way, man.

CAMERA PANS THE ROOM—from Kyle's

271

point of view–and stops on a
glittery pink book tucked behind
a tattered purple teddy bear.

KYLE

Got it.

CUT TO: Jason and Kyle in Jason's room. The
door is bolted with seven locks, and a chair
rests under the doorknob.

ZOOM IN: The book and the first page, written
in curvy letters. "HOT LIPS LIST." Shot from
view of Jason holding the book.

ZOOM OUT: Kyle is looking over Jason's shoulder
at the book.

KYLE

That's it? That's what all this was
for? A hot lips list?

JASON

Ahh, my friend. This is much more
than a book. This is blackmail.

                              KYLE

            (Nodding, then grinning) Hey, Jase.
            (He clears his throat and rubs his
            palms together.) Am I on the list?

                              JASON

            (Rolling his eyes) You're not serious,
            are you?

ZOOM OUT: Jason and Kyle laughing.

I laughed. Brooke and Mel tried to torture us into telling them about where we hid that dumb book. But we never gave it up. Honestly, it wasn't even that interesting. They had rated the "kissable" guys from their class with lipstick kisses: one being "good enough for practice"; five being "steamy tongue-twisting." And the highlighted entries were the ones they'd actually hooked up with—with the corrected lipstick kisses to the side. Big deal.

I wondered if Mrs. Bishop had found the book and sent Brooke to do extra church time. Maybe she found all of Jase's stuff. What did she do with it? What happened to Jason's locker? What does the school do with a dead kid's locker?

It was the last day before Christmas break. The day before any school vacation is a waste. In most classes, we

just hung out and ate candy. Mrs. Beacham decided to have a Shakespearian insult competition. I won a box of caramel chocolates with "Swim with leeches, thou gorbellied, codpiece-sniffing maggot pie!"

After the bell rang, I walked down the empty hallways. Carson High had become a ghost school. Everybody— students, teachers, custodians, secretaries—had run for home as fast as possible. Mr. Cordoba sat alone, working at his desk, like it was another regular day at the library. I opened the door a crack.

"Mr. Caroll, it's nice to see you here. What with all the holiday festivities."

"Yeah. I wanted to return *The Catcher in the Rye* before the break." I'd re-checked it out twice, just to hold on to it.

He scanned the book. "What did you think?"

"I liked it. A lot." I wondered if Jase had liked it as much as I did.

"You sound surprised."

"Well, you wouldn't think a story about some kid's weekend in New York would be so good, but it was."

"Why?"

I fidgeted with my backpack. "I really liked Holden, you know?"

"What did you like about him?"

"Well, he's funny. And real."

"Real?"

"Yeah. Honest. He definitely isn't the type to have to hang out with the popular kids just to be cool."

Mr. Cordoba tapped his fingers on the desk. "Do you know anybody like that?"

I thought about Kohana. "Yeah. I do. But he doesn't have a lot of friends. Funny, huh?"

Mr. Cordoba shut down his computer and looked at me. "Does Holden have a lot of friends?"

I shook my head. "No. It seems like he could use one."

Mr. Cordoba waited and leaned on the desk. He hadn't scratched his temple yet, so that meant I wasn't done talking about the book. He always scratched his temple when he didn't want to talk anymore. He probably wasn't a very good poker player.

"Why?"

"I dunno. He seems kind of lonely."

"That must be hard."

"It is . . . I guess." I blushed.

Mr. Cordoba scratched his temple. "I agree."

"You think Holden would be a good friend?"

"I think *you* would be a good friend to Holden."

I stood there stunned until Mr. Cordoba said, "So— what book are you taking home for the holidays?"

"Um, I dunno. Could you maybe pick out a book you like—really like, though? One you read not because you *had* to read it? Maybe I'll like it, too." I scuffed my shoe

against the carpet. I'd already had to change the duct tape twice. I'd used Dad's because I didn't want to bug Chase about it.

He pulled a book from the shelves and handed it to me. "This is one of my favorites. Let's see if we have the same taste."

I flipped to the front. No Jason.

He took it back and registered it in the system while I fished for my library card at the bottom of my pack.

"Mr. Cordoba?"

"Yes?"

"Did you know Jason? Jason Bishop?"

He nodded.

I turned away from Mr. Cordoba's steady gaze. "Did you know him well? I mean, did you talk about books a lot?"

"No. I didn't know him well."

"That's too bad." I sighed. "Did he check out a lot of books?"

"Some."

I looked around the library. "What other books did he like to read? Do you remember?"

"He spent a lot of time looking at the art books," Mr. Cordoba said, pointing to the reference section. "And he used to check out graphic novels every now and again."

I stared at the flecks of brown in the worn library carpet.

I didn't want Mr. Cordoba to think I was stalking a dead guy. "Okay. Just wondering, you know."

"I understand."

"You do?"

"What people read says a lot about them."

"Yeah. I guess it does." I looked at the book in my hands. "So what does this book say about me: kid who doesn't know what to read?" I laughed.

"Or what does it say about me?"

"Oh. Oh yeah." I looked at the title: *Chronicle of a Death Foretold.*

"Merry Christmas, Mr. Caroll."

"You, too. And thanks." When I walked down the hall, I felt like I carried the secret to who Mr. Cordoba was in my backpack. But I wasn't sure if I wanted to know what that secret was.

42

Since the day with the poinsettia, I hadn't seen Mr. Bishop's car. Snow piled on the Bishops' walk and driveway. I started to get up early to shovel it. Then I shoveled both their next-door neighbors' walks and driveways, too, so Mrs. Bishop would think it was one of them. It was hard to do with a broken hand and in the dark. At least my cast hand had healed quick. Sometimes it took me a couple of hours.

I cradled a hot chocolate against my fingers after one morning of shoveling, inhaling the smell of sticky-sweet marshmallows. I opened *Chronicle of a Death Foretold,* and an envelope dropped out. *Mr. Caroll* was scribbled on the front.

I hadn't gotten a Christmas card from anyone. My Secret Santa in math class never even gave me a present. I

took out the card. It was simple, with a small tree on the front, encircled by the words PEACE ON EARTH. I opened it.

> Dear Mr. Caroll,
>   I wish you peace. Happy Christmas.
>   —Mr. Cordoba

I held the card in my hand, unable to believe that we had ever thought Mr. Cordoba was a heartless assassin. The guy handed out PEACE ON EARTH Christmas cards. No mafia guy ever sends cards. What would Capone have written on his cards?

> Merry Christmas. Hope I don't have to off you this year.
>   —Al

I turned the card over. It smelled like books. Do people always smell like their jobs? If so, it would totally suck to be a proctologist.

Good one, Kyle.

Thanks, Jase.

I smiled and put the card back in the novel.

Christmas Eve loomed over us like some kind of black cloud—like that 1978 horror flick *The Swarm*, where a

279

mass of African bees invades and kills thousands in Houston. Mel and I were anxious. Mom had baked three kinds of desserts to calm her nerves. And it was all Dad's fault. He had invited Uncle Ray and Aunt Phyllis. Having to spend any amount of time with Aunt Phyllis topped Jason's and my "what's worse" list.

"I want everybody to be on their best behavior tonight," Dad said. He looked at Mom when he talked. "I mean everybody!"

When we heard Uncle Ray and Aunt Phyllis's car in the drive, Mel and I bolted upstairs. Mom met us at the top of the stairwell and growled, "Don't you *dare* think of escaping tonight. Now get downstairs and *be nice*."

After dinner, Aunt Phyllis sat down at the piano and started pounding out Christmas carols. At first it was totally embarrassing and lame, but after a while, all of us were singing—even Mom.

"I think she's drinking something a lot stronger than eggnog," Mel whispered.

Mom's cheeks were pink and her eyes looked droopy. "Maybe," I agreed.

Aunt Phyllis and Uncle Ray took Mel's room. Mel took my bed, and I slept on the floor. I slipped into my sleeping bag. Sleeping bags are always the same—same feel, same smell. There's something nice about things that don't change.

I peed in my bag once at summer camp in fourth grade. The next morning, everybody knew who had wet their bags because the sleeping bags were hung up on the camp clothesline.

Jeffrey Mason razzed me, but Jason stepped up. "Listen, purple puke face, I wouldn't mess with Kyle if I were you."

That was a great line: purple puke face. I started to write out the next scene in my head.

UNTITLED: ~~Scene Three~~Scene Four–The sleeping bag
Campers sing "Kumbaya" in the background.

FADE IN: Camera pans a typical summer camp in
the mountains. There's a bonfire, and one
kid's marshmallow goes up in flames.

ARC SHOT of boy and burning marshmallow. A
dizzying look at the hazards of summer camp.

CUT TO: A group stands around the sleeping
bags hanging on the line.

CLOSE-UP: The blue sleeping bag with green
lining. Kyle is written in huge letters
across it.

The camera swish-pans the faces of the
campers using a fish-eye lens. Their faces
are blurry and distorted as they laugh and
point at the sleeping bag.

JASON

(Standing tall) Listen, purple puke
face, I wouldn't mess with Kyle if I
were you.

"Kyle?" Melanie interrupted the memory while I was
thinking about the color of Jason's bag. Was it red or
orange? It bugged me that I couldn't remember.

"Are you asleep?" she asked.

"No." I looked up at Pluto and sighed.

"Can we talk for a sec?"

I propped myself up on my elbow. "Huh?" I hoped Mel
wasn't going to start talking to me about Jake Sanders, her
latest boyfriend. Everybody called the guy Hoover. Since
Mel had started hooking up with him, she wore turtlenecks
a lot.

"It's just— Well, you're different. That's all." Melanie
moved to the end of the bed and peered over at me.

Pluto was starting to blur into Saturn. Everything
seemed too heavy to hold inside. I couldn't move. I couldn't
breathe.

Mel leaned over and grabbed my hand. "I wish we hadn't fought that morning, you know? I mean, it was stupid."

I wished we hadn't fought, too. I nodded.

"I think about it a lot. Sometimes I wonder if things could've been different if only—" Mel wiped her nose. "It's stupid, I guess."

"It's not your fault, Mel."

"I sometimes think it is."

"Why?"

"I was mad at Jason, you know? And I just hated seeing him there that morning."

I sat up. "What for?"

"He'd totally ditched you for those losers. Then he came over and sat at our table, eating Mom's pancakes like everything was the same. Dad even went out to get syrup for him. Like when would that have ever happened in a normal world? King Jason. I wished he'd go away."

And he did.

She wiped away some tears. "Now I feel like shit all the time, because . . ."

I squeezed her hand.

"God, it sucks."

"Mel, it's not like what you thought made a difference. If you had that power, I would've spontaneously combusted about five years ago."

She laughed through her tears.

"Do you ever talk to Brooke?" I asked. Melanie had lost a best friend, too. I never told her how bad I felt about that. I just never knew what to say anymore.

She shook her head.

"That sucks."

"No big deal. She dropped out of cheer— It doesn't matter. Anyway, we were just friends because of habit, you know. It's not like we had a lot in common anymore."

I knew what she meant. Kind of.

"Hold on a sec." Mel ran out of the room and came back in. "Here. It's your Christmas present."

I opened up a gift certificate to Sundance Books. "Sweet, Mel. That's cool."

"Yeah, you've been reading a lot. Maybe if you have any left over, you can invite me for a coffee there."

"Like a ten-dollar latte? That's half the certificate!"

"Cheap ass."

I laughed. Mel brought her hand down on my head and ruffled my hair. She slipped off the bed and sat next to me. "You know, I'm glad you're here. I wouldn't trade you for anything."

Maybe she was worth that ten-dollar latte after all. I leaned into her. "All right. But make it a small latte without all those foo-foo add-ons. And it'd better not be fat-free decaf shit, okay?"

"Deal," she said, and kissed me on the forehead. She

climbed back into bed and whispered, "Merry Christmas, Kyle."

"You, too, Mel." I listened as her breathing steadied. "Thank you," I whispered.

When Mel finally fell asleep, I went to sit at the top of the staircase. The house smelled like pine. The glow of the Christmas tree was the only light left. Last year Jase and I would've been stuffed with Mrs. Bishop's caramel cookies and hot chocolate.

What would Jason wish for you now? Dr. Matthews's question popped into my head and wouldn't leave. I wished I knew the answer.

I went back to bed and listened to the quiet house until the blackness of night lifted.

Merry Christmas, Jase, I thought.

43

At dawn I snuck out. The moon still hung low in the sky. I walked to the Bishops' and tapped on Chase's window.

He popped his head up and peered out. He smooshed his nose against the pane and started to laugh, so that the whole window fogged up.

I put my finger to my lips. "Shhhh." I stomped my feet, trying to keep warm.

"What?" he mouthed.

I motioned him to go to the back door and jumped the side fence to meet him.

"I'm sorry about your dad, Chase." He covered his ears and turned his back to me. I walked around and faced him. "We don't have to talk about that. Okay?"

He uncovered his ears. "Whatcha doin' up so early?" he asked. "Do you need help shoveling today?"

"You know?" I asked.

"I figured it was you."

I lowered my voice. "Does your mom know?"

Chase shook his head. "She doesn't get up that early anymore. She sleeps a lot." He faced the rising sun, squinting in the early-morning light. "Did you know that the sun has been called Helios and sol? Nuclear fusion produces a really cool energy output of three hundred eighty-six billion billion megawatts. And there are over one billion stars in our galaxy. The sun's just one of them. Funny, huh? One in a billion."

"Did you get a new book?"

Chase grinned. "You do know the difference between a solar system and a galaxy, don't you?"

I rubbed my arms to warm up, still stuck on Helios and his 386 billion billion megawatts.

"Anyway, the sun has eight satellites. We like to call them planets. You know Jason had the sun's satellites all messed up on his ceiling. He mixed up Saturn and Jupiter. And Pluto isn't even considered a planet anymore, scientifically speaking. Maybe historically we can talk about Pluto as a planet, but it's not really. I mean, how could Jason *not* know that?"

Since when was Pluto not a planet? "Hey, are the

planets still there? On Jase's ceiling?"

Chase nodded. "Yep."

"Don't take them down. I mean, if you don't have to."

"Mom doesn't touch anything in Jason's room. It's like a museum."

"Chase, I can't stay long. Here, I got you something."

"Wait a sec." Chase ran back into the house.

God, I hope he isn't getting his mom.

He came out and handed me a card. "It's a winter solstice card. I meant to give it to you on December twenty-first, but Dad picked me up that day."

I smiled. "Wow, Chase." I held the construction-paper card in my hand. It had a picture of the sun and some stars. And on the inside he had written, *I like your orange shoes. Keep your head up, Orange Dragon.*

"Mike helped me with it. He's still really into hiring you."

I took a deep breath and tried to control my voice. "Maybe after your gig is over."

Chase's eyes got real big. I cracked a smile.

"Nah, you wouldn't ditch me," he said.

"Never."

"Never."

"Thanks," I said. "It's the best winter solstice card I've ever gotten—the best card, really."

"So how many days has it been?"

"Has what been?"

"The orange shoes? The bet? I told Mom that Jason owed you his 1948 Captain Marvel Adventures number eighty-one if you wore them for a year straight."

"Oh yeah? What'd she say?"

"She didn't say anything. She just cried. She always cries."

I kicked some snow off the back porch. "Yeah, well, the comic books don't really matter."

"So why do you wear 'em?"

I shrugged. "Just because."

"Honoring your bet?"

"I guess so."

"Good enough. Well, I knew you'd like the card." Chase eyed the present I had in my hands.

"Oh, so you want this?"

I handed it over, and he tore open the wrapping paper. "No way! It's a dragon! It's a red dragon!"

"I couldn't find orange."

"That doesn't matter. Orange is a by-product of red and yellow. This is the best!"

"Just don't drag it on the street or anything. Maybe we can fly it at Mills. Saturday. Noon."

"On the sly?" Chase grinned.

"Sure. On the sly." I laughed. "Now go hide it. Don't tell anybody."

Chase crossed his heart. "Boy Scout's honor."

"Chase, you're not a Boy Scout."

"But I have honor."

"Yeah. Happy Christmas, okay?"

"Happy late winter solstice to you." Chase left the wrapping paper soaking in the snow and went inside. I scooped it up and walked by his window. He pressed his whole face against it this time. Then he pulled back and mouthed, "Thank you."

"Any New Year's resolutions, Mr. Caroll?" Mr. Cordoba asked, placing *Chronicle of a Death Foretold* on a pile of books.

"No. I, uh, don't make resolutions—not anymore, anyway."

Mr. Cordoba tapped his finger on the book. He flipped through the pages. "What did you think?"

"I really liked it. Maybe I can read more by that author."

He nodded. "He's Colombian."

"Really?"

"From my hometown."

"Oh, yeah?" No wonder everybody thought he was some kind of mafia guy. Carson City was so lame. Had

Cordoba been from Cuba, everybody probably would've thought he was a commie spy.

"Aracataca. He won the Nobel prize."

"For what?"

"For literature."

"Oh. That's a pretty big deal."

Mr. Cordoba looked at me over his glasses. "Pretty big. So why did you like it?"

"I dunno. I guess I liked how this guy wanted to go back and find out what happened, but it turned out everybody had a different story."

"Memory is tricky, isn't it?"

"It is." I wondered what Chase remembered about Jason. If it was different from what I remembered. I pulled out my notebook. "I wrote this line down: 'The broken mirror of memory.'"

Mr. Cordoba nodded. "That's a great way to describe memories. It's like your director's notebook."

"How?"

"Fourteen versions of the same scene."

"Yeah. I hadn't thought about that. It's just that none of them turned out right."

"You haven't found the right director."

I shook my head. "Not yet."

"You will." Mr. Cordoba watched me intently. Waiting. "Are you going to do homework today?"

"I don't really feel like it."

Mr. Cordoba raised his eyebrows. "Come help me out, then." He handed me a pile of envelopes to lick.

"What are these for?" I passed my tongue across the sticky sweet glue.

"I'm trying to raise money to open a boxing gym in Aracataca."

"So you're a boxer?"

"I was."

Cordoba was actually telling me stuff about himself—not his books. Maybe I'd tell Kohana. I paused. "Do you still box?"

"Just for exercise and training."

"You train boxers?"

"A little—down at the community center gym."

"Were you a good boxer?"

"Some say so."

"Were you pro?"

"Almost."

"What happened?"

"I came here and became a librarian."

Intense! "Why a librarian? I mean, you could've been a boxer. You could've been superfamous or something." Mr. Cordoba looked up from the letters he was folding. "Well, not that a librarian can't be famous. I'm sure there are famous ones out there." I felt my face get hot.

Mr. Cordoba pointed out the books on the shelves. "Because here, every day, I can be anything I want to be. There is no limit to what I can do here"—he tapped his temple—"and here." He pointed to the books.

I shrugged. Weird. After that, we didn't talk for a long time. I just licked and sealed envelopes. The silences with Mr. Cordoba were cool, too.

"Do you need another book, Mr. Caroll?" Mr. Cordoba asked while I gathered my things.

"Sure. That'd be good."

He handed me *The Outsiders.*

"Hey! This is a great Coppola movie."

Cordoba smiled. "I've never seen it."

"You don't like movies?"

"I never know what to watch."

"Oh, c'mon, Mr. Cordoba. I can give you a list a mile long of movies to watch."

"Okay, then, pick one, and I'll watch it this week."

"Narrow it down to one? Let me think." I zipped up my pack and grinned. *"Black Mask."*

"Black Mask?" Mr. Cordoba wrote it down.

"If you have trouble finding it, I can download it for you."

"Thank you, Mr. Caroll. I look forward to watching it."

When I turned to go, I asked, "Mr. Cordoba, um, can I ask you one more thing?"

He nodded.

"Is that how you got the scar? Boxing?"

"No."

My ears prickled. They were probably about the color of Mark's head after his trip to Cancun over the holidays. "Uh, sorry. I just thought . . ."

"See you tomorrow morning. Don't be late."

The sun was about to drop behind the mountains. I rode home as fast as I could, pumping my legs, feeling the burn in my thighs and sweat trickle down my back. My heart pounded, and I think I was smiling.

Mr. Cordoba was a boxer.

45

Everything started going back to normal all around me. Almost like October 8 had never really happened. I worried that I was the only one remembering Jase, keeping him from disappearing forever. After school one day I went to look for Jase's locker. I just wanted to see it. Instead, I found Alex and his friends surrounding Kohana in one of the back hallways. Pinky and Troy held Kohana down while Alex ripped his photography portfolio out of his hands. "Nice pictures, man." Ever since they had taken the heat off me, I'd noticed them hanging around Kohana more. They never did things other than say lame-ass stuff and try to look cool. Kohana didn't put up with their shit, anyway. The day before, when Alex tried to trip Kohana after school, Kohana slammed him into the flagpole. Alex had

been alone. It looked like Alex got his henchmen to take care of things for him again.

Alex showed Kohana's photo to Pinky and Troy. He tore it down the middle. The vein on Kohana's temple pulsated as he tried to break free. I felt the red rage again and raced down the hall. No teachers were around. These guys thought they ruled the fucking world.

I threw myself into Alex, and the portfolio went flying. Pinky and Troy pounced on me. "Get your photos, Kohana! Get 'em!" Kohana ran to his portfolio as Troy kicked me in the stomach. Not this again.

"Oh, look who we have here, guys. A true hero, huh?" Alex stood up, brushing off his pants. His voice quavered. *Fucking pansy.*

Pinky and Troy pulled me up and shoved me into the lockers. My hand throbbed. I'd only had the cast off for a week, and it still hurt—useless for a fight.

Kohana was a step from his portfolio when he turned around. "Leave him alone, assholes."

"How sweet, Clock. You found yourself a little friend." Alex laughed.

Friend. I had never thought that I was Kohana's friend. I just kinda figured he put up with me after school since he didn't have a lot of company.

Alex kept laughing. But nobody else did. Not even Pinky and Troy. Pinky looked at Troy and shrugged, still

holding me against the locker doors.

I felt like I was in a spaghetti western with a really bad script. I looked down the hall for a tumbleweed and listened for Ennio Morricone's theme music.

I tried to push Pinky and Troy off, but they were too strong.

Alex sneered at me. "Yeah, and we know what happens to Kyle's friends."

"I said, 'Leave him alone,'" Kohana said, and shoved Alex against the lockers across the hall. "Back off," he whispered. "Leave us alone. Just back off." Kohana looked from Alex to me. He cocked his head to the side. "What, Alex, you gonna piss yourself again?"

Pinky snorted. "C'mon, guys. They aren't worth it," he said. Kohana let Alex go. "Maybe they'll go off and watch one of Kyle's weird-ass movies together."

How did they know about the movies?

"It was Jase's own fault he died, hanging out with a freak like Kyle," Alex said.

That sent me reeling. I yanked myself free of Troy and Pinky and raced at Alex. The hallways turned red. The rage overtook me, and I don't know what I would've done if I hadn't felt Kohana's hand on my shoulder. "He's not worth it, man. Let it go." Kohana brought me back to the hallway. Alex whimpered. Troy and Pinky didn't move.

Then I saw Alex, really saw him. A pathetic shit of a

friend. And scared. It was like I could see his movie projected ten years into the future. He'd be that guy at the class reunion who still talked about being homecoming king; that guy who'd buy beer for the keggers at the creek, hanging out with the high school kids when his friends were long gone; that guy who wore his letterman jacket after graduation and never let go of the past.

I didn't want to be like him—stuck on a day, stuck in an era.

I watched the three of them walk away. Troy and Pinky walked ahead—the first sign of the end of Alex's golden years.

I sat against the lockers to catch my breath.

Kohana grabbed his portfolio and sat next to me. "You okay?"

"Yeah. You?"

"Yeah. Thanks."

"You, too, man." I rubbed my temples.

"What they say about Jason and stuff. That's not cool. They're losers."

I leaned my head against the lockers. "Fuck, it's complicated." Kohana flipped through his portfolio. "Are your pictures okay?"

"Thanks to you."

"I know they mean a lot to you." I sighed. "Your stories."

Kohana took out his camera and took a picture of the hallway. "This was a good story, too."

"What's the story? Getting picked on by the school tools?"

Kohana shook his head. "No. Friendship." He cleared his throat and smiled.

I wondered if that was okay. Would it be okay with Chase and Jason that I had a friend? Plus I still wasn't completely sure I hadn't shot my last one on purpose. Maybe I ought to come with a "friendship warning label." I closed my eyes and sighed.

"How can you be so okay with things, Kohana? Doesn't it just piss you off?"

He laughed. "Seriously, nobody's worth that."

"Worth what?"

"There's this old Native American thing Gram said to me one time. It sucked at first, growing up here. My mom died. Dad left. He didn't want to be the dad of a deformed kid. I had no friends." Kohana wiped his camera lens. "I didn't see the point of anything, you know. One day Gram said, 'Kohana, I want to know what sustains you from the inside when all else falls away.'"

"Huh?"

Kohana sighed. "That's what I said. I was only eight. But I got it after a while. Everything fell away, you know. And I was alone. So I had to figure it out."

"Figure what out?"

"What sustains me."

We sat in silence for a while.

"Gram gave me this camera, the first one she ever used. She was a professional photographer before I came along."

"Is that what sustains you?"

"No." He shook his head. "It can never be a thing. This is just a tool. But it helps. So that's what you've got to figure out."

What sustains me? I'd have to think on that. "Hey, thanks." I said.

"For what?"

"For your story."

"Yeah, and what about yours?"

"Another time?"

Kohana nodded. "Another time."

"I think you should take a picture of your camera."

Kohana smirked. "Kinda hard to do."

I stood. "Maybe you want to hang out at the library?" I'd never wanted to share that space with anybody before.

Kohana pushed his hair out of his face. "I dunno. I'm not really a group person."

"Three people are a group?"

"Hey, man. I'm used to hanging solo."

"True. It's a good place, though. I'll introduce you to Mr. Cordoba. He seems mean, but he's not. He's a"—I

mumbled the words—"a friend."

"Then he must be pretty okay," Kohana said.

We walked down the hall. "You know, Gram has a friend with a cabin up in Squaw Valley. Sometimes we go for the weekend to hike and mountain bike and stuff."

"Yeah? Sounds cool."

"Maybe you can come next time."

"I'd like that." Then I paused. "Squaw Valley's in California, right?"

"Yeah."

"Shit, man, I'm not sure if I'm allowed to leave the state."

"Oh." He looked disappointed.

"I can ask my PO."

"PO?"

"Parole officer."

Kohana turned to me. I shrugged; then we buckled over, laughing.

46

I started to sleep better at night, but I'd always wake up really early in the morning. The mornings were the hardest. The house was so damned quiet and the neighborhood looked dead, like an empty movie set. Nobody'd show up until seven A.M. to bring it to life. I wished Mr. Cordoba would open the library at five A.M. or something. That would've helped. At least sometimes there was shoveling to do.

One morning, I couldn't take the quiet anymore, so I got dressed and stood outside Chase's window. "Chase," I whispered and tapped on the window.

Nothing.

"Chase!" I flicked a couple of stones at the window.

His head popped up and he rubbed his eyes. "What?"

the side fence.

peeked his head

e at all. Remember?

lippers and robe on."

ut he finally came out all

."

"No yo

"I always brus.   teeth first thing when I wake up. Don't you?"

"Okay. Yeah."

"Breathe on me. I betcha you don't."

"I do, too, Chase."

"Breathe on me."

I breathed.

"You have smelly breath. You didn't brush."

"Okay, so I forgot. It's early. I usually wait until after breakfast."

"How many cavities do you have?"

"Not many."

"How many?"

"I don't know."

"*Hmmph.*"

We sat on the back porch and looked up at the stars. "Can you show me dandelion?"

"You mean *Taraxacum officinale*?"

"Yeah. I never remember the name."

Chase looked around and pointed up to a cluster of stars. "That's it." He turned to me. "That all you need?"

"Are you doing okay? About your dad and all?"

Chase turned away. He got up and said, "I'm going now."

"Wait, Chase." I patted the step beside me. "I read this book a little while ago. It was really weird. It was about this guy who woke up one morning as a bug."

"What kind of bug?"

"Um, an insect."

"More than one million species of insects have been identified. And in all, there are over ten quintillion insects in the world. So you might want to narrow it down."

"Oh. Well, um, the book doesn't really say. But he goes to sleep as a man and wakes up a bug. An insect. But it's not science fiction or anything."

Chase chewed his bottom lip and sat down. "Tell me more."

So I told him about *The Metamorphosis*. We spent about an hour on the porch. The black night turned to the

purple dawn. Porch lights flickered off. "I'd better go, Chase."

"See ya this afternoon, Kyle. Don't be late." Chase pointed to my watch.

"Never."

"Never?"

"Well, almost never."

"Close enough. Don't forget to brush your teeth."

"I won't."

"And Kyle?"

"Yeah?" I had to get back before the Bishops came out, before Mom and Dad were up.

"You can come and tell me about your books whenever you want. You read good books."

"Cool. I'll be back then." I waved from the sidewalk. Chase looked a little like an old man in his tattered robe and slippers. I hoped he wouldn't be too tired at school.

47

Dr. Matthews strummed her fingers on her desk. She'd been losing weight and had gotten thin enough to stop wearing curtain-dresses. She was wearing pants and a sweater. She looked kinda nice. Chubby nice. "New journal?" Dr. Matthews pointed to my notebook.

I nodded.

"And?"

"I'm, um, trying to write the whole movie now. Like you said." I cleared my throat and pretended to be really interested in the books she had on her shelves.

She smiled at me—a real smile. And I told her about the time Jase and I got grounded for taking his grandma's car down the street when we were twelve. How were we supposed to know it wasn't like driving bumper cars?

At first the memories came back one scene at a time. I'd find something, like my old Rollerblades, and that would remind me of the time Jase didn't brake right and he ended up with eight stitches in his forehead. After a while, though, the stories flowed. It was easy to go back in time and find a piece of Jason in practically every object I had in my room.

With my director's notes, I felt like I could edit the bullshit. I didn't care about the times Jase blew off my Friday-night movie marathons. The new notebook let me write about the important stuff.

It was like Kohana and his camera. He could choose which stories he wanted to photograph. It could be anything—from a spray-painted locker to the bottom of somebody's desk. He didn't have to take pictures of the bad stuff. Neither did I.

Kohana sometimes came to the library when he missed the bus. He never bugged me about where I went for a half hour after school, and I never asked him why he liked to sit outside so much. Sometimes I'd wait with Kohana at the flagpole after library time until his grandma came around. He'd show me his pictures. We'd talk about the best angle to take a shot, to film a scene. Or we wouldn't say anything at all.

I almost told him about the notebook a million times, but I didn't want to ruin the magic. It was almost like Jason was coming back to life in the notebook Mr. Cordoba had

given me. I wished, though, that I could take all those memories and bring him back to the Bishops—to Chase.

At the library I spent more time writing than doing homework. Homework was easy, so I usually got it done fast so I could do the other stuff. I had always been a "solid C" student until that last fall. Then I crashed to Fs and rose to Bs. My teachers almost glowed when they handed out semester grades.

"You're really reaching your potential."

"Oh, Kyle, I am so pleased with your effort and academic success this term."

And Mark was right there behind them—proud of *his* success story—his grade contract. Even Mel took me out one night with her new boyfriend, Hoover, after progress reports came. We went out for buffalo wings, then to a movie. Hoover paid for everything. And I ate a lot. I felt kinda bad and offered to pay for at least the movie, and he said something like, "No way. This is your night." He was trying to be gallant or something, which was pretty cool, I guess.

After all the glowing reports and happy teachers, I could probably do milk commercials for Carson City wearing one of those freakish milk moustaches.

I was the boy who shot his friend, and look at me now. Don't let homicide ruin your smile. Drink milk.

309

Mr. Cordoba was the only one who didn't congratulate me.

"I watched *Black Mask*, Mr. Caroll." Mr. Cordoba was working his way through the media center, scanning all the computers for viruses.

"Really?" I was relieved to talk about something—anything—besides my miracle grades. "And?"

"He was quite an unusual librarian."

I laughed. Most librarians probably didn't do kung fu stuff. Most librarians weren't boxers, either. "Did you like it?"

Mr. Cordoba paused. "Yes, I did."

"Good."

"So?" Mr. Cordoba peered over his glasses.

"So what?"

"I could use a recommendation for another movie."

"Sure," I said. It was nice to feel like I knew a lot about something.

"How about one of your favorites. Maybe by one of your favorite directors." Mr. Cordoba said. "One you used in your notebook."

My hands felt clammy. I hated thinking about that notebook. I hated thinking about that scene that none of the directors could get right. Whenever I thought about it too hard, I started questioning myself all over again. I couldn't have done it on purpose. Shit happens, right? Mr.

Cordoba looked up from the computer screen. He was waiting for me to say something.

"Okay. Maybe a Clint Eastwood movie? Not *Dirty Harry* or anything, even though those are pretty tight. You should see this western he directed and starred in. *Unforgiven.*"

Mr. Cordoba scribbled something down on a sticky pad. "Why do you like it?"

"Because it's everything you don't expect from a western, you know? It's about how bad somebody can feel doing what he used to do best."

Mr. Cordoba waited.

"And it has the perfect line in it." I cleared my throat and lowered my voice, trying to do Eastwood. "'It's a hell of a thing, killing a man. You take away all he's got, and all he's ever gonna have. . . .' It's a good movie."

Mr. Cordoba smiled. "Better than your Eastwood impersonation?"

"Much." I grinned. Jase would've nailed it. There wasn't anybody he couldn't impersonate.

"I'll watch it this week."

"Cool." I went back to the tables and pulled out a book to read.

"Mr. Caroll, have you thought about what you're going to do after high school?"

I looked up. "That's another two and a half years

away. That's forever."

"Two and a half years isn't that long."

I shrugged.

"You're a good student. When you want to be one."

So he had seen my grades too. I wondered if there was some kind of "underground Kyle network" that monitored everything I did. Maybe Mark was the big spy of the whole operation, and his secret 007 lover was Dr. Matthews, totally redefining the Bond chick look.

I closed my book. "I dunno. The only reason I had ever really thought about going to college was to room with Jason and try out a ramen noodle diet."

"A ramen noodle diet?"

"Well, you know. Like that fat guy did eating sub sandwiches, and the other guy did for his documentary on McDonald's. Jason and I were going to see how long we could live on ramen noodles. I was going to direct a cool documentary and win awards and stuff. That was the only reason I would really want to go to college—the ramen noodle documentary."

Mr. Cordoba arched his eyebrows. "So what's stopping you?"

"You can't do that kind of stuff alone." I picked at a sticker somebody had stuck on the table. "Anyway, it was Jason's idea. It'd be pretty shitty to steal it. He had a lot of good ones, you know." I bit my lip. "Excuse me. I didn't

312

mean to say *shitty* in the library. Twice."

Mr. Cordoba returned to his desk and sat down. "I bet you have your own ideas as well."

"Nah, not like Jase. I mean, Jason was an animal for insane ideas." I laughed. "The only plan of his that backfired was trying to puff out pond frogs' croakers by sticking straws up their butts and blowing. We thought we were onto something until one of the frogs exploded. We were only seven at the time."

"He sounds like he was a smart guy."

"Yeah. Funny how I ended up being his best friend." All of a sudden my throat felt like it was closing up. My nose burned. I swallowed and counted to twenty. I couldn't have done it on purpose.

"You don't think you were a good friend?"

"Not like in the books." I pointed to *The Outsiders*. "Those guys stood up for each other through it all—never questioned each other."

"And that's how Jason was with you—never questioning? Standing up for you?"

"Yeah. I guess." I thought about Jason hanging out with Alex because I didn't want to go to the "cool" parties; how they called me Shadow and laughed at me and he let them. I glared at Mr. Cordoba. "Jason was a great friend. The best."

"I don't doubt he was, nor do I doubt that you *are*."

"Whatever."

"So, Mr. Caroll, you still haven't answered my question. What would you think you would like to do? After high school?"

How would Jason like to see you?

It wasn't fair. How could I move on and leave everything behind when I stole that from Jase? I shrugged. "I haven't thought about it."

"Think about it."

All I knew was that I had to stick around. I couldn't leave Chase. I couldn't leave Jason and the old man who raked the leaves off his grave. I couldn't just up and go.

At four o'clock, I grabbed my things and took off. For the first time, I felt like the library was going to smother me.

48

I heard hooting early one morning. Chase stood below my window and waved up at me. I threw on a sweatshirt and went outside to meet him.

He had on his bathrobe and slippers full of holes. His nose was bright red from the early-morning chill.

"You're supposed to hoot back."

"What?"

"You're supposed to hoot back. That way I know you've heard the signal."

"Oh. Next time, okay?"

He shook his head and sighed. "Fine."

"What's up? You doing okay?" Mr. Bishop hadn't come back to the house yet. He sometimes came to pick Chase up after school. I wondered where he was living. I wondered if

he'd ever come back. But if I tried to talk to Chase about it, he'd cover his ears and turn away.

"Here." Chase handed me a card. "Happy birthday." He shivered and rubbed his shoulders.

"This is my first birthday card." I traced the orange dragon.

"That was my intention. I was going to come at midnight, but I fell asleep."

"This is perfect. Thank you."

"And this, too." He pulled a yellowed envelope out of his pocket. "I found this in Jason's room."

I looked at Jason's handwriting: *Kyle.*

"Is your mom, um, cleaning out his room?"

Chase shook his head. "No."

We sat on the porch steps, watching the last stars fade away.

"I sit there," he said. "In his room."

I nodded.

"It doesn't smell like him anymore, but I still like it." Chase leaned on me. "I like to pretend he's coming home."

"Me too."

"But he's not."

"I know." I put my arm around Chase.

He got up. "See you this afternoon."

"See you."

"Don't be late."

"Never."

"Almost never," he corrected me, then walked do.
the street, leaving padded footprints in the crystal frost.

Kyle

Jason's writing.

I turned the envelope over in my hands and slipped out a brochure. *Voices of Youth Filmmaker Contest.* Jason had highlighted the application due date: May 7.

I lay on the porch, my shoulder blades digging into the concrete. The first rays of sunlight crept across the street until they worked their way up the steps. Tears pooled in my ears.

"Happy birthday, man," Kohana said, coming up to me before lunch.

"Thanks. How'd you know?"

He held out the *The Carson High Tribune.* "They always print up the birthdays here, a week ahead of time."

"I never noticed."

"I have a lot of quality reading time waiting for Gram when I miss the bus."

"Yeah, I guess so." I read my name: Kyle Michael Caroll, February 2.

"Dude, so are you getting your driver's license today?"

I shook my head. I felt kind of stupid.

"So are you having a party or something?"

"Nah."

Kohana took back the paper. "Well, happy birthday." He walked down the hall toward the cafeteria. I was on my way to the library.

"Um, Kohana?"

"Yeah?"

"Do you maybe want to come over for dinner tonight? Just if you can, you know."

He grinned. "Sure."

"We can pick you up and take you home, if you need."

"Cool."

"Um, seven o'clock okay?"

"Definitely."

On the way out of the library, Mr. Cordoba handed me a small package. "Open it." I guess he read the *The Carson High Tribune* too.

The whole birthday thing is way overrated. It would be cool if we had a system where birthdays were earned. Like if you lived the year right, then you could get older by one year, or even two if you lived the year really perfect. If not, you'd end up staying the same age until you did. That would've made more sense than giving somebody a present just because they happened to get born on some particular day. Especially if that person didn't deserve it.

Mr. Cordoba leaned on the desk.

I opened up a tattered book in Spanish: *Crónica de una*

muerte anunciada. The name *Edgar* was scribbled inside.

"That's the first book I ever owned," he said.

"Your very first book?"

He leaned his elbows on the desk. "It's *Chronicle of a Death Foretold*, in Spanish."

"You read *this* as a kid?"

He laughed. "I got it when I was nineteen."

"Nineteen? You didn't have your own book until you were nineteen?"

"No, I didn't."

"What about school? Didn't they give you books?"

"I didn't go to school in Colombia."

"Really?"

"I had to work. I boxed."

I shook my head. "They let you box instead of going to school?"

"No. I boxed because my family needed money. School didn't come with a paycheck like I got from the ring."

I cradled the book in my hand. "So how'd you learn how to read?"

"When I was eighteen, I was given a few years to think about a lot of things. That's when I decided to study and learned to read. That's when I learned to make peace."

"Peace?"

Mr. Cordoba eyed my notebook. "To make peace with the past." He got up from his desk and motioned me to sit

319

down. He sat down across from me at the table. He pointed to his scar. "This is a memory, a reminder of who I was. I take this to bed with me every night." He scanned the library. "And this is who I am."

"Who were you?" I looked at the scar.

Mr. Cordoba smiled. "A foolish young man who was given a second chance at life."

I stared at the scar on his face. I wondered if Kohana had ever taken a photo of Mr. Cordoba's scar, if he had ever captured that story.

Mr. Cordoba watched me intently, then said, "I choose not to live my life based on one moment." He rubbed his scar.

I ran my fingers over the soft edges of the book, worn like velvet. "So you didn't learn how to read until you were eighteen?"

"No. And I've been trying to catch up ever since."

"And after you learned, this was the first book you ever bought?"

"Actually, my best friend gave it to me."

"And you're giving it to me?" I blushed.

He smiled.

"I don't know what to say. About this."

"'Thank you' will do." He got up from the table.

"Thank you, Mr. Cordoba."

"Happy birthday, Mr. Caroll." He patted my shoulder

and headed back to his office.

That afternoon, even Mark stopped by with a card. "Happy birthday, Kyle. Now that you're sixteen, gotta get you up on a motorcycle one of these days."

Mom set her jaw and scowled. The last thing she needed was for me to join a biker gang.

"Just kidding, Mrs. Caroll." Mark laughed and winked at me. The last of his Cancun sunburn had flaked off. For a while his head had looked like a blotchy billiard cue ball.

We picked Kohana up at seven o'clock. Dad grilled burgers out on the deck. Mom made sweet potato fries. Kohana had three helpings of everything. He turned red every time Mel said anything to him. It was the first time I ever saw the guy flustered.

Mom brought out a double-chocolate fudge cake with chocolate-chip ice cream, my favorite since forever. Everybody sang.

"Make a wish, Kyle," Mel said.

I closed my eyes and blew out all the candles. *I just want things to be okay again. I want Chase and the Bishops to be okay.*

Mom and Dad gave me a key chain and keys to both their cars. Mel gave me a TEAM DUDE BIG LEBOWSKI T-shirt.

Kohana pulled out his photography portfolio. He handed me a photo. "This one's for you."

It was a black-and-white of my shoes, hand-tinted orange. "This is really cool."

Mom, Dad, and Mel crowded around to look at the pictures Kohana had taken. "Those are so good, Kohana," Mel said. "I never thought those shoes of Kyle's would be photogenic." She pinched her nose, and everybody laughed.

Kohana turned magenta. "Thanks."

"They're stories," I interrupted. Then I explained Kohana's philosophy of photography.

"Maybe one day you can tell us the stories," Mom said.

"Sure, Mrs. Caroll." Kohana chewed on his lower lip and fidgeted with the zipper on his portfolio.

Mom smiled at Kohana. "Only if you'd like."

Mom, Dad, and Mel looked at every one of Kohana's pictures, then headed into the kitchen. I got up to help with the dishes. "I got 'em, Kyle," Mel said.

Kohana reorganized his portfolio, leaving a blank spot.

"What picture goes there?" I asked.

"Your shoes."

"You can keep this if you need it." I handed him the photo.

"I have a copy," he said.

"So? Why leave it blank?"

"This is like an anthology. But it can't be complete without your story. No story. No photo."

"Oh." I swallowed.

"Maybe another time."

"Yeah. Maybe."

Dad and I took Kohana home. He talked the entire way about how much he had loved dinner. Mom had made him a leftover bag so he could share with his grandma.

As he was walking into his house, he shouted, "You owe me a story!"

On the way home, Dad turned on the radio and hummed along to some jazz solo. He looked over at me and said, "Anything else you'd like to do?" He motioned to the slice of cake I'd wrapped in aluminum foil and brought with me at the last minute.

"Do you think we could stop by the cemetery?"

Dad nodded. We drove in silence and parked outside the gate. "I think it's closed."

"I know a way in."

"Do you need company?"

I shook my head. "I'd rather go alone. If that's okay."

"Sure." He lit up a cigarette and winked. "Don't tell your mother."

"I won't." I rolled my eyes. It would be easier if they just smoked together.

I slipped through the shadows of the cemetery, unwrapped the cake, and left it next to Chase's M&M's jar.

Happy birthday, man.

Thanks, Jase.

Make a wish?

Yep.

Hope it comes true.

Me, too, Jase.

"Okay." I ran up to Dad. "I'm ready."

I got into the car and Dad cranked up the heat. "It's cold outside."

"Yeah." I cleared my throat. It had felt pretty scratchy all day. "Can you maybe not tell anybody we came by?"

He turned off the radio and touched his forehead to mine, just like he used to do when I was little. I leaned into him and it felt good, like I was ten years old again.

When we got home, I hung Kohana's picture up next to Chase's Orange Dragon drawing. The walls didn't seem so empty anymore.

49

Every day I'd wake up hoping to find Mr. Bishop's car back in the driveway. It didn't make sense to me that he had left Chase and Brooke like that. Jason didn't have a choice, but Mr. Bishop did.

I walked down the winding path to Jason's grave one day and saw Mrs. Bishop on her knees. The snow had melted and the cemetery looked barren. There was a smattering of chalky conversation hearts left over from Valentine's Day. I walked away before she saw me.

I had turned sixteen. Jason never would.

Freeze frame.

The rest of February sucked. The snow was crusty and melted, black and yellow from exhaust fumes and dog piss. And all I did was write, trying to bring Jason back with

every object, every scene. Once in a while I thought about Scene Three, but I was afraid it would bring me back to the way I had felt that night in the shed.

Sometimes the scenes came back so quickly, I felt like I wouldn't be able to write them down fast enough. One afternoon I sat behind the Dumpsters writing about the time Jase helped me organize a B-movie marathon in the backyard. I had gotten seven of the best B-movies to show and was ready with Grandpa's old projector. When we threaded the first film, the movie that started to play definitely wasn't *The Rocky Horror Picture Show*. We didn't get a chance to see too much before Dad ripped it out of the projector and canceled the showing until he reviewed all seven movies. All seven starred a girl named Roxy Lovelace. Apparently we had gotten the wrong shipment. I wrote the scene in a grind-house movie style—like those cheesy seventies movies with bad acting and hot chicks.

"Kyle. Hey, Kyle! *Psst!*"

Chase and Mike were standing together, peeking around the corner. "Hey, guys. Sorry. Didn't see you." I shoved the notebook into my backpack.

"You didn't hear us hoot?" Chase asked.

"I guess not."

Chase crossed his arms. "A little lackadaisical today."

"Nice word, Chase."

"Thanks. I learned it last week."

"Yeah, and he says it every day, all day long." Mike rolled his eyes. "Nobody in Mrs. Perrin's class knows what it means. I don't think she even knows what it means."

Chase glared at Mike. "It means 'lazy.'"

Mike picked at a scab. "Yeah. But who's gonna remember that?"

"I'm going to Mike's."

"Cool." I looked at the time—late for the library again.

"Anyway, I need your help with something," Chase said, turning to me.

"What's going on?"

"Well, Mom is into this heaven–eternal-life stuff, telling me Jason's with me always."

My throat felt dry. I rubbed my eyes. "What does your dad say?"

"Dad stopped going to church the day he left the house. I heard him tell Mom that there is no God."

I couldn't believe I had taken God away from Mr. Bishop too. "Have you tried praying to him? Doesn't Pastor Pretzer help you with that stuff?"

He shook his head. "I saw this thing on the Light Up Your Life channel at Mike's house, that when people die, they leave a soul print."

"A soul print?" I asked.

"There are even soul-print hunters who help people find the place where a person was at the very moment

when their soul left their body."

"On *what* channel?"

"Mike has DISH."

I nodded. "I remember."

"Anyway, it's all really confusing and I can't afford a soul-print hunter. And I have something really important I need Jason to know. I need to get a message to him."

"Jase is always going to be with you, Chase. Just because he's not here"—I motioned to the air—"doesn't mean he's not here." I tapped Chase's heart.

"So do you know how I can talk to him? To feel him here?" Chase touched his heart right where I had.

I thought for a while. No clue. But I couldn't let Chase down again. "I think I might know a way."

Chase's eyes got wide. "You really know how to talk to the dead?"

I did it every day. But I didn't figure that would be a good thing to tell Chase. "Well, I wouldn't say that exactly."

Mike grinned. "Wow, Chase. This is big."

Chase nodded. "How about this Saturday? March eighteenth. Oh seven hundred hours."

"Oh seven hundred?"

"That's military time for seven A.M."

"Oh. Yeah." March 18? I wondered how it was possible that more than five months had gone by. "Oh seven hundred hours. You got it."

Chase turned to Mike. "You've got to get me an invitation to stay over Friday night."

Mike wrinkled his nose. "An invitation? Like a card or something?"

Chase rolled his eyes. "No. Just have your mom call my mom. Okay?"

"Oh. Okay."

I laughed. "Where do you live, Mike?"

Mike gave me detailed instructions on how to get to his house. Chase interrupted, giving me the GPS coordinates.

"Got it, OD?" Mike asked.

"Yeah, I got it."

"You sure?" Chase asked. "I didn't see you write down the coordinates."

It was like we were acting out some James Bond movie. "I'm sure."

"So?" Chase asked. "We're on for Saturday?"

"We're on. I'll pick you two up at seven."

"A.M?"

"Yes. A.M."

"Do I need anything?" Chase asked.

I thought for a while. "Write down the message you need to get to Jason on a piece of paper." It sounded good anyway—like I knew what I was doing.

Chase shook my hand. "I knew I could count on you, Kyle."

50

I pedaled as hard as I could, zigzagging puddles and pot-holes. Maybe Cordoba had some books on talking to the dead. Jesus, that wasn't a conversation I wanted to have with him.

How *could* Chase talk to Jason? I had five days to figure it out.

I wondered if anybody in Carson City could do a séance at the last minute. Would that kind of shit be in the yellow pages? Or maybe I could use Mel's Ouija board. But how seriously can anybody take something made by Parker Brothers? I had to find some way for Chase to send a mes-sage to Heaven.

If there even was a Heaven.

Why had I promised those things to him? Jesus.

I threw open the library doors, trying to catch my

breath. Mr. Cordoba looked up from the paper.

"Sorry." I looked at the clock on the wall and pinched my side.

Mr. Cordoba mumbled and continued reading the paper. I peeled off my sticky sweatshirt, found my seat, and brought out my notebook. The library was empty—the way I liked it. Sometimes it felt like it was there just for me. Then I closed my eyes and thought about the day we took Chase to Rancho San Rafael Park to watch the national kite festival. Colors and shapes dotted the sky like confetti. We lay on the grassy hills of the park, eating cotton candy, watching the kites cartwheel and somersault in the sky.

"KITE," I titled the scene.

Mr. Cordoba cleared his throat in the way he did when he wanted me to pay attention. Phony phlegm. Maybe one day I could write that scene. I laughed to myself, imagining a suspense scene building up to the phony phlegm sound followed by a shrill scream from a beautiful blonde. Very Hitchcock.

"I watched *Unforgiven*," Cordoba said.

"Really?" I put the notebook down. "What'd you think?"

"Interesting choice."

"It's a great western—one of the best."

"Why do you like it so much?"

I bit my lip. "It just makes sense to me. It was like the past was always with him."

331

"So, a man is stuck with his past?"

I thought about my old notebook, the shed, and all the ways I had tried to write the scene. Jason ended up dead every time. I nodded. "Pretty much."

"He can't choose to change?"

"He might change, but everybody else stays the same, you know. So he would have to leave everything to really change. Just like William Munny did in the end."

"Though he left, did his past change?"

"Well, no. But at least he didn't have to face it every day. It's easier to forget that way."

"And you think he'll forget his past?"

"I suppose not."

"So what has changed? What changed in him?"

"Nothing. Everything." I threw my hands up. "I don't know. It's just a movie I like, Mr. Cordoba." A slow ache settled in my heart.

Maybe I could escape to San Francisco and set up a dry-goods store just like William Munny.

Mr. Cordoba pulled out the filmmaker brochure. "This fell out of your backpack yesterday."

The edges of the brochure were curled in from the time I dropped it in the snow when I was visiting Jase. The glossy cover looked smudged and dull.

"Are you thinking about entering?" Mr. Cordoba asked.

"No." I wanted to rip it out of his hands but instead

shoved my fists into my pockets. "It's just a dumb thing somebody gave me."

"Who?"

"Jason." It slipped out. "Um, his brother found it in his room."

Mr. Cordoba raised his eyebrows. "It sounds like Jason knew you quite well."

I shrugged. "No big deal."

"Why won't you enter it?"

Because I have no right. Because I took away all Jase was and was ever gonna be. Because I don't know if I did it on purpose. But how could I explain that to Cordoba? "I need to go."

Mr. Cordoba stood in front of me, holding the brochure in his hands. "Take this. Think about it."

"I don't want it. I gotta go."

Mr. Cordoba didn't move.

"I gotta go," I repeated. My face burned. I bit down on my lip to keep from crying. My fingernails bit into my palms.

Then he grabbed me and held my shoulders. "It was an accident."

"Let me go. Let me go." My voice got lost in my sadness. I tried to pull away, tried to stop the tears, but the harder I tried, the closer he pulled me in.

"Kyle, it was an accident."

I pushed him.

"It was an accident." Mr. Cordoba pulled me tighter.

"How do you know? How do you know I didn't kill him on purpose? How do you know what happened in that shed when I don't even fucking know?"

"I know you. It was an accident."

Then it came—all of Jason flooded out of me. I couldn't push away anymore. Mr. Cordoba held me up. And I cried.

He repeated, "It was an accident."

Was that it? Did that make it okay?

Mr. Cordoba let go of me and helped me sit down. His jacket was soaked. I couldn't look him in the eyes. Couldn't stop crying.

"Kyle, I have something for you." Mr. Cordoba went back to his office and brought out my old notebook.

I pushed it away. "I can't do it. I can't think about that day anymore."

Mr. Cordoba put it in my hands. "You have one director left to write the scene."

I nodded.

"*You* write it. Face it. Find your peace."

I looked at the notebook. "What if," I whispered, choking out the words, "what if I remember, and it wasn't an accident?"

Mr. Cordoba looked really sad all of sudden. He rubbed his temples. His eyes clouded over. "Don't die with Jason."

All night I thought about how I would direct the scene. Even though Jase would never come back, it mattered. I needed to know what happened that day. Cordoba was right. I needed to make peace. I held the notebook close. One more take. It was time to remember, so I wrote:

SCENE THREE: Take Fifteen—Kyle style

FADE IN: Kyle and Jason are going through the shelves. Kyle sees his grandpa's old 8 mm film projector and takes down the box of home movies. He blows dust off the old reels and checks to see if the film is still good.

                    KYLE

          Maybe we can set it up later, huh?

CUT TO: Jason jimmying the lock of a metal box.
Jason doesn't pay attention to Kyle.

                    KYLE

          Whatcha got, Jase?

Jason whistles.

ZOOM IN: The gun in Jason's hand.

                   JASON

          Check this baby out. It's pretty
          tight, huh?

                    KYLE

          Sweet, Jase. That's sweet.

CUT TO: Jason twirls gun around his thumb, a
confident smile on his face.

WIDE ANGLE of shed. Kyle's pajama pants are
stuck to his ankles. Kyle crouches down to
squeeze out the dew. He takes a deep breath

                    336

and stands up again. Jason still twirls the
gun around his thumb.

                    JASON
          (Holds the gun out to Kyle)
          What do you wanna do?

                    KYLE
          (Pulls his hands back—instinctively.)
          I dunno. What are we s'posed to do
          with it?

                    JASON
          (Pulls up T-shirt collar around his
          neck, like a pastor. He scowls.)
          Well, Kyle, let's see what our
          options are. We could A: put the gun
          away and continue to freeze, B: put
          the gun to good use; or C (and my
          personal favorite): rob the local
          convenience store, frame Mel and
          Brooke, move to the Cayman Islands,
          and never, ever have to work again.

                    KYLE
          (Relaxes his shoulders and laughs.)

                    337

We don't work now, you moron. (He
looks at the gun.)

ZOOM IN: Shot of gun in Jason's hands.)

                    KYLE
You wanna shoot it or something?

                    JASON
(Shrugging, looking indifferent)
Maybe we should. I dunno. (Cocks the
gun and slips the cock back into
place.) Why does your dad have a
gun, anyway?

                    KYLE
(Grinning) Maybe Dad's a spy for the
CIA. Maybe he does undercover DEA
shit and the café is a front.

                    JASON
(Rolls his eyes and shakes his
head.) In Carson City?

                    KYLE
(Glaring at Jason) Just because you

hit puberty like three years before
me and probably every other guy our
age in the state, you don't have to
act like a jerk.

JASON

(Raises his eyebrows and grins.)
Dude, whatever. Well? What're we
gonna do?

Kyle hesitates. He squeezes his pajama pants
again. Jason holds the gun out to him.

JASON

Here, Kyle, you take it.

Kyle swallows. He takes the gun from Jason,
but it slips from his frosty hands. His
fingers are stiff. He tries to grab the gun,
to stop it from falling to the ground, so he
grips it tighter, his fingers squeezing the
trigger. There's an explosion in the shed.
Kyle looks at the gun. He touches the barrel
of the gun and jerks his hand back. He looks
up, confused, not quite understanding that the
gun has just gone off.

KYLE

> Oh shit, Jason. Shit, shit, shit,
> shit, shit. Mom and Dad are gonna
> shit.

CUT TO: CLOSE-UP of Kyle's face. Kyle closes his eyes and his lips move, forming the words "Please, God. Please don't let this have happened."

CUT TO: the watch on Kyle's wrist.

ZOOM IN: The time is 9:16 a.m.

FADE OUT: Jason slumped against the workbench, then slowly falling to the floor of the shed. Blood pools beside his body.

> I felt a wave of relief.
> It was an accident.
> It was an accident.

I biked in the chilly spring afternoon to visit Jase. His grave hadn't changed much. The marker had been washed recently. All the spring mud was cleared away. I pulled the Dimex out of my pocket and set it on his marker.

10:46.

I got out the notebook. "I was worried, you know?" I

sat and faced the marker. "But you knew all along. You knew I didn't mean to." I hugged my knees to my chest. "It's been pretty shitty thinking all this time that— Well. You know." I brushed dirt off my knees. "And no, 'shit happens' was not enough information."

I stretched back with my arms under my head, watching the clouds drift by. A cloud covered the sun, blanketing the cemetery in soft shadows. The last rays of sunlight finally broke through, warming my face.

"I'm so sorry, Jase. I'm sorry to have taken your life away like that." I wiped the tears from my eyes and sighed. It felt good to say that. Sorry. It made a difference.

How would Jason like to see you today?

I sat up. "Hey, Jase. I thought maybe I'd write the scene about what I think you'd want for me. If that's okay?"

Spring afternoons were pretty windy, and I had forgotten my jacket. I shivered. "You know, it sure would help if you had one of those standing-up gravestones, because then I could lean on something. Or even a tree."

New shoots of grass pushed through the soil, covering Jason's grave with what looked like tiny green polka dots.

"Maybe we can write this together."

HOW WOULD JASON LIKE TO SEE ME TODAY: *Scenes to write . . .*

- Getting action of any kind
- Cruising the strip up in Reno
- Getting a sweet summer job at the Rage

- Wearing out the orange shoes so I don't win his vintage comic books
- Making a movie instead of just talking about it

I read the last line over.

"See, Jase. That's kinda tricky. I'd need your mom and Chase for this movie I've been writing, and things with your family are pretty bad. Your dad left." The words hung in the air. "I'm sorry about that, too."

"Does he talk back?"

I looked up. Chase held a jar of red M&M's in his hand. "Chase! You don't usually come here during the week."

"Does he answer you?"

"Um, no. Maybe just in my head. Sometimes. I dunno." I closed the notebook and stuffed it into my backpack. "Are you alone?"

Chase shook his head. "Mom's talking to Mr. Peoples."

"Mr. Peoples?"

"The caretaker."

"The rake guy?"

"She's coming, though." He looked behind him. "I'm not allowed to go to Mike's this weekend. It's a Dad weekend. Brooke's with Mom. We alternate. So I can't talk to Jase." He shoved his hands into his pockets.

"We'll do it another day, Chase."

"When?"

"Chase, I gotta go."

Chase grabbed my hand. "But it's important."

"I know." I rubbed my neck. "But you gotta see your dad. That's important too."

"Well, they never ask me."

"Ask you what?"

"What I wanna do."

I sighed. "We'll do it another day. I've really gotta go."

"When? When will we do it?"

"Whenever you can."

"But I never can. They made this calendar of "Chase days." So every weekend I have to go to Virginia City, Ichthyosaur State Park, Sand Mountain, and the Tahoe Rim Trail either with my mom or with my dad. I'll never stay at Mike's again. They're just big bullies disguised as parents."

I squatted down next to him. "Give it time. And when you can, we'll go." Chase looked so small. I squeezed his hand. "I promise. Just say the word." I grabbed the watch and turned to go.

"But it's important. His soul print!" he called after me.

Mrs. Bishop walked up the path. I rushed past her with my head down, staring at the ground.

"Kyle?" Mrs. Bishop said.

I didn't turn around. My throat felt dry and my heart hammered in my chest. I made it to my bike and didn't stop pumping until I was home.

That Tuesday, I waited for Dr. Matthews in her freshly painted waiting room. It was a psychedelic green color. Retro green. Hippy green. Matthews green. Maybe it was her favorite color.

Jason's favorite color was blue. What were his other favorite things? Maybe I could write a scene.

It was an accident.

"Kyle, I'm sorry you had to wait today. Come in." Dr. Matthews peeked out of her office. Some kid pushed past her and grumbled something on the way out.

"It's okay." I was happy to be thinking about Jason's favorites. There were tons of things I could write about. I followed Dr. Matthews into her office. I threw my backpack on the lumpy college couch and sat down.

Dr. Matthews sat next to me.

"You look"—she paused, as if trying to find the right word—"happy. Yes, happy." Dr. Matthews crossed her legs.

She looked happy, too. Like a different person than the one I had first met. Everybody changes, I guessed.

"I'm okay." I thought for a second. "Maybe happy."

"How come?"

"I, um . . ." I chewed on my bottom lip. "I was thinking about that scene again, you know?"

She nodded.

"It was an accident." There. I'd said it. I waited for the world to crumble around me, but the office stayed the same; sunlight streamed through the windows.

"Can you tell me about that day?" she asked.

I told her how the gun slipped from my fingers, wet with frost. I told her how scared I was; how important it was for Jason to have fun that morning and want to hang out. It was an accident.

"Did you know that? That it was an accident?" I asked.

She nodded.

"How?"

"Intuition, I guess." She handed me a Kleenex.

"You know," I said, after I had wiped my nose, "I think Jason would want me to be okay."

"I think so, too. In fact, I think you will be okay," she said.

345

I shrugged. "I guess I don't have much of a choice, huh?"

Dr. Matthews smiled. "We all have choices."

"Yeah," I said. "I guess we do."

Weeks passed as Chase was passed back and forth between the Bishops like a Ping-Pong ball. One afternoon he and Mike came up to the Dumpsters and hooted.

I hooted back.

Chase came around and said, "Kyle, I need serious help."

Mike came and stood behind him.

"What's going on?" I asked.

Chase lowered his voice. "Have you ever planned a prison break?"

"Prison break?"

Mike bit his lower lip and looked from side to side. "Were you really in the can, Orange Dragon?"

I burst out laughing. "Where'd you learn that? Wait . . . FX?"

Mike nodded.

"No. I've never been in jail," I assured him.

Mike looked relieved.

"I told you," Chase said, elbowing Mike. Chase turned to me. "They made me go to Wild Waters last weekend. And I hate getting wet." Chase pointed to the skin peeling on his head and the splotchy calamine lotion on his back. "I got really sunburned, too."

Mike scratched his nose. "I sure would've liked to have gone to Wild Waters. All I did was go to my sister's dumb dance recital."

Chase glared. "Nobody brought the right SPF."

Mike rolled his eyes.

"Hang in there, Chase," I said.

"But what are we going to do about the wardens?"

"The wardens?"

"My parents."

I shook my head. "I don't know. But I'll be here tomorrow."

He sighed. "Yeah. See you, then, I guess. If my skin doesn't peel off beforehand."

I ruffled his hair. "I'll be here." They slumped off across the field. Mike put his arm around Chase. Mike's mom's car pulled up just as they reached the walk.

One night I lay in bed thinking about Kohana's philosophy of photography and how that helped me write the scenes

from Jason's life. There had to be a way to combine photography and film with Jason's stories to make something awesome. Something for Chase. Something that would never be forgotten. If Kohana's portfolio was a photo documentary, maybe I could make a short subject documentary like *Hardwood*. Something that would help me bring Jason back to everybody. I could use old home movies, invent interviews like that guy did in *Good Bye Lenin!* (I didn't figure the Bishops would be too keen on real interviews), and film all the things that meant the most to Jase. I imagined the script for those objects—what I would say. But I'd need help. Nobody can make a film alone.

The brochure for the voices of youth filmmakers documentary short competition was sitting on my desk, its pages fluttering in the wind from my open window. I got dressed, stuffed my backpack, and wheeled my bike out of the garage, cycling down the black streets until I got to Kohana's house. I owed him a story. And I needed his help.

The house was dark except for one window. Muted yellow light glowed behind translucent shades. I tapped on the glass.

The blinds opened and Kohana pressed his face against the pane. "Who's there?"

"It's me. Kyle."

He opened the window. "Your watch still broke?"

I pulled out the watch, a kite, Jason's sketchbook, the filmmaker competition brochure, and my notebook. I took

off my orange shoes and put them beside the other objects. "I want to tell you a story."

We sat on the porch. And I began to talk.

I talked until the first light of dawn stole across the sky. When I finished, Kohana sat silently. He hadn't said anything all night.

He finally turned toward me. "So," he said. "When do we start filming?"

54

The next couple of weeks, Kohana and I worked nonstop before and after school to make Jason's film. Dad let me use his video camera. Kohana even came with me to Chase's school, and we got shots of the Dumpster.

The next day, Chase got picked up by his dad, but he sent a message with Mike that said, *SOS. This weekend, they're making me go to some ice-skating show up at Lawlor Events Center.*

When Kohana read the note, he said, "He has to be part of this, Kyle. We've got to get him to help."

"He's the new Bishop pawn. They don't leave him for a second."

Kohana looked disgusted. "That's too bad."

Late afternoons and into the evening, we used Mr.

Cordoba's multimedia room to edit the footage and cut old home videos into the new material we filmed. It was as if we were getting Jason's life back with every scene we shot.

Kohana knew all sorts of stuff about great camera angles. And I had learned how to make stills and cut moving film into them, creating a "frozen time" effect. The whole documentary had all of Jason's objects frozen, while I walked around them, talking. But I decided to film it so I would always be overexposed—a shadow walking through Jason's world. Over the course of the documentary, my image got clearer. But we needed Chase for the kites and the end.

Mr. Cordoba ordered film books for the library, and as soon as they arrived, he let Kohana and me check them out. I studied the pages of those books whenever I had a chance.

One afternoon, Mike came running to me as soon as he left the school building. "Chase is missing," he gasped.

"Missing?"

"Yeah. My mama was talking to his mama this morning on the phone. Mama asked me about all our favorite hiding spots." Mike wiped the tears out of his eyes. "I think he ran away."

I hugged Mike. "It'll be okay. We'll find him."

Mike shook his head. "He left me this note yesterday. I

didn't read it. It was too long." He handed me a wrinkled piece of paper with jelly stains on it. "There."

I read the note:

April 20 (COPY OF ORIGINAL LETTER DATED APRIL 20 ADDRESSED TO JASON BISHOP)

> Chase Bishop
> 6167 S. Richmond Avenue
> Carson City, NV 58367

Jason Bishop
The Great Beyond

Dear Mr. Bishop (aka Jason) (aka means Also Known As),

I am learning to write letters in class now, so I'm writing you in business letter format. First, I make a brief introduction. Then I state my business. Then I end, cordially, thanking you for your time, reminding you of my business.

How are you? Julian, Marcus, and José don't beat Mike or me up anymore because I contracted the services of Kyle as a bodyguard. We call him Orange

Dragon, or OD. Kyle might be skinny, but he can be pretty intimidating. Plus they think he's a lunatic because he hangs out behind Dumpsters. (Lunatic comes from the word *lunaticus*, meaning "moonstruck"; affected with periodic insanity, dependent on the changes of the moon. Kyle's is more of a permanent thing, but not in a bad way.)

Things at home aren't too good. Mom and Dad fight all the time. And Dad doesn't even live there. So they fight long distance. Brooke cries a lot. And Chip doesn't have much of an appetite. (Chip is my new goldfish who you haven't met yet.)

I don't think things are that great for Kyle either. (But not because of the Dumpster thing. I know that's part of his work as a bodyguard: low-profile stuff.) It's just that he's different than he used to be. He doesn't really smile anymore, and he hasn't invited me over to watch a movie marathon in ages.

I don't know if you're okay or not. I've looked, but I can't find your soul print anywhere. Even Pastor Pretzer can't help me. (Quite honestly, I'm getting a little tired of Sunday school. They made me be a shepherd again in the pageant, and told me that in Jesus's time there were no aeronautical engineers to

visit Baby Jesus. I find that hard to believe, since the Chinese were flying kites in approximately 200 b.c. And if anybody would be given a kite for his birthday, it would be Jesus.) Also, Dad quit church.

I'm writing to tell you I miss you. I think I'll always miss you. I didn't know missing could be forever. Do you know a way for it to go away? This sad feeling I have? Is there a way to find you? So the missing doesn't hurt so much?

Your attention to this matter would be greatly appreciated. Thank you for your valuable time and consideration.

Best regards,
Mr. Bishop (aka Chase)

I read the letter three times. "Mike," I said, "did Chase say anything else to you? About where he wanted to be?"

Mike shook his head. "Only that he wanted to be where Jason was."

My insides turned to ice. No, I shook my head. He wouldn't do that. He would never do that.

"Orange Dragon?" Mike looked really scared.

I fought to catch my breath. "I'll find him, I promise. I'll find him, and I'll see you both here tomorrow."

Mike grabbed my hand. "He's my best friend."

"I know." I hugged Mike again, then tore off on my bike.

The cemetery was empty.

He wasn't flying kites at Mills Park.

I raced home. Running up the porch, I slammed into Mr. and Mrs. Bishop.

My throat froze again, just looking at how thin Mrs. Bishop had gotten—how sad she looked.

"Kyle," she said. "He's gone. We can't find him."

I'm sorry.

I'm sorry.

Jesus, just say it. It's all my fault. I wanted the tape to get reversed—back to the very beginning. Without me Jase would be alive. Chase would never have run away. And everybody's life would've been just right.

"Please help find my baby, Kyle. I can't lose him, too." Her last words were muffled in a sob.

I will.

I watched them head frantically back to their house, the candle lamp glowing in the window. *Jesus, please don't let her light another one.* This couldn't be happening.

Mom was talking on the phone. She motioned for me to sit down. "They've been looking all day. I need someone to stay here. Just in case Chase comes around, okay?"

"All day?" I interrupted. "Why didn't somebody tell me? Shouldn't it be on the news? Shouldn't there be

police officers everywhere?"

She grabbed her car keys. "Dad and I are going with the Bishops. Mel and the cheerleaders are posting flyers all over town."

A knot formed in my throat.

"We're setting up a search-and-rescue post at the community center."

"Did he leave a note? Did he say anything?"

Mom pulled on a sweatshirt. "He said he wanted to be where he could find Jason's soul print. None of us can figure it out. Stay here. Just in case he comes over. We need you by the phone." Mom left.

"Okay." I slumped at the kitchen table.

Soul print. I sighed, relieved it wasn't what I first thought.

Where would Chase look for Jason's soul print? The neighborhood bustled with action. I stood out on the porch, then walked around to the backyard and stared at the shed.

I hooted.

Somebody's lawn mower kicked on, and the familiar smell of fresh-cut grass drifted through the neighborhood.

I hooted again. After hooting two or three times, I finally heard a soft hoot in return. I circled the shed. The cardboard Dad had used to tape up the window was gone. I hooted louder.

Chase's hoot echoed in the shed.

My heart felt lodged in my throat. Memories of that moment flashed through my mind.

I took a deep breath and climbed through the window.

The shed smelled like fertilizer and oil. It smelled like Clorox and gasoline. I inhaled again, expecting to smell Jason, death, the stench of burned matches, but all I smelled was the familiarity of the shed—a place I used to love as a kid.

My eyes took a second to adjust to the darkness. Chase sat cross-legged in the center of the shed.

"Can I sit here?" I asked.

He scooted over to make room.

I avoided crossing over the bleached spot and made my way to Chase. We sat in silence.

"I just wanted to see," he finally said.

I listened.

"Where it happened."

I nodded.

"I thought it would make it better to see. Maybe he would've left his soul print here, and I could talk to him." Chase sniffled and choked out the words. "But he isn't here, either. And I've been waiting since last night."

I swallowed. But I knew there were no words that would make it better for Chase. We were both looking for the same thing, but neither of us knew how to find it. "I'm

so sorry," I finally said.

Chase looked up at me. He leaned his head on my shoulder. We sat for a long time.

"I don't think Dad's coming home," he finally said. "Do you?"

"I don't know, Chase." I squeezed his shoulder. "Maybe."

"Maybe not."

"Maybe not." I sighed.

The light outside the shed changed. I watched through the square of the window as it turned from yellow to a bright orange. "How about if I take you home? A lot of people are really worried." I held out my hand.

He hesitated, then slipped his hand into mine. He had a letter crumpled in his fist. He turned to throw it away in the garbage, and I stopped him. "Do you still want to get a message to Jason?"

Chase turned and looked me in the eyes. "More than anything in this world."

"How about Saturday? Do you think we can meet at Mike's?"

"I dunno. I think I'll be grounded."

"True."

"Maybe I can sneak out."

"And get more grounded?" I asked.

"This is really important."

"Okay. Saturday at seven A.M. I'll tap on your window." I boosted Chase out and followed close behind. We walked out the back gate. "Do you need me to go with you?" I motioned to his house.

He shook his head. "Sometimes a man has to face his fate alone."

What a kid.

He walked home, stepping carefully over the lines in the sidewalk. When he got to his front porch, he turned and waved, then disappeared inside the house.

55

"**C**'mon." I tapped on his window.

Chase peeked out. When he saw me, he grinned and ran to the backyard.

"Did you brush your teeth?" I asked.

"Oh, no!"

"I'm joking! Chase!"

Before I could catch him, he ran back into the house. He came back out. "That was close. Ready?" He grabbed my hand.

"How much time do you have?" I asked.

"About two hours."

"What happens if your mom wakes up and doesn't find you?"

"I've left a note on the kitchen table. It says I went to

do the Carson City historical walk."

"And she'll buy that?"

"Mike and I used to do it every Saturday—before the event calendar. I have the map here." He pulled out a tattered map. It had red markings and highlights all over it. "And the guided tour is in my MP3 player."

I didn't even know there was a Carson City historical walk. "Two hours is plenty of time," I said.

"Maybe next Saturday, you ought to do the historical walk with us." Chase raised his eyebrows.

"I'd like that." And I meant it. "Okay. Let's go." I handed him a helmet. "It's too far to walk. So you get to go for a ride." I hoisted Chase onto the bike.

"Does riding double comply with traffic regulations?"

I laughed. "Sure."

"Really?"

"C'mon, Chase. We don't have all day."

Chase scowled. "Okay. But just this once."

"Okay."

"But ride careful."

"I will."

"And don't tell Mike."

We rode to the graveyard. Rake guy waved at us. When he saw Chase, he came out with a couple of chocolates.

"We come here every Sunday," Chase whispered.

We found Jase's grave. Fresh lilies and daisies covered

it. I wondered if Jason had a favorite flower. I'd never really thought about it before. I didn't have a favorite flower—at least I didn't think so.

We stood there for a while, listening to the silence of the graveyard. I pulled Jason's sketchbook out of my bag and opened it up to the last page. A full-scale comic-book battle.

Finally Chase said, "That's me, isn't it?"

I explained a little. "You're Kite Rider. You're a superhero. A real live superhero."

"Only in Jason's world," he mumbled. "If that were really true, I wouldn't need a bodyguard."

I flipped through the pages and showed him Freeze Frame.

"Hey, you're a superhero too!"

"Yep. With more experience. Maybe I'm supposed to train you."

"Instead of protect me?"

"Maybe."

He grinned. "That sounds better." He rubbed the chalky drawings and smelled his fingers. "Chalk," he whispered.

"Chalk." I closed the notebook. "I just wanted to show this to you. I'm sorry I didn't earlier."

Chase smiled. "It doesn't matter. You're still going to help me talk to Jase, right?"

"Yes."

"Do you think he'll hear me? Get the message?"

"Definitely. Do you have the letter?"

"Yeah." Chase pulled a folded-up note out of his pocket.

"Good." I took a kite out of my backpack. It was one of those cheap, garbage-sack plastic kites. The AM/PM store didn't have a great kite selection.

Chase's eyes got real big. "We're gonna fly a kite. I could've brought the dragon. It's *much* nicer than this one."

"Don't worry about it. Fold your note and put a hole in it. We have to put the string through the hole."

It took Chase about fifteen minutes to find the one spot that didn't have words to put the hole in it. "I want to make sure Jason gets the complete message."

"Okay, sure." It was a good thing we had two hours.

Chase pulled the string through the hole. "That's a lot of string."

"We've got to get the kite as high up as we can—so high we might not even be able to see it."

"And this is gonna work? To get my message out?"

"Yep."

"How do you know about this?"

"I read about it somewhere."

"You read nonfiction?" Chase looked at me sideways.

"Sure, I read everything." I had lately, anyway—anything Mr. Cordoba threw my way.

Chase bit his lip.

"C'mon, Chase. It'll work. I'm gonna run up the path. The wind is pretty decent. We've got to get the kite in the air, okay?"

"Yeah, but don't run over any of the graves, Kyle. You might wake some of these dead people up."

Dead people don't wake up.

"I won't. Don't worry. You hold the kite there." I had Chase hold on. "I'm gonna get it flying, then you'll do the rest."

He nodded.

"When I say, 'Let go!' let go. But not any sooner."

"Okay."

"Ready?"

"Ready!"

I ran up the path, the string trailing behind me. "Let go! Let go!" I shouted. Chase let go just at the right time, and the wind caught the kite, pushing it high above the elm trees and graves.

"C'mon, Chase." Chase caught up to me and grabbed on to the string. "You've got to work the note up to the top of the string, okay? Jiggle it a little in the beginning, and the wind will do the rest. The kite has to fly until the note hits its base."

Chase ran up and down the path; the kite flew high between trees—a plastic red square in the sky. Its colorful

tail zigzagged with gusts of wind. It was perfect April wind for flying a kite.

"Kyle, it's there. The note is there! See it?" He laughed.

"Okay. Now let the string out. Let it out until the very end."

Chase unraveled the extra string until all he had was what was looped around his hand. By then the kite was nothing but a tiny red dot in the sky.

"Come over here." We stood next to Jason's grave. "Now you've gotta think about the person you want to receive the note, okay? Think real hard about Jason."

Chase squeezed his eyes closed.

"When you're ready, let the kite go and let it fly away."

We waited. Chase clutched the kite string, taut from the tug of the almost invisible kite. "Ready?"

Chase sniffled and clutched the string.

"Jason will get your message, Chase. Just think real hard about him. Think about how happy he'll be to hear from you."

"Promise?"

"I promise."

"Boy Scout's honor?"

"Yeah. Boy Scout's honor."

"You're not a Boy Scout." Chase's lip quivered.

"But I have honor." I smiled.

"That's my line," he protested.

"I learn from the best." I winked. "Let go of the kite. It's okay."

"Okay." He inhaled and let go of the kite. He unlooped the string, and it slipped out of his hand and floated away, attached to the kite we couldn't even see anymore. Chase grabbed my hand.

He looked up at me. "I really think he got it."

"Me, too," I said. "This is for you." I handed him the sketchbook.

Chase hugged the sketchbook. "It's him. He's really here." His eyes flooded with tears. "This is the best present ever." He wrapped his small arms around my waist and hugged me. "I'm so lucky to have you."

"I'm lucky to have you, too, Chase." He hugged me harder. "Hey, listen, I was thinking that maybe you could help me with something too, something I have for Jase."

"You wrote him a note, too?"

"No. But I thought I'd leave him this." I pulled out the watch.

Chase grabbed my hand. "It's okay, you know?"

"What's okay?"

"It's okay to let it go."

I nodded and wiped the tears from my eyes. Jesus, Chase made my throat knot up.

He squeezed my hand tighter. "Come on, Kyle."

Together, we put the watch on top of Jason's grave. I

looked at the time—on the watch Chase had given me. "Jase," I whispered. "It's eight thirty-seven."

Then Chase took my hand and we walked back through the heavy silence of the graves.

56

Early on April 23, Chase, Kohana, and I got together. I took off my shoes. "One year," I said. "three hundred and sixty-five days."

"Actually three hundred and sixty-five point two-five days, Kyle," Chase corrected me.

Kohana smiled. He and Chase got along really well. I thought Chase would feel bad that I had a friend, but one day he'd said, "It's just too bad Jason wasn't friends with Kohana, too. He's really nice."

"Are you ready to film?" Kohana asked.

I took a deep breath. We'd already filmed Jason's duffel and sleeping bag. We created a movie poster/comic art montage with all of Jason's favorite comic-book artists, including Kyle Baker and Frank Miller. We had footage

from old home movies that Chase had snuck out of the house: birthdays, Christmases, Little League and stuff. Chase had found the WXYZ volume of the encyclopedia in Jason's room, and we filmed that. Kohana convinced me to open up the papers and film them. Funny. Jase and I had written the same thing:

Kyle: Ten years from now, I'll be hanging out with Jase.

Jason: Ten years from now, I'll be hanging out with Kyle on his birthday. (Hopefully in a bar with really hot women).

My hands shook so bad, I couldn't keep the camera in focus. That day we didn't film any more. I think it made us all sad.

We had even filmed Chase and his kites—running up and down the path of the cemetery sending Jase messages. The only thing I didn't film was Jason's secret stash. I figured it was okay for some scenes to be just between Jase and me.

"Are you ready?" Kohana asked again. "Last scene."

I looked over my director's notes. Chase came over and sat next to me. "He'd like this scene. Even though it might bug him. He never lost a bet, you know."

I laughed. He hadn't. Not with me, anyway. "Ready," I said, and took another deep breath. This was the final

scene. There were no more stills, no more overexposures, no more shadows. Just regular filming—moving forward.

UNTITLED: FINAL SCENE—Orange Chili Shoes
Kyle is sitting in the middle of cans of chili. He doesn't speak. He sits there, waiting for his cue.

> KOHANA (VOICE-OVER)
> We're rolling, Kyle.

> KYLE
> Ready. (Looks into the camera)
> Three hundred and sixty-five point
> two-five days, Jase.

Kyle takes off the shoes. Chase comes into the camera's view and hands Kyle a 1948 Captain Marvel Adventures #81.

> KYLE
> (Shakes his head) You keep this,
> Chase.

> ZOOM IN: on Kyle's face as he flips
> through the pages of the comic book.

CHASE

    (Off camera) A bet's a bet. He'd
    want you to have this.

ZOOM IN: On the comic book.

FADE OUT:

        KYLE (VOICE-OVER)
    It looks like that's a wrap.

Kohana, Chase, and I sat there for a while, just hanging out on the porch. "Hungry?" I finally said, holding up a chili can. Then we all cracked up. It had been a long morning.

"What if we finish editing this afternoon?" Kohana asked.

"Yeah!" Chase jumped up. "Let's go!"

"You think Mr. Cordoba would be okay with that? On a Saturday?"

"We can ask," Kohana said.

We called Mr. Cordoba.

"Can we work in the library today? To finish the movie? I asked. "I know it sounds crazy, but—"

"I'll meet you there in half an hour," Mr. Cordoba interrupted, and hung up the phone.

We hardly recognized Cordoba. He was wearing a pair

of jeans, a Juan Valdez T-shirt, and a paint-splattered baseball cap. He let us work all day, late into the afternoon.

"We're done," I finally said.

Kohana and Chase nodded.

"Let's watch it," said Chase.

"Wait." Kohana went and got Mr. Cordoba.

The four of us sat down and watched as Jason's friendship and memories came to life. When the movie ended, nobody said anything for a while. Then Chase started clapping. I thought I saw Mr. Cordoba wipe his nose with a handkerchief.

"What do you think?" Kohana asked.

Mr. Cordoba said, "I bet the judges in the film competition will love it."

Maybe they would, but that's not why I had made it.

"You did it, man." Kohana took out the DVD, slipped it into the case, and handed it to me. "What are you gonna title it?"

I turned it over in my hands and felt relieved. And sad. But I knew it was going to be okay. *"Freeze Frame."*

"That's a perfect title," Chase whispered.

"Do you boys need a ride home?" Mr. Cordoba said, interrupting the silence of the media room.

"That'd be great, Mr. Cordoba," Kohana said.

We piled into his car. When we got to Kohana's house, he said, "We're going to Squaw next week, Kyle. Can you come?"

"I'd like to," I said.

"You asked your PO?"

"Yeah. He said it wouldn't be a problem."

"Cool." Kohana walked up the path to his house.

On the way home, Chase told Mr. Cordoba about Jason's planets being wrong on the ceiling and how the Mayas had calculated Venus's orbit for 6,000 years and were off by a day or something. Mr. Cordoba told Chase he had a great book about the Incas and their solar calendars that he would get to me to give to him. I loved listening to them, talking about ancient worlds, planets' orbits, and things that made a difference in the world.

57

When I got home, Mel was all ready for the junior prom. "Whaddya think?" She curtsied. She had on a green shiny dress that, I admit, was tight in just the right spots.

"You're real pretty, Mel."

She blushed. "Thanks."

Mom cried when Jake (a.k.a. Hoover) showed up with some massive carnation corsage dyed mint green. She took about a thousand pictures and Dad looked crabby. He did that for the intimidation effect, and since Jake said, "We'll be home by midnight," I think it worked.

Mom and Dad decided to go for a walk.

I stepped outside in the chilly evening air. The clouds had faded into streaks of pastels and purples. It was the time of day when the moon still has to share the sky with the sun.

Mrs. Bishop had already turned on her lamp, waiting for Jase to come home. I walked across the street and worked my way to the porch. I stood there in the dim evening light. My hand trembled when it reached out to ring the bell. I listened to the life unfolding inside. Chase and Brooke were fighting about something. Somebody put dishes in cupboards. What would I say?

Mrs. Bishop opened the door with a damp dish towel in her hands.

For a moment, I thought about running away, but some force kept me on that porch. Her cheeks sagged a little. She looked thin. I knew I had done that to her.

My hands shook as I gave her my DVD. "I'm so sorry," I whispered. "This was the best I could do to bring him back."

She wrapped me in her arms. "I've been waiting for you."

Acknowledgments

Thank you to the supportive communities of children's writers I've been fortunate enough to be involved with: Northern Nevada SCBWI, in particular Ellen, Suzy, Sheryle, Emily, and Katy; my writing family, the Wordslingers, Trish, Christine, Jean, Lisa, and Mandy; and the Blueboarders. Special thanks to my extraordinary family that has always encouraged me: Mom, Dad, Rick, Syd, and Kyra. And finally, I am privileged to work with two of the most amazing professionals in the business: Stephen Barbara, my intrepid agent, who believed in this project from the beginning, and Jill Santopolo, my brilliant editor, who challenged me to take this novel to a whole other level. I am so grateful.

Turn the page for a look at the first chapter of
Heidi Ayarbe's next hard-hitting novel,
COMPROMISED.

F irst they take our flat screen.

And the computers, all of Dad's satellite equipment, stereos, DVDs. Even the George Foreman grill.

I watch from down the street as they pile our things in the rusty trailer. I steady my breathing and walk up the driveway.

Dad sits on the front steps, head leaning against the brick porch. Icy beads of water drip off his beer can.

"You're home early," I say, walking up the driveway.

He nods. "I'm sorry, Maya," and motions to the house.

I pause at the front door, running my hand over the smooth oak. I grasp the brass doorknob before entering, then wander through the stripped rooms—naked sockets, way pre–Best Buy.

The only thing they left is that garage sale microwave that whistles when it's on. I haven't used it for about a year, though, since I don't want to grow an extra ear from electromagnetic waves. Not scientifically viable, but I'm not taking any chances.

I slump next to Dad on the porch. It's not like I'm surprised. We're all creatures of habit and this was bound to happen. But I can't help feeling disappointed. I guess things had been going too well for too long. My chest tightens.

Dad shakes his head. I smell beer on his stale breath.

"It's okay," I say.

He pulls me in close. "That's my girl." Dad pushes my hair back behind my ears and wraps his arm around my shoulders. "You look a lot like her, you know. You have her eyes. Gray."

Yeah. Storm clouds. Sadness. Thanks for comparing me to the chemically imbalanced family member. Who would want to be anything like her? I shrug, pushing the knot from my throat. "Who cares about all that stuff? We'll be fine." We always are.

He smiles. Tired. He always looks tired just before a move.

I scan the block, taking in the variety of decorative flags: everything from cutesy pumpkins to ladybugs. Manicured lawns, ceramic house numbers—it'll be a while before we live in another neighborhood like this.

Dad leaves after I go to bed—like I'm not gonna know. He probably has some loose ends to tie up. I always picture Dad's bungles like a tangled-up small intestine—twenty-odd feet of knots and feces.

After I hear the clatter of the garage door shutting, I raid the dwindling supply of Pepto-Bismol to coat the burn in my stomach.

Hypothesis: If they've taken our TVs, DVDs, and stuff, they'll come back for more.

I just hope we won't be here when they do.

Next they take our car.

They drive up in a mud-caked truck that has ROY'S REPO painted on the side in faded red letters. It actually says ROY' R PO. And they have one of those bullet-hole stickers on the side.

Different guys from the ones before.

The short guy wears army boots, tight jeans, and a tighter T-shirt that says HAVE A BALL AT LEE'S 12TH ANNUAL TESTICLE FESTIVAL. Sheep nuts for dinner. Yum.

The big guy wears jeans and a shirt that rides up his stomach. A sweat-stained baseball cap sits crooked on his head. He scratches his gut and stretches his faded T-shirt down. I watch them through the laundry room window.

"Roy's Repo!" The big guy raps on the door with raw knuckles. "We know you're in there."

I hold my breath, hoping they'll go away. Hoping they'll hop back into their truck and drive away. But I know that's dumb. Hope isn't real—just a circuitry problem in my head.

He bellows, "Mr. Sorenson. We need to talk to you, and we're not going to wait all day."

I duck to keep away from the windows and crouch behind the kitchen counter to phone Dad. The line's dead. My cell service had been "discontinued" too. It's not like I was text queen, anyway. I don't think the only message I got—the one from Genevieve Dodge when I went to one of the science club's lunch meetings that said SCI BTCH GO HOME—justified Dad paying my unlimited texting plan. I think she was miffed that I figured out the

4

joke: What's the chemical name of CH_2O? Seawater. Like who couldn't figure that one out? I stare at the useless phone. I might as well have had two cups with string attached to them.

I slip out the back door and jump the fence to call Dad from Mrs. Velasquez's house. "I think we're having trouble with our phone line," I tell her.

Mrs. Velasquez's eyes narrow. She crosses her arms—that perfect I-told-you-so stance only nags can pull off. She stopped bringing us her homemade flan and sopapillas when Dad made a business deal with her brother. The guy probably should've checked out the nice beachfront property at Lahontan before he went for it. Maybe he didn't have Google Earth or something. Anyway, she's pretty bitter now.

I dial, trying to keep my hand from shaking too much. "They're here."

"I'll be right there." I listen to the click and hum of the line.

Dad drives up in his Beemer. The latest model. He swings open the door and steps into the dry October heat. We're having a weird heat wave in Reno. Last year at this time Dad was all psyched about getting me into

5

skiing. I shade my eyes and watch them talk. The tears are probably just from the glare of the sun. Definitely global warming. But the end of the earth doesn't seem all that important right now.

Dad looks handsome in his pressed suit and starched shirt. He loosens his Italian silk tie and faces the repo guys. As soon as Dad starts to talk, the red splotches on the big guy's face fade. He looks almost apologetic. Dad's got big-time attractive genetics. Some people are genetically more attractive than others. It's their smell, their chemistry—something inherent in that double helix, twenty-three pairs of chromosomes. Most people call it charisma. Whatever you want to call it, Dad has it.

The big guy tugs at his shirt. The short guy turns to the house, eyes me, and winks. He flexes and flares his nostrils.

Dad points to the house. "Misunderstanding, I'm sure," he's saying as he passes me on the porch. "Maya, honey, can you get these gentlemen something cold to drink?"

I nod and go to the kitchen, fishing out two of the coldest Cokes I can find in the cooler. The ice has melted. A piece of lactose-free Velveeta cheese floats and bobs. I

give them the Cokes, making sure there's no skin-to-skin contact. The last thing I need is scabies or some other kind of communicable disease repo guys have buried under their skin.

The big guy hands Dad a letter. "Here's the information, if you want to try to get your car back."

Dad flashes me a look. Panic. Funny. I still don't get how he doesn't see this stuff coming. Supposedly we use about ten percent of our brain capacity. But since the brain's hard drive is never full—with an infinite capacity to learn, taking ten percent of infinity is impossible. Pretty arbitrary, really. The brain's potential, with ten billion neurons and one hundred and twenty billion glial cells, is staggering. Potential, however, is the key word.

Sometimes Dad doesn't seem to reach that potential.

It's out of his hands now.

The repo guys leave dusty footprints all over the carpet. The engine of the truck sputters, then roars to life. We watch as they tow away the car. Dad flinches.

"It's just a car, Dad. Whatever." I try to hide my anger and throw the letter on the table, turning my back to him. I know he's sorry. But sometimes . . . sometimes sorry isn't good enough.

"It's a setback, baby. Nothing more." He moves to me and puts his arm around my shoulder. "Let's go out to dinner."

We don't even have money to pay our phone bill—where will we get the money for dinner? I look down at my designer jeans and trendy shoes. It's not rational to get upset over *things*, but my throat feels like somebody has wedged a grapefruit in it.

"How about going to that steak house we like so much?" Dad pulls out his wallet and flips through his credit cards.

I pry open the lid of the cooler. "Let's just eat grilled cheese sandwiches." I do a mental inventory of the things I can sell. We just need enough to get us a couple of bus tickets to Nowhere, U.S.A.

Dad sits slumped over the kitchen table, his head cradled in his hands. The sandwiches sizzle in the fry pan. At least they haven't cut the gas line. Yet. I pass a sandwich to him on our last Chinet plate and hold mine in a napkin. It'll pass. We'll be okay. We just need about a thousand miles between Dad's latest scam and us.

Before bed, I make the plan. It's always worked before.

Purpose: Keep Dad out of trouble

Hypothesis: If I get all of our money together and get us on a bus ASAP, Dad and I will make it out of Reno safely.

Materials: Money from cache, materials to sell, bus tickets, me, Dad

Procedure:

1) Get money from the cache

2) See how much we need to sell to get to price of tickets

3) Sell necessary items

4) Buy tickets

5) Convince Dad to go with me

6) Get on bus

Variable: Time: How quickly can I do this? How quickly will the cops get here?

Constants: Me and Dad—we never change. He never changes.

The only way for Maya to find home is to hit the streets.

COMPROMISED

HEIDI AYARBE

Maya's life has always been chaotic. Living with a con-man dad, she's spent half of her life on the run. But when her dad ends up in prison and foster care fails, Maya grasps at her last possible hope: a long-lost aunt, who may not even exist.

So with just her wits, an unlikely ally, and twenty dollars in her pocket, she sets off in search of this aunt, navigating the unpredictable four hundred miles to Boise. But life on the streets is tougher than Maya ever imagined. And with each passing day, she begins to wonder if trying to find her aunt—and some semblance of stability—is worth the harrowing journey. Or will Maya compromise, and find a way to survive on her own?

Barack Obama's Speeches

Los discursos de Barack Obama

Ulysses Press

Published in the U.S. by:
ULYSSES PRESS
P.O. Box 3440
Berkeley, CA 94703
www.ulyssespress.com

ISBN 978-1-56975-730-7
Library of Congress Control Number: 2009930126

Printed in the United States by Bang Printing

10 9 8 7 6 5 4 3 2 1

Acquisitions Editor: Keith Riegert
Managing Editor: Claire Chun
Editor: Paula Dragosh
Spanish translation development: Semantics, Inc.
Proofreader: Lauren Harrison
Cover design: Double R Design
Interior design and layout: what!design @ whatweb.com

Distributed by Publishers Group West

Contents/Contenido

Introduction

Most political speeches pass quietly into history as soon as they are delivered. But the words of President Barack Obama, America's landmark first black president and a remarkably inspiring speaker, will be rated among those of America's greatest presidents.

The speeches in this collection include Obama's breakout address to the 2004 Democratic National Convention, famous campaign speeches from his run for the presidency in 2008 and some of his notable speeches during his first year as the nation's forty-fifth president.

The speeches presented in this book and translated into Spanish have been edited to highlight their central themes. Some material on specific policy as well as dated information has been left out. Several speeches, such as the inaugural address and the speech on race in America, are presented intact. Full transcripts of all eleven speeches are available online.

As a United States senator, presidential candidate, and president, Barack Obama has connected today's events with America's complex and multicultural history. He has instilled renewed hope not only to America but the world over.

Introducción

La mayoría de los discursos políticos pasan discretamente a la Historia en cuanto se pronuncian. Pero las palabras del presidente Barack Obama, un hito como el primer presidente de Estados Unidos de raza negra y orador notablemente inspirador, estarán consideradas entre las de los más grandes presidentes de Estados Unidos.

Los discursos en esta colección incluyen el de apertura de Obama de la Convención Nacional Demócrata de 2004, famosos discursos de campaña de su candidatura a la presidencia en 2008 y algunos de sus notables discursos durante su primer año como el cuadragésimo quinto presidente de la nación.

Los discursos que se presentan en este libro traducidos al español han sido editados para destacar sus temas principales. Algunos materiales sobre política específica al igual que información actualizada se han dejado fuera. Varios discursos, como el discurso de toma de posesión y el discurso sobre la raza en Estados Unidos, se presentan intactos. Transcripciones completas de los once discursos están disponibles en línea.

Como senador, candidato a la presidencia, y presidente de los Estados Unidos, Barack Obama ha conectado los acontecimientos de la actualidad con la compleja y multicultural historia de Estados Unidos. Él ha infundido una esperanza renovada no sólo a Estados Unidos sino también a todo el mundo.

Keynote Address
July 27, 2004
Boston, Massachusetts

*At the 2004 Democratic National Convention, Barack Obama,
running for the U.S. Senate in Illinois, took the national
stage with a rousing speech that turned him into a contender for the
Democratic presidential nomination in 2008.*

On behalf of the great state of Illinois, crossroads of a nation, land of Lincoln, let me express my deep gratitude for the privilege of addressing this convention. Tonight is a particular honor for me because, let's face it, my presence on this stage is pretty unlikely.

My father was a foreign student, born and raised in a small village in Kenya. He grew up herding goats, went to school in a tin-roof shack. His father, my grandfather, was a cook, a domestic servant.

But my grandfather had larger dreams for his son. Through hard work and perseverance my father got a scholarship to study in a magical place: America, which stood as a beacon of freedom and opportunity to so many who had come before.

While studying here, my father met my mother. She was born in a town on the other side of the world, in Kansas. Her father worked on oil rigs

Discurso de apertura
27 de julio de 2004
Boston, Massachusetts

En la Convención Demócrata de 2004, Barack Obama, que se presentaba como candidato al Senado de Estados Unidos por Illinois, subió a la escena política con un conmovedor discurso que lo convirtió en competidor demócrata para la nominación presidencial en 2008.

En nombre del gran estado de Illinois, encrucijada de una nación, tierra de Lincoln, permítanme expresar mi profunda gratitud por el privilegio de dirigirme a esta convención. Esta noche es un honor particular para mí porque, seamos sinceros, mi presencia en este escenario es bastante insólita.

Mi padre fue un estudiante extranjero, nacido y criado en un pequeño pueblo en Kenia. Creció conduciendo cabras, fue a la escuela en una choza con tejado de hojalata. Su padre, mi abuelo, era cocinero, sirviente doméstico.

Pero mi abuelo tenía grandes sueños para su hijo. Mediante el duro trabajo y la perseverancia, mi padre obtuvo una beca para estudiar en un lugar mágico: Estados Unidos, que se erigió como un faro de libertad y oportunidad para muchos que habían llegado antes.

Mientras estudiaba aquí, mi padre conoció a mi madre. Ella nació en una ciudad al otro lado del mundo, en Kansas. Su padre trabajó en

and farms through most of the Depression. The day after Pearl Harbor
he signed up for duty, joined Patton's army and marched across Europe.

Back home, my grandmother raised their baby and went to work on a
bomber assembly line. After the war, they studied on the GI Bill, bought
a house through FHA, and moved west in search of opportunity.

And they, too, had big dreams for their daughter, a common dream, born
of two continents. My parents shared not only an improbable love; they
shared an abiding faith in the possibilities of this nation.

They would give me an African name, Barack, or "blessed," believing that
in a tolerant America your name is no barrier to success. They imagined
me going to the best schools in the land, even though they weren't rich,
because in a generous America you don't have to be rich to achieve your
potential. They are both passed away now. Yet, I know that, on this night,
they look down on me with pride.

I stand, grateful for the diversity of my heritage, aware that my parents'
dreams live on in my precious daughters. I stand here knowing that my
story is part of the larger American story, that I owe a debt to all of those
who came before me, and that, in no other country on earth, is my story
even possible.

Our pride is based on a very simple premise, summed up in a declaration
made over two hundred years ago, "We hold these truths to he self-
evident, that all men are created equal. That they are endowed by their
Creator with certain inalienable rights. That among these are life, liberty
and the pursuit of happiness."

plataformas petrolíferas y granjas durante la mayor parte de la Depresión. El día después de Pearl Harbor se alistó en el ejército, se unió a las tropas de Patton y marchó por Europa.

En casa, mi abuela crió a su bebé y fue a trabajar en la cadena de montaje de un bombardero. Después de la guerra, estudiaron en el programa para veteranos de guerra (GI Bill), compraron una casa mediante la Administración General de la Vivienda (FHA), y se mudaron al oeste en busca de oportunidad.

Y también ellos tenían grandes sueños para su hija, un sueño común, nacido de dos continentes. Mis padres compartieron no sólo un amor improbable; compartieron una fe firme en las posibilidades de esta nación.

Ellos me pusieron un nombre africano, Barack, o "bendito", creyendo que en una Norteamérica tolerante el nombre no es barrera alguna para el éxito. Ellos me imaginaron yendo a las mejores escuelas del país, aunque ellos no eran ricos, porque en una Norteamérica generosa uno no tiene que ser rico para alcanzar su potencial. Ahora, ellos dos ya han fallecido; sin embargo sé que, esta noche, ellos me miran con orgullo.

Estoy aquí agradecido por la diversidad de mi herencia, consciente de que los sueños de mis padres siguen viviendo en mis preciosas hijas. Estoy aquí sabiendo que mi historia es parte de la amplia historia de Estados Unidos, que estoy en deuda con todos aquellos que me han precedido, y sabiendo que, en ningún otro país en la tierra, mi historia ni siquiera es posible.

Nuestro orgullo está basado en una premisa muy simple, resumida en una declaración hecha hace más de doscientos años: "Sostenemos como evidentes estas verdades: que todos los hombres son creados iguales. Que son dotados por su Creador de ciertos derechos inalienables. Que entre éstos están: la vida, la libertad y la búsqueda de la felicidad".

That is the true genius of America, a faith in the simple dreams of its people, the insistence on small miracles. That we can tuck in our children at night and know they are fed and clothed and safe from harm. That we can say what we think, write what we think, without hearing a sudden knock on the door. That we can have an idea and start our own business without paying a bribe or hiring somebody's son.

And fellow Americans, Democrats, Republicans, Independents, I say to you tonight: we have more work to do.

More to do for the workers I met in Galesburg, Illinois, who are losing their union jobs at the Maytag plant that's moving to Mexico, and now are having to compete with their own children for jobs that pay seven bucks an hour.

More to do for the father I met who was losing his job and choking back tears, wondering how he would pay $4,500 a month for the drugs his son needs without the health benefits he counted on.

More to do for the young woman in East St. Louis, and thousands more like her, who has the grades, has the drive, has the will, but doesn't have the money to go to college.

Don't get me wrong. The people I meet in small towns and big cities, in diners and office parks, they don't expect government to solve all their problems. They know they have to work hard to get ahead and they want to.

Go into the collar counties around Chicago, and people will tell you they don't want their tax money wasted by a welfare agency or the Pentagon. Go into any inner-city neighborhood, and folks will tell you that government alone can't teach kids to learn.

Esa es la verdadera genialidad de Estados Unidos: una fe en los sencillos sueños de su pueblo, en la insistencia en pequeños milagros. Que podemos llevar a la cama a nuestros hijos por la noche y saber que están alimentados, y vestidos, y seguros del peligro. Que podemos decir lo que pensamos, escribir lo que pensamos sin oír un repentino golpe en la puerta. Que podemos tener una idea y comenzar nuestra propia empresa sin tener que pagar sobornos o contratar al hijo de otra persona.

Y conciudadanos estadounidenses, demócratas, republicanos, independientes, les digo esta noche: tenemos más trabajo que hacer.

Más que hacer por los trabajadores que conocí en Galesburg, Illinois, que están perdiendo sus empleos en la planta Maytag que se traslada a México, y ahora tienen que competir con sus propios hijos por empleos que pagan siete dólares la hora.

Más que hacer por el padre que conocí, que se quedó sin empleo y luchaba por reprimir las lágrimas preguntándose cómo pagaría los 4500 dólares al mes que cuestan las medicinas que su hijo necesita al no tener los beneficios de salud con los que contaba.

Más que hacer por la joven en East St. Louis, y miles más como ella, que tiene las calificaciones, tiene la voluntad, pero no tiene el dinero para estudiar en la Universidad.

No me malentiendan. Las personas que conozco en pequeños pueblos y grandes ciudades, en restaurantes y en parques empresariales, no esperan que el gobierno resuelva todos sus problemas. Ellos saben que tienen que trabajar duro para avanzar, y quieren hacerlo.

Vayan a los condados que rodean Chicago, y la gente les dirá que no quiere que el dinero de sus impuestos lo desperdicie una agencia de beneficencia o el Pentágono. Vayan a cualquier barrio céntrico pobre, y las personas les dirán que solamente el gobierno no puede enseñar a los niños a aprender.

They know that parents have to parent, that children can't achieve unless we raise their expectations and turn off the television sets and eradicate the slander that says a black youth with a book is acting white.

No, people don't expect government to solve all their problems. But they sense, deep in their bones, that with just a change in priorities, we can make sure that every child in America has a decent shot at life, and that the doors of opportunity remain open to all. They know we can do better. And they want that choice.

A while back, I met a young man named Seamus at the VFW Hall in East Moline, Illinois. He was a good-looking kid, six-two or six-three, clear-eyed, with an easy smile. He told me he'd joined the Marines and was heading to Iraq the following week.

As I listened to him explain why he'd enlisted, his absolute faith in our country and its leaders, his devotion to duty and service, I thought this young man was all any of us might hope for in a child. But then I asked myself: Are we serving Seamus as well as he was serving us?

I thought of more than nine hundred service men and women, sons and daughters, husbands and wives, friends and neighbors, who will not be returning to their hometowns. I thought of families I had met who were struggling to get by without a loved one's full income, or whose loved ones had returned with a limb missing or with nerves shattered, but who still lacked long-term health benefits because they were reservists.

When we send our young men and women into harm's way, we have a solemn obligation not to fudge the numbers or shade the truth about why they're going, to care for their families while they're gone, to tend to the

Ellos saben que los padres tienen que educar, que los hijos no pueden rendir a menos que elevemos sus expectativas, y apaguemos los aparatos de televisión, y erradiquemos la difamación que dice que un joven de raza negra con un libro está actuando como un blanco.

No, la gente no espera que el gobierno resuelva todos sus problemas. Pero siente, en lo profundo de su ser, que sólo con un cambio de prioridades podemos asegurar que todos los niños en Estados Unidos tengan un estímulo decente en la vida, y que las puertas de la oportunidad permanezcan abiertas para todos. Ellos saben que podemos mejorar. Y quieren tener esa opción.

Hace algún tiempo conocí a un hombre llamado Seamus en el Salón de Veteranos de Guerras Extranjeras en East Moline, Illinois. Era un hombre bien parecido, de 1,80 ó 1,90 de estatura, de ojos claros y de sonrisa fácil. Me dijo que se había alistado en los Marines y que la siguiente semana partiría para Iraq.

Mientras le escuchaba explicar por qué se había alistado, su absoluta fe en nuestro país y en sus líderes, su devoción a la obligación y el servicio, pensé que ese joven era todo lo que cualquiera de nosotros podría esperar de un niño. Pero después me pregunté: ¿Estamos sirviendo a Seamus tan bien como él nos estaba sirviendo a nosotros?

Pensé en más de novecientos hombres y mujeres de servicio, hijos e hijas, esposos y esposas, amigos y vecinos, quienes no regresarán a sus ciudades natales. Pensé en familias que había conocido que estaban luchando por seguir adelante sin los ingresos de un ser querido, o cuyos seres queridos habían regresado sin uno de sus miembros o con los nervios destrozados, pero que aún carecían de beneficios sanitarios a largo plazo porque eran reservistas.

Cuando enviamos a nuestros jóvenes camino del peligro, tenemos la solemne obligación de no eludir los números o sombrear la verdad sobre el porqué se van, de cuidar de sus familias mientras ellos no están, de atender a

soldiers upon their return, and to never ever go to war without enough troops to win the war, secure the peace, and earn the respect of the world.

Now let me be clear. We have real enemies in the world. These enemies must be found. They must be pursued and they must be defeated.

John Kerry knows this. And just as Lieutenant Kerry did not hesitate to risk his life to protect the men who served with him in Vietnam, President Kerry will not hesitate one moment to use our military might to keep America safe and secure.

John Kerry believes in America. And he knows it's not enough for just some of us to prosper. For alongside our famous individualism, there's another ingredient in the American saga.

A belief that we are connected as one people. If there's a child on the South Side of Chicago who can't read, that matters to me, even if it's not my child. If there's a senior citizen somewhere who can't pay for her prescription and has to choose between medicine and the rent, that makes my life poorer, even if it's not my grandmother. If there's an Arab American family being rounded up without benefit of an attorney or due process, that threatens my civil liberties.

It's that fundamental belief—I am my brother's keeper, I am my sister's keeper—that makes this country work.

It's what allows us to pursue our individual dreams, yet still come together as a single American family. "E pluribus unum." Out of many, one.

Yet even as we speak, there are those who are preparing to divide us, the spin masters and negative ad peddlers who embrace the politics of anything goes. Well, I say to them tonight, there's not a liberal America and a conservative America; there's the United States of America. There's

los soldados cuando regresan, y de nunca ir a la guerra sin suficientes tropas para ganar la guerra, asegurar la paz y ganarnos el respeto del mundo.

Ahora permítanme ser claro. Tenemos enemigos reales en el mundo, y hay que encontrar a esos enemigos. Deben ser perseguidos y deben ser derrotados.

John Kerry sabe esto. Y al igual que el teniente Kerry no dudó en arriesgar su vida para proteger a los hombres que sirvieron con él en Vietnam, el presidente Kerry no dudará ni un momento en utilizar nuestra fuerza militar para mantener a Estados Unidos seguro.

John Kerry cree en Estados Unidos. Y él sabe que no es suficiente que solamente algunos de nosotros prosperemos. Porque junto con nuestro famoso individualismo, hay otro ingrediente en la saga estadounidense.

Una creencia en que estamos conectados como un solo pueblo. Si hay un niño en la parte sur de Chicago que no sabe leer, eso me importa, aunque no sea mi hijo. Si hay una ciudadana de la tercera edad en algún lugar que no puede pagar sus recetas y tiene que escoger entre medicinas y el alquiler, eso empobrece mi vida, aunque ella no sea mi abuela. Si hay una familia árabe estadounidense siendo acorralada sin el beneficio de un abogado o un procesamiento adecuado, eso amenaza mis libertades civiles.

Es esa creencia fundamental—yo soy el guardián de mi hermano, soy el guardián de mi hermana—la que hace que este país funcione.

Es lo que nos permite perseguir nuestros sueños individuales y, aun así, reunirnos como una sola familia estadounidense. "E pluribus unum". De muchos, uno.

Sin embargo, aun mientras hablamos, están quienes se están preparando para dividirnos, los maestros de la interpretación y los vendedores de anuncios negativos que siguen la política del todo vale. Bien, les digo a ellos esta noche que no hay una Norteamérica liberal y una Norteamérica

not a black America and white America and Latino America and Asian America; there's the United States of America.

The pundits like to slice and dice our country into Red States and Blue States; Red States for Republicans, Blue States for Democrats. But I've got news for them, too. We worship an awesome God in the Blue States, and we don't like federal agents poking around our libraries in the Red States. We coach Little League in the Blue States and have gay friends in the Red States.

There are patriots who opposed the war in Iraq and patriots who supported it. We are one people, all of us pledging allegiance to the Stars and Stripes, all of us defending the United States of America.

In the end, that's what this election is about. Do we participate in a politics of cynicism or a politics of hope? I'm not talking about blind optimism here, the almost willful ignorance that thinks unemployment will go away if we just don't talk about it, or the health care crisis will solve itself if we just ignore it. No, I'm talking about something more substantial.

It's the hope of slaves sitting around a fire singing freedom songs; the hope of immigrants setting out for distant shores; the hope of a young naval lieutenant bravely patrolling the Mekong Delta; the hope of a millworker's son who dares to defy the odds; the hope of a skinny kid with a funny name who believes that America has a place for him, too. The audacity of hope!

conservadora; hay los Estados Unidos de América. No hay una Norteamérica negra, una Norteamérica blanca, una Norteamérica latina, una
Norteamérica asiática; hay los Estados Unidos de América.

A los expertos les gusta rebanar y cortar nuestro país en Estados Rojos
y Estados Azules; Estados Rojos para los republicanos, y Estados Azules
para los Demócratas. Pero tengo noticias también para ellos. Nosotros
adoramos a un Dios increíble en los Estados Azules, y no nos gusta que
agentes federales estén curioseando en nuestras bibliotecas en los Estados
Rojos. Entrenamos en las Ligas menores en los Estados Azules y tenemos
amigos homosexuales en los Estados Rojos.

Hay patriotas que se opusieron a la guerra en Iraq y patriotas que la
apoyaron. Somos un solo pueblo, todos nosotros jurando lealtad a las
Estrellas y las Barras, y todos nosotros defendiendo a los Estados Unidos
de América.

Al final, de eso se tratan las elecciones. ¿Participamos en una política de cinismo
o en una política de esperanza? No estoy hablando aquí de optimismo ciego,
de la casi deliberada ignorancia que piensa que el desempleo se eliminará si
sencillamente no hablamos de él, o que la crisis de la asistencia de salud se
resolverá por sí sola si sencillamente la ignoramos. No, estoy hablando sobre
algo más importante.

Es la esperanza de esclavos sentados alrededor de una hoguera cantando cantos
de libertad; la esperanza de inmigrantes que parten para costas distantes; la
esperanza de un joven teniente de marina que patrulla con valentía el delta
del Mekong; la esperanza del hijo de un molinero que se atreve a desafiar
las predicciones; la esperanza de un niño flaco con un nombre chistoso que
cree que Estados Unidos tiene un lugar también para él. ¡La audacia de la
esperanza!

Speech to the
National Council of La Raza
July 22, 2007
Miami, Florida

At the annual conference of the National Council of La Raza, Senator Obama linked the movements started by Cesar Chavez and Dr. Martin Luther King Jr. and promised the nation's largest advocacy group for Hispanics that he would fight for immigration reform.

I have been running for president now for a little over five months. And in that time, I have been inspired by crowds tens of thousands of people strong—many who have come out for the very first political event of their lifetime.

I'd like to take all the credit here myself, but as my wife reminds me every day, I'm just not that great.

The real reason that so many people are coming out and signing up is because they see in this campaign the potential for the change Americans are so hungry for. It's not just the kind of change you hear about in slogans or from politicians every few years; it's the kind of bottom-up, grassroots movement that can transform a nation.

La Raza has always represented this kind of movement. You didn't get your start as some top-down interest group in Washington, you got

Discurso al
Consejo Nacional de La Raza
22 de julio de 2007
Miami, Florida

En la conferencia anual del Consejo Nacional de La Raza, el senador Obama relacionó los movimientos comenzados por César Chávez y el Dr. Martin Luther King Jr. y prometió al mayor grupo del país de defensa de los hispanos que lucharíamos por la reforma de la inmigración.

Hace ya más de cinco meses que me presenté como candidato a la presidencia. Y en ese periodo he sido inspirado mucho por multitudes de cientos de miles de personas, muchas que han acudido al primer evento político en toda su vida.

Me gustaría tomar todo el mérito yo mismo aquí, pero como mi esposa me recuerda cada día, sencillamente no soy tan grande.

La verdadera razón de que estén llegando tantas personas y registrándose es porque ven en esta campaña el potencial para el cambio del que los estadounidenses tenemos tanta hambre. No es sólo el tipo de cambio del que uno oye en eslóganes o de boca de políticos cada pocos años; es el tipo de movimiento de base, de abajo hacia arriba, que puede transformar una nación.

La Raza siempre ha representado este tipo de movimiento. Ustedes no comenzaron como algún grupo de interés de arriba hacia abajo en

your start standing up for the dreams and aspirations of Latinos in farm fields and barrios all across America.

You got your start almost forty years ago in places like Southern California, where farmworkers and their children were beaten because they asked for the right to organize—because they believed that picking grapes all day in the hot sun should be rewarded with a decent wage and protection from deadly pesticides.

And when a man named Cesar Chavez saw this injustice, he knew it wasn't right and so he went about organizing those workers. And one fateful day he decided to draw the eyes of the nation to their cause by sitting down for a hunger strike. He went without food for twenty-five days, and at one point he received a telegram from an Atlanta preacher who was busy leading his own strike of sanitation workers all the way in Memphis, Tennessee.

The telegram from Dr. Martin Luther King Jr. to Cesar Chavez said this: "As brothers in the fight for equality, I extend the hand of fellowship and good will and wish continuing success to you and your members. . . . Our separate struggles are really one. A struggle for freedom, for dignity, and for humanity."

Our separate struggles are really one. It was a belief that Dr. King repeated often when he would say that an injustice anywhere is a threat to justice everywhere. It means that the civil rights movement wasn't just a movement of African Americans, but Latino Americans, and white Americans, and every American who believes that equality and opportunity are not just words to be said but promises to be kept. The civil rights movement was your movement too, and its unfinished work is still the task of every American.

Washington, sino que comenzaron defendiendo los sueños y aspiraciones de los latinos en granjas y barrios por todo Estados Unidos.

Comenzaron hace casi cuarenta años en lugares como California del Sur, donde granjeros y sus hijos eran golpeados porque pedían el derecho a organizarse; porque creían que recoger uvas todo el día bajo el calor del sol debería ser recompensado con un salario decente y protección de pesticidas mortales.

Y cuando un hombre llamado César Chávez vio esta injusticia, supo que no estaba bien, y por eso emprendió la tarea de organizar a esos obreros. Y un fatídico día decidió atraer los ojos del país a su causa sentándose y haciendo una huelga de hambre. Estuvo sin comer durante veinticinco días, y en un punto recibió un telegrama de un predicador de Atlanta que estaba ocupado realizando su propia huelga de obreros de la limpieza en Memphis, Tennessee.

El telegrama del Dr. Martin Luther King Jr. a César Chávez decía lo siguiente: "Como hermanos en la lucha por la igualdad, extiendo la mano del compañerismo y buena voluntad, y les deseo un éxito continuado a usted y a sus miembros... Nuestras batallas por separado son realmente una. Una batalla por la libertad, por la dignidad, y por la humanidad".

Nuestras batallas por separado son realmente una. Era una creencia que el Dr. King repetía con frecuencia cuando decía que una injusticia en cualquier lugar es una amenaza para la justicia en todo lugar. Significa que el movimiento por los derechos no era sólo un movimiento de afroamericanos, sino también de estadounidenses latinos, y estadounidenses blancos, y de cada estadounidense que cree que igualdad y oportunidad no son sólo palabras que hay que decir sino promesas que hay que cumplir. El movimiento por los derechos civiles fue también el movimiento de ustedes, y su obra no finalizada sigue siendo la tarea de todo estadounidense.

Our separate struggles are really one. If there's a child stuck in a crumbling school who graduates without ever learning how to read, it doesn't matter if that child is a Latino from Miami or an African American from Chicago or a white girl from rural Kentucky—she is our child, and her struggle is our struggle.

It doesn't matter if the injustice involves a brown man who's badgered into proving his citizenship again and again or a black man who's pulled over because the car he's driving is too nice—it's injustice either way, and we all have a role in ending it.

Whether you're one of the 45 million Americans without health care in this country, or the one in five African Americans, or the one in three Latinos, it will take all of us to stand up to a drug and insurance industry that spent $1 billion in lobbying to block health care reform. That's the kind of movement we need in America.

It won't be enough to change parties in this election if we don't also change a politics that has tried to divide us for far too long. Because when we spend all our time keeping score of who's up and who's down, the only winners are those who can afford to play the game—those with the most money, and influence, and power.

I was too young to participate in the civil rights movement, but I was inspired by leaders like King and Chavez to become a community organizer. Almost twenty-five years ago, I was hired by a group of churches on the South Side of Chicago to help turn around neighborhoods that had been devastated by the closing of nearby steel plants.

I knew that change wouldn't be easy, but I also knew it would be impossible without bringing folks together and building a movement within the community. So I reached out and formed coalitions between Latino

Nuestras batallas por separado son realmente una. Si hay un niño atascado en una escuela que se desmorona y que se gradúa sin siquiera haber aprendido a leer, no importa si ese niño es un latino de Miami, o un afroamericano de Chicago, o una niña blanca del Kentucky rural; es nuestro niño, y su batalla es nuestra batalla.

No importa si la injusticia implica a un hombre mulato al que han atormentado para que demuestre su ciudadanía una y otra vez, o a un hombre negro al que hacen detener su auto porque ese auto que conduce es demasiado bonito: es injusticia de todos modos, y todos desempeñamos un papel para ponerle fin.

Sea usted uno de los 45 millones de estadounidenses que no tienen asistencia médica en este país, o uno de cada cinco afroamericanos, o uno de cada tres latinos, nos tocará a todos nosotros hacer frente a una industria farmacéutica y de seguros que gastó mil millones de dólares en hacer presión para bloquear la reforma de la asistencia médica. Ese es el tipo de movimiento que necesitamos en Estados Unidos.

No será suficiente con cambiar de partidos en estas elecciones si no cambiamos también una política que ha intentado dividirnos por demasiado tiempo. Porque cuando empleamos todo nuestro tiempo anotando quién asciende y quién desciende, los únicos ganadores son quienes pueden permitirse jugar el partido: quienes tienen más dinero, e influencia, y poder.

Yo era demasiado joven para participar en el movimiento por los derechos civiles, pero fui inspirado por líderes como King y Chávez para convertirme en un organizador comunitario. Hace casi veinticinco años fui contratado por un grupo de iglesias en la parte sur de Chicago para ayudar a recuperar barrios que habían sido devastados por el cierre de fábricas de acero cercanas.

Yo sabía que ese cambio no sería fácil, pero también sabía que sería imposible sin unir a las personas y crear un movimiento dentro de la comunidad. Así que tendí la mano y formé coaliciones entre líderes

leaders and black leaders on every issue from failing schools to illegal dumping to unimmunized children. And together, we made progress. We set up job training and after school programs, and we taught people on the South Side to stand up to their government when it wasn't standing up for them.

But I didn't stop there. When all the cynics said it wasn't possible, I kept building coalitions and making progress throughout my eight years in the Illinois state senate.

They told me I couldn't reform a death penalty system that had sent thirteen innocent people to death row. But we did that. They told me that trying to pass new racial profiling laws to protect black folks and brown folks would stir up too much controversy. But we did that too.

And they doubted whether we could put government back on the side of average people—but we put $100 million worth of tax cuts in the pockets of the low-income workers and passed health care reform that insured another 150,000 children and parents.

So I want you to remember one thing, because you'll be hearing from a lot of candidates today. When I talk about hope; when I talk about change; when I talk about holding America up to its ideals of opportunity and equality, this isn't just the rhetoric of a campaign for me, it's been the cause of my life—a cause I will work for and fight for every day as your president.

I will be a president who remembers that our separate struggles are really one. I will never walk away from the tough battles or the difficult work of bringing people together. And I will never walk away from the 12 million undocumented immigrants who live, work, and contribute to our country every single day.

latinos y líderes negros en cada problema, desde escuelas que fracasaban, vertidos ilegales, hasta niños no inmunizados. Y juntos, hicimos progreso. Establecimos programas de formación laboral y actividades extraescolares, y enseñamos a las personas en la parte sur a hacer frente a su gobierno cuando éste no los estaba defendiendo.

Pero no me detuve ahí. Cuando todos los cínicos decían que no era posible, yo seguí creando coaliciones y haciendo progreso a lo largo de mis ocho años en el senado del estado de Illinois.

Ellos me dijeron que yo no podía reformar un sistema de pena capital que había enviado a trece personas inocentes al corredor de la muerte. Pero hicimos eso. Ellos me dijeron que intentar aprobar nuevas leyes sobre perfiles raciales para proteger a las personas de color y las personas mulatas provocaría demasiada controversia. Pero hicimos eso también.

Y ellos dudaron de que pudiéramos volver a poner al gobierno del lado del pueblo llano; pero hicimos recortes de impuestos por un valor de 100 millones de dólares y los pusimos en los bolsillos de trabajadores con bajos ingresos, y aprobamos una reforma de la asistencia médica que aseguró a otros 150 000 niños y padres.

Por tanto, quiero que recuerden una cosa, porque oirán a muchos candidatos hoy. Cuando yo hablo de esperanza; cuando hablo de cambio; cuando hablo de elevar a Estados Unidos a sus ideales de oportunidad e igualdad, no es sólo la retórica de una campaña para mí; ha sido la causa de mi vida, una causa por la que trabajaré y lucharé cada día como su presidente.

Yo seré un presidente que recuerda que nuestras batallas por separado son realmente una. Nunca me alejaré de las luchas difíciles o del duro trabajo de unir a las personas. Y nunca me alejaré de los 12 millones de inmigrantes indocumentados que viven, trabajan y contribuyen en nuestro país cada día.

There are few better examples of how broken, bitter, and divisive our politics has become than the immigration debate that played out in Washington a few weeks ago.

So many of us—Democrats and Republicans—were willing to compromise in order to pass comprehensive reform that would secure our borders while giving the undocumented a chance to earn their citizenship.

We knew that the American people believe that we are a nation of laws— that we have a right and duty to protect our borders. And we should also crack down on employers who hire undocumented workers so that we can protect jobs and wages.

But the American people also know that we are a nation of immigrants—a nation that has always been willing to give weary travelers from around the world the chance to come here and reach for the dream that so many of us have reached for. That's the America that answered my father's letters and his prayers and brought him here from Kenya so long ago. That's the America we believe in.

But that's the America that the President and too many Republicans walked away from when the politics got tough. Now, there are plenty of people opposed to immigration reform for principled reasons that I happen to disagree with. But this time around, we saw parts of the immigration debate took a turn that was both ugly and racist in a way we haven't seen since the struggle for civil rights.

Well we didn't walk away from injustice then and we won't walk away from it today. I'll keep fighting, and I'll keep attending immigration rallies, and I'll keep believing that we can have a civil debate about immigration where we begin to recognize ourselves in one another.

Hay pocos ejemplos mejores de lo fracturada, amarga y divisiva que se ha vuelto nuestra política que el debate sobre inmigración que se llevó a cabo en Washington hace unas semanas.

Muchos de nosotros—demócratas y republicanos—estuvimos dispuestos a ceder a fin de aprobar una reforma general que asegurase nuestras fronteras a la vez que les diera a los indocumentados una oportunidad de ganarse su ciudadanía.

Sabíamos que el pueblo estadounidense cree que somos una nación de leyes; que tenemos el derecho y la obligación de proteger nuestras fronteras. Y también deberíamos tomar duras medidas contra los patrones que emplean a trabajadores indocumentados, a fin de poder proteger los trabajos y los salarios.

Pero el pueblo estadounidense también sabe que somos una nación de inmigrantes; una nación que siempre ha estado dispuesta a dar a los cansados viajeros de todo el mundo la oportunidad de venir aquí y alcanzar el sueño que tantos de nosotros hemos alcanzado. Ese es el Estados Unidos que respondió las cartas de mi padre y sus oraciones, y le trajo aquí desde Kenia hace mucho tiempo. Ese es el Estados Unidos donde vivimos.

Pero ese es el Estados Unidos del que se alejaron el Presidente y demasiados republicanos cuando la política se puso difícil. Ahora bien, hay muchas personas que se oponen a la reforma de la inmigración por razones basadas en fuertes principios con los que resulta que yo estoy en desacuerdo. Pero en este tiempo, vimos partes del debate sobre inmigración dar un giro tanto feo como racista, de manera que no hemos visto desde la lucha por los derechos civiles.

Bien, nosotros no nos alejamos de la injusticia entonces y no nos alejaremos de ella ahora. Seguiré luchando, y seguiré asistiendo a concentraciones por la inmigración, y seguiré creyendo que podemos tener un debate civil sobre inmigración donde comencemos a reconocernos a nosotros mismos los unos en los otros.

But you and I know that the struggle we share goes far beyond immigration. We don't expect our government to guarantee success and happiness, but when millions of children start the race of life so far behind only because of race, only because of class, that's a betrayal of our ideals. That's not just a Latino problem or an African American problem; that is an American problem that we have to solve.

It's an American problem when Latinos are the most likely to be uninsured even though they make up a disproportionate share of the workforce. It's an American problem when one in four Latinos cannot communicate well with their doctor about what's wrong or fill out medical forms because there are language barriers we refuse to break down. It's an American problem that our health care system is broken and it's time to fix it once and for all.

Let's give our kids everything they could possibly need to have a fighting chance. Let's not pass a law called No Child Left Behind and then leave the money behind. Let's finally invest in what makes the most difference in any child's education—the person standing in the front of the classroom. And let's make sure any child who comes here and studies here and does well in school gets the same chance to attend a public college as anyone else.

And there's one other thing we can do. For millions of Latinos and other Americans, the cornerstone of the American Dream is the ability to own your own home. You work hard for it, and you save for it, and you're willing to sacrifice to buy it.

But there is an army of lenders and brokers out there who are ready and willing to take advantage of your hopes and cheat you out of your dream. They lurk in your neighborhoods and sometimes they even come into your churches and they offer you these subprime mortgage loans.

Pero ustedes y yo sabemos que la batalla que compartimos va mucho más allá de la inmigración. No esperamos que nuestro gobierno garantice el éxito y la felicidad, pero cuando millones de niños comienzan la carrera de la vida tan retrasados solamente debido a la raza, solamente debido a la clase social, eso es una traición a nuestros ideales. No es sólo un problema latino o un problema africano; es un problema norteamericano que tenemos que resolver.

Es un problema norteamericano cuando los latinos son quienes tienen más probabilidades de no estar asegurados aunque representen una parte desproporcionada de la fuerza laboral. Es un problema norteamericano cuando uno de cada cuatro latinos no puede comunicarse bien con su doctor sobre lo que anda mal ni rellenar formularios médicos porque hay barreras de idioma que nos negamos a derrumbar. Es un problema norteamericano que nuestro sistema de asistencia sanitaria esté fracturado, y es momento de repararlo de una vez por todas.

Demos a nuestros niños todo lo que pudieran necesitar para tener una oportunidad de luchar. No aprobemos una ley denominada "Ningún niño queda atrás" y después dejemos atrás el dinero. Invirtamos finalmente en lo que marca la mayor diferencia en la educación de cualquier niño: la persona que está al frente de la clase. Y asegurémonos de que cualquier niño que venga aquí, y estudie aquí, y le vaya bien en la escuela tenga la misma oportunidad de ir a una universidad pública que todos los demás.

Y hay otra cosa que podemos hacer. Para millones de latinos y de otros estadounidenses, la piedra angular del Sueño Americano es la capacidad de ser dueño de su propia casa. Ustedes trabajan duro por ello, y ahorran por ello, y están dispuestos a sacrificarse para adquirirla.

Pero hay un ejército de prestamistas y agentes que están listos y dispuestos a aprovecharse de sus esperanzas y estafarles su sueño. Merodean por sus barrios y a veces hasta entran en sus iglesias y les ofrecen esos préstamos hipotecarios subprime.

They make them sound easy and affordable and they tell you to ignore the fine print and ask you to sign on the dotted line.

A recent report showed that 2.2 million subprime loans made in recent years have failed or will end in foreclosure, costing homeowners as much as $164 billion. Latinos hold up to 40 percent of these mortgages. African Americans hold over half.

This is no accident. These loans are discriminatory, they are dishonest, and it's time for us to treat these fraudulent lenders like the criminals that they are.

A couple of years ago, right around the time of the first immigration debate, I attended a naturalization workshop at a church in Chicago. I walked down the aisle of the church and met people who were clutching their American flags, waiting to be called up so they could start the long process of becoming citizens.

At one point, a little girl came up to me and asked me for my autograph. She said her name was Cristina, that she was studying government, and wanted to show the autograph to her third-grade class.

I told her parents they should be proud of her. And as I watched Cristina translate my words into Spanish for them, I thought for a moment about Dr. King's telegram to Cesar Chavez, and I knew that, in the end, our separate dreams are really one as well.

It's the dream my father had when he arrived here from Kenya. The dream Cristina's parents had for her. And the dream that I have for my own two daughters.

Ellos hacen que suenen fáciles y posibles, y les dicen que ignoren la letra pequeña y firmen en la línea de puntos.

Un reciente informe mostró que 2.2 millones de préstamos subprime hechos en años recientes no han dado resultado o terminarán en juicio hipotecario, costando a los propietarios de casas tanto como 164 millones de dólares. Los latinos tienen hasta el cuarenta por ciento de esas hipotecas, y los afroamericanos más de la mitad.

Eso no es por accidente. Esos préstamos son discriminatorios, son deshonestos, y ya es momento de que tratemos a esos prestamistas fraudulentos como los delincuentes que son.

Hace un par de años, justamente alrededor de la época del primer debate sobre inmigración, asistí a un taller sobre ciudadanía en una iglesia en Chicago. Caminé por el pasillo de la iglesia y encontré a personas que agarraban sus banderas estadounidenses, esperando a que les llamasen para poder comenzar el largo proceso de convertirse en ciudadanos.

En cierto momento, una niña se acercó a mí y me pidió mi autógrafo. Me dijo que se llamaba Cristina, que estaba estudiando el gobierno, y que quería enseñar el autógrafo a su clase de tercer grado.

Yo le dije a sus padres que deberían estar orgullosos de ella. Y mientras observaba a Cristina traducir para ellos mis palabras al español, pensé por un momento en el telegrama del Dr. King a César Chávez, y supe que, al final, nuestros sueños por separado son también realmente uno.

Es el sueño que mi padre tenía cuando llegó aquí desde Kenia. El sueño que los padres de Cristina tenían para ella. Y el sueño que yo tengo para mis dos hijas.

A More Perfect Union speech
March 18, 2008
Philadelphia, Pennsylvania

*At the National Constitution Center, created in 2003
to foster better understanding of the U.S. Constitution, Senator Obama
addressed the controversy over remarks made during sermons
by the pastor of his Chicago church.*

"We the people, in order to form a more perfect union."

Two hundred and twenty-one years ago, in a hall that still stands across the street, a group of men gathered and, with these simple words, launched America's improbable experiment in democracy. Farmers and scholars, statesmen and patriots who had traveled across an ocean to escape tyranny and persecution finally made real their declaration of independence at a Philadelphia convention that lasted through the spring of 1787.

The document they produced was eventually signed but ultimately unfinished. It was stained by this nation's original sin of slavery, a question that divided the colonies and brought the convention to a stalemate until the founders chose to allow the slave trade to continue for at least twenty more years, and to leave any final resolution to future generations.

Discurso "Una unión más perfecta"
18 de marzo de 2008
Philadelphia, Pennsylvania

En el Centro Nacional de la Constitución, creado en 2003
para fomentar un mejor entendimiento de la Constitución de U.S.,
el senador Obama abordó la controversia por comentarios hechos
durante sermones por el pastor de su iglesia en Chicago.

"Nosotros, el pueblo, a fin de formar una unión más perfecta".

Hace doscientos veintiún años, en un salón que sigue estando al otro lado de la calle, un grupo de hombres se reunió y, con estas sencillas palabras, lanzó el improbable experimento de Estados Unidos a la democracia. Granjeros y eruditos, hombres de estado y patriotas que habían viajado atravesando un océano para escapar de la tiranía y la persecución, finalmente hicieron realidad su declaración de independencia en una convención en Filadelfia que duró a lo largo de la primavera de 1787.

El documento que produjeron fue finalmente firmado pero quedó, en definitiva, sin terminar. Estaba manchado por el pecado original de la esclavitud de esta nación, una cuestión que dividió a las colonias y llevó a la convención a un punto muerto hasta que los fundadores escogieron permitir que el mercado de esclavos continuase durante al menos veinte años más, y dejar cualquier resolución final a futuras generaciones.

Of course, the answer to the slavery question was already embedded within our Constitution—a Constitution that had at its very core the ideal of equal citizenship under the law, a Constitution that promised its people liberty, and justice, and a union that could be and should be perfected over time.

And yet words on a parchment would not be enough to deliver slaves from bondage or provide men and women of every color and creed their full rights and obligations as citizens of the United States.

What would be needed were Americans in successive generations who were willing to do their part—through protests and struggle, on the streets and in the courts, through a civil war and civil disobedience and always at great risk—to narrow that gap between the promise of our ideals and the reality of their time.

This was one of the tasks we set forth at the beginning of this campaign— to continue the long march of those who came before us, a march for a more just, more equal, more free, more caring, and more prosperous America.

I chose to run for the presidency at this moment in history because I believe deeply that we cannot solve the challenges of our time unless we solve them together—unless we perfect our union by understanding that we may have different stories, but we hold common hopes; that we may not look the same and we may not have come from the same place, but we all want to move in the same direction—toward a better future for our children and our grandchildren.

Throughout the first year of this campaign, against all predictions to the contrary, we saw how hungry the American people were for this message of unity. Despite the temptation to view my candidacy through a purely racial lens, we won commanding victories in states with some

Desde luego, la respuesta a la cuestión de la esclavitud ya estaba incrustada en nuestra Constitución; una Constitución que tenía en su núcleo mismo el ideal de la ciudadanía igualitaria bajo la ley, una Constitución que prometía a su pueblo libertad y justicia, y una unión que podría ser y debería ser perfeccionada con el tiempo.

Y, sin embargo, palabras sobre un pergamino no serían suficientes para liberar a los esclavos de la esclavitud o proporcionar a hombres y mujeres de todos los colores y credos sus plenos derechos y obligaciones como ciudadanos de los Estados Unidos.

Lo que se necesitó fueron estadounidenses en sucesivas generaciones que estuvieron dispuestos a hacer su parte—mediante protestas y batallas, en las calles y en los tribunales, mediante una guerra civil y desobediencia civil y siempre con gran riesgo—para acortar la brecha que había entre la promesa de nuestros ideales y la realidad de su época.

Esta fue una de las tareas que presentamos al comienzo de esta campaña: continuar la larga marcha de aquellos que nos precedieron, una marcha por un Estados Unidos más justo, más igualitario, más libre, más auxiliador y más próspero.

Escogí presentarme a la presidencia en este momento en la Historia porque creo profundamente que no podemos resolver los desafíos de nuestro tiempo a menos que los resolvamos juntos; a menos que perfeccionemos nuestra unión entendiendo que puede que tengamos historias distintas, pero sostenemos esperanzas comunes; que puede que no tengamos el mismo aspecto y que no hayamos llegado desde el mismo lugar, pero todos queremos movernos en la misma dirección: hacia un futuro mejor para nuestros hijos y nuestros nietos.

A lo largo del primer año de esta campaña, contra todas las predicciones contrarias, vimos el hambre que el pueblo estadounidense tenía de este mensaje de unidad. A pesar de la tentación de ver mi candidatura con unos lentes puramente raciales, ganamos abrumadoras victorias en estados con

of the whitest populations in the country. In South Carolina, where the Confederate flag still flies, we built a powerful coalition of African Americans and white Americans.

This is not to say that race has not been an issue in the campaign. At various stages in the campaign, some commentators have deemed me either "too black" or "not black enough." We saw racial tensions bubble to the surface during the week before the South Carolina primary. The press has scoured every exit poll for the latest evidence of racial polarization, not just in terms of white and black, but black and brown as well.

And yet, it has only been in the last couple of weeks that the discussion of race in this campaign has taken a particularly divisive turn.

On one end of the spectrum, we've heard the implication that my candidacy is somehow an exercise in affirmative action, that it's based solely on the desire of wide-eyed liberals to purchase racial reconciliation on the cheap.

On the other end, we've heard my former pastor, the Reverend Jeremiah Wright, use incendiary language to express views that have the potential not only to widen the racial divide but to denigrate both the greatness and the goodness of our nation, that rightly offend white and black alike.

I have already condemned, in unequivocal terms, the statements of Reverend Wright that have caused such controversy. For some, nagging questions remain.

Did I know him to be an occasionally fierce critic of American domestic and foreign policy? Of course. Did I ever hear him make remarks that could be considered controversial while I sat in church? Yes.

algunas de las mayores poblaciones de blancos del país. En Carolina del Sur, donde sigue ondeando la bandera confederada, establecimos una poderosa coalición de afroamericanos y estadounidenses de raza blanca.

Esto no es decir que la raza no haya sido un escollo en la campaña. En varias etapas en la campaña, algunos comentaristas me han calificado como "demasiado negro" o "no lo bastante negro". Vimos tensiones raciales surgir a la superficie durante la semana anterior a las primarias de Carolina del Sur. La prensa ha batido todas las salidas de las urnas buscando la última evidencia de polarización racial, no sólo en términos de personas blancas y negras, sino también de personas negras y mulatas.

Y sin embargo, ha sido sólo en las dos últimas semanas cuando la discusión de la raza en esta campaña ha adoptado un giro particularmente divisivo.

En un extremo del espectro, hemos oído la insinuación de que mi candidatura es de algún modo un ejercicio en acción afirmativa, que está basada únicamente en el deseo de cándidos liberales de comprar la reconciliación racial a bajo precio.

En el otro extremo, hemos oído a mi anterior pastor, el reverendo Jeremiah Wright, usar lenguaje incendiario para expresar puntos de vista que tienen el potencial no sólo de ampliar la división racial sino también de denigrar tanto la grandeza como la bondad de nuestra nación, que legítimamente ofenden a blancos y negros igualmente.

Ya he condenado, en términos inequívocos, las afirmaciones del reverendo Wright que han causado tal controversia. Para algunos, permanecen las preguntas críticas.

¿Sabía yo que él era ocasionalmente un crítico feroz de la política interior y exterior de Estados Unidos? Claro que sí. ¿Le oí alguna vez hacer comentarios que pudieran ser considerados controvertidos mientras estaba yo sentado en la iglesia? Sí.

Did I strongly disagree with many of his political views? Absolutely—just as I'm sure many of you have heard remarks from your pastors, priests, or rabbis with which you strongly disagreed.

But the remarks that have caused this recent firestorm weren't simply controversial. They weren't simply a religious leader's effort to speak out against perceived injustice. Instead, they expressed a profoundly distorted view of this country—a view that sees white racism as endemic and that elevates what is wrong with America above all that we know is right with America; a view that sees the conflicts in the Middle East as rooted primarily in the actions of stalwart allies like Israel, instead of emanating from the perverse and hateful ideologies of radical Islam.

As such, Reverend Wright's comments were not only wrong but divisive, divisive at a time when we need unity; racially charged at a time when we need to come together to solve a set of monumental problems—two wars, a terrorist threat, a falling economy, a chronic health care crisis, and potentially devastating climate change; problems that are neither black nor white nor Latino nor Asian, but rather problems that confront us all.

Given my background, my politics, and my professed values and ideals, there will no doubt be those for whom my statements of condemnation are not enough. Why associate myself with Reverend Wright in the first place, they may ask? Why not join another church?

And I confess that if all that I knew of Reverend Wright were the snippets of those sermons that have run in an endless loop on the television and YouTube, or if Trinity United Church of Christ conformed to the caricatures being peddled by some commentators, there is no doubt that I would react in much the same way.

¿Estaba yo en fuerte desacuerdo con muchas de sus perspectivas políticas? Totalmente; al igual que estoy seguro de que muchos de ustedes han oído comentarios de sus pastores, sacerdotes o rabinos con los cuales estaban en fuerte desacuerdo.

Pero los comentarios que han causado esta reciente tormenta no fueron simplemente controvertidos. No fueron simplemente el esfuerzo de un líder religioso por expresarse contra la injusticia percibida. En cambio, expresaron una perspectiva profundamente distorsionada de este país; una perspectiva que ve el racismo blanco como endémico y que eleva lo que está mal en Estados Unidos por encima de todo lo que sabemos que está bien en Estados Unidos; una perspectiva que ve los conflictos en Medio Oriente arraigados primordialmente en los actos de leales aliados como Israel, en lugar de emanar de las perversas y odiosas ideologías del islam radical.

Como tales, los comentarios del reverendo Wright no sólo fueron equivocados, sino también divisivos; divisivos en un tiempo en que necesitamos unidad; con carga racial en un tiempo en que necesitamos unirnos para resolver un conjunto de problemas monumental: dos guerras, una amenaza terrorista, una economía en baja, una crisis crónica de la asistencia médica, y un cambio climático potencialmente devastador; problemas que no son ni blancos ni negros, ni latinos ni asiáticos, sino problemas que nos confrontan a todos.

Dado mi trasfondo, mi política, y los valores e ideales que profeso, sin duda habrá aquellos para quienes mis afirmaciones de condena no sean suficientes. Puede que pregunten: ¿Por qué relacionarme con el reverendo Wright en un principio? ¿Por qué no unirme a otra iglesia?

Y confieso que si todo lo que yo conociera del reverendo Wright fueran los fragmentos de esos sermones que han aparecido una y otra vez en la televisión y en YouTube, o si la iglesia Trinity United Church of Christ se conformara a las caricaturas que algunos comentaristas han difundido, no hay duda alguna de que yo reaccionaría de forma muy parecida.

But the truth is, that isn't all that I know of the man. The man I met more than twenty years ago is a man who helped introduce me to my Christian faith, a man who spoke to me about our obligations to love one another, to care for the sick and lift up the poor.

He is a man who served his country as a U.S. Marine, who has studied and lectured at some of the finest universities and seminaries in the country, and who for over thirty years led a church that serves the community by doing God's work here on earth—by housing the homeless, ministering to the needy, providing day care services and scholarships and prison ministries, and reaching out to those suffering from HIV/AIDS.

In my first book, *Dreams from My Father*, I described the experience of my first service at Trinity:

"People began to shout, to rise from their seats and clap and cry out, a forceful wind carrying the reverend's voice up into the rafters. . . . And in that single note—hope!—I heard something else; at the foot of that cross, inside the thousands of churches across the city, I imagined the stories of ordinary black people merging with the stories of David and Goliath, Moses and Pharaoh, the Christians in the lion's den, Ezekiel's field of dry bones.

Those stories—of survival, and freedom, and hope—became our story, my story; the blood that had spilled was our blood, the tears our tears; until this black church, on this bright day, seemed once more a vessel carrying the story of a people into future generations and into a larger world. Our trials and triumphs became at once unique and universal, black and more than black; in chronicling our journey, the stories and songs gave us a means to reclaim memories that we didn't need to feel shame about . . . memories that all people might study and cherish—and with which we could start to rebuild."

Pero lo cierto es que eso no es todo lo que yo conozco de ese hombre. El hombre al que conocí hace más de veinte años es un hombre que ayudó a presentarme la fe cristiana, un hombre que me habló sobre nuestras obligaciones de amarnos unos a otros, de ocuparnos de los enfermos y levantar a los pobres.

Él es un hombre que sirvió a este país como Marine, que ha estudiado y ha dado conferencias en algunas de las mejores universidades y seminarios del país, y quien, por más de treinta años, dirigió una iglesia que sirve a la comunidad haciendo la obra de Dios aquí en la tierra: alojando a los sin hogar, ministrando a los necesitados, proporcionando servicios de asistencia de día, y becas, y ministerios en cárceles, y tendiendo la mano a quienes sufren VIH/SIDA.

En mi primer libro, *Dreams from My Father* [Sueños de mi padre], describí la experiencia de mi primer servicio en Trinity:

"La gente comenzó a gritar, a levantarse de sus asientos y aplaudir, y clamar, un fuerte viendo que elevaba hasta el techo la voz del reverendo… Y en esa única nota—¡esperanza!—oí algo más; a los pies de aquella cruz, en el interior de miles de iglesias por toda la ciudad, imaginé las historias de personas de raza negra comunes y corrientes mezclándose con las historias de David y Goliat, Moisés y Faraón, los cristianos en el foso de los leones, el campo de huesos secos de Ezequiel.

Esas historias—de supervivencia, y libertad, y esperanza—se convirtieron en nuestra historia, en mi historia; la sangre que se había derramado era nuestra sangre, las lágrimas, nuestras lágrimas; hasta que esa iglesia negra, en aquel brillante día, parecía una vez más una embarcación que llevaba la historia de un pueblo a futuras generaciones y a un mundo más grande. Nuestras pruebas y triunfos se convirtieron en un instante en únicos y universales, en negros y más que negros; al hacer una crónica de nuestro viaje, las historias y las canciones nos dieron un medio de reclamar recuerdos de los que no teníamos que sentirnos avergonzados… recuerdos que todas las gentes podrían estudiar y atesorar, y con los cuales podíamos comenzar a reconstruir".

That has been my experience at Trinity. Like other predominantly black churches across the country, Trinity embodies the black community in its entirety—the doctor and the welfare mom, the model student and the former gangbanger. Like other black churches, Trinity's services are full of raucous laughter and sometimes bawdy humor. They are full of dancing, clapping, screaming, and shouting that may seem jarring to the untrained ear.

The church contains in full the kindness and cruelty, the fierce intelligence and the shocking ignorance, the struggles and successes, the love and, yes, the bitterness and bias that make up the black experience in America.

And this helps explain, perhaps, my relationship with Reverend Wright. As imperfect as he may be, he has been like family to me. He strengthened my faith, officiated my wedding, and baptized my children.

Not once in my conversations with him have I heard him talk about any ethnic group in derogatory terms, or treat whites with whom he interacted with anything but courtesy and respect. He contains within him the contradictions—the good and the bad—of the community that he has served diligently for so many years.

I can no more disown him than I can disown the black community. I can no more disown him than I can my white grandmother—a woman who helped raise me, a woman who sacrificed again and again for me, a woman who loves me as much as she loves anything in this world, but a woman who once confessed her fear of black men who passed by her on the street, and who on more than one occasion has uttered racial or ethnic stereotypes that made me cringe.

These people are a part of me. And they are a part of America, this country that I love.

Esa ha sido mi experiencia en Trinity. Al igual que otras iglesias predominantemente negras por todo el país, Trinity representa a la comunidad de raza negra en su totalidad: el doctor y la madre que vive de la beneficencia, el estudiante modelo y el ex pandillero. Al igual que otras iglesias de color, los servicios de Trinity están llenos de estridentes risas y a veces humor subido de tono. Están llenas de danzas, de aplausos, de gritos que pueden parecer discordantes para el oído no entrenado.

La iglesia contiene plenamente la bondad y la crueldad, la intensa inteligencia y la sorprendente ignorancia, las batallas y los éxitos, el amor y, sí, la amargura y el prejuicio que constituyen la experiencia de las personas de color en Estados Unidos.

Y esto ayuda a explicar, quizá, mi relación con el reverendo Wright. Por imperfecto que él pueda ser, para mí ha sido como mi familia. Él fortaleció mi fe, ofició mi boda, y bautizó a mis hijas.

Ni una sola vez en mis conversaciones con él le oí hablar sobre ningún grupo étnico con términos despectivos, o tratar a los blancos con los que se relacionaba con otra cosa que no fuese cortesía y respeto. Él lleva en su interior las contradicciones — las buenas y las malas—de la comunidad a la que ha servido diligentemente por muchos años.

No puedo repudiarlo a él más de lo que puedo repudiar a la comunidad de raza negra. No puedo repudiarlo a él más de lo que puedo repudiar a mi abuela de raza blanca: una mujer que ayudó a criarme, una mujer que se sacrificó una y otra vez por mí, una mujer que me quiere tanto como quiere cualquier otra cosa en este mundo, pero una mujer que en una ocasión confesó su temor a los hombres de raza negra que pasaban a su lado en la calle, y quien en más de una ocasión ha pronunciado estereotipos raciales o étnicos que me horrorizaban.

Esas personas son una parte de mí. Y son una parte de Estados Unidos, este país al que amo.

Some will see this as an attempt to justify or excuse comments that are simply inexcusable. I can assure you it is not.

I suppose the politically safe thing would be to move on from this episode and just hope that it fades into the woodwork. We can dismiss Reverend Wright as a crank or a demagogue, just as some have dismissed Geraldine Ferraro, in the aftermath of her recent statements, as harboring some deep-seated racial bias.

But race is an issue that I believe this nation cannot afford to ignore right now. We would be making the same mistake that Reverend Wright made in his offending sermons about America—to simplify and stereotype and amplify the negative to the point that it distorts reality.

The fact is that the comments that have been made and the issues that have surfaced over the last few weeks reflect the complexities of race in this country that we've never really worked through—a part of our union that we have yet to perfect. And if we walk away now, if we simply retreat into our respective corners, we will never be able to come together and solve challenges like health care, or education, or the need to find good jobs for every American.

Understanding this reality requires a reminder of how we arrived at this point. As William Faulkner once wrote, "The past isn't dead and buried. In fact, it isn't even past."

We do not need to recite here the history of racial injustice in this country. But we do need to remind ourselves that so many of the disparities that exist in the African American community today can be directly traced to inequalities passed on from an earlier generation that suffered under the brutal legacy of slavery and Jim Crow.

Algunos verán esto como un intento de justificar o de excusar comentarios que son sencillamente inexcusables. Puedo asegurarles que no lo es.

Supongo que lo políticamente seguro sería avanzar dejando este episodio y simplemente esperar a que se desvanezca no se sabe dónde. Podemos rechazar al reverendo Wright como excéntrico o demagogo, al igual que algunos han rechazado a Geraldine Ferraro, después de sus recientes afirmaciones, considerando que albergaba algunos prejuicios profundamente arraigados.

Pero la raza es un asunto que creo que esta nación no puede permitirse pasar por alto en este momento. Estaríamos cometiendo el mismo error que cometió el reverendo Wright en sus ofensivos sermones sobre Estados Unidos: simplificar, y estereotipar, y ampliar lo negativo hasta el punto de que distorsione la realidad.

El hecho es que los comentarios que se han hecho y los problemas que han surgido en las últimas semanas reflejan las complejidades de la raza en este país que realmente nunca hemos solucionado, una parte de nuestra unión que aún tenemos que perfeccionar. Y si nos alejamos ahora, si sencillamente nos retiramos a nuestras respectivas esquinas, nunca seremos capaces de unirnos y resolver desafíos como la asistencia médica, o la educación, o la necesidad de encontrar buenos empleos para cada estadounidense.

Entender esta realidad requiere un recordatorio de cómo llegamos hasta este punto. Como escribió en una ocasión William Faulkner: "El pasado no está muerto y enterrado. De hecho, ni siquiera es pasado".

No necesitamos recitar aquí la historia de la injusticia racial en este país; pero sí necesitamos recordarnos a nosotros mismos que muchas de las disparidades que existen en la comunidad afroamericana en la actualidad pueden remontarse directamente a desigualdades transmitidas desde una generación anterior que sufrió bajo el brutal legado de esclavitud y Jim Crow.

Segregated schools were, and are, inferior schools; we still haven't fixed them, fifty years after Brown v. Board of Education, and the inferior education they provided, then and now, helps explain the pervasive achievement gap between today's black and white students.

Legalized discrimination—where blacks were prevented, often through violence, from owning property, or loans were not granted to African American business owners, or black homeowners could not access FHA mortgages, or blacks were excluded from unions, or the police force, or fire departments—meant that black families could not amass any meaningful wealth to bequeath to future generations.

That history helps explain the wealth and income gap between black and white, and the concentrated pockets of poverty that persist in so many of today's urban and rural communities.

A lack of economic opportunity among black men, and the shame and frustration that came from not being able to provide for one's family, contributed to the erosion of black families—a problem that welfare policies for many years may have worsened.

And the lack of basic services in so many urban black neighborhoods—parks for kids to play in, police walking the beat, regular garbage pickup, and building code enforcement—helped create a cycle of violence, blight, and neglect that continues to haunt us.

This is the reality in which Reverend Wright and other African Americans of his generation grew up. They came of age in the late fifties and early sixties, a time when segregation was still the law of the land and opportunity was systematically constricted.

Las escuelas segregadas eran, y son, escuelas inferiores; aún no nos hemos encargado de ellas, cincuenta años después de Brown contra la Junta de Educación, y la educación inferior que proporcionaban, entonces y ahora, ayuda a explicar la generalizada brecha de logros que existe entre los estudiantes de raza negra y blanca en la actualidad.

La discriminación legalizada—en la que se evitaba que personas de raza negra, con frecuencia mediante la violencia, poseyeran propiedades, o no se otorgaban préstamos a dueños de negocios afroamericanos, o donde dueños de casas de raza negra no tenían acceso a préstamos de la Administración General de la Vivienda (FHA), o se excluía a los negros de los sindicatos, o de la policía, o del departamento de bomberos— significaba que familias de raza negra no podían acumular ninguna riqueza significativa para legar a generaciones futuras.

Esa historia ayuda a explicar la brecha en riqueza e ingresos existente entre negros y blancos, y los concentrados bolsillos de pobreza que persisten en tantas de las comunidades urbanas y rurales de la actualidad.

Una falta de oportunidad económica entre hombres de raza negra, y la vergüenza y frustración que conllevaba no poder proveer para la familia, contribuyeron a la erosión de familias de raza negra, un problema que políticas de beneficencia por muchos años pueden haber empeorado.

Y la falta de servicios básicos en muchos barrios urbanos negros—parques donde los niños puedan jugar, policías patrullando, recogida regular de basura, y aplicación del código de construcción—ayudó a crear un ciclo de violencia, de ruina y de descuido que continúa persiguiéndonos.

Esta es la realidad en la que el reverendo Wright y otros afroamericanos de su generación crecieron. Fueron mayores de edad a final de los años cincuenta y principios de los sesenta, un periodo en el cual la segregación seguía siendo la ley de la tierra y la oportunidad era sistemáticamente restringida.

What's remarkable is not how many failed in the face of discrimination but how many men and women overcame the odds; how many were able to make a way out of no way for those like me who would come after them.

But for all those who scratched and clawed their way to get a piece of the American Dream, there were many who didn't make it—those who were ultimately defeated, in one way or another, by discrimination. That legacy of defeat was passed on to future generations—those young men and increasingly young women whom we see standing on street corners or languishing in our prisons, without hope or prospects for the future.

Even for those blacks who did make it, questions of race, and racism, continue to define their worldview in fundamental ways. For the men and women of Reverend Wright's generation, the memories of humiliation and doubt and fear have not gone away, nor have the anger and the bitterness of those years.

That anger may not get expressed in public, in front of white coworkers or white friends. But it does find voice in the barbershop or around the kitchen table. At times, that anger is exploited by politicians, to gin up votes along racial lines, or to make up for a politician's own failings.

And occasionally it finds voice in the church on Sunday morning, in the pulpit and in the pews. The fact that so many people are surprised to hear that anger in some of Reverend Wright's sermons simply reminds us of the old truism that the most segregated hour in American life occurs on Sunday morning.

That anger is not always productive; indeed, all too often it distracts attention from solving real problems; it keeps us from squarely facing our own complicity in our condition and prevents the African American community from forging the alliances it needs to bring about real

Lo notable no es cuántos fracasaron ante la discriminación, sino cuántos hombres y mujeres vencieron las desventajas; cuántos fueron capaces de hacer camino de la nada para aquellos que, como yo, vendrían después de ellos.

Pero por todos aquellos que se abrieron camino escarbando y arañando para conseguir una parte del Sueño Americano, hubo muchos que no lo lograron: quienes fueron finalmente vencidos, de un modo u otro, por la discriminación. Ese legado de derrota fue transmitido a futuras generaciones, esos hombres jóvenes y cada vez más mujeres a quienes vemos de pie en las esquinas de las calles o languideciendo en nuestras cárceles, sin esperanza o perspectivas para el futuro.

Aun para las personas de raza negra que sí lo lograron, cuestiones de raza, y de racismo, continúan definiendo su perspectiva de formas fundamentales. Para los hombres y mujeres de la generación del reverendo Wright, los recuerdos de humillación, y duda, y temor, no se han alejado, ni tampoco la ira y la amargura de aquellos años.

Esa ira puede que no llegue a expresarse en público, delante de compañeros de trabajo blancos o de amigos blancos; pero sí encuentra una voz en la barbería o alrededor de la mesa de la cocina. A veces, esa ira es explotada por políticos, para atrapar votos recurriendo a asuntos raciales, o para compensar los propios fracasos de un político.

Y ocasionalmente se expresa en la iglesia el domingo en la mañana, en el púlpito y en los bancos. El hecho de que tantas personas se sorprendan al oír esa ira en algunos de los sermones del reverendo Wright simplemente nos recuerda el viejo tópico de que la hora de mayor segregación en la vida estadounidense ocurre el domingo en la mañana.

Esa ira no siempre es productiva; además, con demasiada frecuencia distrae la atención de resolver problemas reales; evita que afrontemos de cara nuestra propia complicidad en nuestra condición y evita que la comunidad afroamericana forje las alianzas que necesita para producir un verdadero

change. But the anger is real; it is powerful; and to simply wish it away, to condemn it without understanding its roots, only serves to widen the chasm of misunderstanding that exists between the races.

In fact, a similar anger exists within segments of the white community. Most working- and middle-class white Americans don't feel that they have been particularly privileged by their race. Their experience is the immigrant experience—as far as they're concerned, no one's handed them anything, they've built it from scratch.

They've worked hard all their lives, many times only to see their jobs shipped overseas or their pension dumped after a lifetime of labor. They are anxious about their futures and feel their dreams slipping away; in an era of stagnant wages and global competition, opportunity comes to be seen as a zero-sum game, in which your dreams come at my expense.

So when they are told to bus their children to a school across town; when they hear that an African American is getting an advantage in landing a good job or a spot in a good college because of an injustice that they themselves never committed; when they're told that their fears about crime in urban neighborhoods are somehow prejudiced, resentment builds over time.

Like the anger within the black community, these resentments aren't always expressed in polite company. But they have helped shape the political landscape for at least a generation.

Anger over welfare and affirmative action helped forge the Reagan Coalition. Politicians routinely exploited fears of crime for their own electoral ends. Talk show hosts and conservative commentators built entire careers unmasking bogus claims of racism while dismissing legitimate discussions of racial injustice and inequality as mere political correctness or reverse racism.

cambio. Pero la ira es real; es poderosa; y simplemente desear que desaparezca, condenarla sin entender sus raíces, sólo sirve para ensanchar el abismo de malentendido y desacuerdo que existe entre las razas.

De hecho, una ira parecida existe dentro de segmentos de la comunidad blanca. La mayoría de estadounidenses de raza blanca de clase trabajadora y media no siente que haya sido particularmente privilegiados por su raza. Su experiencia es la experiencia inmigrante: en cuanto a ellos respecta, nadie les ha entregado nada, ellos lo han construido desde cero.

Han trabajado duro toda su vida, muchas veces sólo para ver que sus empleos se trasladan al extranjero o su pensión es rechazada tras toda una vida de trabajo. Están ansiosos por su futuro y sienten que sus sueños se les van de las manos; en una época de salarios congelados y competición global, la oportunidad llega a considerarse un juego de sumar cero, en el cual los sueños de otro llegan a costa mía.

Por tanto, cuando se les dice que lleven en autobús a sus hijos a una escuela al otro extremo de la ciudad; cuando oyen que un afroamericano está obteniendo una ventaja para conseguir un buen empleo o para entrar en una buena universidad debido a una injusticia que él mismo nunca cometió; cuando se les dice que sus temores por la delincuencia en barrios urbanos tienen ciertos prejuicios, se acumula resentimiento con el paso del tiempo.

Al igual que la ira dentro de la comunidad negra, esos resentimientos no siempre se expresan al estar en buena compañía; pero han ayudado a dar forma al paisaje político al menos durante una generación.

La ira en cuanto a la beneficencia y la acción afirmativa ayudó a forjar la Coalición Reagan. Los políticos, por rutina explotaban el miedo a la delincuencia para sus propios fines electorales. Presentadores de programas de entrevistas y comentaristas conservadores han construido sus carreras desenmascarando falsas afirmaciones de racismo y haciendo caso omiso, a la vez, a las discusiones sobre injusticia y desigualdad racial calificándolas de mera corrección política o racismo inverso.

Just as black anger often proved counterproductive, so have these white resentments distracted attention from the real culprits of the middle-class squeeze—a corporate culture rife with inside dealing, questionable accounting practices, and short-term greed; a Washington dominated by lobbyists and special interests; economic policies that favor the few over the many.

And yet, to wish away the resentments of white Americans, to label them as misguided or even racist, without recognizing they are grounded in legitimate concerns—this too widens the racial divide and blocks the path to understanding.

This is where we are right now. It's a racial stalemate we've been stuck in for years. Contrary to the claims of some of my critics, black and white, I have never been so naive as to believe that we can get beyond our racial divisions in a single election cycle or with a single candidacy—particularly a candidacy as imperfect as my own.

But I have asserted a firm conviction—a conviction rooted in my faith in God and my faith in the American people—that working together we can move beyond some of our old racial wounds, and that in fact we have no choice if we are to continue on the path of a more perfect union.

For the African American community, that path means embracing the burdens of our past without becoming victims of our past. It means continuing to insist on a full measure of justice in every aspect of American life.

But it also means binding our particular grievances—for better health care, and better schools, and better jobs—to the larger aspirations of all Americans—the white woman struggling to break the glass ceiling, the white man who's been laid off, the immigrant trying to feed his family.

Al igual que la ira de las personas de color con frecuencia demostró ser contraproducente, así esos resentimientos de las personas blancas distrajeron la atención de los verdaderos culpables de los aprietos de la clase media: abundancia de cultura colectiva con negocios internos, cuestionables prácticas contables, y avaricia a corto plazo; políticas económicas que favorecen a unos pocos sobre los muchos.

Y aun así, querer que desaparezcan los resentimientos de los estadounidenses blancos, catalogarlos de equivocados o incluso racistas, sin reconocer que están arraigados en preocupaciones legítimas; también esto ensancha la división racial y bloquea el camino hacia el entendimiento.

Ahí es donde estamos en este momento. Es un punto muerto racial en el que hemos estado atascados por años. Contrariamente a las reivindicaciones de algunos de mis críticos, blancos y de color, yo nunca he sido tan ingenuo como para creer que podemos ir más allá de nuestras divisiones raciales en un sólo ciclo de elecciones o con una sola candidatura, particularmente una candidatura tan imperfecta como la mía.

Pero he aseverado la firme convicción—una convicción arraigada en mi fe en Dios y en mi fe en el pueblo estadounidense—de que trabajando juntos podemos avanzar más allá de algunas de nuestras viejas heridas raciales, y que, de hecho, no tenemos otra elección si hemos de continuar en el camino de una unión más perfecta.

Para la comunidad afroamericana, ese camino significa aceptar las cargas de nuestro pasado sin convertirnos en víctimas de nuestro pasado. Significa seguir insistiendo en una plena medida de justicia en todos los aspectos de la vida estadounidense.

Pero también significa sujetar nuestras propias reivindicaciones particulares— por una mejor asistencia médica, y mejores escuelas, y mejores empleos—a las aspiraciones más grandes de todos los estadounidenses: la mujer blanca que lucha por romper la barrera invisible que le impide ascender, el hombre blanco que ha sido despedido, el inmigrante que intenta alimentar a su familia.

And it means taking full responsibility for our own lives—by demanding more from our fathers, and spending more time with our children, and reading to them, and teaching them that while they may face challenges and discrimination in their own lives, they must never succumb to despair or cynicism; they must always believe that they can write their own destiny.

Ironically, this quintessentially American—and yes, conservative—notion of self-help found frequent expression in Reverend Wright's sermons. But what my former pastor too often failed to understand is that embarking on a program of self-help also requires a belief that society can change.

The profound mistake of Reverend Wright's sermons is not that he spoke about racism in our society. It's that he spoke as if our society was static; as if no progress has been made; as if this country—a country that has made it possible for one of his own members to run for the highest office in the land and build a coalition of white and black, Latino and Asian, rich and poor, young and old—is still irrevocably bound to a tragic past.

But what we know—what we have seen—is that America can change. That is true genius of this nation. What we have already achieved gives us hope—the audacity to hope—for what we can and must achieve tomorrow.

In the white community, the path to a more perfect union means acknowledging that what ails the African American community does not just exist in the minds of black people, that the legacy of discrimination—and current incidents of discrimination, while less overt than in the past—are real and must be addressed.

Not just with words but with deeds—by investing in our schools and our communities, by enforcing our civil rights laws and ensuring fairness in

Y significa asumir plena responsabilidad de nuestras propias vidas, demandando más de nuestros padres, y pasando más tiempo con nuestros hijos, y leyéndoles historias, y enseñándoles que aunque puede que afronten desafíos y discriminación en sus propias vidas, nunca deben sucumbir a la desesperación o al cinismo; siempre deben creer que ellos pueden escribir su propio destino.

Irónicamente, esta idea estadounidense quintaesencial—y, sí, conservadora—de autoayuda con frecuencia encuentra expresión en los sermones del reverendo Wright. Pero lo que mi anterior pastor frecuentemente no entendía es que embarcarse en un programa de autoayuda también requiere la creencia en que la sociedad puede cambiar.

El profundo error de los sermones del reverendo Wright no es que él hablase sobre racismo en nuestra sociedad. Es que hablaba como si nuestra sociedad fuese estática; como si no se hubiera hecho ningún progreso; como si este país—un país que ha hecho posible que uno de sus propios miembros se presentase al puesto más elevado en la nación y construyera una coalición de blancos y negros, latinos y asiáticos, ricos y pobres, jóvenes y viejos—estuviera irrevocablemente atado a un pasado trágico.

Pero lo que sabemos—lo que hemos visto—es que Estados Unidos puede cambiar. Esa es la verdadera genialidad de esta nación. Lo que ya hemos logrado nos da esperanza—la audacia de la esperanza—para lo que podemos y debemos lograr mañana.

En la comunidad blanca, el camino hacia una unión más perfecta significa reconocer que lo que aflige a la comunidad afroamericana no sólo existe en las mentes de las personas de raza negra, que el legado de discriminación — y los actuales incidentes de discriminación, aunque menos patentes que en el pasado — es real y debe abordarse.

No sólo con palabras sino también con hechos: invirtiendo en nuestras escuelas y nuestras comunidades, haciendo cumplir nuestras leyes sobre

our criminal justice system, by providing this generation with ladders of opportunity that were unavailable for previous generations.

It requires all Americans to realize that your dreams do not have to come at the expense of my dreams, that investing in the health, welfare, and education of black and brown and white children will ultimately help all of America prosper.

In the end, then, what is called for is nothing more, and nothing less, than what all the world's great religions demand—that we do unto others as we would have them do unto us. Let us be our brother's keeper, scripture tells us. Let us be our sister's keeper. Let us find that common stake we all have in one another, and let our politics reflect that spirit as well.

For we have a choice in this country. We can accept a politics that breeds division, and conflict, and cynicism. We can tackle race only as spectacle—as we did in the OJ trial—or in the wake of tragedy, as we did in the aftermath of Katrina—or as fodder for the nightly news.

We can play Reverend Wright's sermons on every channel, every day and talk about them from now until the election, and make the only question in this campaign whether or not the American people think that I somehow believe or sympathize with his most offensive words.

We can pounce on some gaffe by a Hillary supporter as evidence that she's playing the race card, or we can speculate on whether white men will all flock to John McCain in the general election regardless of his policies.

We can do that.

derechos civiles y asegurando justicia en nuestro sistema de justicia criminal, proporcionando a esta generación peldaños de oportunidad que no estaban a disposición de anteriores generaciones.

Requiere que todos los estadounidenses comprendan que sus sueños no tienen que llegar a costa de mis sueños, que invertir en la salud, el bienestar y la educación de niños negros, y mulatos, y blancos, finalmente ayudará a prosperar a todo el país.

Al final, entonces, lo que se requiere no es nada más, ni nada menos, que aquello que todas las grandes religiones del mundo demandan: que hagamos a otros lo que nos gustaría que ellos nos hicieran a nosotros. Seamos el guardián de nuestro hermano, nos dice la escritura. Seamos el guardián de nuestra hermana. Encontremos esa marca común que todos tenemos el uno en el otro, y que nuestra política refleje también ese espíritu.

Porque tenemos una elección en este país. Podemos aceptar una política que alimente la división, y el conflicto, y el cinismo. Podemos abordar la carrera sólo como espectáculo — como hicimos en el juicio a OJ —; o tras la tragedia, como hicimos después del Katrina; o como forraje para las noticias de la noche.

Podemos retransmitir los sermones del reverendo Wright en todas las cadenas, cada día, y hablar de ellos desde ahora hasta las elecciones, y hacer que la única pregunta en esta campaña sea si el pueblo estadounidense piensa o no que yo, de algún modo, creo o comprendo sus palabras más ofensivas.

Podemos abalanzarnos sobre alguna equivocación por parte de algún partidario de Hillary como evidencia de que ella está jugando al programa de carreras, o podemos especular sobre si todos los hombres de raza blanca apoyarán o no a John McCain en las elecciones generales a pesar de cuáles sean sus políticas.

Podemos hacer eso.

But if we do, I can tell you that in the next election, we'll be talking about some other distraction. And then another one. And then another one. And nothing will change.

That is one option. Or, at this moment, in this election, we can come together and say, "Not this time."

This time we want to talk about the crumbling schools that are stealing the future of black children and white children and Asian children and Hispanic children and Native American children. This time we want to reject the cynicism that tells us that these kids can't learn, that those kids who don't look like us are somebody else's problem.

The children of America are not those kids, they are our kids, and we will not let them fall behind in a twenty-first century economy. Not this time.

This time we want to talk about how the lines in the emergency room are filled with whites and blacks and Hispanics who do not have health care, who don't have the power on their own to overcome the special interests in Washington, but who can take them on if we do it together.

This time we want to talk about the shuttered mills that once provided a decent life for men and women of every race, and the homes for sale that once belonged to Americans from every religion, every region, every walk of life.

This time we want to talk about the fact that the real problem is not that someone who doesn't look like you might take your job; it's that the corporation you work for will ship it overseas for nothing more than a profit.

This time we want to talk about the men and women of every color and creed who serve together, and fight together, and bleed together under

Pero si lo hacemos, puedo decirles que, en las siguientes elecciones, estaremos hablando sobre alguna otra distracción. Y después sobre otra. Y después sobre otra. Y nada cambiará.

Esa es una opción. O, en este momento, en estas elecciones, podemos unirnos y decir: "Esta vez no".

Esta vez queremos hablar sobre las escuelas que se desmoronan y que están robando el futuro de niños negros, y niños blancos, y niños asiáticos, y niños hispanos, y niños estadounidenses nativos. Esta vez queremos rechazar el cinismo que nos dice que esos niños no pueden aprender, que esos niños que no son como nosotros son problemas de otras personas.

Los niños de Estados Unidos no son esos niños, son nuestros niños, y no permitiremos que se queden atrás en una economía del siglo XXI. Esta vez no.

Esta vez queremos hablar de que las filas en las salas de urgencias están llenas de blancos, y negros, e hispanos que no tienen asistencia médica, que no tienen la capacidad por sí mismos de vencer los intereses especiales en Washington, pero que pueden enfrentarse a ellos si lo hacemos juntos.

Esta vez queremos hablar de las fábricas cerradas que anteriormente proporcionaban una vida decente a hombres y mujeres de todas las razas, y de las casas que están a la venta y que antes pertenecían a estadounidenses de todas las religiones, todas las regiones, de toda condición social.

Esta vez queremos hablar del hecho de que el verdadero problema no es que alguien que no se parece a uno podría quedarse con su empleo; es que la empresa para la cual usted trabaja enviará ese empleo al extranjero nada más que por obtener un beneficio.

Esta vez queremos hablar de los hombres y mujeres de todo color y credo que sirven juntos, y luchan juntos, y sangran juntos bajo la misma

the same proud flag. We want to talk about how to bring them home from a war that never should've been authorized and never should've been waged, and we want to talk about how we'll show our patriotism by caring for them, and their families, and giving them the benefits they have earned.

I would not be running for president if I didn't believe with all my heart that this is what the vast majority of Americans want for this country. This union may never be perfect, but generation after generation has shown that it can always be perfected.

And today, whenever I find myself feeling doubtful or cynical about this possibility, what gives me the most hope is the next generation—the young people whose attitudes and beliefs and openness to change have already made history in this election.

There is one story in particular that I'd like to leave you with today—a story I told when I had the great honor of speaking on Dr. King's birthday at his home church, Ebenezer Baptist, in Atlanta.

There is a young, twenty-three-year-old white woman named Ashley Baia who organized for our campaign in Florence, South Carolina. She had been working to organize a mostly African American community since the beginning of this campaign, and one day she was at a roundtable discussion where everyone went around telling their story and why they were there.

And Ashley said that when she was nine years old, her mother got cancer. And because she had to miss days of work, she was let go and lost her health care. They had to file for bankruptcy, and that's when Ashley decided that she had to do something to help her mom.

She knew that food was one of their most expensive costs, and so Ashley convinced her mother that what she really liked and really wanted to eat

orgullosa bandera. Queremos hablar de cómo traerlos a casa de una guerra que nunca debiera haberse autorizado y nunca debiera haberse entablado, y queremos hablar de cómo mostraremos nuestro patriotismo ocupándonos de ellos, y de sus familias, y dándoles los beneficios que se han ganado.

Yo no me presentaría a la presidencia si no creyera con todo mi corazón que esto es lo que la inmensa mayoría de estadounidenses quiere para este país. Esta unión puede que nunca sea perfecta, pero generación tras generación ha demostrado que siempre puede perfeccionarse.

Y hoy, siempre que me encuentro a mí mismo sintiendo dudas o cinismo en cuanto a esta posibilidad, lo que me da mayor esperanza es la siguiente generación: los jóvenes cuyas actitudes, y creencias, y apertura al cambio ya han hecho Historia en estas elecciones.

Hay una historia en particular que me gustaría dejarles hoy, una historia que relaté cuando tuve el gran honor de hablar sobre el cumpleaños del Dr. King en su iglesia, Ebenezer Baptist, en Atlanta.

Hay una joven de raza blanca de veintitrés años de edad llamada Ashley Baia que organizó nuestra campaña en Florence, Carolina del Sur. Ella había estado trabajando para organizar a una comunidad principalmente afroamericana desde el comienzo de esta campaña, y un día estaba en una mesa redonda donde cada uno iba relatando su historia y por qué estaba allí.

Y Ashley dijo que cuando ella tenía nueve años, su madre tuvo cáncer. Y debido a que tenía que faltar al trabajo algunos días, la despidieron y perdió su asistencia médica. Ellos tuvieron que presentar bancarrota, y fue entonces cuando Ashley decidió que tenía que hacer algo para ayudar a su mamá.

Ella sabía que los alimentos suponían uno de los mayores gastos, y por tanto Ashley convenció a su madre de que la comida que realmente le

more than anything else was mustard and relish sandwiches. Because that was the cheapest way to eat.

She did this for a year until her mom got better, and she told everyone at the roundtable that the reason she joined our campaign was so that she could help the millions of other children in the country who want and need to help their parents too.

Now Ashley might have made a different choice. Perhaps somebody told her along the way that the source of her mother's problems were blacks who were on welfare and too lazy to work, or Hispanics who were coming into the country illegally. But she didn't. She sought out allies in her fight against injustice.

Anyway, Ashley finishes her story and then goes around the room and asks everyone else why they're supporting the campaign. They all have different stories and reasons. Many bring up a specific issue. And finally they come to this elderly black man who's been sitting there quietly the entire time.

And Ashley asks him why he's there. And he does not bring up a specific issue. He does not say health care or the economy. He does not say education or the war. He does not say that he was there because of Barack Obama.

He simply says to everyone in the room, "I am here because of Ashley." "I'm here because of Ashley." By itself, that single moment of recognition between that young white girl and that old black man is not enough. It is not enough to give health care to the sick, or jobs to the jobless, or education to our children.

But it is where we start. It is where our union grows stronger. And as so many generations have come to realize over the two hundred and twenty-one years since a band of patriots signed that document in Philadelphia, that is where the perfection begins.

gustaba y realmente quería comer más que ninguna otra cosa eran los sándwiches de mostaza. Porque esa era la forma más barata de comer.

Ella hizo eso durante un año hasta que su mamá mejoró, y les dijo a todos en la mesa redonda que la razón por la cual se había unido a nuestra campaña fue para poder ayudar a los millones de otros niños en el país que quieren y necesitan también ayudar a sus padres.

Ahora bien, Ashley podría haber elegido de forma distinta. Quizá alguien le dijera a lo largo del camino que la fuente de los problemas de su madre eran personas de raza negra que estaban en la beneficencia y eran demasiado perezosos para trabajar, o hispanos que llegaban al país ilegalmente. Pero ella no hizo eso. Ella buscó aliados en su lucha contra la injusticia.

De todos modos, Ashley finaliza su historia y después va por la sala y pregunta a todos los demás por qué están apoyando la campaña. Todos tienen diferentes historias y razones. Muchos sacan a relucir un problema concreto. Y finalmente llegan a un anciano de raza negra que ha estado sentado en silencio todo el tiempo.

Y Ashley le pregunta por qué está allí. Y él no habla de un problema concreto; no dice que es la asistencia médica o la economía; no habla de la educación o de la guerra. No dice que estaba allí por Barack Obama. Simplemente dice a todos en la sala: "Estoy aquí por Ashley".

"Estoy aquí por Ashley". Por sí mismo, ese único instante de reconocimiento entre aquella joven de raza blanca y aquel anciano de raza negra no es suficiente. No es suficiente con proporcionar asistencia médica a los enfermos, o empleos a los que no tienen, o educación a nuestros niños.

Pero es ahí donde comenzamos. Es donde nuestra unión se fortalece. Y como muchas generaciones han llegado a comprender durante los doscientos veintiún años desde que un grupo de patriotas firmaron ese documento en Filadelfia, es ahí donde comienza la perfección.

Final Primary Night speech
June 3, 2008
St. Paul, Minnesota

*The battle for the Democratic presidential nomination
between Senator Obama and Senator Hillary Rodham Clinton,
who was trying to become the first woman presidential candidate
from a major party, drew record numbers of voters, but the political
newcomer's message of change won out over the former
First Lady's emphasis on experience.*

Tonight, after fifty-four hard-fought contests, our primary season has finally come to an end.

Sixteen months have passed since we first stood together on the steps of the Old State Capitol in Springfield, Illinois. Thousands of miles have been traveled. Millions of voices have been heard.

And because of what you said—because you decided that change must come to Washington; because you believed that this year must be different than all the rest; because you chose to listen not to your doubts or your fears but to your greatest hopes and highest aspirations, tonight we mark the end of one historic journey with the beginning of another—a journey that will bring a new and better day to America.

Discurso de la noche final de las Primarias

3 de junio de 2008
St. Paul, Minnesota

La batalla por la nominación demócrata a la presidencia entre el senador Obama y la senadora Hillary Rodham Clinton, quien trataba de convertirse en la primera mujer candidata a la presidencia de uno de los principales partidos, atrajo a números sin precedentes de votantes, pero el mensaje político de cambio del recién llegado se impuso al énfasis en la experiencia de la Primera Dama.

Esta noche, después de cincuenta y cuatro duros combates, nuestro periodo de primarias ha llegado a su fin.

Han pasado dieciséis meses desde que por primera vez estuvimos juntos sobre los escalones del Old State Capitol en Springfield, Illinois. Se han viajado cientos de miles de kilómetros; se han oído millones de voces.

Y debido a lo que ustedes dijeron, porque decidieron que el cambio debe llegar a Washington; porque creyeron que este año debe ser diferente de todos los demás; porque escogieron escuchar no a sus dudas o sus temores sino a sus mayores esperanzas y más altas aspiraciones, esta noche marcamos el final de un viaje histórico con el comienzo de otro: un viaje que traerá un nuevo y mejor día a Estados Unidos.

Tonight, I can stand before you and say that I will be the Democratic nominee for president of the United States.

At this defining moment for our nation, we should be proud that our party put forth one of the most talented, qualified field of individuals ever to run for this office. I have not just competed with them as rivals, I have learned from them as friends, as public servants, and as patriots who love America and are willing to work tirelessly to make this country better. They are leaders of this party, and leaders that America will turn to for years to come.

There are those who say that this primary has somehow left us weaker and more divided. Well I say that because of this primary, there are millions of Americans who have cast their ballot for the very first time. There are Independents and Republicans who understand that this election isn't just about the party in charge of Washington, it's about the need to change Washington. There are young people, and African Americans, and Latinos, and women of all ages who have voted in numbers that have broken records and inspired a nation.

All of you chose to support a candidate you believe in deeply. But at the end of the day, we aren't the reason you came out and waited in lines that stretched block after block to make your voice heard. You didn't do that because of me or Senator Clinton or anyone else.

You did it because you know in your hearts that at this moment—a moment that will define a generation—we cannot afford to keep doing what we've been doing. We owe our children a better future. We owe our country a better future. And for all those who dream of that future tonight, I say—let us begin the work together. Let us unite in common effort to chart a new course for America.

Esta noche, puedo estar delante de ustedes y decir que yo seré el nominado demócrata a la presidencia de los Estados Unidos.

En este momento determinante para nuestra nación, deberíamos estar orgullosos de que nuestro partido presentase a los candidatos más talentosos y cualificados que se hayan presentado nunca para este puesto. Yo no he competido con ellos sólo como rivales, he aprendido de ellos como amigos, como servidores públicos, y como patriotas que aman Estados Unidos y están dispuestos a trabajar sin descanso para hacer que este país sea mejor. Ellos son líderes de este partido, y líderes a los que Estados Unidos recurrirá en años venideros.

Hay quienes dicen que estas primarias de algún modo nos han dejado más débiles y más divididos. Bien, digo eso porque en estas primarias hay millones de estadounidenses que han emitido su voto por primera vez. Hay independientes y republicanos que entienden que estas elecciones no se tratan solamente del partido que dirija desde Washington, se tratan de la necesidad de cambiar Washington. Hay jóvenes, y afroamericanos, y latinos, y mujeres de todas las edades que han votado en números que han batido récords y han inspirado a una nación.

Todos ustedes escogieron apoyar a un candidato en el que creen profundamente. Pero al final, nosotros no somos la razón por la que ustedes salieron y esperaron en filas que recorrían bloque tras bloque para hacer oír su voz. Ustedes no hicieron eso por mí, o por la senadora Clinton, o por ninguna otra persona.

Lo hicieron porque saben en sus corazones que en este momento—un momento que definirá a una generación—no podemos permitirnos seguir haciendo lo que hemos estado haciendo. Les debemos a nuestros hijos un futuro mejor. Le debemos a nuestro país un futuro mejor. Y a todos aquellos que sueñan con ese futuro esta noche les digo: comencemos juntos el trabajo. Unámonos en un esfuerzo común por trazar un nuevo rumbo para Estados Unidos.

In just a few short months, the Republican Party will arrive in St. Paul with a very different agenda. They will come here to nominate John McCain, a man who has served this country heroically.

I honor that service, and I respect his many accomplishments, even if he chooses to deny mine. My differences with him are not personal; they are with the policies he has proposed in this campaign.

Because while John McCain can legitimately tout moments of independence from his party in the past, such independence has not been the hallmark of his presidential campaign.

There are many words to describe John McCain's attempt to pass off his embrace of George Bush's policies as bipartisan and new. But change is not one of them.

Change is a foreign policy that doesn't begin and end with a war that should've never been authorized and never been waged. I won't stand here and pretend that there are many good options left in Iraq, but what's not an option is leaving our troops in that country for the next hundred years—especially at a time when our military is overstretched, our nation is isolated, and nearly every other threat to America is being ignored.

We must be as careful getting out of Iraq as we were careless getting in— but start leaving we must.

It's time for Iraqis to take responsibility for their future. It's time to rebuild our military and give our veterans the care they need and the benefits they deserve when they come home. It's time to refocus our efforts on al-Qaeda's leadership and Afghanistan, and rally the world against the common threats of the twenty-first century—terrorism and nuclear weapons, climate change and poverty, genocide and disease. That's what change is.

En sólo unos pocos y cortos meses, el partido republicano llegará a St. Paul con una agenda muy diferente. Ellos vendrán aquí para nominar a John McCain, un hombre que ha servido a este país heroicamente.

Yo honro ese servicio, y respeto sus muchos logros, aun si él escoge negar los míos. Mis diferencias con él no son personales; lo son en cuanto a las políticas que él ha propuesto en esta campaña.

Porque mientras que John McCain puede pregonar legítimamente momentos de independencia de su partido en el pasado, tal independencia no ha sido la marca de su campaña presidencial.

Hay muchas palabras para describir el intento de John McCain de restar importancia a su aceptación de las políticas de George Bush considerándolas bipartidarias y nuevas. Pero el cambio no es una de ellas.

El cambio es una política exterior que no comienza y termina con una guerra que nunca debiera haber sido autorizada y nunca debiera haberse hecho. Yo no estaré aquí y fingiré que quedan muchas buenas opciones en Iraq, y lo que no es una opción es dejar a nuestras tropas en ese país durante los próximos cien años; especialmente en un momento en que nuestro ejército está demasiado forzado, nuestra nación está aislada, y casi todas las demás amenazas a Estados Unidos se están pasando por alto.

Debemos ser tan cautelosos para salir de Iraq como descuidados fuimos para entrar; pero debemos comenzar a salir.

Es momento de que los iraquíes asuman la responsabilidad de su futuro. Es momento de que reconstruyamos nuestro ejército y proporcionemos a nuestros veteranos el cuidado que necesitan y los beneficios que merecen cuando regresen a casa. Es momento de reenfocar nuestros esfuerzos en cuanto al liderazgo de al-Qaeda y Afganistán, y que reunamos al mundo contra las amenazas comunes del siglo XXI: el terrorismo y las armas nucleares, el cambio climático y la pobreza, el genocidio y la enfermedad. Eso es el cambio.

Change is realizing that meeting today's threats requires not just our firepower but the power of our diplomacy—tough, direct diplomacy where the president of the United States isn't afraid to let any petty dictator know where America stands and what we stand for.

We must once again have the courage and conviction to lead the free world. That is the legacy of Roosevelt, and Truman, and Kennedy. That's what the American people want. That's what change is.

Change is building an economy that rewards not just wealth but the work and workers who created it.

It's understanding that the struggles facing working families can't be solved by spending billions of dollars on more tax breaks for big corporations and wealthy CEOs, but by giving the middle class a tax break, and investing in our crumbling infrastructure, and transforming how we use energy, and improving our schools, and renewing our commitment to science and innovation. It's understanding that fiscal responsibility and shared prosperity can go hand in hand, as they did when Bill Clinton was president.

John McCain has spent a lot of time talking about trips to Iraq in the last few weeks, but maybe if he spent some time taking trips to the cities and towns that have been hardest hit by this economy—cities in Michigan, and Ohio, and right here in Minnesota—he'd understand the kind of change that people are looking for.

Maybe if he went to Iowa and met the student who works the night shift after a full day of class and still can't pay the medical bills for a sister who's ill, he'd understand that she can't afford four more years of a health care plan that only takes care of the healthy and wealthy.

Cambio es entender que enfrentarse a las actuales amenazas requiere no sólo la potencia de nuestro fuego sino el poder de nuestra diplomacia: una diplomacia férrea y directa en la que el presidente de los Estados Unidos no tenga miedo a hacer saber a cualquier dictador mezquino en qué postura está Estados Unidos y lo que defendemos.

Una vez más debemos tener la valentía y la convicción de guiar al mundo libre. Ese es el legado de Roosevelt, y Truman, y Kennedy. Eso es lo que quiere el pueblo estadounidense. Eso es el cambio.

Cambio es construir una economía que recompense no sólo la riqueza sino también el trabajo y a los trabajadores que la crearon.

Es entender que las luchas a que se enfrentan las familias trabajadoras no pueden resolverse gastando miles de millones de dólares en más recortes de impuestos para grandes empresas y ricos ejecutivos, sino dando a la clase media un recorte de impuestos, e invirtiendo en nuestra desmoronada infraestructura, y transformando el modo en que utilizamos la energía, y mejorando nuestras escuelas, y renovando nuestro compromiso con la ciencia y la innovación. Es entender que la responsabilidad fiscal y la prosperidad compartida van de la mano, como iban cuando Bill Clinton era presidente.

John McCain ha empleado mucho tiempo hablando de viajes a Iraq en las últimas semanas, pero quizá si emplease algún tiempo haciendo viajes a las ciudades y pueblos que han sido más golpeadas por esta economía —ciudades en Michigan, y Ohio, y justamente aquí en Minnesota—, entendería el tipo de cambio que la gente está buscando.

Quizá si fuese a Iowa y conociese al estudiante que trabaja en el turno de noche después de un día entero de clases y aun así no puede pagar las cuentas médicas de una hermana que está enferma, entendería que ella no puede permitirse otros cuatro años más de un plan de asistencia médica que solamente se ocupa de los sanos y los ricos.

She needs us to pass a health care plan that guarantees insurance to every American who wants it and brings down premiums for every family who needs it. That's the change we need.

Maybe if he went to Pennsylvania and met the man who lost his job but can't even afford the gas to drive around and look for a new one, he'd understand that we can't afford four more years of our addiction to oil from dictators.

That man needs us to pass an energy policy that works with automakers to raise fuel standards, and makes corporations pay for their pollution, and oil companies invest their record profits in a clean energy future—an energy policy that will create millions of new jobs that pay well and can't be outsourced. That's the change we need.

And maybe if he spent some time in the schools of South Carolina or St. Paul or where he spoke tonight in New Orleans, he'd understand that we can't afford to leave the money behind for No Child Left Behind, that we owe it to our children to invest in early childhood education, to recruit an army of new teachers and give them better pay and more support, to finally decide that in this global economy, the chance to get a college education should not be a privilege for the wealthy few but the birthright of every American.

That's the change we need in America. That's why I'm running for president.

The other side will come here in September and offer a very different set of policies and positions, and that is a debate I look forward to. It is a debate the American people deserve.

Ella necesita que aprobemos un plan de asistencia médica que garantice un seguro para cada estadounidense que lo quiera, y que baje las primas a cada familia que lo necesite. Ese es el cambio que necesitamos.

Quizá si fuese a Pennsylvania y conociese al hombre que perdió su empleo pero que ni siquiera puede permitirse la gasolina para salir a buscar uno nuevo, entendería que no podemos permitirnos otros cuatro años más de nuestra adicción al petróleo de dictadores.

Ese hombre necesita que aprobemos una política de energía que trabaje con los fabricantes de vehículos para elevar los estándares del combustible, y que haga que las empresas paguen por la contaminación que producen, y que las compañías petroleras inviertan sus beneficios récord en un futuro con energía limpia; una política energética que cree millones de nuevos empleos con buenos salarios y que no pueda contratar de fuentes ajenas. Ese es el cambio que necesitamos.

Y quizá si pasase algún tiempo en las escuelas de Carolina del Sur o St. Paul, o donde habló esta noche en Nueva Orleans, entendería que no podemos permitirnos dejar atrás el dinero para el programa "Ningún niño dejado atrás", que les debemos a nuestros niños inversiones en la educación primaria, reclutar a un ejército de nuevos maestros y darles mejores salarios y más apoyo, decidir finalmente que en esta economía global, la oportunidad de obtener educación universitaria no debería ser un privilegio de los pocos ricos sino el derecho de nacimiento de todos los estadounidenses.

Ese es el cambio que necesitamos en Estados Unidos. Por eso me presento como candidato a presidente.

El otro bando vendrá aquí en septiembre y ofrecerá un conjunto de políticas y posturas muy diferentes, y ese es un debate que estoy deseando que llegue. Es un debate que el pueblo estadounidense merece.

But what you don't deserve is another election that's governed by fear, and innuendo, and division. What you won't hear from this campaign or this party is the kind of politics that uses religion as a wedge and patriotism as a bludgeon—that sees our opponents not as competitors to challenge but as enemies to demonize. Because we may call ourselves Democrats and Republicans, but we are Americans first. We are always Americans first.

Despite what the good Senator from Arizona said tonight, I have seen people of differing views and opinions find common cause many times during my two decades in public life, and I have brought many together myself.

In our country, I have found that this cooperation happens not because we agree on everything but because behind all the labels and false divisions and categories that define us, beyond all the petty bickering and point-scoring in Washington, Americans are a decent, generous, compassionate people, united by common challenges and common hopes. And every so often, there are moments that call on that fundamental goodness to make this country great again.

So it was for that band of patriots who declared in a Philadelphia hall the formation of a more perfect union, and for all those who gave on the fields of Gettysburg and Antietam their last full measure of devotion to save that same union.

So it was for the Greatest Generation that conquered fear itself and liberated a continent from tyranny, and made this country home to untold opportunity and prosperity.

So it was for the workers who stood out on the picket lines, the women who shattered glass ceilings, the children who braved a Selma bridge for freedom's cause.

Pero lo que ustedes no merecen son otras elecciones que estén gobernadas por el temor, y las insinuaciones, y la división. Lo que ustedes no oirán desde esta campaña o este partido es el tipo de política que utiliza la religión como brecha y el patriotismo como coacción; que ve a nuestros oponentes no como competidores a quienes desafiar sino como enemigos a quienes demonizar. Porque puede que nos denominemos demócratas o republicanos, pero primero somos estadounidenses. Siempre somos primero estadounidenses.

A pesar de lo que el buen senador por Arizona dijo esta noche, yo he visto a personas de diferentes puntos de vista y opiniones encontrar una causa común muchas veces durante mis dos décadas en la vida pública, y yo mismo he unido a muchas de ellas.

En nuestro país, he visto que esta cooperación se produce no porque estemos de acuerdo en todo, sino porque detrás de todas las etiquetas y falsas divisiones y categorías que nos definen, por encima de las insignificantes peleas y de marcar puntos en Washington, los estadounidenses son un pueblo decente, generoso y compasivo, unido por desafíos comunes y esperanzas comunes. Y de vez en cuando, hay momentos que exigen esa bondad fundamental para volver a hacer grande a este país.

Así fue para ese grupo de patriotas que declararon en un salón en Filadelfia la formación de una unión más perfecta, y para todos aquellos que dieron en los campos de Gettysburg y Antietam su más plena medida de dedicación a salvar esa misma unión.

Así fue para la Generación Grande que conquistó al miedo mismo y liberó a un continente de la tiranía, e hizo de este país el hogar de fabulosas oportunidades y prosperidad.

Así fue para los trabajadores que estuvieron en los piquetes, las mujeres que hicieron pedazos los obstáculos para ascender, los niños que hicieron frente a un puente Selma por la causa de la libertad.

So it has been for every generation that faced down the greatest challenges and the most improbable odds to leave their children a world that's better, and kinder, and more just.

And so it must be for us.

America, this is our moment. This is our time.

Our time to turn the page on the policies of the past. Our time to bring new energy and new ideas to the challenges we face. Our time to offer a new direction for the country we love.

I face this challenge with profound humility and knowledge of my own limitations. But I also face it with limitless faith in the capacity of the American people.

Because if we are willing to work for it, and fight for it, and believe in it, then I am absolutely certain that generations from now, we will be able to look back and tell our children that this was the moment when we began to provide care for the sick and good jobs to the jobless; this was the moment when the rise of the oceans began to slow and our planet began to heal; this was the moment when we ended a war and secured our nation and restored our image as the last, best hope on earth.

Así ha sido para cada generación que afrontó los mayores desafíos y las más improbables probabilidades para dejar a sus hijos un mundo que sea mejor, y más agradable, y más justo.

Y así debe ser para nosotros.

Estados Unidos, este es nuestro momento.

Este es nuestro tiempo. Nuestro momento para pasar página en las políticas del pasado. Nuestro momento para aportar nueva energía y nuevas ideas a los desafíos que afrontamos. Nuestro momento para ofrecer una nueva dirección para el país que amamos.

Yo afronto este desafío con profunda humildad y conocimiento de mis propias limitaciones. Pero también lo afronto con una fe ilimitada en la capacidad del pueblo estadounidense.

Porque si estamos dispuestos a trabajar por ello, y a luchar por ello, y a creer en ello, entonces estoy totalmente seguro de que, en próximas generaciones, podremos mirar atrás y decir a nuestros hijos que este fue el momento en que comenzamos a proporcionar cuidado a los enfermos y empleos a quienes no tenían; este fue el momento en que la crecida de los océanos comenzó a ralentizarse y nuestro planeta comenzó a sanar; este fue el momento en que terminamos una guerra, y aseguramos nuestra nación, y restauramos nuestra imagen como la última, la mejor esperanza en la tierra.

A World That Stands as One speech
July 24, 2008
Berlin, Germany

*Following in the footsteps of John F. Kennedy, Ronald Reagan,
and Bill Clinton, Senator Obama went to Berlin to kick off his overseas
campaign tour with an optimistic appeal to tear down the
walls of division worldwide.*

I know that I don't look like the Americans who've previously spoken in this great city. The journey that led me here is improbable. My mother was born in the heartland of America, but my father grew up herding goats in Kenya. His father—my grandfather—was a cook, a domestic servant to the British.

At the height of the Cold War, my father decided, like so many others in the forgotten corners of the world, that his yearning—his dream— required the freedom and opportunity promised by the West. And so he wrote letter after letter to universities all across America until somebody, somewhere answered his prayer for a better life.

That is why I'm here. And you are here because you too know that yearning. This city, of all cities, knows the dream of freedom. And you know that the only reason we stand here tonight is because men and women from both of our nations came together to work, and struggle, and sacrifice for that better life.

Discurso "Un mundo que es uno"
24 de julio de 2008
Berlín, Alemania

Siguiendo los pasos de John F. Kennedy, Ronald Reagan y Bill Clinton, el senador Obama viajó a Berlín para empezar su gira de campaña en el extranjero con un optimista llamamiento a derribar los muros de división en todo el mundo.

Sé que no me parezco a los estadounidenses que han hablado anteriormente en esta gran ciudad. El viaje que me ha traído aquí es improbable. Mi madre nació en el corazón de Estados Unidos, pero mi padre se crió cuidando cabras en Kenia. Su padre—mi abuelo—era cocinero, sirviente doméstico de los británicos.

En plena Guerra Fría, mi padre decidió, como muchos otros en los rincones olvidados del mundo, que su anhelo—su sueño—requería la libertad y la oportunidad prometida por Occidente. Y, por tanto, escribió carta tras carta a universidades por todo Estados Unidos hasta que alguien, en algún lugar, respondió su oración por una vida mejor.

Por eso estoy aquí. Y ustedes están aquí porque también conocen ese anhelo. Esta ciudad, de entre todas las ciudades, conoce el sueño de la libertad. Y ustedes saben que la única razón por la cual estamos aquí esta noche es porque hombres y mujeres de nuestros dos países se unieron para trabajar, y para luchar, y para sacrificarse por esa vida mejor.

Ours is a partnership that truly began sixty years ago this summer, on the day when the first American plane touched down at Templehof.

On that day, much of this continent still lay in ruin. The rubble of this city had yet to be built into a wall. The Soviet shadow had swept across Eastern Europe, while in the West, America, Britain, and France took stock of their losses and pondered how the world might be remade.

This is where the two sides met. And on the twenty-fourth of June, 1948, the Communists chose to blockade the western part of the city. They cut off food and supplies to more than two million Germans in an effort to extinguish the last flame of freedom in Berlin.

The size of our forces was no match for the much larger Soviet Army. And yet retreat would have allowed Communism to march across Europe. Where the last war had ended, another World War could have easily begun. All that stood in the way was Berlin.

And that's when the airlift began—when the largest and most unlikely rescue in history brought food and hope to the people of this city.

The odds were stacked against success. In the winter, a heavy fog filled the sky above, and many planes were forced to turn back without dropping off the needed supplies. The streets where we stand were filled with hungry families who had no comfort from the cold.

But in the darkest hours, the people of Berlin kept the flame of hope burning. The people of Berlin refused to give up. And on one fall day, hundreds of thousands of Berliners came here, to the Tiergarten, and heard the city's mayor implore the world not to give up on freedom.

La nuestra es una colaboración que comenzó verdaderamente hará setenta años este verano, el día en que el primer avión estadounidense aterrizó en Templehof.

En aquel tiempo, gran parte de este continente estaba aún en ruinas. Los escombros de esta ciudad aún tenían que ser convertidos en un muro. La sombra soviética se había extendido por toda Europa Oriental, mientras que en Occidente, Estados Unidos, Gran Bretaña y Francia hacían recuento de sus pérdidas y pensaban en cómo el mundo podría rehacerse.

Ahí es donde se encontraron los dos bandos. Y el día veinticuatro de junio de 1948, los comunistas escogieron bloquear la parte occidental de la ciudad. Interrumpieron el suministro de alimentos y existencias a más de dos millones de alemanes en un esfuerzo por extinguir la última llama de libertad en Berlín.

El tamaño de nuestras fuerzas armadas no estaba a la altura del ejército soviético, mucho más grande. Y, aun así, la retirada habría permitido al comunismo marchar por Europa. Donde la última guerra había terminado, podría haber comenzado fácilmente otra Guerra Mundial. Lo único que se interponía en el camino era Berlín.

Y ahí comenzó el transporte por avión; cuando el rescate más grande y más improbable de la Historia llevó alimentos y esperanza a las personas de esta ciudad.

Las probabilidades estaban en contra del éxito. En el invierno, una densa niebla llenaba el cielo, y muchos aviones se vieron obligados a regresar sin dejar las necesarias provisiones. Las calles donde hoy estamos estaban llenas de familias hambrientas que no encontraban consuelo en el frío.

Pero en los peores momentos, el pueblo de Berlín mantuvo ardiendo la llama de la esperanza. El pueblo de Berlín se negó a abandonar. Y un día de otoño, cientos de miles de berlineses vinieron aquí, al Tiergarten, y escucharon al alcalde de la ciudad implorar al mundo que no renunciase a la libertad.

"There is only one possibility," he said. "For us to stand together united until this battle is won. . . . The people of Berlin have spoken. We have done our duty, and we will keep on doing our duty. People of the world: now do your duty. . . . People of the world, look at Berlin!"

People of the world—look at Berlin!

Look at Berlin, where Germans and Americans learned to work together and trust each other less than three years after facing each other on the field of battle.

Look at Berlin, where the determination of a people met the generosity of the Marshall Plan and created a German miracle, where a victory over tyranny gave rise to NATO, the greatest alliance ever formed to defend our common security.

Look at Berlin, where the bullet holes in the buildings and the somber stones and pillars near the Brandenburg Gate insist that we never forget our common humanity.

Sixty years after the airlift, we are called on again. History has led us to a new crossroad, with new promise and new peril. When you, the German people, tore down that wall—a wall that divided East and West, freedom and tyranny, fear and hope—walls came tumbling down around the world.

From Kiev to Cape Town, prison camps were closed, and the doors of democracy were opened. Markets opened too, and the spread of information and technology reduced barriers to opportunity and prosperity.

"Hay una única posibilidad—dijo él—. Que permanezcamos unidos hasta que se gane esta batalla... El pueblo de Berlín ha hablado. Hemos cumplido con nuestra obligación, y seguiremos cumpliendo con nuestra obligación. Pueblos del mundo: cumplan ahora con su obligación... Pueblos del mundo, ¡miren a Berlín!"

Pueblos del mundo: ¡miren a Berlín!

Miren a Berlín, donde alemanes y estadounidenses aprendieron a trabajar juntos y a confiar el uno en el otro menos de tres años después de enfrentarse el uno al otro en el campo de batalla.

Miren a Berlín, donde la determinación de un pueblo se encontró con la generosidad del Plan Marshall y creó el milagro alemán, donde una victoria sobre la tiranía hizo surgir la OTAN, la mayor alianza jamás formada para defender nuestra seguridad común.

Miren a Berlín, donde los agujeros de las balas en los edificios y las sombrías piedras y pilares cerca de la Puerta de Brandenburgo insisten en que nunca olvidemos nuestra humanidad común.

Setenta años después del transporte con aviones, somos llamados de nuevo. La Historia nos ha llevado a una nueva encrucijada, con una nueva promesa y un nuevo peligro. Cuando ustedes, el pueblo alemán, derribaron ese muro—un muro que dividía Occidente y Oriente, la libertad y la tiranía, el miedo y la esperanza—, otros muros llegaron a venirse abajo por todo el mundo.

Desde Kiev hasta Cape Town, se cerraron campamentos para prisioneros y se abrieron las puertas de la democracia. Los mercados también se abrieron, y la difusión de información y de tecnología redujo barreras de oportunidad y de prosperidad.

The fall of the Berlin Wall brought new hope. But that very closeness has given rise to new dangers—dangers that cannot be contained within the borders of a country or by the distance of an ocean.

The terrorists of September 11th plotted in Hamburg and trained in Kandahar and Karachi before killing thousands from all over the globe on American soil.

As we speak, cars in Boston and factories in Beijing are melting the ice caps in the Arctic, shrinking coastlines in the Atlantic, and bringing drought to farms from Kansas to Kenya.

Poorly secured nuclear material in the former Soviet Union or secrets from a scientist in Pakistan could help build a bomb that detonates in Paris. The poppies in Afghanistan become the heroin in Berlin. The poverty and violence in Somalia breeds the terror of tomorrow. The genocide in Darfur shames the conscience of us all.

In this new world, such dangerous currents have swept along faster than our efforts to contain them. That is why we cannot afford to be divided. No one nation, no matter how large or powerful, can defeat such challenges alone.

None of us can deny these threats or escape responsibility in meeting them. Yet, in the absence of Soviet tanks and a terrible wall, it has become easy to forget this truth. And if we're honest with each other, we know that sometimes, on both sides of the Atlantic, we have drifted apart and forgotten our shared destiny.

In Europe, the view that America is part of what has gone wrong in our world, rather than a force to help make it right, has become all too common. In America, there are voices that deride and deny the importance of Europe's role in our security and our future. Both views

La caída del Muro de Berlín trajo nueva esperanza. Pero precisamente esa cercanía ha dado lugar a nuevos peligros, peligros que no pueden contenerse dentro de las fronteras de un país o por la distancia de un océano.

Los terroristas del 11 de septiembre construyeron su trama en Hamburgo y se entrenaron en Kandahar y Karachi antes de matar a miles de personas de todo el mundo en suelo estadounidense.

Mientras hablamos, autos en Boston y fábricas en Beijing están derritiendo el hielo en el Ártico, haciendo retroceder costas en el Atlántico, y llevando sequía a granjas desde Kansas hasta Kenia.

Material nuclear mal protegido en la anterior Unión Soviética o secretos de un científico en Pakistán podrían ayudar a construir una bomba que detone en París. Las amapolas en Afganistán se convierten en la heroína en Berlín. La pobreza y la violencia en Somalia alimenta el terror del mañana. El genocidio en Darfur avergüenza la conciencia de todos nosotros.

En este nuevo mundo, corrientes muy peligrosas se han extendido con más rapidez que nuestros esfuerzos para contenerlas. Por eso no podemos permitirnos estar divididos. Ninguna nación, sin importar lo grande o poderosa que sea, puede derrotar tales desafíos por sí sola.

Ninguno de nosotros puede negar estas amenazas o escaparse de la responsabilidad de afrontarlas. Sin embargo, en ausencia de tanques soviéticos y un muro terrible, se ha vuelto fácil olvidar esta verdad. Y si somos sinceros unos con otros, sabemos que a veces, por parte de ambos lados del Atlántico, nos hemos alejado y hemos olvidado nuestro destino compartido.

En Europa, el punto de vista de que Estados Unidos es parte de lo que ha ido mal en nuestro mundo, en lugar de ser una fuerza para ayudar a que vaya bien, se ha vuelto demasiado común. En Estados Unidos, hay voces que ridiculizan y niegan la importancia del papel de Europa en

miss the truth—that Europeans today are bearing new burdens and taking more responsibility in critical parts of the world, and that just as American bases built in the last century still help defend the security of this continent, so does our country still sacrifice greatly for freedom around the globe.

Yes, there have been differences between America and Europe. No doubt, there will be differences in the future. But the burdens of global citizenship continue to bind us together. A change of leadership in Washington will not lift this burden.

In this new century, Americans and Europeans alike will be required to do more—not less. Partnership and cooperation among nations is not a choice; it is the one way, the only way, to protect our common security and advance our common humanity.

That is why the greatest danger of all is to allow new walls to divide us from one another.

The walls between old allies on either side of the Atlantic cannot stand. The walls between the countries with the most and those with the least cannot stand. The walls between races and tribes, natives and immigrants, Christian and Muslim and Jew cannot stand. These now are the walls we must tear down.

We know they have fallen before. After centuries of strife, the people of Europe have formed a Union of promise and prosperity. Here, at the base of a column built to mark victory in war, we meet in the center of a Europe at peace. Not only have walls come down in Berlin, but they have come down in Belfast, where Protestant and Catholic found a way to live together; in the Balkans, where our Atlantic alliance ended wars and brought savage war criminals to justice; and in South Africa, where the struggle of a courageous people defeated apartheid.

nuestra seguridad y nuestro futuro. Ambos puntos de vista pasan por alto la verdad: que los europeos en la actualidad soportan nuevas cargas y asumen más responsabilidad en partes críticas del mundo, y que al igual que las bases estadounidenses construidas en el último siglo aún ayudan a defender la seguridad de este continente, así nuestro país sigue haciendo un gran sacrificio por la libertad en todo el planeta.

Sí, ha habido diferencias entre Estados Unidos y Europa. Sin duda, habrá diferencias en el futuro; pero las cargas de la ciudadanía global continúan uniéndonos. Un cambio de liderazgo en Washington no quitará esta carga.

En este nuevo siglo se requerirá a estadounidenses y europeos por igual que hagan más, no menos. La colaboración y la cooperación entre naciones no es una elección; es el único camino, el único camino para proteger nuestra seguridad común y avanzar nuestra humanidad común.

Por eso el mayor peligro de todos es permitir que nuevos muros nos dividan los unos de los otros.

Los muros entre viejos aliados a ambos lados del Atlántico no pueden permanecer. Los muros entre los países con más y los países con menos no pueden permanecer. Los muros entre razas y tribus, entre nativos e inmigrantes, entre cristianos, musulmanes y judíos no pueden permanecer. Esos son ahora los muros que debemos derribar.

Sabemos que han caído antes. Después de siglos de peleas, los pueblos de Europa han formado una Unión de promesa y prosperidad. Aquí, en la base de una columna construida para marcar la victoria en la guerra, nos reunimos en el centro de una Europa en paz. Los muros no sólo han sido derribados en Berlín, sino también en Belfast, donde protestantes y católicos encontraron una manera de vivir juntos; en los Balcanes, donde nuestra alianza Atlántica puso fin a guerras y llevó a salvajes criminales de guerra ante la justicia; y en Sudáfrica, donde la lucha de un pueblo valiente derrotó el apartheid.

So history reminds us that walls can be torn down. But the task is never easy.

True partnership and true progress require constant work and sustained sacrifice. They require sharing the burdens of development and diplomacy, of progress and peace. They require allies who will listen to each other, learn from each other, and, most of all, trust each other.

That is why America cannot turn inward. That is why Europe cannot turn inward. America has no better partner than Europe.

Now is the time to build new bridges across the globe as strong as the one that bound us across the Atlantic. Now is the time to join together, through constant cooperation, strong institutions, shared sacrifice, and a global commitment to progress, to meet the challenges of the twenty-first century. It was this spirit that led airlift planes to appear in the sky above our heads, and people to assemble where we stand today. And this is the moment when our nations—and all nations—must summon that spirit anew.

Now the world will watch and remember what we do here—what we do with this moment. Will we extend our hand to the people in the forgotten corners of this world who yearn for lives marked by dignity and opportunity, by security and justice? Will we lift the child in Bangladesh from poverty, shelter the refugee in Chad, and banish the scourge of AIDS in our time?

Will we stand for the human rights of the dissident in Burma, the blogger in Iran, or the voter in Zimbabwe? Will we give meaning to the words "never again" in Darfur?

Por tanto, la Historia nos recuerda que se pueden derribar muros. Pero la tarea no es nunca fácil.

La verdadera colaboración y el verdadero progreso requieren trabajo constante y sacrificio sostenido. Requieren compartir las cargas del desarrollo y la diplomacia, del progreso y de la paz. Requieren aliados que se escuchen unos a otros, que aprendan unos de otros y, sobre todo, que confíen unos en otros.

Por eso Estados Unidos no puede volverse hacia el interior. Por eso Europa no puede volverse hacia el interior. Estados Unidos no tiene mejor colaborador que Europa.

Ahora es el momento de construir nuevos puentes a lo largo del planeta tan fuertes como el que nos une cruzando el Atlántico. Ahora es el momento de reunirnos, mediante la cooperación constante, fuertes instituciones, sacrificio compartido, y un compromiso global con el progreso, para afrontar los desafíos del siglo XXI. Fue este espíritu el que condujo a que aparecieran aviones en el cielo sobre nuestras cabezas, y que personas se reunieran donde estamos en este día. Y este es el momento en que nuestras naciones—todas las naciones—deben pedir ese espíritu de nuevo.

Ahora el mundo observará y recordará lo que hagamos aquí; lo que hagamos con este momento. ¿Extenderemos nuestra mano a las personas en los rincones olvidados de este mundo que anhelan vidas marcadas por la dignidad y la oportunidad, por la seguridad y la justicia? ¿Salvaremos al niño en Bangladesh de la pobreza, daremos cobijo al refugiado en Chad, y desterraremos el azote del SIDA en nuestra época?

¿Defenderemos los derechos humanos de los disidentes en Burma, de quien escribe un blog en Irán, o del votante en Zimbabwe? ¿Daremos significado a las palabras "nunca más" en Darfur?

Will we acknowledge that there is no more powerful example than the one each of our nations projects to the world? Will we reject torture and stand for the rule of law? Will we welcome immigrants from different lands and shun discrimination against those who don't look like us or worship like we do, and keep the promise of equality and opportunity for all of our people?

People of Berlin—people of the world—this is our moment. This is our time.

I know my country has not perfected itself. At times, we've struggled to keep the promise of liberty and equality for all of our people. We've made our share of mistakes, and there are times when our actions around the world have not lived up to our best intentions.

But I also know how much I love America. I know that for more than two centuries, we have strived—at great cost and great sacrifice—to form a more perfect union; to seek, with other nations, a more hopeful world.

Our allegiance has never been to any particular tribe or kingdom—indeed, every language is spoken in our country; every culture has left its imprint on ours; every point of view is expressed in our public squares.

What has always united us—what has always driven our people, what drew my father to America's shores—is a set of ideals that speak to aspirations shared by all people: that we can live free from fear and free from want, that we can speak our minds and assemble with whomever we choose and worship as we please.

These are the aspirations that joined the fates of all nations in this city. These aspirations are bigger than anything that drives us apart.

¿Reconoceremos que no hay ejemplo más poderoso que aquel que cada una de nuestras naciones proyecta al mundo? ¿Rechazaremos la tortura y defenderemos el imperio de la ley? ¿Daremos la bienvenida a inmigrantes de diferentes tierras y rechazaremos la discriminación contra quienes no se parecen a nosotros o adoran como nosotros, y mantendremos la promesa de igualdad y oportunidad para todo nuestro pueblo?

Pueblo de Berlín—pueblos del mundo—, este es nuestro momento. Este es nuestro tiempo.

Sé que mi país no se ha perfeccionado a sí mismo. A veces, hemos luchado para mantener la promesa de libertad e igualdad para todo nuestro pueblo. Hemos cometido nuestra parte de errores, y hay veces en que nuestros actos alrededor del mundo no han estado a la altura de nuestras mejores intenciones.

Pero también sé cuánto amo a Estados Unidos. Sé que durante más de dos siglos nos hemos esforzado—con gran coste y gran sacrificio—por formar una unión más perfecta; por buscar, junto con otras naciones, un mundo más esperanzador.

Nuestra lealtad nunca ha sido a cualquier tribu o reino en particular; además, en nuestro país se hablan todos los idiomas; toda cultura ha dejado su huella en la nuestra; todo punto de vista se expresa en nuestras plazas públicas.

Lo que siempre nos ha unido—lo que siempre ha impulsado a nuestro pueblo, lo que atrajo a mi padre a las costas de Estados Unidos—es un conjunto de ideales que hablan a aspiraciones compartidas por todas las personas: que podemos vivir libres del miedo y libres de la carencia, que podemos expresar nuestras ideas, y reunirnos con quien queramos, y adorar como nos agrade.

Esas son las aspiraciones que unen los destinos de todas las naciones en esta ciudad. Esas aspiraciones son mayores que ninguna otra cosa que nos aleje.

It is because of these aspirations that the airlift began. It is because of these aspirations that all free people—everywhere—became citizens of Berlin. It is in pursuit of these aspirations that a new generation—our generation—must make our mark on the world.

A causa de esas aspiraciones comenzó el transporte por avión. A causa de esas aspiraciones todas las personas libres—en todas partes—se hicieron ciudadanos de Berlín. En la búsqueda de esas aspiraciones, una nueva generación—nuestra generación—debe dejar nuestra huella en el mundo.

The American Promise speech
August 28, 2008
Denver, Colorado

*More than eighty thousand people packed Mile High Stadium
to hear the nation's first African American presidential candidate for
a major party deliver his acceptance speech at the Democratic
National Convention. It was only the second time that such a speech
was given in a stadium—the first was in 1960, when
John F. Kennedy accepted the nomination in Los Angeles at the
Memorial Coliseum.*

Four years ago, I stood before you and told you my story—of the brief union between a young man from Kenya and a young woman from Kansas who weren't well-off or well-known but shared a belief that in America, their son could achieve whatever he put his mind to.

It is that promise that has always set this country apart—that through hard work and sacrifice, each of us can pursue our individual dreams but still come together as one American family, to ensure that the next generation can pursue their dreams as well.

That's why I stand here tonight. Because for two hundred and thirty-two years, at each moment when that promise was in jeopardy, ordinary men and women—students and soldiers, farmers and teachers, nurses and janitors—found the courage to keep it alive.

Discurso "La promesa estadounidense"

28 de agosto de 2008
Denver, Colorado

Más de ochenta mil personas abarrotaron el estadio Mile High para oír al primer candidato afroamericano a la presidencia del país de un partido importante dar su discurso de aceptación en la Convención Nacional Demócrata. Fue la segunda vez que un discurso así se daba en un estadio; la primera fue en 1960, cuando John F. Kennedy aceptó la nominación en Los Ángeles en el Memorial Coliseum.

Hace cuatro años estuve delante de ustedes y les relaté mi historia: de la breve unión entre un joven de Kenia y una joven de Kansas que no eran acomodados ni conocidos pero compartían la creencia de que, en Estados Unidos, su hijo podía lograr cualquier cosa que se propusiera.

Es esa promesa la que siempre ha puesto aparte a este país: que por medio del trabajo duro y el sacrificio, cada uno de nosotros puede perseguir sus sueños individuales y al mismo tiempo estar unidos como familia estadounidense, para asegurar que la siguiente generación pueda también perseguir sus sueños.

Por eso estoy aquí esta noche. Porque durante doscientos treinta y dos años, en cada momento en que esa promesa estuvo en peligro, hombres y mujeres comunes y corrientes—estudiantes y soldados, granjeros y maestros, enfermeras y conserjes—encontraron la valentía para mantenerla viva.

We meet at one of those defining moments—a moment when our nation is at war, our economy is in turmoil, and the American promise has been threatened once more.

Tonight, more Americans are out of work and more are working harder for less. More of you have lost your homes and even more are watching your home values plummet. More of you have cars you can't afford to drive, credit card bills you can't afford to pay, and tuition that's beyond your reach.

These challenges are not all of government's making. But the failure to respond is a direct result of a broken politics in Washington and the failed policies of George W. Bush.

America, we are better than these last eight years. We are a better country than this.

Tonight, I say to the American people, to Democrats and Republicans and Independents across this great land—enough!

This moment—this election—is our chance to keep, in the twenty-first century, the American promise alive. Because next week, in Minnesota, the same party that brought you two terms of George Bush and Dick Cheney will ask this country for a third. And we are here because we love this country too much to let the next four years look like the last eight. On November 4, we must stand up and say: "Eight is enough."

Senator McCain likes to talk about judgment, but really, what does it say about your judgment when you think George Bush has been right more than 90 percent of the time? I don't know about you, but I'm not ready to take a 10 percent chance on change.

Nos reunimos en uno de esos momentos decisivos; un momento en que nuestra nación está en guerra, nuestra economía está alborotada, y la promesa estadounidense ha sido amenazada una vez más.

Esta noche, más estadounidenses están sin empleo y más trabajan más duro por menos salario. Más de ustedes han perdido sus casas y aún más están viendo cómo el valor de su casa cae en picada. Más de ustedes tienen autos que no pueden permitirse conducir, facturas de tarjetas de crédito que no pueden permitirse pagar, y tasas de matrículas que están por encima de su alcance.

Estos desafíos no son todos obra del gobierno. Pero no responder a ellos es un resultado directo de una política fracturada en Washington y de las políticas fallidas de George W. Bush.

Estados Unidos, somos mejores que estos últimos ocho años. Somos un mejor país que esto.

Esta noche, le digo al pueblo estadounidense, a demócratas, y republicanos, y a independientes a lo largo de esta gran tierra: ¡ya basta!

Este momento—estas elecciones—son nuestra oportunidad para mantener viva, en el siglo XXI, la promesa estadounidense. Porque la próxima semana, en Minnesota, el mismo partido que les proporcionó dos mandatos de George Bush y Dick Cheney pedirá a este país un tercero. Y estamos aquí porque amamos demasiado a este país para permitir que los próximos cuatro años sean como los últimos ocho. El 4 de noviembre debemos ponernos en pie y decir: "Con ocho basta".

Al senador McCain le gusta hablar sobre juicio, pero en realidad, ¿qué dice eso sobre el juicio de ustedes cuando piensan que George Bush ha estado en lo correcto más del noventa por ciento del tiempo? No sé de ustedes, pero yo no estoy preparado para aceptar un diez por ciento de posibilidad de cambio.

The truth is, on issue after issue that would make a difference in your lives—on health care and education and the economy—Senator McCain has been anything but independent.

He said that our economy has made "great progress" under this president. He said that the fundamentals of the economy are strong. And when one of his chief advisers—the man who wrote his economic plan—was talking about the anxiety Americans are feeling, he said that we were just suffering from a "mental recession" and that we've become, and I quote, "a nation of whiners."

A nation of whiners? Tell that to the proud autoworkers at a Michigan plant who, after they found out it was closing, kept showing up every day and working as hard as ever, because they knew there were people who counted on the brakes that they made. Tell that to the military families who shoulder their burdens silently as they watch their loved ones leave for their third or fourth or fifth tour of duty.

These are not whiners. They work hard and give back and keep going without complaint. These are the Americans that I know.

Now, I don't believe that Senator McCain doesn't care what's going on in the lives of Americans. I just think he doesn't know.

Why else would he define middle class as someone making under five million dollars a year? How else could he propose hundreds of billions in tax breaks for big corporations and oil companies but not one penny of tax relief to more than one hundred million Americans? How else could he offer a health care plan that would actually tax people's benefits, or an education plan that would do nothing to help families pay for college, or a plan that would privatize Social Security and gamble your retirement?

Lo cierto es que en cuanto a asunto tras asunto que marcarían una diferencia en sus vidas—sobre asistencia médica, y educación, y la economía—, el senador McCain ha sido cualquier cosa menos independiente.

Él dijo que nuestra economía ha hecho "un gran progreso" bajo este presidente. Él dijo que los puntos fundamentales de la economía son fuertes. Y cuando uno de sus principales consejeros—el hombre que redactó su plan económico—hablaba sobre la ansiedad que los estadounidenses están sintiendo, él dijo que solamente estábamos sufriendo de "recesión mental" y que nos hemos convertido, y cito sus palabras, "en una nación de quejumbrosos".

¿Una nación de quejumbrosos? Que les digan eso a los trabajadores orgullosos en la fábrica de autos en la planta de Michigan quienes, después de enterarse de que iba a cerrar, siguieron acudiendo cada día a trabajar tan duro como siempre, porque sabían que había personas que confiaban en los frenos que ellos fabricaban. Que les digan eso a las familias de los militares que soportan sus cargas en silencio mientras ven a sus seres queridos irse a su tercero, o cuarto, o quinto turno de responsabilidad.

Ellos no son quejumbrosos. Trabajan duro, y contribuyen, y siguen adelante sin quejarse. Esos son los estadounidenses que conozco.

Ahora bien, no creo que al senador McCain no le importe lo que sucede en las vidas de los estadounidenses. Sencillamente creo que él no lo sabe.

¿Si no, por qué definiría a la clase media como personas que ganan menos de cinco millones de dólares al año? ¿De qué otra manera podría proponer una deducción impositiva de cientos de millones de dólares para grandes corporaciones y compañías petroleras, sin ofrecer ni siquiera un centavo de reducción fiscal para más de cien millones de estadounidenses? ¿Cómo no podría ofrecer un plan de asistencia médica que realmente gravase los beneficios de las personas, o un plan de educación que no hiciese nada para ayudar a las familias a pagar la universidad, o un plan que privatizase la Seguridad Social y arriesgase la jubilación?

It's not because John McCain doesn't care. It's because John McCain doesn't get it.

For over two decades, he's subscribed to that old, discredited Republican philosophy—give more and more to those with the most and hope that prosperity trickles down to everyone else. In Washington, they call this the Ownership Society, but what it really means is—you're on your own.

Out of work? Tough luck. No health care? The market will fix it.

Born into poverty? Pull yourself up by your own bootstraps—even if you don't have boots. You're on your own.

Well it's time for them to own their failure. It's time for us to change America.

You see, we Democrats have a very different measure of what constitutes progress in this country.

We measure progress by how many people can find a job that pays the mortgage; whether you can put a little extra money away at the end of each month so you can someday watch your child receive her college diploma.

We measure the strength of our economy not by the number of billionaires we have or the profits of the Fortune 500 but by whether someone with a good idea can take a risk and start a new business, or whether the waitress who lives on tips can take a day off to look after a sick kid without losing her job—an economy that honors the dignity of work.

No es porque a John McCain no le importe. Es porque John McCain no lo entiende.

Durante más de dos décadas, él ha sido partidario de esa vieja y desacreditada filosofía republicana: dar cada vez más a quienes más tienen y esperar que la prosperidad vaya llegando a todos los demás. En Washington, denominan a esto la Sociedad de la Propiedad, pero lo que realmente significa es: uno está solo.

¿Ha perdido su empleo? Mala suerte. ¿No tiene asistencia médica? El mercado lo solucionará.

¿Ha nacido en la pobreza? Repóngase con sus propios esfuerzos, aunque no tenga esfuerzos. Está usted solo.

Bien, es momento de que ellos se adueñen de su propio fracaso. Es momento de que cambiemos Estados Unidos.

Miren, nosotros los demócratas tenemos una medida muy distinta de lo que constituye progreso en este país.

Nosotros medimos el progreso por cuántas personas pueden encontrar un empleo que les permita pagar la hipoteca; si pueden ahorrar un poco de dinero extra al final de cada mes para algún día poder ver a sus hijos recibir su título universitario.

Nosotros medimos la fortaleza de nuestra economía no por el número de multimillonarios que tenemos o por los beneficios del Fortune 500, sino por si alguien que tenga una buena idea puede arriesgarse y comenzar un nuevo negocio, o si la camarera que vive de las propinas puede tomarse un día libre para cuidar de un hijo enfermo sin por eso perder su empleo; una economía que honra la dignidad del trabajo.

The fundamentals we use to measure economic strength are whether we are living up to that fundamental promise that has made this country great—a promise that is the only reason I am standing here tonight.

Because in the faces of those young veterans who come back from Iraq and Afghanistan, I see my grandfather, who signed up after Pearl Harbor, marched in Patton's Army, and was rewarded by a grateful nation with the chance to go to college on the GI Bill.

In the face of that young student who sleeps just three hours before working the night shift, I think about my mom, who raised my sister and me on her own while she worked and earned her degree, who once turned to food stamps but was still able to send us to the best schools in the country with the help of student loans and scholarships.

When I listen to another worker tell me that his factory has shut down, I remember all those men and women on the South Side of Chicago who I stood by and fought for two decades ago after the local steel plant closed.

And when I hear a woman talk about the difficulties of starting her own business, I think about my grandmother, who worked her way up from the secretarial pool to middle management, despite years of being passed over for promotions because she was a woman.

She's the one who taught me about hard work. She's the one who put off buying a new car or a new dress for herself so that I could have a better life. She poured everything she had into me. And although she can no longer travel, I know that she's watching tonight, and that tonight is her night as well.

Los puntos fundamentales que utilizamos para medir la fortaleza económica son si estamos a la altura de esa promesa básica que ha hecho grande a este país; una promesa que es la única razón de que yo esté aquí esta noche.

Porque delante de los rostros de esos jóvenes veteranos que regresaron de Iraq y de Afganistán veo a mi abuelo, que se alistó después de Pearl Harbor, marchó en el Ejército de Patton, y fue recompensado por una nación agradecida con la oportunidad de estudiar en la universidad en el programa para veteranos de guerra (GI Bill).

Delante del rostro de ese joven estudiante que duerme sólo tres horas antes de irse a trabajar en el turno de la noche pienso en mi mamá, que nos crió a mi hermana y a mí por sí sola a la vez que trabajaba y obtenía su título, que en una ocasión recurrió a los cupones de comida pero fue capaz de mandarnos a las mejores escuelas del país con la ayuda de préstamos y becas para estudiantes.

Cuando escucho a otro trabajador decirme que su empresa ha cerrado, recuerdo a todos esos hombres y mujeres del lado sur de Chicago a quienes apoyé y con quienes luché hace dos décadas después de que la fábrica local de acero cerrase.

Y cuando oigo a una mujer hablar de las dificultades de comenzar su propio negocio pienso en mi abuela, que se abrió camino trabajando desde el secretariado hasta la gerencia intermedia, a pesar de años de que la saltasen en los ascensos porque era una mujer.

Ella es quien me enseñó sobre el trabajo duro. Ella es quien posponía la compra de un nuevo auto o un nuevo vestido para ella misma a fin de que yo pudiera tener una vida mejor. Ella infundió en mí todo lo que tenía. Y aunque ella ya no puede viajar, sé que me está viendo esta noche, y esta noche es también su noche.

I don't know what kind of lives John McCain thinks that celebrities lead, but this has been mine. These are my heroes. Theirs are the stories that shaped me. And it is on their behalf that I intend to win this election and keep our promise alive as president of the United States.

What is that promise?

It's a promise that says each of us has the freedom to make of our own lives what we will, but that we also have the obligation to treat each other with dignity and respect.

It's a promise that says the market should reward drive and innovation and generate growth, but that businesses should live up to their responsibilities to create American jobs, look out for American workers, and play by the rules of the road.

Ours is a promise that says government cannot solve all our problems, but what it should do is that which we cannot do for ourselves—protect us from harm and provide every child a decent education, keep our water clean and our toys safe, invest in new schools and new roads and new science and technology.

Our government should work for us, not against us. It should help us, not hurt us. It should ensure opportunity not just for those with the most money and influence but for every American who's willing to work.

That's the promise of America—the idea that we are responsible for ourselves, but that we also rise or fall as one nation; the fundamental belief that I am my brother's keeper, I am my sister's keeper.

Yo no sé qué tipo de vida cree John McCain que llevan las celebridades, pero esta ha sido la mía. Las de ellos son las historias que me moldearon; y por causa de ellos intento ganar estas elecciones y mantener viva nuestra promesa como presidente de los Estados Unidos.

¿Cuál es esa promesa?

Es una promesa que dice que cada uno de nosotros tiene la libertad de hacer de su propia vida lo que quiera, pero que también tenemos la obligación de tratarnos unos a otros con dignidad y respeto.

Es una promesa que dice que el mercado debería recompensar el empuje y la innovación, y generar crecimiento, pero que los negocios deberían estar a la altura de sus responsabilidades de crear empleos estadounidenses, buscar obreros estadounidenses, y jugar según el reglamento.

La nuestra es una promesa que dice que el gobierno no puede resolver todos nuestros problemas, pero que sí debería hacer lo que nosotros no podemos hacer por nosotros mismos: protegernos del daño y proporcionar a cada niño una educación decente, mantener limpia nuestra agua y seguros nuestros juguetes, invertir en nuevas escuelas, en nuevas carreteras, en nueva ciencia y tecnología.

Nuestro gobierno debería trabajar para nosotros, y no contra nosotros. Debería ayudarnos, y no dañarnos. Debería asegurar oportunidad no sólo para quienes tienen más dinero e influencia, sino para cada estadounidense que esté dispuesto a trabajar.

Esa es la promesa de Estados Unidos: la idea de que somos responsables de nosotros mismos, pero que también ascendemos o caemos como una sola nación; la creencia fundamental en que yo soy el guardián de mi hermano, yo soy el guardián de mi hermana.

And Democrats, we must also admit that fulfilling America's promise will require more than just money. It will require a renewed sense of responsibility from each of us to recover what John F. Kennedy called our "intellectual and moral strength."

Yes, government must lead on energy independence, but each of us must do our part to make our homes and businesses more efficient. Yes, we must provide more ladders to success for young men who fall into lives of crime and despair.

But we must also admit that programs alone can't replace parents, that government can't turn off the television and make a child do her homework, that fathers must take more responsibility for providing the love and guidance their children need.

Individual responsibility and mutual responsibility—that's the essence of America's promise.

And just as we keep our keep our promise to the next generation here at home, so must we keep America's promise abroad. If John McCain wants to have a debate about who has the temperament, and judgment, to serve as the next commander in chief, that's a debate I'm ready to have.

For while Senator McCain was turning his sights to Iraq just days after 9/11, I stood up and opposed this war, knowing that it would distract us from the real threats we face.

When John McCain said we could just "muddle through" in Afghanistan, I argued for more resources and more troops to finish the fight against the terrorists who actually attacked us on 9/11, and made clear that we must take out Osama bin Laden and his lieutenants if we have them in our sights.

Y, demócratas, también debemos admitir que cumplir la promesa estadounidense requerirá algo más que solamente dinero. Requerirá un renovado sentimiento de responsabilidad por parte de cada uno de nosotros para recobrar lo que John F. Kennedy llamó nuestra "fortaleza intelectual y moral".

Sí, el gobierno debe liderar en independencia energética, pero cada uno de nosotros debe aportar su parte para hacer que nuestros hogares y empresas sean más eficientes. Sí, debemos proporcionar más peldaños para el éxito para jóvenes que caen en vidas de delincuencia y desesperación.

Pero también debemos admitir que solamente los programas no pueden sustituir a los padres, que el gobierno no puede apagar el televisor y hacer que un niño haga sus tareas de la escuela, que los padres deben asumir mayor responsabilidad de proporcionar el amor y la dirección que sus hijos necesitan.

La responsabilidad individual y la responsabilidad mutua: esa es la esencia de la promesa de Estados Unidos.

Y al igual que mantenemos nuestra promesa a la siguiente generación aquí en casa, así debemos mantener la promesa estadounidense en el extranjero. Si John McCain quiere realizar un debate sobre quién tiene el temperamento, y el juicio, para servir como el siguiente comandante en jefe, ese es un debate que yo estoy listo para realizar.

Porque mientras el senador McCain dirigía su mirada hacia Iraq pocos días después del 11 de septiembre, yo me levanté y me opuse a esa guerra, sabiendo que nos distraería de las verdaderas amenazas que afrontamos.

Cuando John McCain dijo que simplemente podíamos "lograrlo de algún modo" en Afganistán, yo me peleé por más recursos y más tropas para terminar la lucha contra los terroristas que realmente nos atacaron el 11 de septiembre, y aclaré que debemos eliminar a Osama bin Laden y sus tenientes si los tenemos a la vista.

John McCain likes to say that he'll follow bin Laden to the Gates of Hell—but he won't even go to the cave where he lives.

And today, as my call for a time frame to remove our troops from Iraq has been echoed by the Iraqi government and even the Bush administration, even after we learned that Iraq has a $79 billion surplus while we're wallowing in deficits, John McCain stands alone in his stubborn refusal to end a misguided war.

That's not the judgment we need. That won't keep America safe. We need a president who can face the threats of the future, not keep grasping at the ideas of the past.

America, our work will not be easy. The challenges we face require tough choices, and Democrats as well as Republicans will need to cast off the worn-out ideas and politics of the past.

For part of what has been lost these past eight years can't just be measured by lost wages or bigger trade deficits. What has also been lost is our sense of common purpose—our sense of higher purpose. And that's what we have to restore.

We may not agree on abortion, but surely we can agree on reducing the number of unwanted pregnancies in this country. The reality of gun ownership may be different for hunters in rural Ohio than for those plagued by gang violence in Cleveland, but don't tell me we can't uphold the Second Amendment while keeping AK-47s out of the hands of criminals.

I know there are differences on same-sex marriage, but surely we can agree that our gay and lesbian brothers and sisters deserve to visit the person they love in the hospital and to live lives free of

A John McCain le gusta decir que él seguirá a bin Laden hasta las puertas del infierno; pero ni siquiera irá hasta la cueva donde él vive.

Y hoy, cuando mi llamado a establecer un marco de tiempo para retirar a nuestras tropas de Iraq ha recibido eco por parte del gobierno iraní y hasta de la administración Bush, incluso después de que nos enterásemos de que Iraq tiene un superávit de 79 mil millones de dólares mientras que nosotros nadamos en déficits, John McCain está solo en su obstinada negativa a poner fin a una guerra equivocada.

Ese no es el juicio que necesitamos. Eso no mantendrá seguro a Estados Unidos. Necesitamos un presidente que pueda afrontar las amenazas del futuro y no seguir aferrándose a las ideas del pasado.

Estados Unidos, nuestro trabajo no será fácil. Los desafíos que afrontamos requieren difíciles elecciones, y demócratas al igual que republicanos necesitarán descartar las agotadas ideas y políticas del pasado.

Porque parte de lo que se ha perdido en estos últimos ocho años no puede medirse simplemente por salarios perdidos o mayores déficits en el mercado. Lo que también se ha perdido es nuestro sentimiento de propósito común, nuestro sentimiento de un propósito más elevado. Y eso es lo que tenemos que recuperar.

Puede que no estemos de acuerdo en el aborto, pero seguramente podemos estar de acuerdo en reducir el número de embarazos no deseados en este país. La realidad de la posesión de armas de fuego puede que sea diferente para los cazadores en la Ohio rural que para quienes están inundados de violencia pandillera en Cleveland, pero no me digan que no podemos mantener la Segunda Enmienda a la vez que mantenemos las AK-47 lejos de las manos de delincuentes.

Sé que hay diferencias sobre el matrimonio entre personas del mismo sexo, pero seguramente podemos estar de acuerdo en que nuestros hermanos gays y nuestras hermanas lesbianas merecen visitar a la persona a la que aman en

discrimination. Passions fly on immigration, but I don't know anyone who benefits when a mother is separated from her infant child or an employer undercuts American wages by hiring illegal workers.

This too is part of America's promise—the promise of a democracy where we can find the strength and grace to bridge divides and unite in common effort.

I know there are those who dismiss such beliefs as happy talk. They claim that our insistence on something larger, something firmer and more honest in our public life is just a Trojan horse for higher taxes and the abandonment of traditional values.

And that's to be expected. Because if you don't have any fresh ideas, then you use stale tactics to scare the voters. If you don't have a record to run on, then you paint your opponent as someone people should run from.

You make a big election about small things.

And you know what—it's worked before. Because it feeds into the cynicism we all have about government. When Washington doesn't work, all its promises seem empty. If your hopes have been dashed again and again, then it's best to stop hoping and settle for what you already know.

I get it. I realize that I am not the likeliest candidate for this office. I don't fit the typical pedigree, and I haven't spent my career in the halls of Washington.

But I stand before you tonight because all across America something is stirring. What the naysayers don't understand is that this election has never been about me. It's been about you.

el hospital y vivir vidas libres de discriminación. Las pasiones se elevan con respecto a la inmigración, pero no conozco a nadie que se beneficie cuando una madre es separada de su hijo pequeño o cuando un patrón rebaja los salarios a los estadounidenses al contratar a trabajadores ilegales.

También esto es parte de la promesa estadounidense, la promesa de una democracia donde podamos encontrar la fortaleza y la gracia para tender un puente sobre las divisiones y unirnos en un esfuerzo común.

Sé que están quienes descartan tales creencias catalogándolas de charla feliz. Ellos afirman que nuestra insistencia en algo mayor, algo más firme y más honesto en nuestra vida pública es simplemente un caballo de Troya para más impuestos y el abandono de los valores tradicionales.

Y eso hay que esperarlo. Porque si no hay ninguna idea nueva, entonces uno utiliza viejas tácticas para asustar a los votantes. Si uno no tiene un testimonio del que hablar, entonces pinta a su oponente como alguien de quien la gente debería alejarse.

Uno hace unas importantes elecciones de cosas pequeñas.

¿Y saben qué? Ha funcionado antes. Porque alimenta el cinismo que todos tenemos en cuanto al gobierno. Cuando Washington no funciona, todas sus promesas parecen vacías. Si las esperanzas de ustedes han sido aplastadas una y otra vez, entonces es mejor dejar de esperar y conformarse con lo que ya conocen.

Lo comprendo. Entiendo que yo no soy el candidato con más probabilidades para este cargo. Yo no encajo dentro del típico pedigrí, y no he pasado mi carrera en los pasillos de Washington.

Pero estoy delante de ustedes esta noche porque en todo Estados Unidos algo se está moviendo. Lo que los pesimistas no entienden es que estas elecciones nunca se han tratado de mí. Se han tratado de ustedes.

For eighteen long months, you have stood up, one by one, and said enough to the politics of the past. You understand that in this election, the greatest risk we can take is to try the same old politics with the same old players and expect a different result.

You have shown what history teaches us—that at defining moments like this one, the change we need doesn't come from Washington. Change comes to Washington. Change happens because the American people demand it—because they rise up and insist on new ideas and new leadership, a new politics for a new time.

America, this is one of those moments.

I believe that as hard as it will be, the change we need is coming. Because I've seen it. Because I've lived it.

I've seen it in Illinois, when we provided health care to more children and moved more families from welfare to work. I've seen it in Washington, when we worked across party lines to open up government and hold lobbyists more accountable, to give better care for our veterans and keep nuclear weapons out of terrorist hands.

And I've seen it in this campaign. In the young people who voted for the first time, and in those who got involved again after a very long time. In the Republicans who never thought they'd pick up a Democratic ballot, but did.

I've seen it in the workers who would rather cut their hours back a day than see their friends lose their jobs, in the soldiers who reenlist after losing a limb, in the good neighbors who take a stranger in when a hurricane strikes and the floodwaters rise.

Durante dieciocho largos meses ustedes se han levantado, uno por uno, y han dicho basta a las políticas del pasado. Ustedes entienden que, en estas elecciones, el mayor riesgo que podemos correr es intentar las viejas políticas con los mismos viejos jugadores y esperar un resultado diferente.

Ustedes han demostrado lo que la Historia nos enseña: que en momentos decisivos como estos, el cambio que necesitamos no viene de Washington. El cambio llega a Washington. El cambio sucede porque el pueblo estadounidense lo demanda; porque se levantan e insisten en nuevas ideas y nuevo liderazgo, en una nueva política para un tiempo nuevo.

Estados Unidos, este es uno de esos momentos.

Yo creo que, por difícil que será, el cambio que necesitamos está llegando. Porque lo he visto. Porque lo he vivido.

Lo he visto en Illinois, cuando proporcionamos asistencia médica a más niños y pasamos a más familias de la beneficencia al trabajo. Lo he visto en Washington, cuando trabajamos cruzando líneas partidistas para abrir el gobierno y demandar más responsabilidad a los grupos de presión, para dar un mejor cuidado a nuestros veteranos y mantener las armas nucleares lejos de manos terroristas.

Y lo he visto en esta campaña. En los jóvenes que votaron por primera vez y en quienes participaron de nuevo después de mucho tiempo. En los republicanos que nunca pensaron que podrían elegir un voto demócrata, pero lo hicieron.

Lo he visto en los trabajadores que preferirían trabajar un día menos antes de que sus amigos perdieran sus empleos, en los soldados que se alistan otra vez después de perder uno de sus miembros, en los buenos vecinos que aceptan en su casa a un extraño cuando llega un huracán y suben las riadas.

This country of ours has more wealth than any nation, but that's not what makes us rich. We have the most powerful military on earth, but that's not what makes us strong. Our universities and our culture are the envy of the world, but that's not what keeps the world coming to our shores.

Instead, it is that American spirit—that American promise—that pushes us forward even when the path is uncertain, that binds us together in spite of our differences, that makes us fix our eye not on what is seen but what is unseen, that better place around the bend.

That promise is our greatest inheritance. It's a promise I make to my daughters when I tuck them in at night and a promise that you make to yours—a promise that has led immigrants to cross oceans and pioneers to travel west, a promise that led workers to picket lines and women to reach for the ballot.

And it is that promise that forty-five years ago today brought Americans from every corner of this land to stand together on the Mall in Washington, before Lincoln's Memorial, and hear a young preacher from Georgia speak of his dream.

The men and women who gathered there could've heard many things. They could've heard words of anger and discord. They could've been told to succumb to the fear and frustration of so many dreams deferred.

But what the people heard instead—people of every creed and color, from every walk of life—is that in America, our destiny is inextricably linked. That together, our dreams can be one.

"We cannot walk alone," the preacher cried. "And as we walk, we must make the pledge that we shall always march ahead. We cannot turn back."

Este país nuestro tiene más riqueza que ninguna otra nación, pero no es eso lo que nos hace ricos. Tenemos el ejército más poderoso de la tierra, pero no es eso lo que nos hace fuertes. Nuestras universidades y nuestra cultura son la envidia del mundo, pero eso no es lo que sigue haciendo que el mundo venga a nuestras costas.

En cambio, es ese espíritu estadounidense—esa promesa estadounidense— el que nos empuja hacia delante aun cuando el sendero es incierto, el que nos une a pesar de nuestras diferencias, el que nos hace fijar nuestros ojos no en lo que se ve sino en lo que no se ve, en ese lugar mejor tras la curva.

Esa promesa es nuestra mayor herencia. Es una promesa que yo hago a mis hijas cuando las llevo a sus camas en la noche, y una promesa que ustedes les hacen a sus hijos: una promesa que ha guiado a inmigrantes a cruzar océanos y a pioneros a viajar hacia el oeste, una promesa que llevó a los trabajadores a los piquetes y a mujeres a lograr el derecho a voto.

Y es esa promesa la que hace cuarenta y cinco años trajo a estadounidenses de todos los rincones a esta tierra para estar juntos en el Mall en Washington, delante del Lincoln's Memorial, y oír a un joven predicador de Georgia hablar de su sueño.

Los hombres y mujeres que se reunieron allí podrían haber oído muchas cosas. Podrían haber oído palabras de ira y de discordia. Les podrían haber dicho que sucumbieran al miedo y a la frustración de tantos sueños postergados.

Pero lo que la gente oyó, por el contrario—personas de todo credo y color, de toda condición social—, es que en Estados Unidos, nuestro destino está inextricablemente unido. Que juntos, nuestros sueños pueden ser uno.

"No podemos caminar solos—gritó el predicador—; y mientras caminamos, debemos hacer la promesa de que siempre marcharemos hacia delante. No podemos volver atrás".

America, we cannot turn back. Not with so much work to be done.

Not with so many children to educate and so many veterans to care for. Not with an economy to fix and cities to rebuild and farms to save. Not with so many families to protect and so many lives to mend. America, we cannot turn back. We cannot walk alone.

At this moment, in this election, we must pledge once more to march into the future. Let us keep that promise—that American promise—and in the words of scripture hold firmly, without wavering, to the hope that we confess.

Estados Unidos, no podemos volver atrás. No con todo el trabajo que queda por hacer.

No con tantos niños que educar y tantos veteranos a los que cuidar. No con una economía que remodelar, y ciudades que reconstruir, y granjas que salvar. No con tantas familias que proteger y tantas vidas que mejorar. Estados Unidos, no podemos volver atrás. No podemos caminar solos.

En este momento, en estas elecciones, debemos prometer una vez más marchar hacia el futuro. Mantengamos esa promesa—esa promesa estadounidense—, y en palabras de la escritura mantengamos firme, sin fluctuar, la esperanza que confesamos.

Election Night speech
Grant Park, Illinois
November 4, 2008

*Despite a victory that inspired many Americans to pour into
the streets in celebration, Senator Obama, the nation's first African
American to be elected president, delivered a serious speech
that reflected the many challenges facing the country.*

If there is anyone out there who still doubts that America is a place where all things are possible, who still wonders if the dream of our founders is alive in our time, who still questions the power of our democracy, tonight is your answer.

It's the answer told by lines that stretched around schools and churches in numbers this nation has never seen; by people who waited three hours and four hours, many for the very first time in their lives, because they believed that this time must be different, that their voice could be that difference.

It's the answer spoken by young and old, rich and poor, Democrat and Republican, black, white, Latino, Asian, Native American, gay, straight, disabled and not disabled—Americans who sent a message to the world that we have never been a collection of Red States and Blue States: we are, and always will be, the United States of America.

Discurso "Noche electoral"
Grant Park, Illinois
4 de noviembre de 2008

A pesar de una victoria que inspiró a muchos estadounidenses a echarse a las calles para celebrarla, el senador Obama, el primer afroamericano del país en ser elegido presidente, pronunció un serio discurso que reflejaba los muchos desafíos que afronta el país.

Si hay alguien ahí que aún dude de que Estados Unidos es un lugar donde todo es posible, que aún se pregunte si el sueño de nuestros fundadores está vivo en nuestra época, que aún se cuestione el poder de nuestra democracia, esta noche es su respuesta.

Es la respuesta dada por filas de personas formadas alrededor de escuelas y de iglesias en números que esta nación no ha visto nunca; por personas que esperaron tres y cuatro horas, muchos por primera vez en su vida, porque creían que esta vez debía ser diferente, que su voz podía marcar esa diferencia.

Es la respuesta pronunciada por jóvenes y viejos, ricos y pobres, demócratas y republicanos, negros, blancos, latinos, asiáticos, indígenas norteamericanos, homosexuales, heterosexuales, discapacitados y no discapacitados: estadounidenses que han enviado al mundo el mensaje de que nunca hemos sido una colección de Estados Rojos y Estados Azules; somos, y siempre seremos, los Estados Unidos de América.

It's the answer that led those who have been told for so long by so many to be cynical, and fearful, and doubtful of what we can achieve to put their hands on the arc of history and bend it once more toward the hope of a better day.

It's been a long time coming, but tonight, because of what we did on this day, in this election, at this defining moment, change has come to America.

I would not be standing here tonight without the unyielding support of my best friend for the last sixteen years, the rock of our family and the love of my life, our nation's next First Lady, Michelle Obama. Sasha and Malia, I love you both so much, and you have earned the new puppy that's coming with us to the White House. And while she's no longer with us, I know my grandmother is watching, along with the family that made me who I am. I miss them tonight and know that my debt to them is beyond measure.

I was never the likeliest candidate for this office. We didn't start with much money or many endorsements. Our campaign was not hatched in the halls of Washington—it began in the backyards of Des Moines and the living rooms of Concord and the front porches of Charleston.

It was built by working men and women who dug into what little savings they had to give five dollars and ten dollars and twenty dollars to this cause.

It grew strength from the young people who rejected the myth of their generation's apathy; who left their homes and their families for jobs that offered little pay and less sleep; from the not-so-young people who braved the bitter cold and scorching heat to knock on the doors of perfect strangers; from the millions of Americans who volunteered, and organized, and proved that more than two centuries later, a government of the people, by the people and for the people has not perished from this earth.

Es la respuesta que condujo a aquellos a quienes muchos les habían dicho por mucho tiempo que fuesen cínicos, y temerosos, y dudosos de lo que podemos lograr, a poner sus manos en el arco de la Historia y dirigirlo una vez más hacia la esperanza de un tiempo mejor.

Ha tardado mucho tiempo en llegar, pero esta noche, debido a lo que hemos hecho este día, en estas elecciones, en este momento determinante, el cambio ha llegado a Estados Unidos.

Yo no estaría aquí esta noche sin el apoyo incondicional de mi mejor amiga durante los últimos dieciséis años, la roca de nuestra familia y el amor de mi vida, la próxima Primera Dama de nuestra nación: Michelle Obama. Sasha y Malia, las amo mucho a las dos, y se han ganado el nuevo perrito que irá con nosotros a la Casa Blanca. Y aunque ya no está con nosotros, sé que mi abuela nos está viendo, junto con la familia que me convirtió en quién soy. Esta noche los extraño, y sé que mi deuda con ellos está por encima de toda medida.

Yo nunca fui el candidato más probable para este puesto. No comenzamos con mucho dinero o con muchos respaldos. Nuestra campaña no estuvo ideada en los pasillos de Washington; comenzó en los patios de Des Moines, y en las salas de estar de Concord, y en los porches de Charleston.

Fue desarrollada por mujeres y hombres trabajadores que rebuscaron entre los pequeños ahorros que tenían para dar cinco dólares, y diez dólares, y veinte dólares a esta causa.

Cobró fuerza de los jóvenes que rechazaron el mito de la apatía de su generación; que dejaron sus hogares y sus familias por empleos que ofrecían poco salario y menos horas de sueño; de las personas no tan jóvenes que hicieron frente al gélido frío y al sofocante calor para llamar a las puertas de perfectos desconocidos; de los millones de estadounidenses que se ofrecieron voluntarios, y se organizaron, y demostraron que más de dos siglos después, un gobierno del pueblo, por el pueblo y para el pueblo no ha perecido en esta tierra.

This is your victory. I know you didn't do this just to win an election, and I know you didn't do it for me. You did it because you understand the enormity of the task that lies ahead.

For even as we celebrate tonight, we know the challenges that tomorrow will bring are the greatest of our lifetime—two wars, a planet in peril, the worst financial crisis in a century. Even as we stand here tonight, we know there are brave Americans waking up in the deserts of Iraq and the mountains of Afghanistan to risk their lives for us.

There are mothers and fathers who will lie awake after their children fall asleep and wonder how they'll make the mortgage, or pay their doctor's bills, or save enough for college. There is new energy to harness and new jobs to be created, new schools to build and threats to meet and alliances to repair.

The road ahead will be long. Our climb will be steep. We may not get there in one year or even one term, but America—I have never been more hopeful than I am tonight that we will get there. I promise you—we as a people will get there.

There will be setbacks and false starts. There are many who won't agree with every decision or policy I make as president, and we know that government can't solve every problem.

But I will always be honest with you about the challenges we face. I will listen to you, especially when we disagree. And above all, I will ask you join in the work of remaking this nation the only way it's been done in America for two hundred and twenty-one years—block by block, brick by brick, calloused hand by calloused hand.

What began twenty-one months ago in the depths of winter must not end on this autumn night. This victory alone is not the change we seek—it is only the chance for us to make that change. And that cannot happen if we go back to the way things were. It cannot happen without you.

Esta es su victoria. Sé que ustedes no hicieron esto sólo para ganar unas elecciones, y sé que no lo hicieron por mí. Lo hicieron porque ustedes entienden la enormidad de la tarea que tenemos por delante.

Porque incluso al celebrar esta noche, sabemos que los desafíos que traerá el mañana son los mayores de toda nuestra vida: dos guerras, un planeta en peligro, la peor crisis financiera del siglo. Aun mientras estamos aquí esta noche, sabemos que hay valientes estadounidenses despertándose en los desiertos de Iraq y en las montañas de Afganistán para arriesgar sus vidas por nosotros.

Hay madres y padres que se quedarán despiertos después de que sus hijos se queden dormidos y se preguntarán cómo van a pagar la hipoteca, o las facturas del doctor, o cómo van a ahorrar lo suficiente para la universidad. Hay nueva energía que utilizar y nuevos empleos que crear, nuevas escuelas que construir, y amenazas que afrontar, y alianzas que conciliar.

El camino que tenemos por delante será largo. Nuestra escalada será empinada. Puede que no lleguemos allí en un año o ni siquiera en un mandato, pero Estados Unidos: nunca he estado tan esperanzado como lo estoy esta noche de que llegaremos allí. Les prometo que, como pueblo, llegaremos allí.

Habrá reveses y salidas en falso. Hay muchos que no estarán de acuerdo con toda decisión o política que yo haga como presidente, y sabemos que el gobierno no puede resolver todos los problemas.

Pero siempre seré sincero con ustedes en cuanto a los desafíos que afrontamos. Les escucharé, especialmente cuando no estemos de acuerdo. Y sobre todo, les pediré que se unan a la tarea de remodelar esta nación de la única forma en que se ha hecho en Estados Unidos durante doscientos veintiún años: bloque a bloque, ladrillo a ladrillo, mano callosa a mano callosa.

Lo que comenzó hace veintiún meses en lo más profundo del invierno no debe terminar en esta noche de otoño. Esta victoria solamente no es el cambio que buscamos; es sólo la oportunidad para poder realizar ese cambio. Y eso no puede suceder si regresamos a la forma en que eran las cosas. No puede suceder sin ustedes.

So let us summon a new spirit of patriotism, of service and responsibility where each of us resolves to pitch in and work harder and look after not only ourselves, but each other.

Let us remember that if this financial crisis taught us anything, it's that we cannot have a thriving Wall Street while Main Street suffers—in this country, we rise or fall as one nation; as one people.

Let us resist the temptation to fall back on the same partisanship and pettiness and immaturity that has poisoned our politics for so long. Let us remember that it was a man from this state who first carried the banner of the Republican Party to the White House—a party founded on the values of self-reliance, individual liberty, and national unity.

Those are values we all share, and while the Democratic Party has won a great victory tonight, we do so with a measure of humility and determination to heal the divides that have held back our progress. As Lincoln said to a nation far more divided than ours, "We are not enemies, but friends...though passion may have strained it must not break our bonds of affection." And to those Americans whose support I have yet to earn—I may not have won your vote, but I hear your voices, I need your help, and I will be your President too.

And to all those watching tonight from beyond our shores, from parliaments and palaces to those who are huddled around radios in the forgotten corners of our world—our stories are singular, but our destiny is shared, and a new dawn of American leadership is at hand. To those who would tear this world down—we will defeat you. To those who seek peace and security—we support you.

And to all those who have wondered if America's beacon still burns as bright—tonight we proved once more that the true strength of our nation comes not from the might of our arms or the scale of our wealth, but from

Por tanto, pidamos un nuevo espíritu de patriotismo, de servicio y responsabilidad, donde cada uno de nosotros decida echar una mano, y trabajar más duro, y no cuidar sólo de nosotros mismos sino también unos de otros.

Recordemos que si esta crisis económica nos ha enseñado algo, es que no podemos tener un Wall Street próspero mientras Main Street sufre; en este país, nos elevamos o caemos como una sola nación; como un sólo pueblo.

Resistamos la tentación de regresar al mismo partidismo, y estrechez de miras e inmadurez que han envenenado nuestra política por tanto tiempo. Recordemos que fue un hombre de este estado quien por primera vez llevó la bandera del Partido Republicano a la Casa Blanca, un partido fundado sobre los valores de la independencia, la libertad individual y la unidad nacional.

Esos son valores que todos compartimos, y aunque el Partido Demócrata ha logrado una gran victoria esta noche, lo hacemos con un mensaje de humildad y de determinación a sanar las divisiones que han retenido nuestro progreso. Como dijo Lincoln a una nación mucho más dividida que la nuestra: "No somos enemigos, sino amigos… aunque la pasión pueda haber dañado, no debe romper nuestros lazos de afecto". Y a aquellos estadounidenses cuyo apoyo aún tengo que ganarme: puede que no haya obtenido su voto, pero oigo sus voces, necesito su ayuda, y seré también el Presidente de ustedes.

Y a todos los que nos están viendo esta noche desde más allá de nuestras costas, desde parlamentos y palacios hasta los que están reunidos en torno a aparatos de radio en los rincones olvidados de nuestro mundo: nuestras historias son singulares, pero nuestro destino es compartido, y un nuevo amanecer de liderazgo estadounidense se acerca. A aquellos que querrían derribar este mundo: les derrotaremos. A aquellos que buscan la paz y la seguridad: les apoyamos.

Y a todos aquellos que se han preguntado si el faro de Estados Unidos sigue brillando con toda su fuerza: esta noche hemos demostrado una vez más que la verdadera fuerza de nuestra nación proviene no de la

the enduring power of our ideals: democracy, liberty, opportunity, and unyielding hope.

For that is the true genius of America—that America can change. Our union can be perfected. And what we have already achieved gives us hope for what we can and must achieve tomorrow.

This election had many firsts and many stories that will be told for generations. But one that's on my mind tonight is about a woman who cast her ballot in Atlanta. She's a lot like the millions of others who stood in line to make their voice heard in this election except for one thing— Ann Nixon Cooper is 106 years old.

She was born just a generation past slavery; a time when there were no cars on the road or planes in the sky; when someone like her couldn't vote for two reasons—because she was a woman and because of the color of her skin.

And tonight, I think about all that she's seen throughout her century in America—the heartache and the hope; the struggle and the progress; the times we were told that we can't, and the people who pressed on with that American creed: Yes we can.

At a time when women's voices were silenced and their hopes dismissed, she lived to see them stand up and speak out and reach for the ballot. Yes we can.

When there was despair in the dust bowl and depression across the land, she saw a nation conquer fear itself with a New Deal, new jobs and a new sense of common purpose. Yes we can.

potencia de nuestras armas o de la escala de nuestra riqueza, sino del perdurable poder de nuestros ideales: democracia, libertad, oportunidad y una esperanza inquebrantable.

Porque esa es la verdadera genialidad de Estados Unidos: que Estados Unidos puede cambiar. Nuestra unión puede perfeccionarse. Y lo que ya hemos logrado nos da esperanza para lo que podemos y debemos lograr mañana.

Estas elecciones tuvieron muchos primeros y muchas historias que se relatarán durante generaciones. Pero una que está en mi mente esta noche es acerca de una mujer que emitió su voto en Atlanta. Ella es muy parecida a los millones de personas que estuvieron en las filas para hacer oír su voz en estas elecciones a excepción de una sola cosa: Ann Nixon Cooper tiene 106 años de edad.

Ella nació solamente a una generación de distancia de la esclavitud del pasado; una época en que no había autos en las carreteras ni aviones en el cielo; cuando alguien como ella no podía votar por dos razones: porque era una mujer y a causa del color de su piel.

Y esta noche, pienso en todo lo que ella ha visto a lo largo de su siglo de vida en Estados Unidos: el dolor y la esperanza; la lucha y el progreso; las veces en que nos dijeron que no podemos, y las personas que prosiguieron con ese credo estadounidense: Sí podemos.

En una época en que las voces de las mujeres eran silenciadas y sus esperanzas rechazadas, ella vivió para verlas elevarse y para llegar a votar. Sí podemos.

Cuando había desesperación en el terreno erosionado por el viento y depresión por toda la tierra, ella vio a una nación conquistar el miedo con un New Deal, nuevos empleos y un nuevo sentimiento de propósito común. Sí podemos.

When the bombs fell on our harbor and tyranny threatened the world, she was there to witness a generation rise to greatness and a democracy was saved. Yes we can.

She was there for the buses in Montgomery, the hoses in Birmingham, a bridge in Selma, and a preacher from Atlanta who told a people that "We Shall Overcome." Yes we can.

A man touched down on the moon, a wall came down in Berlin, a world was connected by our own science and imagination. And this year, in this election, she touched her finger to a screen, and cast her vote, because after 106 years in America, through the best of times and the darkest of hours, she knows how America can change. Yes we can.

America, we have come so far. We have seen so much. But there is so much more to do.

So tonight, let us ask ourselves—if our children should live to see the next century; if my daughters should be so lucky to live as long as Ann Nixon Cooper, what change will they see? What progress will we have made?

This is our chance to answer that call. This is our moment.

This is our time—to put our people back to work and open doors of opportunity for our kids; to restore prosperity and promote the cause of peace; to reclaim the American Dream and reaffirm that fundamental truth—that out of many, we are one; that while we breathe, we hope, and where we are met with cynicism, and doubt, and those who tell us that we can't, we will respond with that timeless creed that sums up the spirit of a people: Yes We Can.

Cuando las bombas caían sobre nosotros y la tiranía amenazaba al mundo, ella estuvo ahí para ser testigo de cómo una generación ascendía a la grandeza y se salvaba la democracia. Sí podemos.

Ella estuvo ahí para los autobuses en Montgomery, las mangueras en Birmingham, un puente en Selma, y un predicador de Atlanta que le dijo a un pueblo: "Nosotros venceremos". Sí podemos.

Un hombre pisó la luna, un muro se derribó en Berlín, un mundo fue conectado mediante nuestra propia ciencia e imaginación. Y este año, en estas elecciones, ella tocó una pantalla con su dedo, y emitió un voto, porque después de 106 años en Estados Unidos, a lo largo de los mejores tiempos y de las horas más oscuras, ella sabe que Estados Unidos puede cambiar. Sí podemos.

Estados Unidos, hemos llegado hasta aquí. Hemos visto mucho. Pero hay mucho más por hacer.

Por tanto, esta noche, hagámonos esta pregunta: si nuestros hijos vivieran hasta ver el próximo siglo; si mis hijas fueran tan afortunadas para vivir tanto tiempo como Ann Nixon Cooper, ¿qué cambios verán? ¿qué progreso habremos hecho?

Esta es nuestra oportunidad de responder a ese llamado. Este es nuestro momento.

Esta es nuestra hora: para hacer regresar a nuestro pueblo al trabajo y a puertas abiertas de oportunidad para nuestros hijos; para restaurar la prosperidad y fomentar la causa de la paz; para reclamar el Sueño Americano y reafirmar esa verdad fundamental, que, de muchos, somos uno; que mientras respiremos, tenemos esperanza, y donde nos encontremos con cinismo, y con duda, y con aquellos que nos dicen que no podemos, responderemos con ese credo intemporal que resume el espíritu de un pueblo: Sí podemos.

Inaugural Address

January 20, 2009
Washington, D.C.

Millions of people went to Washington, D.C., to attend this historic inauguration and heard President Obama deliver a traditional message of national renewal that called for a new era of responsibility and placed unusual emphasis on energy and the environment.

I stand here today humbled by the task before us, grateful for the trust you have bestowed, mindful of the sacrifices borne by our ancestors. I thank President Bush for his service to our nation, as well as the generosity and cooperation he has shown throughout this transition.

Forty-four Americans have now taken the presidential oath. The words have been spoken during rising tides of prosperity and the still waters of peace. Yet every so often the oath is taken amid gathering clouds and raging storms.

At these moments, America has carried on not simply because of the skill or vision of those in high office but because We the People have remained faithful to the ideals of our forebearers and true to our founding documents.

Discurso de investidura
20 de enero de 2009
Washington, D.C.

Millones de personas fueron a Washington, D.C., para asistir a esta histórica investidura y oír al presidente Obama dar un tradicional mensaje de renovación nacional que llamaba a una nueva era de responsabilidad y hacía un inusual hincapié en la energía y el medioambiente.

~ ~

Estoy aquí hoy humilde por la tarea que tenemos por delante, agradecido por la confianza que me han otorgado, consciente de los sacrificios que nuestros antecesores soportaron. Doy gracias al presidente Bush por su servicio a nuestra nación, al igual que por la generosidad y la cooperación que él ha demostrado a lo largo de esta transición.

Cuarenta y cuatro estadounidenses han realizado hasta ahora el juramento presidencial. Las palabras se han pronunciado durante elevadas mareas de prosperidad y las quietas aguas de la paz. Sin embargo, de vez en cuando el juramento se hace en medio de crecientes nubes y fuertes tormentas.

En estos momentos, Estados Unidos ha seguido adelante no sólo por la capacidad o la visión de aquellos que ocupan altos cargos, sino porque "nosotros, el pueblo" hemos permanecido fieles a los ideales de nuestros antepasados y fieles a nuestros documentos fundacionales.

So it has been. So it must be with this generation of Americans.

That we are in the midst of crisis is now well understood. Our nation is at war, against a far-reaching network of violence and hatred. Our economy is badly weakened, a consequence of greed and irresponsibility on the part of some, but also our collective failure to make hard choices and prepare the nation for a new age.

Homes have been lost; jobs shed; businesses shuttered. Our health care is too costly; our schools fail too many; and each day brings further evidence that the ways we use energy strengthen our adversaries and threaten our planet.

These are the indicators of crisis, subject to data and statistics. Less measurable but no less profound is a sapping of confidence across our land—a nagging fear that America's decline is inevitable and that the next generation must lower its sights.

Today I say to you that the challenges we face are real. They are serious and they are many. They will not be met easily or in a short span of time. But know this, America—they will be met.

On this day, we gather because we have chosen hope over fear, unity of purpose over conflict and discord.

On this day, we come to proclaim an end to the petty grievances and false promises, the recriminations and worn-out dogmas, that for far too long have strangled our politics.

We remain a young nation, but in the words of scripture, the time has come to set aside childish things.

Así ha sido. Así debe ser con esta generación de estadounidenses.

Que estamos en medio de una crisis ahora se entiende muy bien. Nuestra nación está en guerra, contra una red de gran alcance de violencia y de odio. Nuestra economía está muy debilitada, una consecuencia de la avaricia y la irresponsabilidad por parte de algunos, pero también de nuestro fracaso colectivo a la hora de tomar decisiones difíciles y preparar a la nación para una nueva era.

Se han perdido hogares; se han recortado empleos; se han cerrado negocios. Nuestra asistencia médica es demasiado costosa; nuestras escuelas les fallan a demasiados; y cada día muestra mayor evidencia de que las formas en que usamos la energía fortalecen a nuestros adversarios y amenazan nuestro planeta.

Esos son los indicadores de la crisis, sujetos a datos y a estadísticas. Menos mensurable pero no menos profundo es un agotamiento de confianza por toda nuestra tierra: un inquietante temor de que el declive de Estados Unidos sea inevitable y que la siguiente generación deba rebajar sus miras.

Hoy les digo que los desafíos que afrontamos son reales; son graves, y son muchos. No se les hará frente fácilmente o en un corto periodo de tiempo. Pero, Estados Unidos, debes saber que se les hará frente.

En este día, nos reunimos porque hemos escogido la esperanza por encima del temor, la unidad por encima del conflicto y la discordia.

En este día, venimos a proclamar un final a las quejas triviales y a las falsas promesas, a las recriminaciones y a los gastados dogmas, que por demasiado tiempo han estrangulado nuestra política.

Seguimos siendo una nación joven, pero en palabras de la Escritura, ha llegado el momento de dejar a un lado las cosas de niños.

The time has come to reaffirm our enduring spirit, to choose our better history, to carry forward that precious gift, that noble idea, passed on from generation to generation: the God-given promise that all are equal, all are free, and all deserve a chance to pursue their full measure of happiness.

In reaffirming the greatness of our nation, we understand that greatness is never a given. It must be earned.

Our journey has never been one of shortcuts or settling for less. It has not been the path for the fainthearted—for those who prefer leisure over work or seek only the pleasures of riches and fame. Rather, it has been the risk takers, the doers, the makers of things—some celebrated but more often men and women obscure in their labor, who have carried us up the long, rugged path toward prosperity and freedom.

For us, they packed up their few worldly possessions and traveled across oceans in search of a new life.

For us, they toiled in sweatshops and settled the West, endured the lash of the whip and plowed the hard earth.

For us, they fought and died, in places like Concord and Gettysburg, Normandy and Khe Sahn.

Time and again these men and women struggled and sacrificed and worked till their hands were raw so that we might live a better life. They saw America as bigger than the sum of our individual ambitions, greater than all the differences of birth or wealth or faction.

This is the journey we continue today. We remain the most prosperous, powerful nation on earth.

Ha llegado el momento de reafirmar nuestro espíritu perdurable, de escoger nuestra mejor historia, de llevar adelante ese precioso don, esa noble idea, transmitidos de generación a generación: la promesa dada por Dios de que todos son iguales, todos son libres, y todos merecen una oportunidad para perseguir su plena medida de felicidad.

Al reafirmar la grandeza de nuestra nación, entendemos que esa grandeza nunca es un hecho reconocido. Tiene que ganarse.

Nuestro viaje nunca ha sido de atajos o de conformarnos con menos. No ha sido el camino para los apocados: para quienes prefieren el tiempo libre en lugar del trabajo o buscan sólo los placeres de las riquezas y la fama. En cambio, han sido los arriesgados, los hacedores, los creadores de cosas, algunos de ellos celebrados pero con mayor frecuencia hombres y mujeres poco conocidos en su labor, quienes nos han llevado por el largo y accidentado camino hacia la prosperidad y la libertad.

Por nosotros, ellos empacaron sus pocas posesiones terrenales y viajaron cruzando océanos en busca de una nueva vida.

Por nosotros, ellos trabajaron duro en fábricas donde eran explotados y establecieron el Oeste, soportaron el azote del látigo y araron la dura tierra.

Por nosotros, ellos pelearon y murieron, en lugares como Concord y Gettysburg, Normandy y Khe Sahn.

Una y otra vez aquellos hombres y mujeres batallaron, y se sacrificaron, y trabajaron hasta que sus manos estuvieron ásperas a fin de que nosotros pudiésemos vivir una vida mejor. Ellos vieron a Estados Unidos como mayor que la suma de nuestras ambiciones individuales, más grande que todas las diferencias de nacimiento, o de riqueza, o de facción.

Este es el viaje que continuamos hoy. Seguimos siendo la nación más próspera y poderosa de la tierra.

Our workers are no less productive than when this crisis began. Our minds are no less inventive, our goods and services no less needed than they were last week or last month or last year. Our capacity remains undiminished.

But our time of standing pat, of protecting narrow interests and putting off unpleasant decisions—that time has surely passed. Starting today, we must pick ourselves up, dust ourselves off, and begin again the work of remaking America.

For everywhere we look, there is work to be done. The state of the economy calls for action, bold and swift, and we will act—not only to create new jobs but to lay a new foundation for growth.

We will build the roads and bridges, the electric grids and digital lines that feed our commerce and bind us together. We will restore science to its rightful place and wield technology's wonders to raise health care's quality and lower its cost.

We will harness the sun and the winds and the soil to fuel our cars and run our factories. And we will transform our schools and colleges and universities to meet the demands of a new age. All this we can do. And all this we will do.

Now, there are some who question the scale of our ambitions—who suggest that our system cannot tolerate too many big plans. Their memories are short. For they have forgotten what this country has already done, what free men and women can achieve when imagination is joined to common purpose, and necessity to courage.

What the cynics fail to understand is that the ground has shifted beneath them—that the stale political arguments that have consumed us for so long no longer apply.

Nuestros trabajadores no son menos productivos que cuando comenzó esta crisis. Nuestras mentes no son menos inventivas, nuestros bienes y servicios no son menos necesarios de lo que eran la semana pasada, o el mes pasado, o el año pasado. Nuestra capacidad no ha disminuido.

Pero nuestro tiempo de seguir en lo mismo, de proteger limitados intereses y de posponer decisiones desagradables, ese tiempo sin duda ha pasado. Comenzando hoy, debemos ponernos en pie, sacudirnos el polvo, y comenzar de nuevo la tarea de rehacer Estados Unidos.

Porque dondequiera que miremos, hay trabajo por hacer. El estado de la economía llama a la acción, valiente y rápida, y actuaremos; no sólo para crear nuevos empleos sino también para poner un nuevo cimiento para el crecimiento.

Construiremos las carreteras y los puentes, los tendidos eléctricos y las líneas digitales que empujan nuestro comercio y nos unen. Volveremos a situar a la ciencia en su lugar legítimo y manejaremos las maravillas de la tecnología para elevar la calidad de la asistencia médica y disminuir sus costos.

Utilizaremos el sol, y los vientos, y el terreno para repostar nuestros vehículos y hacer funcionar nuestras fábricas. Y transformaremos nuestras escuelas, institutos y universidades para satisfacer las demandas de una nueva era. Podemos hacer todo esto. Y haremos todo esto.

Ahora bien, hay algunos que cuestionan la escala de nuestras ambiciones, que sugieren que nuestro sistema no puede tolerar demasiados grandes planes. Sus memorias son malas; porque han olvidado lo que este país ya ha hecho, lo que hombres y mujeres libres pueden lograr cuando la imaginación se une al propósito común, y la necesidad al coraje.

Lo que los cínicos no entienden es que el terreno ha cambiado bajo sus pies; que los viejos argumentos políticos que nos han consumido durante tanto tiempo ya no se aplican.

The question we ask today is not whether our government is too big or too small but whether it works—whether it helps families find jobs at a decent wage, health care they can afford, a retirement that is dignified. Where the answer is yes, we intend to move forward. Where the answer is no, programs will end.

And those of us who manage the public's dollars will be held to account— to spend wisely, reform bad habits, and do our business in the light of day—because only then can we restore the vital trust between a people and their government.

Nor is the question before us whether the market is a force for good or ill. Its power to generate wealth and expand freedom is unmatched, but this crisis has reminded us that without a watchful eye, the market can spin out of control—and that a nation cannot prosper long when it favors only the prosperous.

The success of our economy has always depended not just on the size of our gross domestic product but on the reach of our prosperity, on the ability to extend opportunity to every willing heart—not out of charity but because it is the surest route to our common good.

As for our common defense, we reject as false the choice between our safety and our ideals. Our Founding Fathers, faced with perils we can scarcely imagine, drafted a charter to ensure the rule of law and the rights of man, a charter expanded by the blood of generations. Those ideals still light the world, and we will not give them up for expedience's sake.

And so to all other peoples and governments who are watching today, from the grandest capitals to the small village where my father was born: know that America is a friend of each nation and every man, woman, and

La pregunta que hacemos hoy no es si nuestro gobierno es demasiado grande o demasiado pequeño, sino si funciona: si ayuda a las familias a encontrar empleos con salarios decentes, una asistencia médica que puedan permitirse, una jubilación que sea digna. Donde la respuesta sea sí, nuestra intención es avanzar. Donde la respuesta sea no, los programas terminarán.

Y a aquellos de nosotros que manejamos los dólares públicos se nos pedirá que rindamos cuentas—gastar sabiamente, reformar malos hábitos, y hacer nuestros negocios a la luz del día—, porque solamente entonces podremos restaurar la confianza vital entre un pueblo y su gobierno.

La pregunta tampoco es si el mercado es una fuerza para bien o para mal. Su poder de generar riqueza y expandir la libertad no tiene par, pero esta crisis nos ha recordado que, sin un ojo supervisor, el mercado puede descontrolarse, y que una nación no puede prosperar mucho tiempo cuando favorece solamente a los prósperos.

El éxito de nuestra economía siempre ha dependido no sólo del tamaño de nuestro producto interior bruto, sino del alcance de nuestra prosperidad, de la capacidad de extender la oportunidad a todo corazón dispuesto; no por caridad, sino porque es la ruta más segura hacia nuestro bien común.

En cuanto a nuestra defensa común, rechazamos como falsa la elección entre nuestra seguridad y nuestros ideales. Nuestros Padres Fundadores, cuando se enfrentaron con peligros que nosotros apenas podemos imaginar, redactaron una constitución para asegurar el imperio de la ley y los derechos del hombre, una constitución ampliada mediante la sangre de generaciones. Esos ideales siguen iluminando el mundo, y no renunciaremos a ellos por causa de la conveniencia.

Por tanto, a todos los demás pueblos y gobiernos que nos están viendo hoy, desde las mayores capitales hasta la pequeña aldea donde mi padre nació: sepan que Estados Unidos es una amiga de cada nación y cada

child who seeks a future of peace and dignity, and we are ready to lead once more.

Recall that earlier generations faced down fascism and communism not just with missiles and tanks but with the sturdy alliances and enduring convictions. They understood that our power alone cannot protect us, nor does it entitle us to do as we please. Instead, they knew that our power grows through its prudent use; our security emanates from the justness of our cause, the force of our example, the tempering qualities of humility and restraint.

We are the keepers of this legacy. Guided by these principles once more, we can meet those new threats that demand even greater effort—even greater cooperation and understanding between nations.

We will begin to responsibly leave Iraq to its people and forge a hard-earned peace in Afghanistan. With old friends and former foes, we'll work tirelessly to lessen the nuclear threat and roll back the specter of a warming planet.

We will not apologize for our way of life, nor will we waver in its defense, and for those who seek to advance their aims by inducing terror and slaughtering innocents, we say to you now that our spirit is stronger and cannot be broken; you cannot outlast us, and we will defeat you.

For we know that our patchwork heritage is a strength, not a weakness. We are a nation of Christians and Muslims, Jews and Hindus—and nonbelievers.

We are shaped by every language and culture, drawn from every end of this earth, and because we have tasted the bitter swill of civil war and segregation, and emerged from that dark chapter stronger and more united, we cannot help but believe that the old hatreds shall someday pass; that the lines of tribe shall soon dissolve; that as the world grows

hombre, mujer y niño que busquen un futuro de paz y dignidad, y estamos preparados para liderar una vez más.

Recordemos que anteriores generaciones amilanaron al fascismo y al comunismo no sólo con misiles y tanques, sino con fuertes alianzas y perdurables convicciones. Ellos entendieron que solamente nuestro poder no puede protegernos, ni nos da derecho a hacer lo que queramos. En cambio, sabían que nuestro poder crece mediante su uso prudente; nuestra seguridad emana de la justicia de nuestra causa, la fuerza de nuestro ejemplo, las atenuantes cualidades de la humildad y la moderación.

Nosotros somos los guardas de este legado. Guiados por estos principios una vez más, podemos afrontar estas nuevas amenazas y demandar un esfuerzo aún mayor, una cooperación y un entendimiento aún mayores entre las naciones.

Comenzaremos a dejar Iraq responsablemente en manos de su propio pueblo y forjar una paz ganada con mucho esfuerzo en Afganistán. Con viejos amigos y anteriores enemigos, trabajaremos sin descanso para reducir la amenaza nuclear y hacer retroceder el espectro de un planeta en calentamiento.

No nos disculparemos por nuestro modo de vida, ni tampoco vacilaremos a la hora de defenderlo, y para aquellos que pretendan hacer avanzar sus objetivos induciendo al terror y masacrando a inocentes, les decimos ahora que nuestro espíritu es más fuerte y no puede ser quebrantado; ustedes no pueden sobrevivir a nosotros, y nosotros les derrotaremos.

Porque sabemos que nuestro mosaico de herencia es una fortaleza y no una debilidad. Somos una nación de cristianos y musulmanes, de judíos e hindúes; y de no creyentes.

Somos moldeados por todo idioma y cultura, traídos desde todos los rincones de esta tierra, y debido a que hemos gustado el amargo trago de la guerra civil y la segregación, y hemos surgido de ese oscuro capítulo más fuertes y más unidos, no podemos evitar creer que los viejos odios pasarán algún día; que las líneas tribales pronto se difuminarán; que a medida que el mundo es más

smaller, our common humanity shall reveal itself; and that America must play its role in ushering in a new era of peace.

To the Muslim world, we seek a new way forward, based on mutual interest and mutual respect. To those leaders around the globe who seek to sow conflict or blame their society's ills on the West—know that your people will judge you on what you can build, not what you destroy. To those who cling to power through corruption and deceit and the silencing of dissent, know that you are on the wrong side of history, but that we will extend a hand if you are willing to unclench your fist.

To the people of poor nations, we pledge to work alongside you to make your farms flourish and let clean waters flow, to nourish starved bodies and feed hungry minds. And to those nations like ours that enjoy relative plenty, we say we can no longer afford indifference to the suffering outside our borders, nor can we consume the world's resources without regard to effect. For the world has changed, and we must change with it.

As we consider the road that unfolds before us, we remember with humble gratitude those brave Americans who, at this very hour, patrol far-off deserts and distant mountains. They have something to tell us, just as the fallen heroes who lie in Arlington whisper through the ages.

We honor them not only because they are guardians of our liberty but because they embody the spirit of service, a willingness to find meaning in something greater than themselves. And yet, at this moment—a moment that will define a generation—it is precisely this spirit that must inhabit us all.

For as much as government can do and must do, it is ultimately the faith and determination of the American people on which this nation relies. It

pequeño, nuestra común humanidad se revelará; y que Estados Unidos debe desempeñar su papel para dar entrada a una nueva era de paz.

Para el mundo musulmán: buscamos un nuevo camino para avanzar, basado en el interés mutuo y en el respeto mutuo. A aquellos líderes en todo el mundo que buscan sembrar conflicto o culpar a Occidente de los males de su sociedad: sepan que su pueblo les juzgará por lo que puedan construir, y no por lo que puedan destruir. A aquellos que se aferran al poder mediante la corrupción, el engaño y haciendo callar a los disidentes; sepan que están ustedes en el lado equivocado de la Historia, pero que extenderemos una mano si están dispuestos a aflojar su puño.

A las personas de naciones pobres: nos comprometemos a trabajar a su lado para hacer que sus granjas se desarrollen y conseguir que tengan agua potable, para nutrir cuerpos desnutridos y alimentar mentes hambrientas. Y para aquellas naciones como la nuestra que disfrutan de una relativa abundancia, les decimos que ya no podemos permitirnos la indiferencia a quienes sufren fuera de nuestras fronteras, ni tampoco podemos consumir los recursos del mundo sin tener en cuenta el efecto. Porque el mundo ha cambiado, y nosotros debemos cambiar con él.

Al considerar el camino que se extiende delante de nosotros, recordemos con humilde gratitud a esos valientes estadounidenses que, en este mismo momento, patrullan lejanos desiertos y distantes montañas. Ellos tienen algo que decirnos, al igual que los héroes caídos que yacen en Arlington susurran en todas las épocas.

Les honramos no sólo porque son guardianes de nuestra libertad, sino también porque ellos representan el espíritu de servicio, una disposición a encontrar significado en algo más grande que ellos mismos. Y así, en este momento—un momento que definirá una generación—, es precisamente ese espíritu el que debe habitar en todos nosotros.

Porque por mucho que el gobierno pueda hacer, y deba hacer, es en definitiva la fe y la determinación del pueblo estadounidense sobre lo

is the kindness to take in a stranger when the levees break, the selflessness of workers who would rather cut their hours than see a friend lose their job, which sees us through our darkest hours. It is the firefighter's courage to storm a stairway filled with smoke, but also a parent's willingness to nurture a child, that finally decides our fate.

Our challenges may be new. The instruments with which we meet them may be new. But those values on which our success depends—honesty and hard work, courage and fair play, tolerance and curiosity, loyalty and patriotism—these things are old. These things are true.

They have been the quiet force of progress throughout our history. What is demanded then is a return to these truths. What is required of us now is a new era of responsibility—a recognition, on the part of every American, that we have duties to ourselves, our nation, and the world, duties that we do not grudgingly accept but rather seize gladly, firm in the knowledge that there is nothing so satisfying to the spirit, so defining of our character, than giving our all to a difficult task.

This is the price and the promise of citizenship.

This is the source of our confidence—the knowledge that God calls on us to shape an uncertain destiny.

This is the meaning of our liberty and our creed—why men and women and children of every race and every faith can join in celebration across this magnificent mall, and why a man whose father less than sixty years ago might not have been served at a local restaurant can now stand before you to take a most sacred oath.

que esta nación se apoya. Es la bondad de aceptar a un extraño cuando los diques se rompen, la falta de egoísmo de trabajadores que prefieren recortar sus horas de trabajo antes de ver a un amigo perder su empleo, lo que nos ayuda a atravesar nuestros peores momentos. Es el valor del bombero que sube por una escalera llena de humo, pero también la disposición de un padre a alimentar a su hijo, lo que finalmente decide nuestro destino.

Nuestros desafíos puede que sean nuevos. Los instrumentos con los cuales los afrontemos puede que sean nuevos. Pero esos valores de los cuales depende el éxito—honestidad y trabajo duro, coraje y juego limpio, tolerancia y curiosidad, lealtad y patriotismo—, esas cosas son viejas; esas cosas son verdaderas.

Han sido la callada fortaleza del progreso a lo largo de nuestra historia. Lo que se demanda, por tanto, es un regreso a esos principios. Lo que se requiere de nosotros ahora es una nueva era de responsabilidad: un reconocimiento, por parte de cada estadounidense, de que tenemos obligaciones con nosotros mismos, con nuestra nación y con el mundo, obligaciones que no aceptamos de mala gana sino que agarramos con alegría, firmes en el conocimiento de que no hay nada tan satisfactorio para el espíritu, que defina tanto nuestro carácter, que entregar nuestro todo a una tarea difícil.

Este es el precio y la promesa de la ciudadanía.

Esta es la fuente de nuestra confianza: el conocimiento de que Dios nos llama a moldear un destino incierto.

Este es el significado de nuestra libertad y nuestro credo, la razón de que hombres, mujeres y niños de toda raza y de toda creencia puedan unirse en celebración en este magnífico lugar, y la razón de que un hombre cuyo padre hace menos de setenta años no podía recibir servicio en un restaurante local pueda ahora estar delante de ustedes para hacer un sagrado juramento.

So let us mark this day with remembrance, of who we are and how far we have traveled.

In the year of America's birth, in the coldest of months, a small band of patriots huddled by dying campfires on the shores of an icy river. The capital was abandoned. The enemy was advancing. The snow was stained with blood.

At a moment when the outcome of our revolution was most in doubt, the father of our nation ordered these words be read to the people:

> "Let it be told to the future world . . . that in the depth of winter, when nothing but hope and virtue could survive . . . that the city and the country, alarmed at one common danger, came forth to meet [it]."

America. In the face of our common dangers, in this winter of our hardship, let us remember these timeless words. With hope and virtue, let us brave once more the icy currents and endure what storms may come.

Let it be said by our children's children that when we were tested we refused to let this journey end, that we did not turn back nor did we falter, and with eyes fixed on the horizon and God's grace upon us, we carried forth that great gift of freedom and delivered it safely to future generations.

Por tanto, marquemos este día con recuerdo, de quiénes somos y hasta dónde hemos llegado.

En el año del nacimiento de Estados Unidos, en los meses más fríos, un pequeño grupo de patriotas se reunían alrededor de fogatas casi extintas en las riberas de un río helado. La capital estaba abandonada. El enemigo estaba avanzando. La nieve estaba manchada de sangre.

En un momento en que el resultado de nuestra revolución estaba más en duda, el padre de nuestra nación ordenó que las siguientes palabras se leyeran al pueblo:

"Que se diga al mundo futuro... que en lo más crudo del invierno, cuando nada sino la esperanza y la virtud podía sobrevivir... que la ciudad y el país, alarmados ante un peligro común, respondieron para afrontarlo".

Estados Unidos. Ante nuestros peligros comunes, en este invierno de nuestra dificultad, recordemos estas palabras intemporales. Con esperanza y virtud, hagamos frente una vez más a las heladas corrientes y soportemos las tormentas que puedan llegar.

Que los hijos de nuestros hijos digan que cuando fuimos probados, nos negamos a permitir que este viaje finalizase, que no volvimos atrás ni vacilamos, y que con ojos fijos en el horizonte y la gracia de Dios sobre nosotros, seguimos sosteniendo ese gran regalo de la libertad y lo llevamos con seguridad a futuras generaciones.

A New Beginning speech
June 4, 2009
Cairo, Egypt

On a five-day trip through the Middle East, President Obama chose to address Muslims worldwide with a talk that highlighted the importance of Islam and the responsibility that people of all religions have to work together for peace and prosperity.

For over a thousand years, Al-Azhar has stood as a beacon of Islamic learning, and for over a century, Cairo University has been a source of Egypt's advancement. Together, you represent the harmony between tradition and progress.

We meet at a time of tension between the United States and Muslims around the world—tension rooted in historical forces that go beyond any current policy debate. The relationship between Islam and the West includes centuries of coexistence and cooperation, but also conflict and religious wars.

More recently, tension has been fed by colonialism that denied rights and opportunities to many Muslims, and a Cold War in which Muslim-majority countries were too often treated as proxies without regard to their own aspirations. Moreover, the sweeping change brought by modernity and globalization led many Muslims to view the West as hostile to the traditions of Islam.

Discurso "Un nuevo comienzo"
4 de junio de 2009
Cairo, Egipto

En un viaje de cinco días por el Medio Oriente, el presidente Obama escogió dirigirse a musulmanes en todo el mundo con una charla que destacó la importancia del islam y la responsabilidad que las personas de todas las religiones tienen de trabajar juntas por la paz y la prosperidad.

Por más de mil años, Al-Azhar se ha erigido como un faro de aprendizaje islámico, y por más de una década la Universidad de Cairo ha sido una fuente de avance de Egipto. Juntos, ustedes representan la armonía entre tradición y progreso.

Nos reunimos en un momento de tensión entre los Estados Unidos y los musulmanes en todo el mundo; una tensión arraigada en fuerzas históricas que están por encima de cualquier debate político actual. La relación entre el islam y Occidente incluye siglos de coexistencia y cooperación, pero también de conflicto y guerras religiosas.

Más recientemente, la tensión se ha visto alimentada por el colonialismo que negó derechos y oportunidades a muchos musulmanes, y una Guerra Fría en la cual los países de mayoría musulmana fueron tratados con demasiada frecuencia como apoderados sin considerar sus propias aspiraciones. Además, el cambio radical producido por la modernidad y la globalización condujo a muchos musulmanes a considerar Occidente hostil a las tradiciones del islam.

Violent extremists have exploited these tensions in a small but potent minority of Muslims. The attacks of September 11, 2001, and the continued efforts of these extremists to engage in violence against civilians have led some in my country to view Islam as inevitably hostile not only to America and Western countries but also to human rights. This has bred more fear and mistrust.

So long as our relationship is defined by our differences, we will empower those who sow hatred rather than peace and who promote conflict rather than the cooperation that can help all of our people achieve justice and prosperity. This cycle of suspicion and discord must end.

I have come here to seek a new beginning between the United States and Muslims around the world, one based on mutual interest and mutual respect, on the truth that America and Islam are not exclusive and need not be in competition. Instead, they overlap and share common principles—principles of justice and progress, tolerance and the dignity of all human beings.

I do so recognizing that change cannot happen overnight. No single speech can eradicate years of mistrust, nor can I answer in the time that I have all the complex questions that brought us to this point. But I am convinced that to move forward, we must say openly the things we hold in our hearts, and that too often are said only behind closed doors.

There must be a sustained effort to listen to each other, to learn from each other, to respect one another, and to seek common ground. As the Holy Koran tells us, "Be conscious of God and speak always the truth." That is what I will try to do—to speak the truth as best I can, humbled by the task before us and firm in my belief that the interests we share as human beings are far more powerful than the forces that drive us apart.

Extremistas violentos han explotado esas tensiones en una pequeña pero potente minoría de musulmanes. Los ataques del 11 de septiembre de 2001, y los continuados esfuerzos de esos extremistas por tomar parte en la violencia contra civiles, ha llevado a algunos en mi país a considerar al islam inevitablemente hostil no sólo a Estados Unidos y los países occidentales, sino también a los derechos humanos. Esto ha engendrado más temor y desconfianza.

Mientras nuestra relación esté definida por nuestras diferencias, capacitaremos a quienes siembran odio en lugar de paz, y a quienes promueven el conflicto en lugar de la cooperación que puede ayudar a toda nuestra gente a lograr justicia y prosperidad. Este círculo de sospecha y discordia debe terminar.

He venido aquí para buscar un nuevo comienzo entre los Estados Unidos y los musulmanes en todo el mundo, un comienzo basado en el interés mutuo y el respeto mutuo, en la verdad de que Estados Unidos y el islam no son exclusivos y no tienen por qué estar en competición. En cambio, coinciden y comparten principios comunes: principios de justicia y progreso, de tolerancia y de la dignidad de todos los seres humanos.

Y lo hago reconociendo que el cambio no puede suceder de la noche a la mañana. Ningún discurso puede erradicar años de desconfianza, ni tampoco puedo yo responder en el tiempo que tengo todas las preguntas que nos han traído hasta este punto. Pero estoy convencido de que, para avanzar, debemos decir abiertamente las cosas que tenemos en nuestros corazones, y que con demasiada frecuencia se dicen solamente tras puertas cerradas.

Debe haber un esfuerzo sostenido para escucharnos los unos a los otros, para aprender los unos de los otros, para respetarnos mutuamente, y para buscar un terreno común. Como nos dice el Santo Corán: "Ten conciencia de Dios y habla siempre la verdad". Eso es lo que intentaré hacer: hablar la verdad lo mejor que pueda, humillado ante la tarea que tenemos por delante y firme en mi creencia de que los intereses que compartimos como seres humanos son mucho más potentes y profundos que las fuerzas que nos separan.

Part of this conviction is rooted in my own experience. I am a Christian, but my father came from a Kenyan family that includes generations of Muslims. As a boy, I spent several years in Indonesia and heard the call of the azaan at the break of dawn and the fall of dusk. As a young man, I worked in Chicago communities where many found dignity and peace in their Muslim faith.

As a student of history, I also know civilization's debt to Islam. It was Islam—at places like Al-Azhar University—that carried the light of learning through so many centuries, paving the way for Europe's Renaissance and Enlightenment. It was innovation in Muslim communities that developed the order of algebra, our magnetic compass and tools of navigation, our mastery of pens and printing, our understanding of how disease spreads and how it can be healed.

Islamic culture has given us majestic arches and soaring spires, timeless poetry and cherished music, elegant calligraphy and places of peaceful contemplation. And throughout history, Islam has demonstrated through words and deeds the possibilities of religious tolerance and racial equality.

I know, too, that Islam has always been a part of America's story. The first nation to recognize my country was Morocco. In signing the Treaty of Tripoli in 1796, our second President John Adams wrote, "The United States has in itself no character of enmity against the laws, religion or tranquility of Muslims."

And since our founding, American Muslims have enriched the United States. They have fought in our wars, served in government, stood for civil rights, started businesses, taught at our universities, excelled in our sports arenas, won Nobel Prizes, built our tallest building, and lit the Olympic Torch.

Parte de esta convicción está arraigada en mi propia experiencia. Yo soy cristiano, pero mi padre provenía de una familia keniana que incluye generaciones de musulmanes. Cuando yo era un muchacho, pasé varios años en Indonesia y oía la llamada del azaan al amanecer y a la caída del atardecer. Cuando era joven, trabajé en comunidades en Chicago donde muchos encontraban dignidad y paz en su fe musulmana.

Como estudiante de Historia, también sé la deuda que la civilización tiene con el islam. Fue el islam —en lugares como la Universidad Al-Azhar— el portador de la luz del aprendizaje durante muchos siglos, preparando el terreno para el Renacimiento y la Ilustración de Europa. Fue la innovación en comunidades musulmanas la que desarrolló el orden del álgebra, nuestra brújula magnética e instrumentos de navegación, nuestro dominio de la pluma y la imprenta, nuestro entendimiento sobre cómo se propagan las enfermedades y cómo pueden curarse.

La cultura islámica nos ha dado majestuosos arcos y altísimas agujas, intemporal poesía y preciada música, elegante caligrafía y lugares de pacífica contemplación. Y, a lo largo de la Historia, el islam ha demostrado por medio de palabras y obras las posibilidades de la tolerancia religiosa y la igualdad racial.

Sé también que el islam siempre ha sido parte de la historia de Estados Unidos. La primera nación en reconocer a mi país fue Marruecos. En la firma del Tratado de Trípoli en 1796, nuestro segundo Presidente, John Adams, escribió: "Los Estados Unidos no tienen en sí mismos carácter alguno de enemistad contra las leyes, la religión o la tranquilidad de los musulmanes".

Y desde nuestra fundación, los musulmanes estadounidenses han enriquecido a los Estados Unidos. Ellos han luchado en nuestras guerras, han servido en el gobierno, han defendido los derechos civiles, han comenzado negocios, han enseñado en nuestras universidades, se han destacado en nuestros estadios deportivos, han ganado premios Nobel, han construido nuestros edificios más altos, y han encendido la Antorcha Olímpica.

And when the first Muslim American was recently elected to Congress, he took the oath to defend our Constitution using the same Holy Koran that one of our Founding Fathers—Thomas Jefferson—kept in his personal library.

So I have known Islam on three continents before coming to the region where it was first revealed. That experience guides my conviction that partnership between America and Islam must be based on what Islam is, not on what it isn't. And I consider it part of my responsibility as president to fight against negative stereotypes of Islam wherever they appear.

But that same principle must apply to Muslim perceptions of America. Just as Muslims do not fit a crude stereotype, America is not the crude stereotype of a self-interested empire.

The United States has been one of the greatest sources of progress that the world has ever known. We were born out of revolution against an empire. We were founded on the ideal that all are created equal, and we have shed blood and struggled for centuries to give meaning to those words—within our borders and around the world. We are shaped by every culture, drawn from every end of the earth, and dedicated to a simple concept: *E pluribus unum*, "Out of many, one."

Much has been made of the fact that an African American with the name Barack Hussein Obama could be elected president. But my personal story is not so unique. The dream of opportunity for all people has not come true for everyone in America, but its promise exists for all who come to our shores.

Moreover, freedom in America is indivisible from the freedom to practice one's religion. That is why there is a mosque in every state of our union,

Y cuando el primer musulmán estadounidense fue recientemente elegido al Congreso, hizo el juramento de defender nuestra Constitución utilizando el mismo Santo Corán que uno de nuestros padres fundadores—Thomas Jefferson—conservaba en su biblioteca personal.

Por tanto, he conocido el islam en tres continentes antes de llegar a la región donde fue revelado por primera vez. Esa experiencia guía mi convicción de que la colaboración entre Estados Unidos y el islam debe basarse en lo que es el islam, y no en lo que no es. Y considero parte de mi responsabilidad como presidente el luchar contra estereotipos negativos del islam dondequiera que aparezcan.

Pero ese mismo principio debe aplicarse a las percepciones que los musulmanes tienen de Estados Unidos. Al igual que los musulmanes no encajan en un burdo estereotipo, Estados Unidos no es el burdo estereotipo de un imperio que actúa en interés propio.

Los Estados Unidos han sido una de las mayores fuentes de progreso que el mundo haya conocido jamás. Nacimos de la revolución contra un imperio. Fuimos fundados sobre el ideal de que todos somos creados iguales, y hemos derramado sangre y luchado durante siglos para dar significado a esas palabras: dentro de nuestras fronteras y alrededor del mundo. Somos moldeados por todas las culturas, traídos desde cada rincón de la tierra, y dedicados a un concepto simple: E pluribus unum, "De muchos, uno".

Se ha dado mucha importancia al hecho de que un afroamericano con el nombre de Barack Hussein Obama pudiera ser elegido presidente. Pero mi historia personal no es tan singular. El sueño de la oportunidad para todas las personas no se ha hecho realidad para todo el mundo en Estados Unidos, pero su promesa existe para todos aquellos que llegan a nuestras costas.

Es más, la libertad en Estados Unidos es indivisible de la libertad de practicar la religión de cada uno. Por eso hay una mezquita en cada estado

and over 1,200 mosques within our borders. That is why the U.S. government has gone to court to protect the right of women and girls to wear the hijab, and to punish those who would deny it.

So let there be no doubt: Islam is a part of America. And I believe that America holds within her the truth that regardless of race, religion, or station in life, all of us share common aspirations—to live in peace and security; to get an education and to work with dignity; to love our families, our communities, and our God. These things we share. This is the hope of all humanity.

Of course, recognizing our common humanity is only the beginning of our task. Words alone cannot meet the needs of our people. These needs will be met only if we act boldly in the years ahead and if we understand that the challenges we face are shared, and our failure to meet them will hurt us all.

This is a difficult responsibility to embrace. For human history has often been a record of nations and tribes subjugating one another to serve their own interests. Yet in this new age, such attitudes are self-defeating. Given our interdependence, any world order that elevates one nation or group of people over another will inevitably fail.

So whatever we think of the past, we must not be prisoners of it. Our problems must be dealt with through partnership; progress must be shared.

The first issue that we have to confront is violent extremism.

In Ankara I made clear that America is not—and never will be—at war with Islam. We will, however, relentlessly confront violent extremists who pose a grave threat to our security. We reject the same thing that people

de nuestra unión, y más de 1200 mezquitas dentro de nuestras fronteras. Por eso el gobierno de los Estados Unidos ha ido a los tribunales para proteger el derecho de las mujeres y las niñas a llevar el hiyab, y para castigar a quienes quieran negárselo.

Por tanto, que no haya duda: el islam es parte de Estados Unidos. Y creo que Estados Unidos sostiene la verdad de que, a pesar de la raza, la religión, o el rango en la vida, todos nosotros compartimos aspiraciones comunes: vivir en paz y seguridad; obtener una educación y trabajar con dignidad; amar a nuestras familias, nuestras comunidades y a nuestro Dios. Todas esas cosas compartimos. Esta es la esperanza de toda la humanidad.

Desde luego, reconocer nuestra común humanidad es sólo el comienzo de nuestra tarea. Solamente las palabras no pueden cubrir las necesidades de nuestro pueblo. Esas necesidades serán cubiertas sólo si actuamos con valentía en los próximos años y si entendemos que los desafíos que afrontamos son compartidos, y que no cubrirlas nos hará daño a todos.

Esta es una responsabilidad difícil de aceptar. Porque la historia humana con frecuencia ha sido una trayectoria de naciones y tribus subyugándose unas a otras para servir a sus propios intereses. Sin embargo, en esta nueva era, tales actitudes son contraproducentes. Dada nuestra independencia, cualquier orden mundial que eleve a una nación o grupo de personas sobre otro, fracasará inevitablemente.

Por tanto, pensemos lo que pensemos del pasado, no debemos ser prisioneros de él. Nuestros problemas deben tratarse mediante la colaboración; el progreso debe ser compartido.

El primer asunto que tenemos que confrontar es el extremismo violento.

En Ankara dejé claro que Estados Unidos no está—y nunca estará—en guerra con el islam. Sin embargo, confrontaremos de modo implacable a los extremistas violentos que representen una grave amenaza para nuestra

of all faiths reject: the killing of innocent men, women, and children. And it is my first duty as president to protect the American people.

The situation in Afghanistan demonstrates America's goals and our need to work together. Over seven years ago, the United States pursued al-Qaeda and the Taliban with broad international support. We did not go by choice; we went because of necessity.

I am aware that some question or justify the events of 9/11. But let us be clear: al-Qaeda killed nearly three thousand people on that day. The victims were innocent men, women, and children from America and many other nations who had done nothing to harm anybody.

Make no mistake: we do not want to keep our troops in Afghanistan. We seek no military bases there. It is agonizing for America to lose our young men and women. It is costly and politically difficult to continue this conflict.

We would gladly bring every single one of our troops home if we could be confident that there were not violent extremists in Afghanistan and Pakistan determined to kill as many Americans as they possibly can. But that is not yet the case.

That's why we're partnering with a coalition of forty-six countries. And despite the costs involved, America's commitment will not weaken. Indeed, none of us should tolerate these extremists. Their actions are irreconcilable with the rights of human beings, the progress of nations, and with Islam.

The Holy Koran teaches that whoever kills an innocent, it is as if he has killed all mankind, and whoever saves a person, it is as if he has saved all mankind. The enduring faith of over a billion people is so much bigger than the narrow hatred of a few. Islam is not part of the

seguridad. Rechazamos lo mismo que las personas de todas las creencias rechazan: la matanza de hombres, mujeres y niños inocentes. Y es mi primera tarea como presidente proteger al pueblo estadounidense.

La situación en Afganistán demuestra los objetivos de Estados Unidos y nuestra necesidad de trabajar juntos. Hace más de siete años, los Estados Unidos persiguieron a al-Qaeda y a los talibanes con un amplio apoyo internacional. No lo hicimos por elección; lo hicimos por necesidad.

Soy consciente de que algunos cuestionan o justifican los acontecimientos del 11 de septiembre. Pero seamos claros: al-Qaeda mató casi a tres mil personas aquel día. Las víctimas eran hombres, mujeres y niños inocentes de Estados Unidos y de muchas otras naciones que no habían hecho nada para hacer daño a nadie.

No nos equivoquemos: no queremos mantener a nuestras tropas en Afganistán; no buscamos tener bases militares allí. Es muy doloroso para Estados Unidos perder a nuestros jóvenes soldados. Es costoso y políticamente difícil continuar con este conflicto.

Con mucho gusto haríamos regresar a casa a cada una de nuestras tropas si pudiéramos tener confianza en que no habría extremistas violentos en Afganistán y en Pakistán decididos a matar tantos estadounidenses como puedan. Pero ese no es todavía el caso.

Por eso estamos colaborando en una coalición de cuarenta y seis países. Y a pesar de los costos implícitos, el compromiso de Estados Unidos no se debilitará. De hecho, ninguno de nosotros debería tolerar a esos extremistas. Sus actos son irreconciliables con los derechos de los seres humanos, con el progreso de las naciones, y con el islam.

El Santo Corán enseña que quien mate a un inocente es como si hubiera matado a toda la humanidad, y quien salve a una persona es como si hubiera salvado a toda la humanidad. La fe duradera de más de mil millones de personas es mucho más grande que el estrecho odio de unos

problem in combating violent extremism—it is an important part of promoting peace.

Let me also address the issue of Iraq. Unlike Afghanistan, Iraq was a war of choice that provoked strong differences in my country and around the world.

Although I believe that the Iraqi people are ultimately better off without the tyranny of Saddam Hussein, I also believe that events in Iraq have reminded America of the need to use diplomacy and build international consensus to resolve our problems whenever possible. Indeed, we can recall the words of Thomas Jefferson, who said: "I hope that our wisdom will grow with our power, and teach us that the less we use our power the greater it will be."

And finally, just as America can never tolerate violence by extremists, we must never alter our principles. 9/11 was an enormous trauma to our country. The fear and anger that it provoked was understandable, but in some cases, it led us to act contrary to our ideals.

We are taking concrete actions to change course. I have unequivocally prohibited the use of torture by the United States, and I have ordered the prison at Guantánamo Bay closed by early next year.

So America will defend itself respectful of the sovereignty of nations and the rule of law. And we will do so in partnership with Muslim communities that are also threatened. The sooner the extremists are isolated and unwelcome in Muslim communities, the sooner we will all be safer.

The second major source of tension is the situation between Israelis, Palestinians, and the Arab world.

cuantos. El islam no es parte del problema para combatir el extremismo violento; es una importante parte del fomento de la paz.

Permítanme que también aborde el asunto de Iraq. Contrariamente a la de Afganistán, la de Iraq fue una guerra por elección que provocó fuertes diferencias en mi país y en todo el mundo.

Aunque yo creo que el pueblo iraquí está definitivamente mejor sin la tiranía de Saddam Hussein, también creo que los acontecimientos en Iraq han recordado a Estados Unidos la necesidad de utilizar la diplomacia y de desarrollar un consenso internacional para resolver nuestros problemas siempre que sea posible. De hecho, podemos recordar las palabras de Thomas Jefferson, que dijo: "Espero que nuestra sabiduría crezca junto con nuestro poder, y nos enseñe que cuanto menos utilicemos nuestro poder, mayor será".

Y finalmente, al igual que Estados Unidos nunca puede tolerar la violencia perpetrada por extremistas, nunca debemos alterar nuestros principios. El 11 de septiembre fue un enorme trauma para nuestro país. El temor y la ira que provocó eran comprensibles, pero, en algunos casos, nos condujo a actuar contrariamente a nuestros ideales.

Estamos adoptando actos concretos para cambiar de curso. He prohibido rotundamente que los Estados Unidos utilicen la tortura, y he ordenado que la prisión en Guantánamo Bay sea cerrada a principios del año próximo.

Por tanto, Estados Unidos se defenderá manteniendo el respeto por la soberanía de las naciones y el imperio de la ley. Y lo haremos en colaboración con las comunidades musulmanas que también están amenazadas. Cuanto antes sean aislados y no bienvenidos los extremistas en las comunidades musulmanas, antes estaremos todos más seguros.

La segunda fuente importante de tensión es la situación entre israelíes, palestinos y el mundo árabe.

America's strong bonds with Israel are well known. This bond is unbreakable. It is based on cultural and historical ties, and the recognition that the aspiration for a Jewish homeland is rooted in a tragic history that cannot be denied.

Around the world, the Jewish people were persecuted for centuries, and anti-Semitism in Europe culminated in an unprecedented Holocaust. Tomorrow, I visit Buchenwald, which was part of a network of camps where Jews were enslaved, tortured, shot, and gassed to death by the Third Reich. Six million Jews were killed—more than the entire Jewish population of Israel today.

Denying that fact is baseless, ignorant, and hateful. Threatening Israel with destruction—or repeating vile stereotypes about Jews—is deeply wrong and only serves to evoke in the minds of Israelis this most painful of memories while preventing the peace that the people of this region deserve.

On the other hand, it is also undeniable that the Palestinian people— Muslims and Christians—have suffered in pursuit of a homeland. For more than sixty years they have endured the pain of dislocation. Many wait in refugee camps in the West Bank, Gaza, and neighboring lands for a life of peace and security that they have never been able to lead. They endure the daily humiliations—large and small—that come with occupation.

So let there be no doubt: the situation for the Palestinian people is intolerable. America will not turn our backs on the legitimate Palestinian aspiration for dignity, opportunity, and a state of their own.

For decades, there has been a stalemate: two peoples with legitimate aspirations, each with a painful history that makes compromise elusive. It is easy to point fingers—for Palestinians to point to the displacement brought by Israel's founding and for Israelis to point to the constant hostility and attacks throughout its history from within its borders as well as beyond. But if we see this conflict only from one side or the other, then

Los fuertes vínculos de Estados Unidos con Israel son bien conocidos. Este vínculo es inquebrantable. Está basado en lazos culturales e históricos, y en el reconocimiento de que la aspiración de una tierra natal judía está arraigada en una trágica historia que no puede negarse.

Alrededor del mundo, el pueblo judío fue perseguido durante siglos, y el anti-semitismo en Europa culminó en un Holocausto sin precedentes. Mañana visito Buchenwald, que fue parte de una red de campos donde los judíos fueron esclavizados, torturados y asesinados por disparos y por gas por el Tercer Reich. Murieron seis millones de judíos, más que toda la población judía de Israel en la actualidad.

Negar el hecho es infundado, ignorante y odioso. Amenazar a Israel con la destrucción—o repetir viles estereotipos sobre los judíos—es profundamente equivocado, y sólo sirve para evocar en las mentes de los israelíes este recuerdo tan doloroso a la vez que para impedir la paz que el pueblo de esa región merece.

Por otro lado, es también innegable que el pueblo palestino—musulmanes y cristianos—ha sufrido en la búsqueda de una tierra propia. Por más de setenta años han soportado el dolor del desplazamiento. Muchos esperan en campos de refugiados en la Franja Occidental, Gaza, y tierras vecinas una vida de paz y seguridad que nunca han podido llevar. Soportan las humillaciones diarias—grandes y pequeñas—que conlleva la ocupación.

Por tanto, que no haya duda alguna: la situación del pueblo palestino es intolerable. Estados Unidos no dará la espalda a la legítima aspiración palestina a tener dignidad, oportunidad y un estado propio.

Durante décadas ha habido un punto muerto: dos pueblos con aspiraciones legítimas, cada uno de ellos con una dolorosa historia que hace que el compromiso sea esquivo. Es fácil señalar; los palestinos señalar al desplazamiento producido por la fundación de Israel, y los israelíes señalar a la constante hostilidad y los ataques a lo largo de su historia desde dentro de sus fronteras al igual que desde fuera. Pero si vemos este

we will be blind to the truth: the only resolution is for the aspirations of both sides to be met through two states, where Israelis and Palestinians each live in peace and security.

That is in Israel's interest, Palestine's interest, America's interest, and the world's interest.

Palestinians must abandon violence. Resistance through violence and killing is wrong and does not succeed. For centuries, black people in America suffered the lash of the whip as slaves and the humiliation of segregation.

But it was not violence that won full and equal rights. It was a peaceful and determined insistence on the ideals at the center of America's founding. This same story can be told by people from South Africa to South Asia, from Eastern Europe to Indonesia.

It's a story with a simple truth: that violence is a dead end. It is a sign of neither courage nor power to shoot rockets at sleeping children or to blow up old women on a bus. That is not how moral authority is claimed—that is how it is surrendered.

Now is the time for Palestinians to focus on what they can build. The Palestinian Authority must develop its capacity to govern, with institutions that serve the needs of its people. Hamas does have support among some Palestinians, but it also has responsibilities. To play a role in fulfilling Palestinian aspirations and to unify the Palestinian people, Hamas must put an end to violence, recognize past agreements, and recognize Israel's right to exist.

At the same time, Israelis must acknowledge that just as Israel's right to exist cannot be denied, neither can Palestine's. The United States does not accept the legitimacy of continued Israeli settlements. This construction

conflicto solamente desde un lado o desde el otro, entonces estaremos ciegos a la verdad: la única resolución es que las aspiraciones de ambas partes se cumplan por medio de dos estados, donde israelíes y palestinos vivan cada uno de ellos en paz y seguridad.

Eso le conviene a Israel, le conviene a Palestina, le conviene a Estados Unidos, y le conviene al mundo.

Los palestinos deben abandonar la violencia. La resistencia mediante la violencia y el asesinato está mal y no consigue el éxito. Durante siglos, el pueblo de raza negra en Estados Unidos sufrió los azotes del látigo como esclavo y la humillación de la segregación.

Pero no fue la violencia la que consiguió derechos plenos e igualitarios; fue la pacífica y decidida insistencia en los ideales que estaban en el núcleo de la fundación de Estados Unidos. Esta misma historia la pueden relatar personas desde Sudáfrica hasta Sudasia, desde Europa Oriental hasta Indonesia.

Es una historia con una sencilla verdad: que la violencia es un callejón sin salida. No es una señal ni de valentía ni de poder disparar cohetes a niños que duermen o hacer volar por los aires a ancianas que van en autobús. No es así como se reivindica la autoridad moral; así es como se rinde.

Ahora es momento de que los palestinos se enfoquen en lo que pueden construir. La Autoridad Palestina debe desarrollar su capacidad de gobernar, con instituciones que sirvan a las necesidades de su pueblo. Hamás sí tiene apoyo entre algunos palestinos, pero también tiene responsabilidades. Para desempeñar un papel a la hora de cumplir las aspiraciones palestinas y unificar al pueblo palestino, Hamás debe poner fin a la violencia, reconocer los acuerdos del pasado, y reconocer el derecho de Israel a existir.

Al mismo tiempo, los israelíes deben reconocer que, al igual que no puede negarse el derecho de Israel a existir, tampoco puede negarse el de los palestinos. Los Estados Unidos no aceptan la legitimidad de asentamientos

violates previous agreements and undermines efforts to achieve peace. It is time for these settlements to stop.

Israel must also live up to its obligations to ensure that Palestinians can live, and work, and develop their society. And just as it devastates Palestinian families, the continuing humanitarian crisis in Gaza does not serve Israel's security; neither does the continuing lack of opportunity in the West Bank. Progress in the daily lives of the Palestinian people must be part of a road to peace, and Israel must take concrete steps to enable such progress.

Finally, the Arab states must recognize that the Arab Peace Initiative was an important beginning, but not the end of their responsibilities. The Arab-Israeli conflict should no longer be used to distract the people of Arab nations from other problems. Instead, it must be a cause for action to help the Palestinian people develop the institutions that will sustain their state, to recognize Israel's legitimacy, and to choose progress over a self-defeating focus on the past.

America will align our policies with those who pursue peace and say in public what we say in private to Israelis and Palestinians and Arabs. We cannot impose peace. But privately, many Muslims recognize that Israel will not go away. Likewise, many Israelis recognize the need for a Palestinian state.

It is time for us to act on what everyone knows to be true.

Too many tears have flowed. Too much blood has been shed. All of us have a responsibility to work for the day when the mothers of Israelis and Palestinians can see their children grow up without fear; when the Holy Land of three great faiths is the place of peace that God intended it to be; when Jerusalem is a secure and lasting home for Jews and Christians and Muslims, and a place for all of the children of Abraham to mingle peacefully together as in the story of Isra, when Moses, Jesus, and Mohammad (peace be upon them) joined in prayer.

israelíes continuados. Esa construcción viola anteriores acuerdos y mina los esfuerzos por lograr la paz. Es momento de que esos asentamientos terminen.

Israel también debe estar a la altura de sus obligaciones para asegurarse de que los palestinos puedan vivir, y trabajar, y desarrollar su sociedad. Y al igual que destruye a familias palestinas, la continuada crisis humanitaria en Gaza no es útil para la seguridad de Israel; y tampoco la continua falta de oportunidad en la Franja Occidental. El progreso en las vidas cotidianas del pueblo palestino debe ser parte de un camino hacia la paz, e Israel debe dar pasos concretos para hacer posible tal progreso.

Finalmente, los estados árabes deben reconocer que la Iniciativa Árabe de Paz fue un importante comienzo, pero no el final de sus responsabilidades. El conflicto árabe-israelí ya no debería utilizarse para distraer al pueblo de las naciones árabes de otros problemas. En cambio, debe ser una causa para actuar y ayudar al pueblo palestino a desarrollar las instituciones que sostendrán su estado, reconocer la legitimidad de Israel, y escoger el progreso por encima de un contraproducente enfoque en el pasado.

Estados Unidos alineará sus políticas con las de quienes persigan la paz y digan en público lo que les decimos en privado a israelíes, palestinos y árabes. No podemos imponer la paz; pero, en privado, muchos musulmanes reconocen que Israel no se irá. De igual modo, muchos israelíes reconocen la necesidad de un estado palestino.

Es momento de que actuemos según lo que todos saben que es cierto.

Se han vertido demasiadas lágrimas. Se ha derramado demasiada sangre. Todos nosotros tenemos la responsabilidad de trabajar para el día en que las madres de israelíes y palestinos puedan ver a sus hijos crecer sin temor; cuando la Tierra Santa de tres grandes religiones sea el lugar de paz que Dios quiso que fuera; cuando Jerusalén sea un hogar seguro y duradero para judíos, cristianos y musulmanes, y un lugar para que todos los hijos de Abraham se mezclen pacíficamente como en la historia de Isra, cuando Moisés, Jesús y Mahoma (paz sea sobre ellos) se unieron en oración.

The third source of tension is our shared interest in the rights and responsibilities of nations on nuclear weapons.

This issue has been a source of tension between the United States and the Islamic Republic of Iran. For many years, Iran has defined itself in part by its opposition to my country, and there is indeed a tumultuous history between us.

In the middle of the Cold War, the United States played a role in the overthrow of a democratically elected Iranian government. Since the Islamic Revolution, Iran has played a role in acts of hostage taking and violence against U.S. troops and civilians. This history is well known.

Rather than remain trapped in the past, I have made it clear to Iran's leaders and people that my country is prepared to move forward. The question, now, is not what Iran is against but what future it wants to build.

I understand those who protest that some countries have weapons that others do not. No single nation should pick and choose which nations hold nuclear weapons. That is why I strongly reaffirmed America's commitment to seek a world in which no nations hold nuclear weapons.

And any nation—including Iran—should have the right to access peaceful nuclear power if it complies with its responsibilities under the nuclear Non-Proliferation Treaty. That commitment is at the core of the treaty, and it must be kept for all who fully abide by it. And I am hopeful that all countries in the region can share in this goal.

The fourth issue that I will address is democracy.

I know there has been controversy about the promotion of democracy in recent years, and much of this controversy is connected to the war in Iraq. So let me be clear: no system of government can or should be imposed on one nation by any other.

La tercera fuente de tensión es nuestro interés compartido en los derechos y responsabilidades de las naciones con respecto a las armas nucleares.

Este asunto ha sido una fuente de tensión entre los Estados Unidos y la República Islámica de Irán. Por muchos años, Irán se ha definido a sí misma, en parte, por su oposición a mi país, y hay, de hecho, una tumultuosa historia entre nosotros.

En mitad de la Guerra Fría, los Estados Unidos desempeñaron un papel en el derrocamiento de un gobierno iraní democráticamente elegido. Desde la Revolución Islámica, Irán ha desempeñado un papel en actos de secuestros y violencia contra las tropas y civiles estadounidenses. Esta historia es bien conocida.

En lugar de permanecer atrapado en el pasado, he dejado claro a los líderes y al pueblo iraní que mi país está preparado para avanzar. La cuestión, ahora, no es en contra de qué está Irán, sino qué futuro quiere construir.

Entiendo a quienes protestan diciendo que algunos países tienen armas que otros no tienen. Ninguna nación por sí sola debería escoger qué países tienen armas nucleares. Por eso reafirmé con firmeza el compromiso de Estados Unidos de buscar un mundo en el cual ninguna nación tenga armas nucleares.

Y cualquier nación—incluyendo Irán—debería tener el derecho a tener acceso a la potencia nuclear pacífica si acata sus responsabilidades bajo el Tratado de No Proliferación. Ese compromiso está en el núcleo del tratado, y debe ser mantenido por todos los que lo cumplen plenamente. Y tengo la esperanza de que todos los países en la región puedan hacer su parte en este objetivo.

El cuarto asunto del que hablaré es la democracia.

Sé que ha habido controversia acerca del fomento de la democracia en años recientes, y gran parte de esta controversia está relacionada con la guerra en Iraq. Por tanto, permítanme ser claro: ninguna nación puede ni debe imponer ningún sistema de gobierno a otra.

That does not lessen my commitment, however, to governments that reflect the will of the people. Each nation gives life to this principle in its own way, grounded in the traditions of its own people. America does not presume to know what is best for everyone, just as we would not presume to pick the outcome of a peaceful election.

But I do have an unyielding belief that all people yearn for certain things: the ability to speak your mind and have a say in how you are governed; confidence in the rule of law and the equal administration of justice; government that is transparent and doesn't steal from the people; the freedom to live as you choose. Those are not just American ideas, they are human rights, and that is why we will support them everywhere.

There is no straight line to realize this promise. But this much is clear: governments that protect these rights are ultimately more stable, successful, and secure. Suppressing ideas never succeeds in making them go away.

America respects the right of all peaceful and law-abiding voices to be heard around the world, even if we disagree with them. And we will welcome all elected, peaceful governments—provided they govern with respect for all their people.

This last point is important because there are some who advocate for democracy only when they are out of power; once in power, they are ruthless in suppressing the rights of others. No matter where it takes hold, government of the people and by the people sets a single standard for all who hold power: you must maintain your power through consent, not coercion; you must respect the rights of minorities, and participate with a spirit of tolerance and compromise; you must place the interests of your people and the legitimate workings of the political process above your party. Without these ingredients, elections alone do not make true democracy.

The fifth issue that we must address together is religious freedom.

Eso no disminuye mi compromiso, sin embargo, con los gobiernos que reflejan la voluntad del pueblo. Cada nación da vida a este principio a su propia manera, arraigada en las tradiciones de su propio pueblo. Estados Unidos no pretende saber lo que es mejor para todos, al igual que no nos atreveríamos a forzar el resultado de unas elecciones pacíficas.

Pero sí tengo la creencia inflexible de que todas las personas anhelan ciertas cosas: la capacidad de decir lo que piensan y tener voz en cuanto a la forma de ser gobernadas; confianza en el imperio de la ley y la administración igualitaria de justicia; un gobierno que sea transparente y no robe al pueblo; la libertad de vivir del modo en que escojan. Estas no son solamente ideas estadounidenses; son derechos humanos, y por eso los apoyaremos en todas partes.

No hay una sola línea para cumplir esta promesa. Pero lo que sí está claro es que los gobiernos que protegen estos derechos son finalmente más estables, exitosos y seguros. Suprimir las ideas nunca tiene éxito para hacer que se vayan.

Estados Unidos respeta el derecho de todas las voces pacíficas y cumplidoras de la ley a ser oídas alrededor del mundo, aunque estemos en desacuerdo con ellas. Y recibiremos a todos los gobiernos elegidos y pacíficos, siempre que gobiernen con respeto hacia todo su pueblo.

Este último punto es importante porque hay algunos que defienden la democracia sólo cuando no están en el poder; una vez que suben al poder, son despiadados al suprimir los derechos de otros. Sin importar dónde se mantenga, el gobierno del pueblo y para el pueblo establece un patrón para todo el que ostenta el poder: debe mantener su poder mediante el consentimiento y no la coacción; debe respetar los derechos de las minorías, y participar con un espíritu de tolerancia y de compromiso; debe poner los intereses de su pueblo y el funcionamiento legítimo del proceso político por encima de su partido. Sin estos ingredientes, solamente unas elecciones no constituyen la verdadera democracia.

El quinto asunto que debemos abordar juntos es la libertad religiosa.

Islam has a proud tradition of tolerance. We see it in the history of Andalusia and Cordoba during the Inquisition. I saw it firsthand as a child in Indonesia, where devout Christians worshiped freely in an overwhelmingly Muslim country. That is the spirit we need today.

People in every country should be free to choose and live their faith based on the persuasion of the mind, heart, and soul. This tolerance is essential for religion to thrive, but it is being challenged in many different ways.

Among some Muslims, there is a disturbing tendency to measure one's own faith by the rejection of another's. The richness of religious diversity must be upheld—whether it is for Maronites in Lebanon or the Copts in Egypt. And fault lines must be closed among Muslims as well, as the divisions between Sunni and Shia have led to tragic violence, particularly in Iraq.

Freedom of religion is central to the ability of peoples to live together. We must always examine how we protect it. For instance, in the United States, rules on charitable giving have made it harder for Muslims to fulfill their religious obligation. That is why I am committed to working with American Muslims to ensure that they can fulfill zakat.

Likewise, it is important for Western countries to avoid impeding Muslim citizens from practicing religion as they see fit—for instance, by dictating what clothes a Muslim woman should wear. We cannot disguise hostility toward any religion behind the pretense of liberalism.

The sixth issue that I want to address is women's rights.

I know there is debate about this issue. I reject the view of some in the West that a woman who chooses to cover her hair is somehow less equal, but I do believe that a woman who is denied an education is denied

El islam tiene una orgullosa tradición de tolerancia. La vemos en la historia de Andalucía y de Córdoba durante la Inquisición. Yo la vi de primera mano cuando era niño en Indonesia, donde cristianos devotos adoraban con libertad en un país de inmensa mayoría musulmana. Ese es el espíritu que necesitamos hoy.

Las personas en todos los países deberían ser libres para escoger y vivir su fe basadas en la persuasión de la mente, el corazón y el alma. Esta tolerancia es esencial para que la religión prospere, pero está siendo desafiada de muchas formas distintas.

Entre algunos musulmanes, hay una inquietante tendencia a medir la fe propia por el rechazo de la fe de otro. La riqueza de la diversidad religiosa debe defenderse, ya sea para los maronitas en Líbano o para los coptos en Egipto. Y deben cerrarse fallas entre los musulmanes también, ya que las divisiones entre suníes y chiíes han llevado a una trágica violencia, particularmente en Iraq.

La libertad de religión es fundamental para que las personas puedan convivir; y siempre debemos examinar cómo la protegemos. Por ejemplo, en los Estados Unidos, las normas sobre donativos benéficos han hecho más difícil que los musulmanes cumplan con su obligación religiosa. Por eso estoy comprometido a trabajar con los musulmanes estadounidenses para asegurar que ellos puedan cumplir con el zakat.

De igual modo, es importante que los países occidentales eviten dificultar el que los ciudadanos musulmanes practiquen la religión como ellos consideren oportuno; por ejemplo, dictando qué tipo de ropa debería vestir una mujer musulmana. No podemos disfrazar la hostilidad hacia cualquier religión tras el pretexto del liberalismo.

El sexto asunto que quiero tratar es el de los derechos de las mujeres.

Sé que hay debate sobre este asunto. Rechazo el punto de vista de algunos en Occidente de que una mujer que escoja cubrir su cabello es, de algún modo, menos igual; pero sí creo que a una mujer a quien se le niegue

equality. And it is no coincidence that countries where women are well educated are far more likely to be prosperous.

Now let me be clear: issues of women's equality are by no means simply an issue for Islam. In Turkey, Pakistan, Bangladesh, and Indonesia, we have seen Muslim-majority countries elect a woman to lead. Meanwhile, the struggle for women's equality continues in many aspects of American life, and in countries around the world.

Our daughters can contribute just as much to society as our sons, and our common prosperity will be advanced by allowing all humanity—men and women—to reach their full potential. I do not believe that women must make the same choices as men to be equal, and I respect those women who choose to live their lives in traditional roles. But it should be their choice.

Finally, I want to discuss economic development and opportunity.

I know that for many, the face of globalization is contradictory. The Internet and television can bring knowledge and information, but also offensive sexuality and mindless violence. Trade can bring new wealth and opportunities, but also huge disruptions and changing communities.

In all nations—including my own—this change can bring fear. Fear that because of modernity we will lose of control over our economic choices, our politics, and most importantly our identities—those things we most cherish about our communities, our families, our traditions, and our faith.

But I also know that human progress cannot be denied. There need not be contradiction between development and tradition. Countries like Japan and South Korea grew their economies while maintaining distinct

una educación se le niega la igualdad. Y no es coincidencia que los países donde las mujeres reciben una buena educación tengan muchas más probabilidades de ser prósperos.

Ahora bien, permítanme ser claro: los problemas de la igualdad de las mujeres no son, de ninguna manera, un asunto simplemente para el islam. En Turquía, Pakistán, Bangladesh e Indonesia, hemos visto países de mayoría musulmana elegir a una mujer para dirigirlo. Mientras tanto, la lucha por la igualdad de las mujeres continúa en muchos aspectos de la vida estadounidense, y en países por todo el mundo.

Nuestras hijas pueden aportar a la sociedad tanto como nuestros hijos, y nuestra prosperidad común avanzará al permitir que toda la humanidad —hombres y mujeres—alcance su pleno potencial. No creo que las mujeres tengan que hacer las mismas elecciones que los hombres para ser iguales, y respeto a las mujeres que escogen vivir su vida desempeñando papeles tradicionales. Pero debería ser elección de ellas.

Finalmente, quiero hablar de desarrollo económico y oportunidad.

Sé que, para muchos, el rostro de la globalización es contradictorio. El Internet y la televisión pueden aportar conocimiento e información, pero también sexualidad ofensiva y violencia sin sentido. El mercado puede aportar nueva riqueza y oportunidades, pero también inmensas alteraciones y comunidades cambiantes.

En todos los países—incluyendo el mío propio—este cambio puede producir temor. Temor a que, debido a la modernidad, perderemos el control de nuestras opciones económicas, nuestra política, y lo más importante, nuestras identidades: las cosas que más atesoramos de nuestras comunidades, nuestras familias, nuestras tradiciones y nuestra fe.

Pero también sé que el progreso humano no puede negarse. No tiene por qué haber contradicción entre desarrollo y tradición. Países como Japón y Corea del Sur desarrollaron sus economías a la vez que mantuvieron

cultures. The same is true for the astonishing progress within Muslim-majority countries from Kuala Lumpur to Dubai. In ancient times and in our times, Muslim communities have been at the forefront of innovation and education.

This is important because no development strategy can be based only on what comes out of the ground, nor can it be sustained while young people are out of work. Many Gulf states have enjoyed great wealth as a consequence of oil, and some are beginning to focus it on broader development.

But all of us must recognize that education and innovation will be the currency of the twenty-first century, and in too many Muslim communities there remains underinvestment in these areas. I am emphasizing such investments within my country. And while America in the past has focused on oil and gas in this part of the world, we now seek a broader engagement.

I know there are many—Muslim and non-Muslim—who question whether we can forge this new beginning. Some are eager to stoke the flames of division, and to stand in the way of progress. Some suggest that it isn't worth the effort—that we are fated to disagree, and civilizations are doomed to clash. Many more are simply skeptical that real change can occur.

There is so much fear, so much mistrust. But if we choose to be bound by the past, we will never move forward. And I want to particularly say this to young people of every faith, in every country—you, more than anyone, have the ability to remake this world.

All of us share this world for but a brief moment in time. The question is whether we spend that time focused on what pushes us apart or whether we commit ourselves to an effort—a sustained effort—to find common

culturas distintivas. Lo mismo es cierto del sorprendente progreso dentro de países de mayoría musulmana, desde Kuala Lumpur hasta Dubai. En épocas antiguas, y en nuestras épocas, las comunidades musulmanas han estado en primera línea de la innovación y la educación.

Esto es importante porque ninguna estrategia de desarrollo puede estar basada únicamente en lo que sale de la tierra, ni tampoco puede sostenerse mientras los jóvenes no tengan trabajo. Muchos estados del Golfo han disfrutado de gran riqueza como consecuencia del petróleo, y algunos están comenzando a enfocarlo en un desarrollo más amplio.

Pero todos nosotros debemos reconocer que la educación y la innovación serán la moneda del siglo XXI, y en demasiadas comunidades musulmanas sigue habiendo infrainversión en estas áreas. Estoy haciendo hincapié en tales inversiones dentro de mi propio país. Y aunque Estados Unidos en el pasado se ha enfocado en el petróleo y el gas en esta parte del mundo, ahora buscamos un compromiso más amplio.

Sé que hay muchos—musulmanes y no musulmanes—que cuestionan si podemos forjar este nuevo comienzo. Algunos están impacientes por atizar las llamas de la división, e interponerse en el camino del progreso. Algunos sugieren que no vale la pena el esfuerzo, que estamos destinados a estar en desacuerdo, y que las civilizaciones están condenadas a enfrentarse. Muchos más son simplemente escépticos en cuanto a que pueda producirse un cambio real.

Hay mucho temor, y mucha desconfianza. Pero si escogemos estar atados por el pasado, nunca avanzaremos. Y quiero decir esto particularmente a los jóvenes de todos los credos, en todos los países: ustedes, más que nadie, tienen la capacidad de rehacer este mundo.

Todos nosotros compartimos este mundo sólo durante un breve momento en el tiempo. La cuestión es si pasaremos ese tiempo enfocados en lo que nos separa o si nos comprometemos a hacer un esfuerzo—un esfuerzo

ground, to focus on the future we seek for our children, and to respect the dignity of all human beings.

It is easier to start wars than to end them. It is easier to blame others than to look inward, to see what is different about someone than to find the things we share.

But we should choose the right path, not just the easy path. There is also one rule that lies at the heart of every religion—that we do unto others as we would have them do unto us.

This truth transcends nations and peoples—a belief that isn't new; that isn't black or white or brown; that isn't Christian, or Muslim, or Jew. It's a belief that pulsed in the cradle of civilization and that still beats in the heart of billions. It's a faith in other people, and it's what brought me here today.

We have the power to make the world we seek, but only if we have the courage to make a new beginning, keeping in mind what has been written. The Holy Koran tells us, "O mankind! We have created you male and a female; and we have made you into nations and tribes so that you may know one another."

The Talmud tells us: "The whole of the Torah is for the purpose of promoting peace."

The Holy Bible tells us, "Blessed are the peacemakers, for they shall be called sons of God."

The people of the world can live together in peace. We know that is God's vision. Now, that must be our work here on earth.

sostenido—para encontrar un terreno común, para enfocarnos en el futuro que buscamos para nuestros hijos, y para respetar la dignidad de todos los seres humanos.

Es más fácil comenzar guerras que ponerles fin. Es más fácil culpar a otros que mirar en el interior, ver lo que es diferente en otra persona que encontrar las cosas que compartimos.

Pero deberíamos escoger el camino correcto, y no el camino fácil. Hay también una regla que yace en el corazón de todas las religiones: que hagamos a los demás lo que nos gustaría que ellos nos hicieran a nosotros.

Esta verdad rebasa naciones y personas: una creencia que no es nueva; que no es blanca, ni negra, ni marrón; que no es cristiana, o musulmana, o judía. Es una creencia que latió en la cuna de la civilización y que sigue latiendo en el corazón de miles de millones. Es una fe en otras personas, y es lo que me ha traído aquí hoy.

Tenemos la capacidad de formar el mundo que buscamos, pero sólo si tenemos la valentía de realizar un nuevo comienzo, teniendo en mente lo que ha sido escrito. El Santo Corán nos dice: "¡Oh humanidad! Les hemos creado varón y hembra; y les hemos convertido en naciones y tribus para que puedan conocerse unos a otros".

El Talmud nos dice: "Toda la Torá tiene el propósito de fomentar la paz".

La Santa Biblia nos dice: "Bienaventurados los pacificadores, porque ellos serán llamados hijos de Dios".

Las personas del mundo pueden convivir en paz. Sabemos que esa es la visión de Dios. Ahora, esa debe ser nuestra tarea aquí en la tierra.

Back to School speech
September 8, 2009
Arlington, Virginia

There was a time when it was a great honor to have the president of the United States visit with schoolchildren. But President Obama's talk at Wakefield High School created an uproar over whether it was appropriate for him to speak to these students and thousands of others, from kindergarten to high school, tuning in from across the country.

I know that for many of you, today is the first day of school. And for those of you in kindergarten, or starting middle or high school, it's your first day in a new school, so it's understandable if you're a little nervous.

I imagine there are some seniors out there who are feeling pretty good right now, with just one more year to go. And no matter what grade you're in, some of you are probably wishing it were still summer, and you could've stayed in bed just a little longer this morning.

I know that feeling. When I was young, my family lived in Indonesia for a few years, and my mother didn't have the money to send me where all the American kids went to school. So she decided to teach me extra lessons herself, Monday through Friday—at 4:30 in the morning.

Discurso "Vuelta a la escuela"
8 de septiembre de 2009
Arlington, Virginia

Hubo un tiempo en que era un gran honor que el presidente de los Estados Unidos visitara a los escolares. Pero la charla del presidente Obama en Wakefield High School creó un alboroto acerca de si era apropiado que él hablase a esos estudiantes y a otros miles, desde kinder hasta secundaria, que sintonizaron desde todos los rincones del país.

Sé que para muchos de ustedes hoy es el primer día de clases. Y para los que están en kinder, o que comienzan la preparatoria o la secundaria, es su primer día en una nueva escuela, así que es comprensible que estén un poco nerviosos.

Imagino que hay algunos veteranos que se sienten bastante bien en este momento, a quienes les queda sólo un año más. Y sin importar en qué grado estén, a algunos de ustedes probablemente les gustaría que aún fuese verano y haber podido quedarse en la cama un poco más de tiempo esta mañana.

Conozco ese sentimiento. Cuando yo era joven, mi familia vivió en Indonesia por unos años, y mi mamá no tenía el dinero para enviarme donde todos los niños estadounidenses iban a la escuela. Por tanto, decidió enseñarme lecciones extra ella misma, de lunes a viernes, a las 4:30 de la madrugada.

Now I wasn't too happy about getting up that early. A lot of times, I'd fall asleep right there at the kitchen table. But whenever I'd complain, my mother would just give me one of those looks and say, "This is no picnic for me either, buster."

So I know some of you are still adjusting to being back at school. But I'm here today because I have something important to discuss with you. I'm here because I want to talk with you about your education and what's expected of all of you in this new school year.

Now I've given a lot of speeches about education. And I've talked a lot about responsibility.

I've talked about your teachers' responsibility for inspiring you and pushing you to learn.

I've talked about your parents' responsibility for making sure you stay on track, and get your homework done, and don't spend every waking hour in front of the TV or with that Xbox.

I've talked a lot about your government's responsibility for setting high standards, supporting teachers and principals, and turning around schools that aren't working where students aren't getting the opportunities they deserve.

But we can have the most dedicated teachers, the most supportive parents, and the best schools in the world—and none of it will matter unless all of you fulfill your responsibilities. Unless you show up to those schools; pay attention to those teachers; listen to your parents, grandparents, and other adults; and put in the hard work it takes to succeed.

And that's what I want to focus on today: the responsibility each of you has for your education. I want to start with the responsibility you have to yourself.

Ahora bien, a mí no me entusiasmaba tener que levantarme tan temprano. Muchas veces me quedaba dormido sobre la mesa de la cocina. Pero siempre que me quejaba, mi madre me lanzaba una de esas miradas y me decía: "Esto tampoco es ningún picnic para mí, amigo".

Así que sé que algunos de ustedes aún se están ajustando al regresar a la escuela. Pero hoy estoy aquí porque tengo algo importante que decirles. Estoy aquí porque quiero hablar con ustedes acerca de su educación y de lo que se espera de todos ustedes en este nuevo año escolar.

Ahora bien, he dado muchos discursos sobre educación; y hemos hablado mucho sobre responsabilidad.

He hablado mucho sobre la responsabilidad que tienen sus maestros de inspirarles e impulsarles a aprender.

He hablado sobre la responsabilidad que tienen sus padres de asegurarse de que ustedes sigan adelante, y que hagan sus tareas, y que no pasen cada hora que están despiertos delante de la televisión o con la Xbox.

He hablado mucho sobre la responsabilidad que tiene su gobierno de establecer estándares elevados, de apoyar a maestros y directores, y de remodelar las escuelas que no estén funcionando y donde los alumnos no estén obteniendo las oportunidades que merecen.

Pero podemos tener los maestros más dedicados, los padres que más apoyan, y las mejores escuelas del mundo; y nada de eso importará a menos que todos ustedes cumplan con sus responsabilidades. A menos que ustedes asistan a esas escuelas; presten atención a esos maestros; escuchen a sus padres, abuelos, y otros adultos; y hagan el trabajo duro que se necesita para tener éxito.

Y en eso quiero enfocarme hoy: la responsabilidad que cada uno de ustedes tiene de su educación. Quiero comenzar con la responsabilidad que tienen de ustedes mismos.

Every single one of you has something you're good at. Every single one of you has something to offer. And you have a responsibility to yourself to discover what that is. That's the opportunity an education can provide.

And no matter what you want to do with your life—I guarantee that you'll need an education to do it. You want to be a doctor, or a teacher, or a police officer? You want to be a nurse or an architect, a lawyer or a member of our military? You're going to need a good education for every single one of those careers.

You can't drop out of school and just drop into a good job. You've got to work for it and train for it and learn for it.

And this isn't just important for your own life and your own future. What you make of your education will decide nothing less than the future of this country. What you're learning in school today will determine whether we as a nation can meet our greatest challenges in the future.

We need every single one of you to develop your talents, skills, and intellect so you can help solve our most difficult problems. If you don't do that—if you quit on school—you're not just quitting on yourself, you're quitting on your country.

Now I know it's not always easy to do well in school. I know a lot of you have challenges in your lives right now that can make it hard to focus on your schoolwork.

I get it. I know what that's like. My father left my family when I was two years old, and I was raised by a single mother who struggled at times to pay the bills and wasn't always able to give us things the other kids had.

There were times when I missed having a father in my life. There were times when I was lonely and felt like I didn't fit in.

Cada uno de ustedes tiene algo que se le da bien. Cada uno de ustedes tiene algo que ofrecer. Y tienen una responsabilidad hacia ustedes mismos de descubrir qué es eso. Esa es la oportunidad que una educación puede proporcionar.

Y no importa lo que ustedes quieran hacer con su vida; les garantizo que necesitarán una educación para hacerlo. ¿Quieres ser doctor, o maestro, u oficial de policía? ¿Quieres ser enfermera o arquitecto, abogado o uno de nuestros militares? Vas a necesitar una buena educación para cada una de esas carreras.

No puedes abandonar la escuela y sencillamente dejarte caer en un buen empleo. Hay que trabajar duro por ello, y formarse para ello, y aprender para ello.

Y esto no sólo es importante para su propia vida y su propio futuro. Lo que ustedes hagan de su educación decidirá nada menos que el futuro de este país. Lo que están aprendiendo ahora en la escuela determinará si, como nación, podemos lograr nuestros mayores desafíos en el futuro.

Necesitamos que cada uno de ustedes desarrolle sus talentos, capacidades e intelecto a fin de poder ayudar a resolver nuestros problemas más difíciles. Si no hacen eso—si abandonan la escuela—, no sólo se están abandonando a ustedes mismos, sino que también abandonan a su país.

Ahora bien, sé que no siempre es fácil ir bien en la escuela. Sé que muchos de ustedes tienen desafíos en sus vidas en este momento que pueden hacer que les resulte difícil enfocarse en su trabajo en la escuela.

Lo entiendo. Sé lo que es eso. Mi padre abandonó a mi familia cuando yo tenía dos años, y fui educado por una madre soltera que a veces batallaba para pagar las facturas y que no siempre podía darnos cosas que los demás niños tenían.

Había veces en que yo extrañaba tener un padre en mi vida. Había veces en que me sentía solo y pensaba que no encajaba.

So I wasn't always as focused as I should have been. I did some things I'm not proud of and got into more trouble than I should have. And my life could have easily taken a turn for the worse.

But I was fortunate. I got a lot of second chances and had the opportunity to go to college, and law school, and follow my dreams.

My wife, our First Lady Michelle Obama, has a similar story. Neither of her parents had gone to college, and they didn't have much. But they worked hard, and she worked hard, so that she could go to the best schools in this country.

Some of you might not have those advantages. Maybe you don't have adults in your life who give you the support that you need. Maybe someone in your family has lost their job, and there's not enough money to go around. Maybe you live in a neighborhood where you don't feel safe or have friends who are pressuring you to do things you know aren't right.

But the circumstances of your life—what you look like, where you come from, how much money you have, what you've got going on at home—that's no excuse for neglecting your homework or having a bad attitude. That's no excuse for talking back to your teacher, or cutting class, or dropping out of school. That's no excuse for not trying.

Where you are right now doesn't have to determine where you'll end up. No one's written your destiny for you. Here in America, you write your own destiny. You make your own future.

That's what young people like you are doing every day all across America.

Por eso no siempre estaba tan enfocado como debería haber estado. Hice algunas cosas de las que no estoy orgulloso, y me metí en más problemas de los que debería haber tenido. Y mi vida fácilmente podría haber dado un giro para peor.

Pero fui afortunado. Tuve muchas segundas oportunidades y tuve la posibilidad de ir a la Universidad, y a la facultad de Derecho, y de perseguir mis sueños.

Mi esposa, nuestra Primera Dama Michelle Obama, tiene una historia similar. Ni su padre ni su madre fueron a la universidad, y no tenían mucho. Pero ellos trabajaron duro, y ella trabajó duro, para poder ir a las mejores escuelas en este país.

Algunos de ustedes puede que no hayan tenido esas ventajas. Quizá no tengan personas adultas en su vida que les den el apoyo que necesitan. Quizá alguien en su familia haya perdido su empleo y no haya dinero suficiente. Quizá vivan en un barrio donde no se sienten seguros, o tengan amigos que les presionan a hacer cosas que ustedes saben que no están bien.

Pero las circunstancias de su vida—su aspecto, de dónde provienen, cuánto dinero tienen, lo que sucede en su hogar—no son una excusa para descuidar sus tareas o para tener una mala actitud. No son una excusa para responder a su maestro, o para faltar a clase, o para abandonar la escuela. No son una excusa para no intentarlo.

Donde están en este momento no tiene por qué determinar dónde terminarán. Nadie ha escrito su destino por ustedes. Aquí en Estados Unidos, ustedes escriben su propio destino. Ustedes moldean su propio futuro.

Eso es lo que jóvenes como ustedes están haciendo cada día en todo Estados Unidos.

Young people like Jazmin Perez, from Roma, Texas. Jazmin didn't speak English when she first started school. Hardly anyone in her hometown went to college, and neither of her parents had gone either. But she worked hard, earned good grades, got a scholarship to Brown University, and is now in graduate school, studying public health, on her way to being Dr. Jazmin Perez.

I'm thinking about Andoni Schultz, from Los Altos, California, who's fought brain cancer since he was three. He's endured all sorts of treatments and surgeries, one of which affected his memory, so it took him much longer—hundreds of extra hours—to do his schoolwork. But he never fell behind, and he's headed to college this fall.

And then there's Shantell Steve, from my hometown of Chicago, Illinois. Even when bouncing from foster home to foster home in the toughest neighborhoods, she managed to get a job at a local health center, start a program to keep young people out of gangs, and she's on track to graduate high school with honors and go on to college.

Jazmin, Andoni, and Shantell aren't any different from any of you. They faced challenges in their lives just like you do. But they refused to give up. They chose to take responsibility for their educations and set goals for themselves. And I expect all of you to do the same.

That's why today, I'm calling on each of you to set your own goals for your education—and to do everything you can to meet them.

Your goal can be something as simple as doing all your homework, paying attention in class, or spending time each day reading a book. Maybe you'll decide to get involved in an extracurricular activity or volunteer in your community. Maybe you'll decide to stand up for kids who are being teased or bullied because of who they are or how they look, because you

Jóvenes como Jazmin Perez, de Roma, Texas. Jazmin no hablaba inglés cuando comenzó a ir a la escuela. Casi nadie en su ciudad natal fue a la universidad, y ni su padre ni su madre habían ido tampoco. Pero ella trabajó duro, sacó buenas calificaciones, consiguió una beca para la Universidad Brown, y ahora está en la escuela de posgrado, estudiando salud pública, de camino a convertirse en la Dra. Jazmin Perez.

Estoy pensando en Andoni Schultz, de Los Altos, California, quien ha batallado con un cáncer cerebral desde que tenía tres años de edad. Él ha soportado todo tipo de tratamientos y cirugías, una de las cuales afectó a su memoria, de modo que necesitó mucho más tiempo—cientos de horas extra—para hacer sus tareas de la escuela. Pero él nunca se quedó atrás, y este otoño irá a la universidad.

Y también está Shantell Steve, de mi ciudad natal de Chicago, Illinois. Aunque fue de casa de acogida en casa de acogida en los barrios más difíciles, ella se las arregló para conseguir un empleo en un centro de salud local, comenzar un programa para mantener a los jóvenes fuera de las pandillas, y ahora está en curso a graduarse de secundaria con honores y después ir a la universidad.

Jazmin, Andoni y Shantell no son distintos a cualquiera de ustedes. Ellos afrontaron desafíos en sus vidas al igual que ustedes los afrontan. Pero ellos se negaron a rendirse. Escogieron asumir responsabilidad por su educación y establecer metas para sí mismos. Y espero que todos ustedes hagan lo mismo.

Por eso, hoy, estoy llamando a cada uno de ustedes a establecer sus propias metas para su educación, y a hacer todo lo que puedan para alcanzarlas.

Su meta puede ser algo tan sencillo como hacer todas sus tareas de la escuela, prestar atención en clase, o pasar tiempo cada día leyendo un libro. Quizá decidirán participar en una actividad extraescolar o hacer trabajo voluntario en su comunidad. Quizá decidirán defender a chicos que estén recibiendo burlas o intimidación debido a quiénes son o debido a su aspecto, porque

believe, like I do, that all kids deserve a safe environment to study and learn. Maybe you'll decide to take better care of yourself so you can be more ready to learn.

Whatever you resolve to do, I want you to commit to it. I want you to really work at it.

I know that sometimes you get the sense from TV that you can be rich and successful without any hard work—that your ticket to success is through rapping or basketball or being a reality TV star, when chances are, you're not going to be any of those things.

But the truth is, being successful is hard.

You won't love every subject you study. You won't click with every teacher. Not every homework assignment will seem completely relevant to your life right this minute. And you won't necessarily succeed at everything the first time you try.

That's OK. Some of the most successful people in the world are the ones who've had the most failures.

J. K. Rowling's first Harry Potter book was rejected twelve times before it was finally published. Michael Jordan was cut from his high school basketball team, and he lost hundreds of games and missed thousands of shots during his career. But he once said, "I have failed over and over and over again in my life. And that is why I succeed."

These people succeeded because they understand that you can't let your failures define you—you have to let them teach you. You have to let them show you what to do differently next time. If you get into trouble, that doesn't mean you're a troublemaker, it means you need to try harder to behave. If you get a bad grade, that doesn't mean you're stupid, it just means you need to spend more time studying.

ustedes creen, al igual que yo, que todos los niños y niñas merecen un ambiente seguro para estudiar y aprender. Quizá decidirán cuidar mejor de ustedes mismos a fin de poder estar más preparados para aprender.

Cualquier cosa que resuelvan hacer, quiero que se comprometan a hacerla. Quiero que realmente trabajen en ello.

Sé que a veces la televisión les hace tener el sentimiento de que pueden ser ricos y exitosos sin nada de trabajo duro; que su boleto hacia el éxito se lo dará el rap, o el básquet, o ser una estrella de un reality de televisión, cuando lo más probable es que no lleguen a ser ninguna de esas cosas.

Pero lo cierto es que ser exitoso es duro.

No les gustarán todas las asignaturas que estudien. No se conectarán con todos los maestros. No todas las tareas que les asignen parecerán totalmente relevantes para sus vidas en este momento. Y no necesariamente tendrán éxito en todo la primera vez que lo intenten.

Eso está bien. Algunas de las personas más exitosas en el mundo son las que más fracasos han tenido.

El primer libro de Harry Potter de J. K. Rowling fue rechazado doce veces antes de ser finalmente publicado. A Michael Jordan lo dejaron fuera de su equipo de básquet en la secundaria, y perdió cientos de partidos y falló miles de tiros durante su carrera. Pero él dijo en una ocasión: "He fracasado una y otra vez en mi vida. Y por eso tengo éxito".

Esas personas tuvieron éxito porque entienden que uno no puede dejar que sus fracasos le definan; tiene que dejar que esos fracasos le enseñen. Tienen que dejar que les muestren qué hacer de modo distinto la próxima vez. Si se meten en problemas, eso no significa que sean ustedes personas problemáticas; significa que tienen que intentar con más fuerza comportarse bien. Si obtienen una mala nota, eso no significa que sean estúpidos; sólo significa que necesitan pasar más tiempo estudiando.

No one's born being good at things, you become good at things through hard work. You're not a varsity athlete the first time you play a new sport. You don't hit every note the first time you sing a song. You've got to practice.

It's the same with your schoolwork. You might have to do a math problem a few times before you get it right, or read something a few times before you understand it, or do a few drafts of a paper before it's good enough to hand in.

Don't be afraid to ask questions. Don't be afraid to ask for help when you need it. I do that every day.

Asking for help isn't a sign of weakness, it's a sign of strength. It shows you have the courage to admit when you don't know something and to learn something new. So find an adult you trust—a parent, grandparent, or teacher; a coach or counselor—and ask them to help you stay on track to meet your goals.

And even when you're struggling, even when you're discouraged, and you feel like other people have given up on you—don't ever give up on yourself. Because when you give up on yourself, you give up on your country.

The story of America isn't about people who quit when things got tough. It's about people who kept going, who tried harder, who loved their country too much to do anything less than their best.

It's the story of students who sat where you sit 250 years ago, and went on to wage a revolution and found this nation. Students who sat where you sit 75 years ago who overcame a Depression and won a world war, who fought for civil rights and put a man on the moon. Students who sat where you sit 20 years ago who founded Google, Twitter, and Facebook and changed the way we communicate with each other.

Nadie nace siendo bueno en cosas; uno llega a ser bueno en cosas mediante el trabajo duro. Uno no es un deportista universitario la primera vez que prueba un deporte nuevo. Uno no da bien todas las notas la primera vez que canta una canción. Hay que practicar.

Y lo mismo pasa con el trabajo escolar. Puede que tengan que repetir un problema de matemáticas varias veces antes de solucionarlo, o leer algo varias veces antes de entenderlo, o hacer varios bocetos sobre papel antes de que sea lo bastante bueno para entregarlo.

No tengan miedo a hacer preguntas. No tengan miedo a pedir ayuda cuando la necesiten. Yo lo hago cada día.

Pedir ayuda no es un signo de debilidad, es un signo de fortaleza. Demuestra que tienen el valor de admitir cuando no saben algo y de aprender algo nuevo. Por tanto, busquen a un adulto en quien confíen—padre, madre, abuelo o maestro; entrenador o consejero—y pídanle ayuda para mantenerse en el curso de alcanzar sus metas.

Y hasta cuando batallen, cuando estén desalentados y sientan que han decepcionado a otras personas, nunca se decepcionen a ustedes mismos. Porque cuando se decepcionan a ustedes mismos, decepcionan a su país.

La historia de los Estados Unidos no habla de personas que abandonaron cuando las cosas se pusieron difíciles. Habla de personas que siguieron adelante, que lo intentaron con más fuerza, que amaban a su país demasiado para hacer algo menor que su mejor esfuerzo.

Es la historia de alumnos que se sentaron hace 250 años donde ustedes se sientan, y pasaron a llevar a cabo una revolución y fundaron esta nación. Alumnos que se sentaron hace 75 años donde ustedes se sientan, y que se sobrepusieron a una Depresión y ganaron una guerra mundial, quienes lucharon por los derechos civiles y llevaron al hombre a pisar la luna. Alumnos que se sentaron hace 20 años donde ustedes se sientan, y que fundaron Google, Twitter y Facebook y cambiaron la forma en que nos comunicamos unos con otros.

So today, I want to ask you, what's your contribution going to be? What problems are you going to solve? What discoveries will you make? What will a president who comes here in twenty or fifty or one hundred years say about what all of you did for this country?

Your families, your teachers, and I are doing everything we can to make sure you have the education you need to answer these questions. I'm working hard to fix up your classrooms and get you the books, equipment, and computers you need to learn.

But you've got to do your part, too. So I expect you to get serious this year. I expect you to put your best effort into everything you do. I expect great things from each of you.

So don't let us down—don't let your family or your country or yourself down. Make us all proud. I know you can do it.

Por tanto, hoy quiero preguntarles: ¿Cuál va a ser su contribución? ¿Qué problemas van a resolver ustedes? ¿Qué descubrimientos harán? ¿Qué dirá un presidente que venga aquí en veinte, o cincuenta, o cien años acerca de lo que todos ustedes hicieron por este país?

Sus familias, sus maestros y yo estamos haciendo todo lo que podemos para asegurarnos de que ustedes tengan la educación que necesitan para responder a esas preguntas. Estoy trabajando duro para acondicionar sus clases y conseguirles los libros, los equipos y las computadoras que necesiten para aprender.

Pero también ustedes tienen que hacer su parte. Por tanto, espero que se pongan serios este año. Espero que aporten su mejor esfuerzo a todo lo que hagan. Espero grandes cosas de cada uno de ustedes.

Así que no nos decepcionen; no decepcionen a su familia, ni a su país, ni a ustedes mismos. Hagan que todos estemos orgullosos. Sé que pueden hacerlo.

Health Care speech
September 9, 2009
Washington, D.C.

*Before a joint session of Congress, President Obama spoke about
his plan to reform health care coverage, one of the most complicated and
controversial issues in American political life.*

I am not the first president to take up this cause, but I am determined to
be the last.

It has now been nearly a century since Theodore Roosevelt first called for
health care reform. And ever since, nearly every president and Congress,
whether Democrat or Republican, has attempted to meet this challenge
in some way. A bill for comprehensive health reform was first introduced
by John Dingell Sr. in 1943. Sixty-five years later, his son continues to
introduce that same bill at the beginning of each session.

Our collective failure to meet this challenge has led us to a breaking
point. Everyone understands the extraordinary hardships that are placed
on the uninsured, who live every day just one accident or illness away
from bankruptcy. These are not primarily people on welfare. These are
middle-class Americans.

Discurso "Asistencia médica"
9 de septiembre de 2009
Washington, D.C.

Antes de una sesión conjunta del Congreso, el presidente Obama hablo sobre su plan para reformar la cobertura de la asistencia médica, uno de los asuntos más complicados y controvertidos en la vida política de Estados Unidos.

No soy el primer presidente que se ocupa de esta causa, pero estoy decidido a ser el último.

Ya ha transcurrido casi un siglo desde que Theodore Roosevelt llamó por primera vez a una reforma de la asistencia médica. Y desde entonces, casi cada presidente y Congreso, ya fueran demócratas o republicanos, ha intentado hacer frente a este desafío de alguna manera. Un proyecto de ley para una reforma general de la salud fue presentado por primera vez por John Dingell Sr. en 1943. Sesenta y cinco años después, su hijo continúa presentando ese mismo proyecto de ley al comienzo de cada sesión.

Nuestro fracaso colectivo en hacer frente a este desafío nos ha conducido a un punto límite. Todos entienden las extraordinarias dificultades que soportan quienes no tienen seguro, quienes viven cada día sólo a un accidente o una enfermedad de distancia de la bancarrota. No son principalmente personas que viven de la beneficencia. Son estadounidenses de clase media.

We are the only advanced democracy on earth—the only wealthy nation—that allows such hardships for millions of its people. There are now more than thirty million American citizens who cannot get coverage.

But the problem that plagues the health care system is not just a problem of the uninsured. Those who do have insurance have never had less security and stability than they do today.

More and more Americans worry that if you move, lose your job, or change your job, you'll lose your health insurance too. More and more Americans pay their premiums, only to discover that their insurance company has dropped their coverage when they get sick, or won't pay the full cost of care. It happens every day.

One man from Illinois lost his coverage in the middle of chemotherapy because his insurer found that he hadn't reported gallstones that he didn't even know about. They delayed his treatment, and he died because of it. Another woman from Texas was about to get a double mastectomy when her insurance company canceled her policy because she forgot to declare a case of acne. By the time she had her insurance reinstated, her breast cancer had more than doubled in size.

That is heartbreaking, it is wrong, and no one should be treated that way in the United States of America.

Then there's the problem of rising costs. We spend one-and-a-half times more per person on health care than any other country, but we aren't any healthier for it.

This is one of the reasons that insurance premiums have gone up three times faster than wages. It's why so many employers—especially small businesses—are forcing their employees to pay more for insurance,

Nosotros somos la única democracia avanzada en la tierra — la única nación rica — que permite que millones de sus habitantes soporten tales dificultades. Ahora hay más de treinta millones de ciudadanos estadounidenses que no pueden obtener cobertura.

Pero el problema que plaga el sistema de asistencia médica no es sólo un problema de quienes no están asegurados. Quienes sí tienen seguro nunca han tenido menos seguridad y estabilidad de las que tienen en la actualidad.

Cada vez más estadounidenses se preocupan de que si uno se traslada, pierde su empleo o cambia de empleo, pierda su seguro de enfermedad también. Cada vez más estadounidenses pagan sus primas sólo para descubrir que su compañía de seguros ha recortado su cobertura cuando se enferman, o que no pagarán el costo total de la asistencia. Eso sucede cada día.

Un hombre de Illinois perdió su cobertura en mitad de la quimioterapia porque su aseguradora descubrió que no había informado de cálculos biliares que él ni siquiera sabía que tenía. Retrasaron su tratamiento, y él murió a causa de eso. Otra mujer de Texas estaba a punto de someterse a una doble masectomía cuando su compañía de seguros canceló su póliza porque ella olvidó declarar un caso de acné. Cuando volvió a tener su seguro, su cáncer de mama había duplicado su tamaño.

Eso es desgarrador, está mal, y nadie debería ser tratado de ese modo en los Estados Unidos de América.

También está el problema de los costos cada vez mayores. Gastamos un uno y medio más por persona en asistencia médica que cualquier otro país, pero no estamos más sanos por eso.

Esta es una de las razones de que las primas de seguros hayan ascendido tres veces más rápidamente que los salarios. Por eso tantos patrones— especialmente en negocios pequeños—están obligando a sus empleados

or are dropping their coverage entirely. It's why so many aspiring entrepreneurs cannot afford to open a business in the first place, and why American businesses that compete internationally—like our automakers—are at a huge disadvantage. And it's why those of us with health insurance are also paying a hidden and growing tax for those without it—about $1000 per year that pays for somebody else's emergency room and charitable care.

Finally, our health care system is placing an unsustainable burden on taxpayers. When health care costs grow at the rate they have, it puts greater pressure on programs like Medicare and Medicaid. If we do nothing to slow these skyrocketing costs, we will eventually be spending more on Medicare and Medicaid than every other government program combined. Put simply, our health care problem is our deficit problem. Nothing else even comes close.

There are those on the left who believe that the only way to fix the system is through a single-payer system like Canada's, where we would severely restrict the private insurance market and have the government provide coverage for everyone. On the right, there are those who argue that we should end the employer-based system and leave individuals to buy health insurance on their own.

I have to say that there are arguments to be made for both approaches. But either one would represent a radical shift that would disrupt the health care most people currently have. Since health care represents one-sixth of our economy, I believe it makes more sense to build on what works and fix what doesn't, rather than try to build an entirely new system from scratch.

We have seen many in this chamber work tirelessly for the better part of this year to offer thoughtful ideas about how to achieve reform. Of the

a pagar más por el seguro, o están recortando toda su cobertura. Por eso tantos empresarios en potencia no pueden permitirse abrir un negocio en un principio, y por eso los negocios estadounidenses que compiten internacionalmente—como nuestros fabricantes de vehículos—tienen una inmensa desventaja. Y por eso aquellos que tenemos seguro de enfermedad también estamos pagando un impuesto oculto y creciente por él: unos 1000 dólares al año que paga las urgencias y la ayuda benéfica de alguna otra persona.

Finalmente, nuestro sistema de asistencia médica está colocando una carga insostenible sobre los contribuyentes. Cuando los costos de la medicina crecen al ritmo en que lo han hecho, eso pone una mayor presión sobre programas como Medicare y Medicaid. Si no hacemos nada para ralentizar estos costos tan elevados, finalmente estaremos gastando más en Medicare y Medicaid que en todos los demás programas del gobierno combinados. En palabras sencillas, el problema de nuestra asistencia médica es nuestro problema de déficit. Ningún otro asunto siquiera se acerca.

En la izquierda, están quienes creen que la única forma de fijar el sistema es mediante un sistema de único pagador como el de Canadá, donde restringiríamos severamente el mercado de los seguros privados y haríamos que el gobierno proporcionase cobertura para todos. En la derecha, están quienes argumentan que deberíamos poner fin al sistema basado en el patrón y dejar que los individuos contraten seguros de enfermedad ellos mismos.

Tengo que decir que hay razones que alegar para ambos enfoques. Pero cualquiera de los dos representaría un cambio radical que interrumpiría la asistencia médica que la mayoría de las personas tienen actualmente. Ya que la salud representa una sexta parte de nuestra economía, creo que tiene más sentido construir sobre lo que funciona y arreglar lo que no funciona, en lugar de intentar construir un sistema totalmente nuevo desde cero.

Hemos visto a muchos en esta cámara trabajar sin descanso durante la mejor parte de este año para ofrecer ideas meditadas sobre cómo lograr la reforma.

five committees asked to develop bills, four have completed their work, and the Senate Finance Committee announced today that it will move forward next week. That has never happened before.

Our overall efforts have been supported by an unprecedented coalition of doctors and nurses, hospitals, seniors' groups, and even drug companies— many of whom opposed reform in the past. And there is agreement in this chamber on about 80 percent of what needs to be done, putting us closer to the goal of reform than we have ever been.

But what we have also seen in these last months is the same partisan spectacle that only hardens the disdain many Americans have toward their own government. Instead of honest debate, we have seen scare tactics.

Some have dug into unyielding ideological camps that offer no hope of compromise. Too many have used this as an opportunity to score short-term political points, even if it robs the country of our opportunity to solve a long-term challenge. And out of this blizzard of charges and countercharges, confusion has reigned.

Well the time for bickering is over. The time for games has passed.

Now is the season for action. Now is when we must bring the best ideas of both parties together, and show the American people that we can still do what we were sent here to do. Now is the time to deliver on health care.

The plan I'm announcing tonight would meet three basic goals.

It will provide more security and stability to those who have health insurance. It will provide insurance to those who don't. And it will

De los cinco comités a quienes les pidieron que desarrollaran proyectos de ley, cuatro han completado su trabajo, y el Comité de Finanzas del Senado anunció hoy que avanzará la semana siguiente. Eso nunca antes ha sucedido.

Nuestros esfuerzos generales han sido apoyados por una coalición sin precedente de doctores y enfermeras, hospitales, grupos de veteranos y hasta empresas farmacéuticas, muchos de los cuales se opusieron a la reforma en el pasado. Y hay acuerdo en esta cámara aproximadamente en un ochenta por ciento sobre lo que hay que hacer, llevándonos más cerca del objetivo de la reforma de lo que nunca antes hemos estado.

Pero lo que también hemos visto en estos últimos meses es el mismo espectáculo partidista que sólo endurece el desprecio que muchos estadounidenses tienen hacia su propio gobierno. En lugar de un debate honesto, hemos visto tácticas alarmistas.

Algunos se han introducido en inflexibles bandos ideológicos que no ofrecen esperanza alguna de compromiso. Demasiadas personas han utilizado eso como una oportunidad para marcar puntos políticos a corto plazo, aunque robe al país nuestra oportunidad de resolver un desafío a largo plazo. Y por ese aluvión de acusaciones y contraacusaciones ha reinado la confusión.

Bien, el periodo de las discusiones ha terminado. Ha pasado el momento de los juegos.

Ahora es la época de la acción. Ahora es cuando debemos reunir las mejores ideas de ambos partidos, y mostrar al pueblo estadounidense que aún podemos hacer aquello que nos enviaron a hacer. Ahora es el momento de producir resultados en la asistencia médica.

El plan que estoy anunciando esta noche cumpliría tres objetivos básicos.

Proporcionará mayor seguridad y estabilidad a quienes tienen seguro de enfermedad. Proporcionará seguro a quienes no lo tienen. Y retardará

slow the growth of health care costs for our families, our businesses, and our government.

It's a plan that asks everyone to take responsibility for meeting this challenge—not just government and insurance companies but employers and individuals. And it's a plan that incorporates ideas from senators and congressmen, from Democrats and Republicans—and yes, from some of my opponents in both the primary and general election.

Here are the details that every American needs to know about this plan.

First, if you are among the hundreds of millions of Americans who already have health insurance through your job, Medicare, Medicaid, or the VA, nothing in this plan will require you or your employer to change the coverage or the doctor you have. Let me repeat this: nothing in our plan requires you to change what you have.

What this plan will do is to make the insurance you have work better for you. Under this plan, it will be against the law for insurance companies to deny you coverage because of a pre-existing condition.

As soon as I sign this bill, it will be against the law for insurance companies to drop your coverage when you get sick or water it down when you need it most.

They will no longer be able to place some arbitrary cap on the amount of coverage you can receive in a given year or a lifetime. We will place a limit on how much you can be charged for out-of-pocket expenses, because in the United States of America, no one should go broke because they get sick. And insurance companies will be required to cover, with no extra charge, routine checkups and preventive care, like mammograms and colonoscopies—because there's no reason we shouldn't be catching diseases like breast cancer and colon cancer before they get worse. That makes sense, it saves money, and it saves lives.

el crecimiento de los costos de salud para nuestras familias, nuestras empresas y nuestro gobierno.

Es un plan que pide a cada uno que se haga responsable de hacer frente a este desafío; no sólo al gobierno y las compañías de seguros, sino también a empresarios e individuos. Y es un plan que incorpora ideas de senadores y congresistas, tanto demócratas como republicanos; y, sí, de algunos de mis oponentes en las elecciones primarias y también generales.

Aquí están los detalles que todo estadounidense necesita saber acerca de este plan.

En primer lugar, si usted está entre los cientos de millones de estadounidenses que ya tienen seguro médico mediante su trabajo, Medicare, Medicaid o el VA, nada en este plan requerirá que ni usted ni su patrón cambien la cobertura o el médico que ya tienen. Permitan que lo repita: nada en nuestro plan requiere que usted cambie lo que ya tiene.

Lo que este plan hará es que el seguro que usted tiene le funcione mejor. Bajo este plan, será contra la ley que las compañías de seguros le nieguen cobertura debido a una enfermedad preexistente.

En cuanto yo firme esta ley, será contra la ley que las compañías de seguros recorten su cobertura cuando usted se enferme o la suavicen cuando usted más lo necesite.

Ellos ya no podrán poner alguna cláusula arbitraria sobre la cantidad de cobertura que puede usted recibir en un año en particular o en toda la vida. Pondremos un límite a cuánto pueden cobrarle por gastos perdidos, porque en los Estados Unidos de América nadie debería arruinarse porque se enferme. Y se requerirá a las compañías de seguros que cubran, sin cargos extra, los chequeos rutinarios y la asistencia preventiva, como mamogramas y colonoscopias; porque no hay razón por la cual no debiéramos detectar enfermedades como el cáncer de mama y el cáncer de colon antes de que empeoren. Eso tiene sentido, ahorra dinero, y salva vidas.

That's what Americans who have health insurance can expect from this plan—more security and stability.

Now, if you're one of the tens of millions of Americans who don't currently have health insurance, the second part of this plan will finally offer you quality, affordable choices. If you lose your job or change your job, you will be able to get coverage. If you strike out on your own and start a small business, you will be able to get coverage.

We will do this by creating a new insurance exchange—a marketplace where individuals and small businesses will be able to shop for health insurance at competitive prices. Insurance companies will have an incentive to participate in this exchange because it lets them compete for millions of new customers. As one big group, these customers will have greater leverage to bargain with the insurance companies for better prices and quality coverage.

This is how large companies and government employees get affordable insurance. It's how everyone in this Congress gets affordable insurance. And it's time to give every American the same opportunity that we've given ourselves.

For those individuals and small businesses who still cannot afford the lower-priced insurance available in the exchange, we will provide tax credits, the size of which will be based on your need. And all insurance companies that want access to this new marketplace will have to abide by the consumer protections I already mentioned. This exchange will take effect in four years, which will give us time to do it right.

In the meantime, for those Americans who can't get insurance today because they have preexisting medical conditions, we will immediately offer low-cost coverage that will protect you against financial ruin if you become seriously ill. This was a good idea when Senator John McCain proposed it in the campaign, it's a good idea now, and we should embrace it.

Eso es lo que los estadounidenses que tienen seguro médico pueden esperar de este plan: mayor seguridad y estabilidad.

Ahora bien, si es usted uno de los millones de estadounidenses que actualmente no tienen seguro médico, la segunda parte de este plan finalmente le ofrecerá calidad y opciones razonables. Si pierde usted su empleo o cambia de empleo, podrá obtener cobertura. Si usted vuela con sus propias alas y comienza un pequeño negocio, podrá obtener cobertura.

Haremos eso creando un nuevo intercambio de seguros: un mercado donde individuos y pequeñas empresas podrán contratar un seguro médico a precios competitivos. Las compañías de seguros tendrán un incentivo por participar en este intercambio porque les permite competir por millones de nuevos clientes. Como un gran grupo, esos clientes tendrán una mayor influencia para negociar con las compañías de seguros mejores precios y cobertura de calidad.

Así es como las grandes empresas y los empleados del gobierno obtienen seguros razonables. Es como todos en este Congreso obtienen seguros razonables. Y es momento de dar a cada estadounidense la misma oportunidad que nos hemos dado a nosotros mismos.

Para aquellos individuos y pequeñas empresas que no puedan permitirse los seguros más baratos disponibles en el intercambio proporcionaremos créditos fiscales, el tamaño de los cuales se basará en sus necesidades. Y todas las compañías de seguros que quieran tener acceso a este nuevo mercado tendrán que atenerse a las protecciones al consumidor que ya he mencionado. Este intercambio tendrá efecto en cuatro años, los cuales nos darán tiempo para hacerlo bien.

Mientras tanto, para aquellos estadounidenses que no puedan tener un seguro en la actualidad porque tienen enfermedades preexistentes, ofreceremos de inmediato cobertura a bajo costo que les protegerá de la ruina económica si enferman de gravedad. Esta fue una buena idea cuando el senador John McCain la propuso en la campaña, es una buena idea ahora, y deberíamos aceptarla.

Now, even if we provide these affordable options, there may be those—particularly the young and healthy—who still want to take the risk and go without coverage. There may still be companies that refuse to do right by their workers. The problem is, such irresponsible behavior costs all the rest of us money.

That's why under my plan, individuals will be required to carry basic health insurance—just as most states require you to carry auto insurance. Likewise, businesses will be required to either offer their workers health care or chip in to help cover the cost of their workers.

There will be a hardship waiver for those individuals who still cannot afford coverage, and 95 percent of all small businesses, because of their size and narrow profit margin, would be exempt from these requirements.

But we cannot have large businesses and individuals who can afford coverage game the system by avoiding responsibility to themselves or their employees. Improving our health care system only works if everybody does their part.

While there remain some significant details to be ironed out, I believe a broad consensus exists for the aspects of the plan I just outlined: consumer protections for those with insurance, an exchange that allows individuals and small businesses to purchase affordable coverage, and a requirement that people who can afford insurance get insurance.

And I have no doubt that these reforms would greatly benefit Americans from all walks of life, as well as the economy as a whole. Still, given all the misinformation that's been spread over the past few months, I realize that many Americans have grown nervous about reform. So tonight I'd like to address some of the key controversies that are still out there.

Ahora bien, aunque proporcionemos estas opciones razonables, puede que haya personas—particularmente los jóvenes y sanos—que aun así quieran correr el riesgo y no tener cobertura. Puede que siga habiendo empresas que se nieguen a hacer lo correcto por sus trabajadores. El problema es que tal conducta irresponsable nos cuesta dinero al resto de nosotros.

Por eso, bajo mi plan, se requerirá a los individuos que tengan un seguro médico básico, al igual que la mayoría de los estados requieren que se tenga un seguro del auto. Igualmente, se requerirá a las empresas que, o bien ofrezcan a sus trabajadores asistencia médica, o bien contribuyan para ayudar a cubrir el costo de sus trabajadores.

Habrá una cláusula de descargo para aquellos individuos que, aun así, no puedan permitirse la cobertura, y el noventa y cinco por ciento de todas las pequeñas empresas, debido a su tamaño y al estrecho margen de beneficios, estará exento de cumplir esos requisitos.

Pero no podemos tener grandes empresas e individuos que pueden permitirse tener seguro y que juegan con el sistema evitando responsabilidades consigo mismos o con sus empleados. La mejora de nuestro sistema de asistencia médica sólo funciona si todo el mundo hace su parte.

Aunque quedan algunos detalles importantes que limar, creo que existe un amplio consenso en los aspectos del plan que acabo de bosquejar: protecciones al consumidor para quienes tienen seguro, un intercambio que permita que individuos y pequeñas empresas contraten una cobertura razonable, y el requisito de que las personas que puedan permitirse un seguro lo tengan.

Y no tengo duda de que estas reformas beneficiarían mucho a los estadounidenses de todas las condiciones sociales, al igual que a la economía en general. Aun así, dada toda la mala información que se ha difundido durante los últimos meses, comprendo que muchos estadounidenses se hayan puesto nerviosos por la reforma. Por tanto, esta noche me gustaría hablar de algunas de las controversias clave que siguen estando ahí.

Some of people's concerns have grown out of bogus claims spread by those whose only agenda is to kill reform at any cost. The best example is the claim, made not just by radio and cable talk show hosts but by prominent politicians, that we plan to set up panels of bureaucrats with the power to kill off senior citizens. Such a charge would be laughable if it weren't so cynical and irresponsible. It is a lie, plain and simple.

There are also those who claim that our reform effort will insure illegal immigrants. This, too, is false—the reforms I'm proposing would not apply to those who are here illegally. And one more misunderstanding I want to clear up—under our plan, no federal dollars will be used to fund abortions, and federal conscience laws will remain in place.

My health care proposal has also been attacked by some who oppose reform as a "government takeover" of the entire health care system. As proof, critics point to a provision in our plan that allows the uninsured and small businesses to choose a publicly sponsored insurance option, administered by the government just like Medicaid or Medicare.

So let me set the record straight. My guiding principle is, and always has been, that consumers do better when there is choice and competition. Unfortunately, in thirty-four states, 75 percent of the insurance market is controlled by five or fewer companies. In Alabama, almost 90 percent is controlled by just one company.

Without competition, the price of insurance goes up and the quality goes down. And it makes it easier for insurance companies to treat their customers badly—by cherry-picking the healthiest individuals and trying to drop the sickest; by overcharging small businesses who have no leverage; and by jacking up rates.

Algunas de las preocupaciones de las personas han surgido de afirmaciones falsas difundidas por aquellos cuyo único plan es matar la reforma a cualquier costo. El mejor ejemplo es la afirmación, hecha no sólo por la radio y los programas de entrevistas en la televisión por cable, sino por destacados políticos, de que planeamos establecer paneles de burócratas con la capacidad de acabar con las personas de la tercera edad. Tal acusación sería ridícula si no fuera tan cínica e irresponsable. Es una mentira, llana y simple.

Están también quienes afirman que nuestra reforma asegurará a los inmigrantes ilegales. También eso es falso: las reformas que propongo no se aplicarán a quienes estén aquí ilegalmente. Y otro malentendido que quiero aclarar: bajo nuestro plan, ningún dólar federal se utilizará para financiar abortos, y las leyes federales de conciencia seguirán en su lugar.

Mi propuesta de asistencia médica también ha sido atacada por algunos que se oponen a la reforma como una "toma de posesión gubernamental" de todo el sistema de asistencia médica. Como prueba, los críticos señalan una prestación en nuestro plan que permite que quienes no tienen seguro y las pequeñas empresas escojan una opción de seguro financiada públicamente, administrada por el gobierno al igual que Medicaid o Medicare.

Por tanto, permítanme aclararlo. Mi principio director es, y siempre ha sido, que a los consumidores les va mejor cuando hay opciones y competencia. Desgraciadamente, en treinta y cuatro estados el setenta y cinco por ciento del mercado de los seguros está controlado por cinco empresas o menos. En Alabama, casi el noventa por ciento está controlado por una sola empresa.

Sin competencia, el precio de los seguros asciende y la calidad disminuye. Y hace más fácil que las compañías de seguros traten mal a sus clientes, al escoger con el máximo cuidado a los individuos más sanos y tratar de dejar fuera a los más enfermos; al cobrar más de la cuenta a las pequeñas empresas que no tienen influencia; y al aumentar las tarifas.

Insurance executives don't do this because they are bad people. They do it because it's profitable.

As one former insurance executive testified before Congress, insurance companies are not only encouraged to find reasons to drop the seriously ill; they are rewarded for it. All of this is in service of meeting what this former executive called "Wall Street's relentless profit expectations."

Now, I have no interest in putting insurance companies out of business. They provide a legitimate service and employ a lot of our friends and neighbors. I just want to hold them accountable. The insurance reforms that I've already mentioned would do just that.

But an additional step we can take to keep insurance companies honest is by making a not-for-profit public option available in the insurance exchange. Let me be clear—it would only be an option for those who don't have insurance. No one would be forced to choose it, and it would not impact those of you who already have insurance.

Despite all this, the insurance companies and their allies don't like this idea. They argue that these private companies can't fairly compete with the government. And they'd be right if taxpayers were subsidizing this public insurance option. But they won't be.

I have insisted that like any private insurance company, the public insurance option would have to be self-sufficient and rely on the premiums it collects. But by avoiding some of the overhead that gets eaten up at private companies by profits, excessive administrative costs and executive salaries, it could provide a good deal for consumers.

It would also keep pressure on private insurers to keep their policies affordable and treat their customers better, the same way public colleges and universities provide additional choice and competition to students

Los ejecutivos de seguros no hacen eso porque sean malas personas. Lo hacen porque les proporciona beneficios.

Como un anterior ejecutivo de seguros testificó delante del Congreso, las compañías de seguros no sólo son alentadas a encontrar razones para dejar fuera a los gravemente enfermos; se les recompensa por ello. Todo esto se hace para ayudar a cumplir lo que este anterior ejecutivo denominó "las implacables expectativas de beneficio de Wall Street".

Ahora bien, no tengo interés alguno en que las compañías de seguros quiebren, pues ellas proporcionan un servicio legítimo y emplean a muchos de nuestros amigos y vecinos. Sólo quiero que sean responsables. Las reformas de los seguros que ya he mencionado harían precisamente eso.

Pero un paso adicional que podemos dar para hacer que las compañías de seguros sigan siendo honestas es poner a disposición una opción pública de no-beneficios en el intercambio de seguros. Permítanme ser claro: sólo sería una opción para quienes no tienen seguro. Nadie sería obligado a escogerla, y no tendría impacto en aquellos de ustedes que ya tienen seguro.

A pesar de todo esto, a las compañías de seguros y a sus alianzas no les gusta esta idea. Ellos argumentan que esas compañías privadas no pueden competir justamente con el gobierno. Y tendrían razón si los contribuyentes estuvieran subsidiando esta opción de seguros públicos; pero no lo harán.

He insistido en que, al igual que cualquier compañía privada de seguros, la opción de seguro público tendría que ser autosuficiente y sostenerse de las primas que cobre. Pero al evitar parte del gasto general que los beneficios, los excesivos costos administrativos y los salarios de los ejecutivos consumen en las compañías privadas, podría proporcionar un buen trato para los consumidores.

También mantendría la presión sobre las aseguradoras privadas para mantener sus pólizas razonables y tratar mejor a sus clientes, del mismo modo en que las escuelas y universidades públicas proporcionan mayores

without in any way inhibiting a vibrant system of private colleges and universities.

It's worth noting that a strong majority of Americans still favor a public insurance option of the sort I've proposed tonight. But its impact shouldn't be exaggerated—by the Left, the Right, or the media. It is only one part of my plan and should not be used as a handy excuse for the usual Washington ideological battles.

To my progressive friends, I would remind you that for decades, the driving idea behind reform has been to end insurance company abuses and make coverage affordable for those without it. The public option is only a means to that end—and we should remain open to other ideas that accomplish our ultimate goal.

And to my Republican friends, I say that rather than making wild claims about a government takeover of health care, we should work together to address any legitimate concerns you may have.

Finally, let me discuss an issue that is a great concern to me, to members of this chamber, and to the public—and that is how we pay for this plan.

Here's what you need to know. First, I will not sign a plan that adds one dime to our deficits—either now or in the future. Period. And to prove that I'm serious, there will be a provision in this plan that requires us to come forward with more spending cuts if the savings we promised don't materialize.

Part of the reason I faced a trillion-dollar deficit when I walked in the door of the White House is because too many initiatives over the last decade were not paid for—from the Iraq War to tax breaks for the wealthy. I will not make that same mistake with health care.

opciones y competencia a los estudiantes sin inhibir de ninguna manera un vibrante sistema de escuelas y universidades privadas.

Vale la pena observar que una fuerte mayoría de estadounidenses siguen estando a favor de una opción de seguro público del tipo que he propuesto esta noche. Pero no debería exagerarse su impacto, ni por la Derecha, ni por la Izquierda, ni por los medios de comunicación. Es sólo una parte de mi plan, y no debería utilizarse como una útil excusa para las usuales batallas ideológicas de Washington.

A mis amigos progresistas les recordaría que, durante décadas, la idea impulsora tras la reforma ha sido poner fin a los abusos de las compañías de seguros y hacer que quienes no tienen cobertura puedan permitirse tenerla. La opción pública es sólo un medio para llegar a ese fin; y deberíamos seguir abiertos a otras ideas que logren nuestro objetivo final.

Y a mis amigos republicanos les digo que en lugar de hacer afirmaciones disparatadas sobre que un gobierno adquiera la asistencia médica, deberíamos trabajar juntos para abordar cualquier preocupación legítima que puedan ustedes tener.

Finalmente, permitan que hable de un asunto que es una gran preocupación para mí, para los miembros de esta cámara, y para el público; y es cómo pagamos este plan.

Lo siguiente es lo que deben saber. En primer lugar, no firmaré un plan que añada ni una sola moneda a nuestros déficits, ya sea ahora o en el futuro. Punto. Y para demostrar que hablo en serio, habrá una estipulación en este plan que requiera que hagamos más recortes en el gasto si los ahorros que prometimos no se materializan.

Parte de la razón por la cual me enfrenté a un déficit de un billón de dólares cuando entré por la puerta de la Casa Blanca es que demasiadas iniciativas a lo largo de la última década no se pagaron; desde la guerra de Iraq hasta recortes fiscales para los ricos. Yo no cometeré ese error con la asistencia médica.

Second, we've estimated that most of this plan can be paid for by finding savings within the existing health care system—a system that is currently full of waste and abuse. Right now, too much of the hard-earned savings and tax dollars we spend on health care doesn't make us healthier. That's not my judgment—it's the judgment of medical professionals across this country. And this is also true when it comes to Medicare and Medicaid.

More than four decades ago, this nation stood up for the principle that after a lifetime of hard work, our seniors should not be left to struggle with a pile of medical bills in their later years. That is how Medicare was born. And it remains a sacred trust that must be passed down from one generation to the next. That is why not a dollar of the Medicare trust fund will be used to pay for this plan.

The only thing this plan would eliminate is the hundreds of billions of dollars in waste and fraud, as well as unwarranted subsidies in Medicare that go to insurance companies—subsidies that do everything to pad their profits and nothing to improve your care. And we will also create an independent commission of doctors and medical experts charged with identifying more waste in the years ahead.

These steps will ensure that you—America's seniors—get the benefits you've been promised. They will ensure that Medicare is there for future generations.

And we can use some of the savings to fill the gap in coverage that forces too many seniors to pay thousands of dollars a year out of their own pocket for prescription drugs. That's what this plan will do for you.

So don't pay attention to those scary stories about how your benefits will be cut—especially since some of the same folks who are spreading these tall tales have fought against Medicare in the past and just this year

En segundo lugar, hemos calculado que la mayor parte de este plan puede pagarse encontrando ahorros dentro del sistema de salud existente, un sistema que actualmente está lleno de malgasto y abuso. En este momento, gran parte de los ahorros tan difíciles de conseguir y de los dólares de los impuestos que gastamos en asistencia médica no nos hacen estar más sanos. Esa no es mi opinión; es la opinión de los profesionales médicos en todo el país. Y esto también es cierto cuando se trata de Medicare y Medicaid.

Hace más de cuatro décadas esta nación defendió el principio de que, después de toda una vida de duro trabajo, nuestros ciudadanos de la tercera edad no deberían quedarse batallando con un montón de facturas médicas en sus últimos años. Así nació Medicaid. Y sigue siendo una sagrada confianza que debemos transmitir de una generación a la siguiente. Por eso ni un sólo dólar de los fondos de Medicaid se utilizará para pagar este plan.

Lo único que este plan eliminaría son los cientos de miles de millones de dólares en malgasto y fraude, al igual que injustificados subsidios en Medicare que van a parar a compañías de seguros; subsidios que hacen todo para aumentar sus beneficios y nada para mejorar la asistencia. Y también crearemos una comisión independiente de doctores y expertos médicos con el encargo de identificar más malgasto en los próximos años.

Estos pasos asegurarán que ustedes—los jubilados de Estados Unidos— obtengan los beneficios que les han prometido. Asegurarán que Medicare esté ahí para futuras generaciones.

Y podemos utilizar algunos de los ahorros para rellenar el hueco en la cobertura que obliga a demasiados jubilados a pagar miles de dólares al año de su propio bolsillo para adquirir medicinas con receta. Eso es lo que este plan hará por ustedes.

Así que no presten atención a esas aterradoras historias sobre cómo se recortarán sus beneficios, especialmente ya que algunas de las mismas personas que están difundiendo esos cuentos han luchado contra Medicare

supported a budget that would have essentially turned Medicare into a privatized voucher program. That will never happen on my watch.

I will protect Medicare.

Reducing the waste and inefficiency in Medicare and Medicaid will pay for most of this plan. Much of the rest would be paid for with revenues from the very same drug and insurance companies that stand to benefit from tens of millions of new customers.

This reform will charge insurance companies a fee for their most expensive policies, which will encourage them to provide greater value for the money—an idea that has the support of Democratic and Republican experts. And according to these same experts, this modest change could help hold down the cost of health care for all of us in the long-run.

Finally, many in this chamber—particularly on the Republican side of the aisle—have long insisted that reforming our medical malpractice laws can help bring down the cost of health care.

I don't believe malpractice reform is a silver bullet, but I have talked to enough doctors to know that defensive medicine may be contributing to unnecessary costs. So I am proposing that we move forward on a range of ideas about how to put patient safety first and let doctors focus on practicing medicine.

Add it all up, and the plan I'm proposing will cost around $900 billion over ten years—less than we have spent on the Iraq and Afghanistan wars, and less than the tax cuts for the wealthiest few Americans that Congress passed at the beginning of the previous administration. Most of these

en el pasado, y precisamente este año apoyaron un presupuesto que esencialmente habría convertido Medicare en un programa privatizado de bonos. Eso nunca sucederá bajo mi supervision.

Yo protegeré Medicare.

Reducir el malgasto y la ineficacia en Medicare y Medicaid pagará la mayor parte de este plan; y gran parte del resto se pagará con ingresos precisamente de los mismos medicamentos y compañías de seguros que siguen ahí para beneficiarse de cientos de millones de nuevos clientes.

Esta reforma cargará a las compañías de seguros una cuota por sus políticas más caras, la cual les alentará a proporcionar mayor calidad por el dinero: una idea que tiene el apoyo de expertos demócratas y republicanos. Y según estos mismos expertos, este modesto cambio podría ayudar a mantener bajos los costos de la asistencia médica para todos nosotros a la larga.

Finalmente, muchos en esta cámara—en particular en el lado republicano del pasillo—han insistido por mucho tiempo en que reformar nuestras leyes de negligencia médica puede ayudar a disminuir el costo de la asistencia médica.

Yo no creo que la reforma de estas leyes sea un remedio mágico, pero he hablado con suficientes doctores como para saber que la medicina defensiva puede estar contribuyendo a que haya costos innecesarios. Por tanto, estoy proponiendo que avancemos sobre un abanico de ideas sobre cómo poner la seguridad del paciente en primer lugar y dejar que los doctores se enfoquen en practicar la medicina.

Sumemos todo, y el plan que estoy proponiendo costará alrededor de 900 mil millones de dólares en diez años: menos de lo que hemos gastado en las guerras de Iraq y Afganistán, y menos que los recortes fiscales para los pocos estadounidenses más ricos que el Congreso aprobó al comienzo

costs will be paid for with money already being spent—but spent badly—in the existing health care system.

This is the plan I'm proposing. It's a plan that incorporates ideas from many of the people in this room tonight—Democrats and Republicans.

And I will continue to seek common ground in the weeks ahead. If you come to me with a serious set of proposals, I will be there to listen. My door is always open.

But know this: I will not waste time with those who have made the calculation that it's better politics to kill this plan than improve it. I will not stand by while the special interests use the same old tactics to keep things exactly the way they are.

If you misrepresent what's in the plan, we will call you out. And I will not accept the status quo as a solution. Not this time. Not now.

In 1933, when over half of our seniors could not support themselves and millions had seen their savings wiped away, there were those who argued that Social Security would lead to socialism. But the men and women of Congress stood fast, and we are all the better for it.

In 1965, when some argued that Medicare represented a government takeover of health care, members of Congress, Democrats and Republicans, did not back down. They joined together so that all of us could enter our golden years with some basic peace of mind.

Our predecessors understood that government could not, and should not, solve every problem. They understood that there are instances when

de la anterior administración. La mayoría de esos costos se pagarán con dinero que ya se está gastando—pero se ha gastado mal—en el sistema de asistencia médica existente.

Este es el plan que estoy proponiendo. Es un plan que incorpora ideas de muchas de las personas que están en esta sala esta noche: demócratas y republicanos.

Y seguiré buscando terreno común en las próximas semanas. Si ustedes acuden a mí con un serio conjunto de propuestas, yo estaré ahí para escuchar. Mi puerta siempre está abierta.

Pero sepan esto: no desperdiciaré tiempo con quienes ya han calculado que es una mejor política matar este plan que mejorarlo. No daré mi apoyo mientras los intereses especiales utilizan las mismas tácticas de siempre para mantener las cosas exactamente del modo en que están.

Si ustedes tergiversan lo que está en el plan, los retaremos. Y no aceptaré el status quo como una solución. Esta vez no. Ahora no.

En 1933, cuando más de la mitad de nuestros jubilados no podían sostenerse a sí mismos y millones habían visto esfumarse sus ahorros, hubo quienes argumentaron que la Seguridad Social conduciría al socialismo. Pero los hombres y las mujeres del Congreso se mantuvieron firmes, y todos nosotros estamos mejor por ello.

En 1965, cuando algunos argumentaron que Medicare representaba una adquisición por parte del gobierno de la asistencia médica, miembros del Congreso, demócratas y republicanos, no se echaron atrás. Se unieron para que todos nosotros pudiéramos entrar en nuestros años dorados con algo de paz mental fundamental.

Nuestros antecesores entendieron que el gobierno no podía, y no debería, resolver todos los problemas. Ellos entendieron que hay ocasiones en que

the gains in security from government action are not worth the added constraints on our freedom.

But they also understood that the danger of too much government is matched by the perils of too little; that without the leavening hand of wise policy, markets can crash, monopolies can stifle competition, and the vulnerable can be exploited.

And they knew that when any government measure, no matter how carefully crafted or beneficial, is subject to scorn; when any efforts to help people in need are attacked as un-American; when facts and reason are thrown overboard and only timidity passes for wisdom, and we can no longer even engage in a civil conversation with each other over the things that truly matter—that at that point we don't merely lose our capacity to solve big challenges. We lose something essential about ourselves.

What was true then remains true today. I understand how difficult this health care debate has been. I know that many in this country are deeply skeptical that government is looking out for them. I understand that the politically safe move would be to kick the can farther down the road—to defer reform one more year, or one more election, or one more term.

But that's not what the moment calls for. That's not what we came here to do. We did not come to fear the future. We came here to shape it.

I still believe we can act even when it's hard. I still believe we can replace acrimony with civility, and gridlock with progress. I still believe we can do great things, and that here and now we will meet history's test.

los beneficios en seguridad debido a la acción del gobierno no compensan las restricciones añadidas a nuestra libertad.

Pero también entendieron que el peligro de que haya demasiado gobierno se iguala a los peligros de tener muy poco; que sin el toque de una política sabia, los mercados pueden quebrar, los monopolios pueden suprimir la competencia, y los vulnerables pueden ser explotados.

Y ellos sabían que cuando cualquier medida del gobierno, sin importar lo cuidadosamente creada o lo beneficiosa que sea, está sujeta al menosprecio; cuando cualquier esfuerzo por ayudar a las personas necesitadas es atacado como anti-estadounidense; cuando los hechos y la razón se tiran por la borda y sólo la timidez pasa por sabiduría, y ya no podemos ni siquiera participar en una conversación civilizada unos con otros sobre las cosas que verdaderamente importan, que en ese punto no sólo perdemos nuestra capacidad de resolver grandes desafíos; perdemos algo esencial en cuanto a nosotros mismos.

Lo que era cierto entonces sigue siendo cierto hoy. Yo entiendo lo difícil que ha sido este debate sobre asistencia médica. Sé que muchos en este país son profundamente escépticos en cuanto a que el gobierno esté mirando por sus intereses. Entiendo que el movimiento políticamente seguro sería dar una patada a la lata en la carretera: posponer la reforma un año más, o unas elecciones más, o un mandato más.

Pero no es eso lo que el momento reclama. No es eso lo que vinimos a hacer. No hemos venido a temer al futuro. Hemos venido para moldearlo.

Sigo creyendo que podemos actuar aun cuando sea difícil. Sigo creyendo que podemos sustituir la acritud por cortesía, y el punto muerto por progreso. Sigo creyendo que podemos hacer grandes cosas, y que aquí y ahora haremos frente a la prueba de la Historia.